THE PALACE

CHRYSANTHA'S ESTATE

THE DARKNESS WITHIN US

ALSO BY TRICIA LEVENSELLER

The Shadows Between Us

Daughter of the Pirate King
Daughter of the Siren Queen
Vengeance of the Pirate Queen

Blade of Secrets
Master of Iron

Warrior of the Wild

THE
DARKNESS
WITHIN
US

TRICIA LEVENSELLER

FEIWEL AND FRIENDS

NEW YORK

A Feiwel and Friends Book
An imprint of Macmillan Publishing Group, LLC
120 Broadway, New York, NY 10271 • fiercereads.com

Our books may be purchased in bulk for promotional, educational, or business use. Please contact your local bookseller or the Macmillan Corporate and Premium Sales Department at (800) 221-7945 ext. 5442 or by email at MacmillanSpecialMarkets@macmillan.com.

Library of Congress Cataloging-in-Publication Data is available.

First edition, 2024
Book design by Liz Dresner and Meg Sayre
Map illustration © 2024 by Virginia Allyn
Feiwel and Friends logo designed by Filomena Tuosto
Printed in China

ISBN 978-1-250-84077-6
10 9 8 7 6 5 4 3 2 1

For Rachel and Holly,
Thank you for making my dreams come true.

➤─◦─◄

THERE'S NO SUCH THING AS A BAD IDEA,
JUST POORLY EXECUTED AWESOME ONES.
—Damon Salvatore, *The Vampire Diaries,*
Season 2, Episode 15

CHAPTER

I

My husband is taking too long to die.

I sit at his bedside, ever the dutiful wife, watching his breath squeeze out of his chest, praying that each one will be his last.

For gods' sake, the man is pushing sixty-four years of age. He's plagued with all manner of diseases from a life of debauchery and indulgence and devils know what else. Yet Hadrian Demos, the Duke of Pholios, clings to life as though there's still something it has to offer him—a bedridden, lecherous old man with nothing going for him except for the sight of my face day after day.

Pholios shifts, as if my thoughts have roused him, and I check over my shoulder, ensuring that Kyros is still stationed in the room, before scooting my chair back an inch. I cast my gaze down to the ground and wait.

"Chrysantha," the old man groans.

"I'm here, husband." I reach out and take one of his spotted, hairy hands, wrapping it in both of mine.

"You look beautiful today," he says.

"Thank you."

I manage not to roll my eyes, for it's how he greets me every morning, as though paying me compliments will get him what he really wants from me, his nineteen-year-old wife.

Pholios smacks his lips together. "Water."

I turn to the pitcher on the bedside table, only to discover it has nothing left.

"You must have been quite thirsty in the night, Your Grace," I say. "I'll refill your cup."

"Kyros can do it."

The hairs on the back of my neck stand on end, and I force my face to remain a mask of indifference. Living with the duke often feels like I've got an iron band around my lungs. It tightens the moment I realize I'm about to be alone with him.

Kyros, the handsome young footman, locks eyes with me. Sympathy and regret radiate from him, but I subtly nod my encouragement. The last thing I want is my friend getting fired for disobeying orders.

"At once, Your Grace," he says. "I will return shortly." The last bit is meant for me.

The moment he leaves the opulent master suite of the Pholios Manor, my husband jerks free of my hold and reaches for my breasts.

Long used to the duke's antics, I stand and turn to make my escape, but not quickly enough. He manages to swat my rump before I'm out of arm's reach. I keep my gaze on the ground.

It's the best tactic for hiding my true thoughts.

"Shall I read to you today?" I ask.

Pholios grunts. "No. No more books. Come back over here."

"More books, you said? Let me go select one." I glide to the opposite side of the room, where a line of shelves decorates the wall.

"Damnable nitwit," Pholios says. "I paid your father seven thousand necos for you. Such a waste."

"I'm sorry, husband." The band squeezes tighter.

"I don't want you to be sorry. I want you to hike up those skirts and climb onto this bed to do your wifely duty."

A so-called duty that he has been unable to force me to perform thanks to his illness.

"What duty could be more important than caring for my husband?" I ask.

He doesn't think me cheeky. No one does. I've worked long and hard to secure the reputation of a simpleton. It's saved me more times than I can count. It's how I manipulated my father into marrying me to a dying wealthy duke. If only I'd known then what I'd signed up for. Pholios didn't reveal his true nature to me until after we were married. I thought he merely wanted a bedside companion until he joined the devils in one of their hells.

"Your *nightly* duty," the duke clarifies.

"It's daytime, husband."

"I know that!" His coughs fill the room, and I ignore them while I take my time staring at the rows of books. I already know which one I will select, but I'm in no hurry to step within reaching distance once again. Not until Kyros is back in the room.

Pholios may be a foul creature, but he likes to keep up appearances in front of his staff. Either he knows what he's doing is wrong and wants to maintain some sort of reputation or he thinks matters of the bedroom should be kept private. Either way, when others are around, he keeps his hands to himself, though Kyros has walked in on plenty of untoward occurrences. I've been grabbed, pinched, slapped, and pawed at more times than I can count in the last two months of my life, which also happens to be the length of my marriage.

But it will all be worth it as soon as Pholios is dead. The duke has no children of his own, no relatives to inherit his title, which means that upon his death, all of this will be mine. The manor, the dukedom, the servants, the *money*. All mine to do with as I please, and no man will ever be able to decide my fate again. I will be a dowager duchess forevermore.

Forever free.

That future is so close I can taste it. Just a few more weeks. A month at most. Pholios can't have much longer left.

And then I won't have to hide who I really am anymore.

When I hear the soft steps of Kyros returning, I select the book of poetry from the shelf. The footman looks relieved to find me on the other side of the room. His sympathy is unnecessary—I can handle the old man—but it is kind, nonetheless. I return to my chair as Kyros finishes assisting the duke in taking a drink. Pholios nearly chokes when he reads the title on the tome I hold.

"No," he says. "I hate poetry."

Which is precisely why I chose it. "It will clear your head, Your Grace. Poetry livens the soul."

He grumbles some more but quiets as I start reading. I think he likes the sound of my voice, though he mostly stares at my chest while I read, so I raise the book a little higher. After about ten minutes of this, Pholios's snores fill the room once more.

"Are you all right, Your Grace?" Kyros asks me, his tone a gentle murmur so as not to wake the duke.

"Well enough, Kyros, and you?" I close the book and turn in my chair to properly observe the man. Even in his livery, he is quite hand-some. He wears the traditional white shirt and stockings with gloves and boots. He's always clean and pristine, with the best posture. His strong chin bears the most adorable dimple in the center, and his green eyes always seem bright. Combed-back, sun-kissed hair hangs past his ears, and his strong form puts many footmen to shame.

Day after day, it's just me and Kyros stuck in this suite, seeing to the duke and his every need. On occasion, Kyros's young son makes an appearance, desperate to show us frogs he's caught in the property's pond or the rocks he's found in the woods. The boy knows to be quiet in case the duke is sleeping, careful to catch our attention and drag us from the room for brief moments to see his prizes.

I always relish the opportunity.

"Very well, Your Grace." Kyros politely does not speak of my marriage with the duke and what I'm subjected to. He has the common sense to know that I have no wish to talk of such humiliation. "Nico learned a new word this morning," he says instead, to bring the conversation to brighter topics.

I smile at that. "And what is the word?"

"Indignant."

"Such a big word for a four-year-old."

"Don't let him hear you say that. He's four and a half, and not a day less."

In the time we've spent together in this room, I've learned quite a bit about Kyros and his past. He had a son at seventeen. He and the child's mother weren't married, and when she became pregnant, she made it very clear that she had no interest in raising a child. Though the law makes no such demands of single men, Kyros took up the role of father alone.

"Where is Nico now?" I ask.

"In the kitchens, helping Cook. You know how he has a sweet tooth."

"I shall have to track him down later. I look forward to hearing him try to work *indignant* into a sentence."

Doran, another footman, enters the room, brandishing a salver with a single letter upon it.

"A letter for you, Duchess," he says in a loud voice, waking Pholios once more. I wish to chide the man, but I keep a wan smile in place.

"Thank you, Doran," I say as I stand and retrieve the folded parchment.

"I'll have breakfast now, Kyros. Go fetch it," the duke says, alert once more.

Though I'm sure both servants leave the room, I don't notice. I'm too busy staring at the handwriting on the letter.

It's my sister's.

Alessandra never writes me. I barely write her—only when I wish to amuse myself by chastising her. She thinks me a puffed-up imbecile, which I find all the more entertaining. Alessandra has always been too obvious about what she wants and how she'll go about getting it. Right now, she's attempting to woo the Shadow King.

I chuckle quietly to myself. If he didn't want me, then he's certainly not going to want her. It's not a matter of vanity. I may have gotten Mother's looks, but that's no matter. A pretty face will only get you so far. What's most important is that I'm the better actress. I can pretend to be what men want. And what men want most, I've discovered, is someone they think they can control. So I pretend to be docile. I pretend to be obedient. When men think they can control you, they don't watch you as closely. When they think you're stupid, they're not so careful about the things they'll say in front of you.

But Alessandra? I could always tell what she was thinking. Although, I will admit that I hadn't thought her capable of murder. When the truth about what happened to her first lover came out, I was caught by surprise. And even more shocking was the king's immediate pardoning of her.

It's my fault the two of us aren't close. We've always been in competition for our father's attention. His whole world was Mother, but when she died when I was twelve and Alessandra eleven, I knew his love would either transfer to Alessandra or to me. He only ever had enough room in his heart for one woman at a time, so I snatched it up before Alessandra even knew what was happening. She would have done the same if she could.

We live in a world where men decide everything. Where we live. When we receive money. Who we will marry. I knew my best chance of achieving happiness was to wrap my father around my finger. It was her or me.

I chose me.

I feel a little guilty at times, but that won't matter when I finally have what I want. When I'm rich and beholden to no man, I can do whatever I wish, including cultivating a relationship with my sister if I choose.

I unfold the letter and read its contents:

Dear Chrysantha,

I wanted to extend a personal invitation to my wedding. Kallias and I are marrying in six months' time. My coronation is to be held the same day, right after the marriage ceremony.

You will attend, yes? Or are you too busy playing nursemaid to your wrinkled husband? Surely you can spare some time for the biggest day in your only sister's life? Send your reply along speedily, and I shall save you a front-row seat to this trollop's wedding to the Shadow King.

All my best,
Alessandra

There's a thundering in my ears, and I don't notice until it's too late that I've crushed the letter within my grasp.

The king.

My little sister is wedding the damned king.

He didn't want me, but he wants her. *Her!* The murderess.

All this time I've spent plotting, planning, trying to achieve something for myself. I've been molested, degraded, verbally assaulted day after day, and for what? Thus far, I have nothing to show for it.

Meanwhile, Alessandra has slept with so many men that I've lost count. I've called her much worse than a trollop in the past. It was my way of telling her to be cautious. She had to be careful with her reputation if she was to secure a good future for herself. And it made me feel better, when the jealousy over her finding companionship while I was fighting for survival on my own would nearly overcome me. Because I thought carrying on as she did would prevent me from marrying into wealth.

But somehow she won a *king*. She will become an actual *queen*. She'll have untold resources and money and *everything*. No one will ever touch her, not when she's wedded to the most powerful man in the world.

My temperature spikes, and red tinges the world.

She won.

How could she have won? She didn't do anything! She didn't earn it. She didn't even know we were playing the same game and how, how, how, damn it?

During my frantic musings, I hadn't realized I'd drawn closer to the bed. Pholios strikes like a snake, gripping my hip through my dress, and trying to pull me closer.

In my fury, I smack his hand away without thinking.

The duke and I both freeze.

"Did you just strike me?" he asks.

"I had an itch, Your Grace."

He grunts and has the audacity to look offended, but I can tell a foul thought has taken root in his mind when he suddenly smiles.

"Come closer, wife, and I shall forgive it."

"Closer?" I ask.

"Yes, lean over the bed. My comforter has come untucked on the other side. You must fix it."

My face is a mask of emptiness, and my soul burns. I've been trapped in this house too long, stuck in this room with the duke staring at me while he licks his lips and tries to coax me closer. Meanwhile, my sister is living a life of luxury and perfection and freedom. On the damned Shadow King's arm. I had failed to woo him during my stay at the palace, so I thought I'd settled for the next best thing.

I will settle no longer.

The iron band around my lungs snaps. My brain detaches from the rest of my body, and my limbs move without my consciously saying so.

I do as the duke bid earlier. I hike up my skirts and sit astride him. His eyes bulge from their sockets before he has the good sense to reach out with both hands, wrapping them around my waist. He tries to force me into just the position he wants; then he makes his best attempts at thrusting his hips up into me, layers and layers of clothing and bedding thankfully still separating us.

But my focus is on the extra pillow beside his head. I lean down for it, and Pholios's fingers go to cup my breasts. The pressure is bruising, but I don't sit up until I've got the pillow. Even then, it's only to adjust my position.

I smother him with the down-filled cushion.

That which had started to go hard beneath me suddenly goes limp. Pholios's cries of distress are eaten by the pillow, and his feeble body barely moves beneath mine. His hands finally leave my chest to reach for my arms, trying to force them away from himself.

I don't let up the pressure.

"Isn't this what you wanted, husband? Am I finally good for something now?"

If Alessandra can get everything she wants despite murdering a man, then why can't I? Her face rises in my vision, and I close my eyes against it, against every foul thing this man has ever done to me.

Never again.

Even when his pathetic resistance ceases, I don't get up right away. I sit there atop my dead husband, lost in some kind of dark limbo between before and after.

Before, I wasn't a violent person. Before, I'd been patience person-ified.

Now, I'm free. Now, I can be whatever I want.

Starting with a murderess, just like my sister. I have stooped to her level. The thought finally drives me to action. I right myself, place the pillow back in its position, and smooth out the duke's hair. He looks so peaceful in death.

I hope he finds no peace wherever I've just sent him.

As I return to my chair, I notice a figure in the doorway. Kyros's son, Nico, stands there, crumbs on his chin.

He looks between me and the duke.

I catch my breath.

CHAPTER

2

Nico puts his finger to his lips, the signal I usually give him when the duke is sleeping. I relax instantly. Of course he doesn't think anything different.

He whispers, "Catch me if you can, Duchess." Then he bolts back out the doorway.

I give chase.

"Did you really just come find me with crumbs on your chin and no sweets to share?" I call after him.

Nico shrieks with laughter. He is surprisingly fast for being so little. He slides down the banister at the stairs, while I have to take them slowly because of the heaviness of my skirts. When I hit the ground, I take off at a run once more, finally gaining on the boy. He pumps his little arms, and just before I'm upon him, Kyros rounds the corner with the duke's breakfast tray.

I scoop Nico up into my arms and twirl him in the air. His giggles lighten my heart, and I reach down with one arm to tickle his tummy before setting him back on the floor. His laughter feels so right in this large manor. It is finally a place where we can all be happy. The duke is dead.

Dead.

Dead.

Dead.

I don't think there's a sweeter word.

"What are you two up to?" Kyros asks.

"Father, the duchess was indignant that I didn't bring sweet rolls to share with her."

"I would have tickled you, too, for such an oversight," Kyros says.

"I'll get more for us all!" Nico darts for the kitchens.

Kyros has nothing but love in his eyes as he watches the child run away. "We best return quickly, before the duke grows incensed, Your Grace."

I say, "He fell back asleep, so I thought to escape for a moment."

Kyros nods in understanding, and together, we return to the master suite.

It is hours before anyone realizes the duke isn't breathing.

⋗┈⬦┈◯┈⬦┈⋖

IN THE DAYS THAT FOLLOW, nothing bad happens. No one suspects a thing. The man was dying anyway. Why should foul play be involved? Besides, everyone thinks me too stupid to even conceive of murder. I've made sure of that.

I wear black to the funeral, manage fake tears on Pholios's behalf, keep my face buried in a silk handkerchief gifted to me by the dead man himself with our initials embroidered on it. Father comforts me and brings me flowers; he even asks if there's anything he can do to help manage the estate. He's quite pleased with me, since my brideprice saved him from ruination. Father may be an earl, but his estate was bankrupt. *I* was bankrupt until I married Pholios.

Now his fortune is mine to do with as I choose. No man can tell me how to spend it. Not even my own father.

I've done it.

I've attained what so few women have managed.

True freedom.

The first thing I decide to do with that freedom is explore the estate and get to know my staff. Pholios never let me venture far from him. I was to take all my meals at his bedside. I was to be there when he woke up and long after he fell asleep. The duke mentioned many times that he was going to get his money's worth out of me. I was his property, he said.

In the end, I think he realized he was sorely mistaken about who had control over whom.

"Your Grace, it is so good to see you again," Mrs. Lagos, the house-keeper, says when she meets with me in the parlor.

I have seen her only a few times since I first set foot inside this dreary manor, when all the staff greeted me in the entryway as their new lady.

Mrs. Lagos looks about as formidable as a kitten, at four feet, eleven inches tall, but gods help anyone who tries to defy her claim that she's an even five (I overheard a particularly nasty conversation to that effect). Her hair is black as night, and her skin is white as ivory. With oval eyes and not a wrinkle in sight, it's impossible to guess her age, and I dare not ask her.

"You as well, Mrs. Lagos. Thank you for meeting with me."

"Of course. How can I be of service?"

"I would like to make some changes to the estate. I hoped you might be up for helping me."

"Certainly. What changes?"

I want my staff to adore me. I want them to *want* me to be their mistress. It's the best way to ensure a seamless transition, and I don't want anyone to question the control I now have. There is a very simple means to achieve that from the start.

"I'd like to raise the wages of the staff by twenty percent."

Mrs. Lagos blinks slowly, as though she didn't quite hear me. Then she grins. "You and I are going to get on well, Your Grace."

"Excellent, because I have plans for lots of redecorating . . ."

First things first, the master suite. I order it gutted. Every single item is moved to storage, from the bed to the draperies to the carpet. I refurbish the entire room so it looks like Pholios never once stepped foot in it. I want it free of anything that could possibly remind me of him.

I've always been fond of pink, and I find a delightful bedspread in a dusty rose that immediately draws my attention at Matilda's Shop. I decorate the whole room to match. White wallpaper with sporadic chrysanthemums, after my namesake. A white oak four-poster bed with mesh hangings. Gold filigreed armchairs with plump white cushions. An elaborate vanity, painted ivory with more gold knobs. I have the ceiling painted with the colors of the daytime sky with rosy-cheeked cherubs darting through the clouds.

While that's being done, Mrs. Lagos prepares the rest of the manor for renovation. I don't want any reminders of the horrible man who once darkened this home, so she sees to it that all the old paintings and vases and any other heirlooms of the Pholios family are removed to the attic, until they can be sold. Until my yearlong mourning period deemed mandatory by society is up, I'm not permitted to attend events or take social calls.

And yet, not even a week goes by before the letters start pouring in. I glance over mere snippets before tossing them all in a pile near the fireplace.

I was saddened to hear of your husband's death, Your Grace. Should you need any comforting, I hope you will call on me.

This from the Earl of Barlas.

Do not dwell on sadness, Your Grace. It is best to look on the future with hope. Might I call on you soon?

From the Earl of Varela.

I have admired you from afar for so long. Now that you are free to choose your own path, might I throw my hat in the running?

From the Duke of Simos.

And then one terribly embarrassing bit that makes my cheeks blush.

A woman in your position deserves all the pleasures life has to offer. Be my mistress, Duchess Pholios, and I will keep you satisfied.

From the Baron of Moros, who is already married.

I'll not be anyone's mistress. I'm done with men telling me what to do, whether it's in the bedroom or not. The correspondences remain thoroughly ignored, though I do read them from time to time when I feel in need of revitalizing. It is a boost to one's self esteem, even if such attentions are unwanted.

At least from powerful men.

For years I've dreamed of the day when I will be the one with the power, free to seek out relationships of my own choosing. I have been alone all my life, denied the simple pleasures of romantic companionship as a highborn lady. The second my mourning period is over, I have every intention of putting an end to that loneliness.

I will take a lover.

A handsome, poor—yet skilled—lover who will dote on me and love me and want nothing from me except for the earthly comforts I can give him.

Men take mistresses all the time, and as a dowager duchess, I may do the same. It is unconventional but not unheard of. I will have the power and standing to withstand any scrutiny I receive as a result. And besides, I'll obviously find someone who can manage to be discreet.

But that's not an option for another eleven months and two weeks. In the meantime, I focus on making new friends around the manor or supervising the improvements to the estate. Handymen can be heard hammering and sawing at all hours during the day. Painters and carpenters and mason workers come and go under the watchful eye of Mrs. Lagos and my staff. It'll take months, or even years, before the entire place is refurbished, but that's to be expected when I've inherited an estate only second in size to the royal palace of Naxos.

Alessandra's palace.

>–·◆›·—O—·‹◆·–·—‹

After Mrs. Lagos, the footmen are the next to be won over. Kyros properly introduces me to the rest of them, and they are delighted to hear that I'm interested in learning how to play the game of hach.

"You want to play a card higher yet in the same suit," Doran explains while Kyros looks over my shoulder.

I grab a queen of rubies.

Kyros leans down by my ear. "Not that one. It's too high. You want to save it. Play this one."

He sets the six of rubies face up on the table, beating the five played earlier in the round.

"I think she gets it," Plutus says with a glare as I scoop up his card. "You can stop helping her now."

"Don't be a bad sport," Kyros fires back. "You've been playing this game for years. She's just learning."

"You're the one who invited her. If she can't keep up, that's her problem." Realizing what he's just said, Plutus pales. "Forgive me, Your Grace, I forgot—"

"It's quite all right, Plutus. Perhaps if I make things a bit more interesting, your mood might improve." I pull a necos from my pocket and lay it on the table.

"We can't match that," Doran says, staring at the coin.

"Then play what you do have. Did I not just raise all your wages? Or are you afraid that I'll take all your money?"

I don't win a single game that night, but I demand a rematch for the next.

Kyros and Nico join me for picnics on the lawns when the sun is out, where the little boy will pick wildflowers for me, and Kyros and I will talk about everything and nothing. Nico shows me his favorite trees to climb, and I show him which fruits are ripe for picking—as well as which poisonous plants to stay away from. Sometimes, I teach the boy lessons at the piano, which I've always been fond of playing. I spared no expense in upgrading the fine instrument.

"You spoil him," Kyros dares to suggest a few weeks into my new dowagerhood.

"Giving a child music is not spoiling. Besides, I like spending time with him."

A large cloud streaks across the sun, dampening the rich verdancy of the trees and surrounding lawns. Kyros leans back on two hands atop our picnic blanket.

"And is that how you imagined spending your time as a dowager? Teaching a servant's child to play piano?"

"I certainly imagined a lot less complaining from the child's father."

Kyros crooks a grin. "In earnest, though, are you happy?"

"Happier than I ever remember being."

"You don't leave the estate often. I thought you'd want to be away with people of your own station. Or inviting them over at the very least. Instead, you spend your days baking with Cook, playing cards with the footmen, and teaching Nico the piano."

"That's hardly all. I've just formed a book club with Damasus, Karla, and Tekla. We're exchanging novels before meeting up to discuss them."

Kyros laughs. "A duchess who discusses books with her butler and maids."

"Laugh all you want, but I am right where I want to be. My father forced me to attend every social function, primp and preen at every ball, tolerate the presence of every foul man. Now I spend my days with who I wish when I wish. My servants are the finest individuals I've ever had the pleasure of knowing. I don't need to seek out the false flattery of noblewomen or the unwanted attention of gentlemen. I read when I wish. I'm out in nature when I wish. I enjoy the company of my horse, a four-year-old boy, and yes, my butler, in addition to everyone else on this estate. It is perfection, and what can be improved, I'm already well on my way to renovating. Now, will you stop scolding me and let me enjoy my hard-earned comforts?"

"Of course, Your Grace."

Kyros's warm smile matches mine, and I recline onto the soft cotton of the checkered blanket. There is a feeling of levity in my chest, and it takes me some time to place it.

This is what it feels like to be happy, I realize.

Speaking my thoughts and having someone else care to listen. No men trying to boss me about or control me. Doing activities I actually enjoy. Being myself around people who care.

This. All of this was worth every hardship I suffered since my mother died.

I am untouchable, and it feels so good I could almost fly.

>⊷⊶◦⊷⊶⊰

WHEN I LEAVE THE ESTATE, it is a different matter entirely.

I'm required to wear black in public as a symbol of my grief. Over a month after the duke's death, I don an ebony dress with a simple hoop skirt and a tight bodice. Long sleeves. No veil. The whole thing looks depressing, yet it's what I must be seen in while I run my errands. Just ten and a half more months and I can do away with this charade, too.

I'm in the chandlers', selecting new candles for the dining room, with a row of footmen behind me to assist with my purchases, when someone approaches me from the side.

"Your Grace?"

I turn to find Lady Evadne Petrakis, daughter of a marquis, doing some shopping of her own. We run in the same social circles, so naturally we've met countless times, but I wouldn't call her a friend. She's more like a frequent acquaintance. Not that it's easy to call anyone a friend when I have hidden my true self from the world for seven years.

"Lady Petrakis, how are you?"

"I'm wonderful! And you? You must be so proud of your sister. Marrying the king!"

I force a smile to my lips. "The king was bound to pick someone eventually. What of you? Has anything of note happened in my absence from events? I've missed out on so much gossip since my wedding."

"A few betrothal announcements, but nothing else of note. Nothing scandalous ever happens now with all the future queen's new edicts."

"Edicts?" Alessandra is making laws? Her?

"Oh yes. Women don't have to wait for marriage before taking part in . . . intimate relations. Fathers are no longer allowed to accept brideprices for their daughters. In fact, they're required to pay their daughters dowries upon their marriages to whomever they please, a sum reasonable to the father's yearly wage."

"What?"

"Oh yes. Some noblemen were rather upset about it, but the king had them beheaded for the threats they dared to throw toward the future queen. No one utters so much as a hint of protest against the new laws now."

"How many new laws have there been?" I ask.

"I've lost count, to be honest. Just last week she decreed that lands and titles are to pass down to the eldest heir, regardless of sex. Oh, and younger daughters no longer have to wait until older daughters are out in society before attending events as they please."

I blink several times, processing her words. "And the king just allows this?"

"He encourages it. His name appears beside hers on every new law. The people say he's utterly smitten by his future bride and would never deny her anything. They're already calling her the Shadow Queen."

More of that anger and bitterness claws its way through me. Alessandra was supposed to be a bargaining chip, like me. A way for Father to get out of debt and save his lands. But she's making laws and gaining favor with all the women of the court. She has freedom and happiness—in exchange for what? What has she suffered? She hasn't *earned* it. Not like I have.

I remind myself that I have everything I want now. I'm happy. That is all that matters. I take a fortifying breath and feel calm once more.

"Oh dear," Evadne says, "did I speak too quickly? I know you have a hard time with that sometimes."

Yes, because everyone thinks I'm an idiot. I'm an idiot while Alessandra is a powerful monarch.

"I'm all right," I say. "Just a bit dazed. I think I'll pay for my merchandise and go."

"All right, then. It was lovely chatting with you. I'm hosting an event in a few months' time, by the way. I'll send an invitation. Any relation of the Shadow Queen's is welcome at my estate."

"Thank you," I say, "but I'm not permitted to attend events until my mourning is over. The duke died, you will recall."

"Oh, that's another thing the future queen has done away with. Women don't have to undergo a mourning period. Nor do you have to wear black." She looks over my dress with sympathy. "You are, of course, free to make your own decision regarding the matter, but no one expects you to show respect to a man almost four times your age. Good day, Duchess."

When I look down at the two long-stemmed candles in my grasp, I find that I've snapped them both in half with my grip.

As Lady Petrakis exits the shop, I stare after her. Why haven't I read the papers? How could I have let all of this sneak up on me? When living with the duke, I always escaped to literature. To fiction, where I could pretend to be going on grand adventures or solving an intricate mystery alongside my favorite heroines.

I've missed so much. Alessandra snuck up on me.

It's not that I ever wanted power or to rule anything, really. I only ever wanted my own freedom. Now I have it, but it feels . . . cheapened. It feels like less when I compare it to what my sister has.

And now I have no excuse not to attend her damned wedding.

If I simply skip it, she'll know she's won. That I'm too ashamed or jealous to attend. I can't let her think that at all.

Really, what has she won? Constant scrutiny from those she rules over. A life of catering to her husband. So much responsibility.

I'm *glad* the Shadow King didn't pick me. Being a dowager duchess is far superior. I'm not like Alessandra, who is petty and vain and self-centered. I don't need attention and pampering. All I've ever wanted is to be left alone to control my life. I have that, so it's time to start exercising more control. More changes.

I'll expand the library. More books, yes, that's what I need. I don't have to mourn? Fine. Good. Great.

Then I won't wait any longer to find myself a lover.

Alessandra has her king, a man who will soon tire of her antics and eventually seek to control her, but imagine if I showed up to her wedding with a man of my own in tow? One who obeys me. One who is there to please me. One who is far more handsome than Kallias Maheras.

That ought to get her attention.

With my new resolve, I approach the pay station.

The man behind the counter asks for my account number. After I recite it, he checks through his records before placing a forced smile on his face.

I know that look. He's about to deliver uncomfortable news.

"Forgive me, Your Grace, but it seems your account is maxed out. We have yet to receive payment for your last order of items."

I don't even blink. "How is that possible?" I signed over the amount just last week.

"There was some sort of holdup with your solicitor."

Is that so?

Not a muscle on my face changes as I order my footmen to place my merchandise on the counter. "I will return shortly," I inform the man.

⋗⋯⬦⋯○⋯⬦⋯⋖

"Change of plans, Kyros. We're bound for Vander's next."

"Very good, Your Grace." He hands me into the carriage, and after a ten-minute ride, we arrive outside the solicitor's.

"You may accompany me inside, Kyros."

My friend follows behind me, and though I don't need him at my back, it feels good to have someone there.

"You're about to see a different side of me," I warn him. "Prepare yourself."

"Sounds exciting."

I march up the stairs of the building and bypass a frazzled secretary once inside, before letting myself into Vander's office.

He looks up from his desk in surprise.

"Mr. Vander," the secretary says, rushing into the room behind me. "Her Grace, the Duchess of Pholios, has arrived."

"Yes, I can see that. Please be seated, Your Grace. The door, Alasdair." The reedy man behind the desk adjusts his spectacles.

The door closes behind us. I take a seat in the offered chair, Kyros hovering over my shoulder. I adopt my usual tone and demeanor with men: casual and aloof.

"Mr. Vander, there seems to be some sort of mistake. I tried to pay for some items at the chandlers' but was denied due to an overdue payment. Did you perhaps forget to send the money?"

The man steeples his fingers atop the desk as he eyes me like a fish he's caught for supper.

"Oh, Your Grace, you have simply overspent. I noticed you've ordered quite a bit of changes to the estate. You have exceeded your monthly allotment. I've slated the overdue payment for next month, along with a surcharge to the agency for the fees that naturally accrue with such an oversight on your part."

At my silence, the man continues. "Fear not, Your Grace. Mathematics are extremely difficult to master. The occasional slipup is understandable, but you have me to handle all that. I shall make sure you're taken care of. Perhaps you'd like to discuss a budget? Or maybe you'd like me to approve your purchases before you make them in the future?"

Kyros has gone rigid behind me, as though he wishes to say something. I stand from my chair.

"Are you quite finished condescending to me?" I ask, my tone still neutral.

Vander looks surprised by the question. "Forgive me if my tone was too harsh, Your Grace. I only wish to help."

"Help, you say? Perhaps you'd like to help me find a new solicitor, then?"

"Your—Your Grace?"

I place my hands on the man's desk and lean forward, my voice turning sharper than a knife. "Tell me, Mr. Vander, does your wife know about the clubs you frequent at night?"

He blinks. "What are you—"

"How about the woman you're keeping on Sixth Street? You know, the one you visit every other weekend when you're supposed to be out of town visiting a wealthy client?"

"How do you—?"

"Tell me the answer to this mathematical equation, would you? If you take your wife and add the knowledge I intend to divulge to her, what does that equal?"

He's finally speechless.

"Or how about this one? If I subtract my business from your establishment and then use my considerable reach as a *duchess* to convince the rest of the nobility to move their business elsewhere, too, what does that equal?"

His face pales.

"Did you think me some easy mark? The poor, simple, newly widowed woman too overwhelmed by her new responsibility? My monthly income would put the *Shadow King* to shame, and you think I've overrun my accounts by refurbishing the estate? I could buy dozens of estates on my income. I've been through the account books, the dukedom's revenue, and Pholios's usual expenditures. Then there are the new investments I had you arrange, which have nearly *doubled* the estate's revenue. Or did you think I wouldn't check up on those?

"And you? You *do not* tell me what to do with my money. Pholios is dead. His entire fortune and holdings are *mine*. You will pay the chandlers the sum owed to them. Plus a generous sum to make up for the mistake, which will come from *your* account. Not mine. This will not happen again. I will not be forced to come to these wretched offices again to remind you of your place. If you so much as misplace a single necos in the future, you will not like the consequences. Do you understand me?"

The silence is so acute I can hear Vander swallow. "I understand."

"Your Grace."

"I understand, Your Grace."

"Good. I look forward to a long and profitable relationship for us both. Good day, Mr. Vander."

Kyros opens the door for me, and I don't look back as I exit.

Only once we're outside does he say anything.

"I wanted to clap."

I offer him a small smile as I turn my head. Then I bow as though I just finished some grand performance and received my standing ovation.

"Different side of you, indeed," Kyros says. "You are sensational."

I have never once blushed in a man's presence, but I've never been complimented on something that matters before. It's quite heady.

Before I can respond, Kyros asks, "Why continue to do business with him? Why not carry out your threat?"

"Because I've put him in his place now. He will not try to take advantage of me again. Besides, any new solicitor I sign with will try the same thing. Then I'll have to go through this scenario all over again."

"And how did you know all of that information? About his mistress and the clubs?"

"He joked about it with Pholios while we were drawing up the papers for the marriage agreement."

"And he forgot you were there?"

"He thought me irrelevant."

"How is that possible?"

I take the remaining steps to the carriage, and Kyros reaches for the door. "Because it's what I wanted him to think."

Kyros shakes his head as I duck inside. "And what is it that you want me to think?"

"That I'm your very capable employer."

"I already knew that," he says as he shuts the door.

CHAPTER
3

When I arrive back home, I ring for Medora, my lady's maid.

"Yes, Your Grace?" she asks as she lets herself into the room. She's older than I, at twenty-seven. Her skin is a creamy peach, while mine is a dark beige. Medora has a bigger bust than I, and she's much thinner about her middle.

"Would you help me out of this hideous dress?" I ask.

"Of course."

"Perhaps we could use it as fuel for my hearth fire tonight?"

She harrumphs. "Might as well burn its weight in bank notes, Your Grace, for it likely cost as much."

"I don't care. I can't stand the sight of it for one second longer. Apparently, I had no reason to wear black all this time." I tell her about my run-in with Lady Petrakis.

"Perhaps we burn this one, but might I suggest relocation for the others? Such fine material would feed families."

"Very well. See to it, but I want to watch this one burn."

When I step out of it, Medora throws the heavy dress atop the ashes in the hearth. "There. What would you like to wear instead?"

I skip over to the wardrobe that matches the rest of my room. White finish. Gold handles. Sweeping designs of trailing flowers. More chrysanthemums.

I begin to flip through dress after dress. Without any preamble, I ask, "Medora, have you ever had a lover?"

She doesn't miss a beat. "A few, Your Grace."

"I'm thinking of taking one."

"Truly? Who?"

"I don't know yet, but I intend to find someone. And quickly."

Before my sister's wedding.

"Falling in love can take time, Your Grace."

I consider a bright green day dress with long sleeves, before sliding it aside and looking at the next. "You misunderstand me. I have no intention of falling in love. I only want a lover."

"Oh," she says in response, as though she doesn't quite understand.

So I help her. "Men in my position are permitted mistresses. So why not me? I'm wealthy, titled, and sick of spending my nights alone. I want a mistress. The male equivalent of one. What would you call that?"

"I don't think there is a word for that."

"Then perhaps we should make one."

For a moment, there isn't a sound except for hangers slinging across the rack in my wardrobe.

"Let me make sure I've got this right," Medora says. "You want to keep a man in the way men traditionally keep women? Exchanging sex for housing, clothing, and all other possessions? No love involved?"

"Precisely." I mean, it wouldn't hurt if my lover fell head over heels in love with me, but I intend to remain at a distance.

I step away from the wardrobe with a pale orange dress with sheer sleeves that extend to my elbows and ribbons that tie into neat bows at my back.

"What do you think of that?" I ask her.

"I think it's brilliant, Your Grace! As long as you're careful, why shouldn't you carry on as a powerful man in your position?"

"Careful?" I ask.

"For two reasons. One, as the woman, you will still bear all the responsibilities if you become pregnant. And two, despite you having the upper hand as far as money and reputation, the man you choose will likely be much stronger than you. I don't wish to see any harm come to you."

The way Medora looks out for me is heartwarming. I've, of course, already thought of such things. I have come all this way, risen as high as I can go, and yet, because women are the child bearers, we are left with all the consequences of pregnancy. Not the man, who is the reason for a woman becoming pregnant in the first place.

I will place an order for contraceptives before starting any physical relationship.

As for Medora's second concern, it hasn't escaped my notice that I'll have to place my trust in a man if I'm to do this. He won't be like Pholios, weaker than me due to illness. I'll have to choose someone who will not abuse me, who will heed my wishes when we are behind closed doors. Even then, I could choose someone who seems kind and then proves to be entirely different when we're alone, just as Pholios was. Luckily, my staff consists of many footmen with impressive physiques, bless Mrs. Lagos for hiring them. I will have them within hearing distance, should I need aid.

It's sad that such things have to be considered, but if I'm to do this, I need to do it the right way.

I step into my dress and turn around so Medora can do up the back. I imagine myself at Alessandra's wedding, all eyes on me, not the bride. On me, not the queen.

"I promise to be careful," I tell her. "Time to take next steps, then. I suppose I should interview some candidates."

"Perhaps you need not choose someone so soon."

"What do you mean?"

"May I speak my mind, Your Grace?"

"Please do."

The fabric at my back tightens as she does another clasp. "Perhaps you might take some time to figure out what you like. Men don't start by taking mistresses. They sample first."

"Sample?"

"Yes, at brothels and the like."

"Oh."

I think on that for a while. Even when I'm fully dressed, I don't yet turn. *Visit a brothel. Sample. Learn what I like.*

It's a good idea.

Nerves and excitement clash in a delicious dance in my belly. I'm going to do this. I'm really going to do this.

I will have everything I've ever wanted.

IT DOESN'T TAKE MUCH digging to find the perfect place. Not only has Alessandra been busy making her new edicts, but the people of Naxos have quickly made changes to accommodate the new laws. Women no longer have to wait until marriage to engage in sexual relations?

Then why not open a brothel dedicated to serving female clientele? Zanita's boasts its "welcoming environment, enthusiastic and healthy workers, and complete discretion for any noblewoman wishing to partake," according to the article in the paper Medora shows me. Its grand opening was just two weeks ago.

I arrange for a carriage to take me that very night.

Everything is lit by candles, rather than electricity, which of course adds a sensual air to the main receiving room. Having never been to a brothel before, I wasn't sure what to expect, but something tells me this place is much classier than those the poor attend.

For one, all the prostitutes are more clothed than I expected. The men wear *very* tight pants. Some wear suspenders without shirts underneath. Others are barefoot with buttoned-down shirts left open. Everything is meant to entice, rather than give anything away. It's tasteful while slightly scandalous.

Second, there are so many more male prostitutes than women, but there are female workers present, too. Many women of the nobility prefer female to male lovers, so it's no surprise that Zanita's has some of each. They all lounge on chairs and cushioned ottomans, talking or playing games of cards. You'd think this were no more than a gaming hall. It's so relaxed and normal, clearly meant to ease the gentler patrons.

"Welcome," the madam says, stepping forward out of the crowd. I assume she's the madam, since she looks a bit older. "I'm Zanita. How can I help you?"

I hand over a hefty purse. "I'm here to sample your male workers."

"Of course, my lady."

"Your Grace," I correct her.

"Please forgive the oversight, Your Grace. It shan't happen again." Lady Zanita snaps her fingers. "Gentlemen, if you please."

The men in the room immediately stop what they're doing and line up against the far wall, shoulder to shoulder.

"Your advertisement claimed discretion," I say, turning away from the dozens of well-muscled men.

"Indeed, Your Grace."

"I would like to pay for house calls."

"That's not a problem. Who would you like to have accompany you home tonight?"

When it's my first time? "Someone patient and gentle."

"You will have to be more specific than that, Your Grace. These are professionals, all trained to see to your needs, not their own. Any one of them is capable of performing a perfect first-time experience."

Is that so? Well, then.

I take a few steps closer and walk down the line of men. Some have pale ivory skin, some medium tones, like mine, and some so dark that their skin shines beautifully in the light. I make eye contact with each man. Some offer cheeky smiles, others wink, still more bite their lips as they look me up and down, making me feel wanted.

Professionals, indeed.

"Do you like working here?" I ask one at random. The question may be strange, but it feels like something I need to be sure of.

"Payment for sex?" the ebony-skinned man responds. "Isn't that every man's dream? Though it's a special treat when someone as beautiful as you walks through those doors."

I return my attention back to the madam. "I will try them all, starting with this one." I point to the man who spoke.

"What's your name?" I ask.

"Sandros, love, and what shall I call you?"

I rather like that word on his lips, so I say, "Love works just fine."

>—⋅⟨⟩⋅•O•⋅⟨⟩⋅—<

Two months fly by in absolute bliss. Zanita was right. Each and every one of her workers is capable. I find that it is less their looks that impress me, since they're all so beautiful, but more what they uniquely offer.

Thaddeus gives sensual massages before each session, claiming he loves to feel every inch of me before we start. Kallen likes to snuggle after lovemaking, cradling my body against his while I drift off to sleep. Soterios is determined to see to my needs three times before he lets himself get lost, saying women are a wonder in how they can perform again and again in rapid succession.

But Sandros is perhaps my favorite. Not just because he gave me a perfect, nearly painless first experience, but because he will spend hours kissing me during each session. As though he is ravenous for me. As though I am special to him.

And I show him that he is special to me by offering him gifts: sapphire cuff links, silk suits, expensive colognes, and anything else I'd love to see him wear. But my favorite is at night when he wears nothing at all.

I feel more relaxed and free than ever as I go about my life. I cannot wait to see the look on Alessandra's face when I show up with Sandros in tow at her wedding.

While the workers toil the days away refurbishing the interior of the manor, I set my mind to the estate grounds. There is much to plan. Hedge mazes and gazebos and flowers. Water fountains, paving stones, and everything else I can think of. I meet with botanists and gardeners, more carpenters and stone masons.

The hedge maze is already nearly done. I paid extra to have mature plants transplanted here. The water fountain plumbing has been finished. I'm just waiting on the mason to finish the sculpture: a beautiful horse with its front legs kicking into the air.

New flowers and tree blossoms bring a sweet scent to the air, and the lawns are visibly greener, thanks to the professional who made some adjustments to the seed and soil.

The estate is already mine in name, but now it is looking it in appearance, too.

"You have a lovely smile, Your Grace," Medora says as she helps me out of a new day dress in a pink pastel color, and into a nightgown of soft silk. I feel like I'm floating when I wear it, so I ordered ten of the exact same one in different colors. Tonight's is a dazzling lavender with straps instead of sleeves.

"Thank you, Medora. It is nice to have reasons to smile every day."

"Your smiles aren't the only ones gracing the dukedom. You might not be aware of all the good your raises have done for the staff, but the footman, Doran, was able to pay for a treatment his mother desperately needed to help her back. Kyros bought new shoes for Nico. The lad is growing faster than Kyros can keep up with. I helped my parents make ends meet when they were short on their rent this month. You've done some real good here, Your Grace."

Her words warm my heart. "I want this place to be a safe haven for everyone who lives here. I want all my staff to lack nothing they need." They all deserve to feel safe and happy. I hadn't realized how crucial that was until I finally began to experience it for myself.

Just after Medora leaves the room, Sandros appears in the doorway.

The look he gives me as he takes in my revealing nightgown makes my toes curl.

"I'm almost ready," I say as I enter my washroom. "Make yourself comfortable." I pull the spring flowers from my hair and brush it, my teeth, and take care of my nightly routine. While I wash my face, I think I might hear a sound over the running water. Perhaps Sandros moved across the room?

But as I dry my face on a pink towel, I hear a shout and the sounds of a scuffle.

My body goes rigid as a blast of fear shoots up my spine. I do a quick survey of my bathroom before my eyes land on my toothbrush. The handle is made out of silver, and the end comes to a slight point.

Holding my feeble weapon behind my back, I exit the washroom.

Only to find a man, one who is most assuredly *not* Sandros, sitting on my now-rumpled bed.

CHAPTER

4

At my intake of breath, the intruder turns, as though I were the one who startled him, and draws two weapons simultaneously. The movement is so fast I can barely follow it. One moment, his hands are bare; in the next, he holds a revolver in his right hand and a wicked, serrated dagger in his left.

My back hits the wall near the open washroom door, as that knife is raised to my neck while the gun presses to my temple.

I don't move; I don't speak. I can barely breathe, for fear of the steel against my skin. He looms over me, his figure terrifyingly muscular. I can feel every hard angle of his body pressed against me. Too much of him, really, since I'm wearing so little.

His expression is dangerous, murderous, and there's something about it that I recognize in myself. A determination to do what it takes to get what he wants.

"Who the hell are you?" the stranger bites out, his voice impatient and violent, yet wearied somehow as well.

"Me?" I choke out, outraged. "Who are you? What are you doing in my bedroom? Unhand me at once or I shall scream for the servants!"

Where *are* my servants? How did he get past the entire staff?

My right hand is pinned between me and the wall. I try to wiggle it free.

"*Your* bedroom?" he asks incredulously.

"Yes, *my* bedroom." My manor. My safe space. Invaded.

Since he's armed, and I still can't access my weapon, I try a tactful approach. "If you're looking for a handout, you can go to the kitchens, where the staff can find some food for you." And Kyros can give him a boot to the ass on his way out the door.

Finally, my hand comes free, and I rotate my arm, bringing the pointed tip into contact with his body.

The man looks down, where I've got silver pressed against his manhood. Hopefully he can't tell it's not actually a knife from his viewpoint. Still, I could do some damage with it.

"Back away from me now," I snap at him.

The man scoffs, as though he finds me a trifling insect, but he releases me. He takes five steps backward, though he doesn't lower the revolver. It's still pointing right at my head.

Now that I've finally gained some distance, I'm able to appraise him properly. I don't recognize his face. It's . . . stern, tanned. Handsome, even. His eyes are like daggers with sharpened edges. His lips are much too full to be reasonable. He has a round chin that cuts to a sharp jaw in a way that manages to look both boyish and manly. Hooded eyes rest beneath ragged tawny-brown hair. He looks my age, though he's taller and definitely stronger.

"Do I look like I'm in need of handouts?" he asks, his voice deep enough to negate anything boyish about him at all.

I lower my eyes to take in his soiled, worn clothing—though atop it all is an impressive, floor-length black leather jacket. Then I dart back up to note the dirt streaks on his cheeks, the wild, rumpled hair, and reply, "Yes!"

The man rolls his eyes. "I've been traveling. It took months to get here, which means I'm short on patience. Now, whoever you are, get the hell out of my house."

"I beg your pardon! I am Lady Chrysantha Demos, Duchess of Pholios, and you cannot order me to leave my own home!"

At that, the man jerks up straight and does a sweep of my body. "*You're* the dowager duchess? You can't be older than . . ."

"Nineteen," I say.

He opens and shuts his mouth a few times but finally reholsters both weapons. "They told me the old man left a widow, but I didn't think you'd be so . . . young. What are you doing in the master suite?"

That is *it*! "You do not get to barge into my manor and threaten me with weapons. You don't get to ask me questions as though I'm some suspect when you're the criminal. Who do you think you are?"

The man cocks his head to the side. "Vander didn't tell you?"

"Tell. Me. What?" The words come through gritted teeth. If I have to pay another visit to that dreadful man, I swear I will ruin him.

The intruder looks heavenward as he says, "My name is Eryx Demos. Hadrian Demos was my grandfather. I'm the new Duke of Pholios. I've just arrived from overseas to take up my lands and title."

My heart stops beating in my chest, and my skin goes cold. "What?" I whisper.

"This is my estate, and these are my rooms," he says, returning his gaze to me.

"No," I say, quietly at first. Then: "No! Pholios had no children. No heirs. This is some kind of horrible scam! I shall send for Vander at once."

"You do that, but he'll tell you the same thing I just did." Eryx places a hand on the back of his neck and cracks it.

"Why wouldn't he have told me this before?"

"How should I know? All Vander told me about you was that you're a bit—uh . . . simple."

Did Vander put this into motion before or after I paid him a visit about trying to steal money from me? Is this payback for putting him in his place? Or did he think me such an easy mark that he made plans to have a man of his choosing pretend to be the duke's grandson so the two could pilfer the earnings of the estate?

And I have no doubt that this is some ruse, because I *know* Pholios had no heirs. That's precisely why I picked him.

"Vander must have me confused with someone else," I say. "For I can assure you I am quite competent and capable of running this estate."

"Yes, I can see you've made all kinds of . . . interesting changes." He surveys the room with distaste. "No matter. I'm sure we can return most of this horrid furniture. Restore the room to its manly glory."

Did he just say *manly glory*?

"You won't be returning anything. The money I've spent is mine. This manor is mine. And you will not take it from me, you insolent child!"

"I am eighteen," he says through clenched teeth. A surprise, I thought him at least a year older.

"Ah, my junior by a year," I say haughtily.

"I doubt that. When's your birthday?"

"November."

"You have five months on me, Duchess. That hardly warrants calling me a child." His calm tone only infuriates me.

"And yet, you're not of age. I'm closer to twenty-one than you are, which means the estate will remain in my hands until then." I don't know what to believe. I don't really even know what I'm saying anymore. The world has tilted, and I'm trying to keep from falling.

Eryx laughs. "Oh, no you don't. Listen here, vixen. This is my birthright. I bear the title of duke, whether or not I'm of age. I outrank you, *dowager*. We will take this matter to the king if need be, but I'm not backing down."

"Go ahead. The king is about to become my brother-in-law."

Which really just means that I'm royally screwed. For Kallias is clearly being puppeted by Alessandra, and she's not about to do me any favors. I called her a trollop the last time I wrote her.

But the lie is worth it when I see a hitch in his calm facade.

Perhaps it's just my imagination, but for the briefest moment, I swear I see the supposed duke's eyes change color, lightening from a deep brown to bright amber, but it must just be the light, because I blink and there is no change at all. Eryx looks impossibly more tired than when I first spotted him in the room. His fingers slide through his hair as he sighs heavily.

"You picked the wrong mark," I say. "I will see you and Vander in prison by tomorrow."

Calmly, resolutely, he extends his right hand forward, where I note for the first time that he's wearing a ring.

Pholios's seal.

How the hell did he get that? It was on Pholios's hand when he died. Wasn't it?

Well, that at least explains how he got past the servants.

At my stunned silence, Eryx says, "We can resume this argument in the morning. I've had a long day. I need rest."

"Well, you're not doing it in here."

"Wouldn't dream of it. All the pink is giving me a headache. Have a good night in this room, Duchess. It won't be yours for much longer." He smiles a grin that makes him seem more dangerous than before.

The door bursts open, and no fewer than ten of my footmen barrel into the room in various stages of undress.

This time, Eryx doesn't grab his dagger or pistol. He just appraises the men calmly.

"No need for that," Eryx says. He steps over something on the floor on his way to the door. The footmen let him pass, awaiting my instructions.

Only then do I notice that Sandros is knocked out cold on the bedside rug.

In my outrage and surprise over the intruder, I'd forgotten about him completely. "Take Sandros to the connecting suite and ring for the doctor, please."

Four men carry out the order, hauling Sandros between them.

Kyros turns to me. "Damasus called for us. Said that some man with the duke's seal was walking about the manor. He had two goons with him, which is why the staff couldn't warn you right away. Are you all right, Your Grace?"

What a question.

I had my perfect life, and now some man-child has come to take it away.

How can he exist? He *can't* exist. I specifically chose the duke because he had no children. No cousins. *No one* to pass the estate on to.

Yet here is someone claiming otherwise.

This can't be right. This can't be it.

I *killed* for this!

I've earned it.

Finding some measure of calm, I say, "I will be."

If Vander and Eryx think I'm just going to hand over this estate, they are sorely mistaken. They have no idea who they're dealing with. The pretend duke may have caught me by surprise, but starting tomorrow I will be prepared.

I return my toothbrush to the washroom. My footmen shuffle out the room, but I ask if a couple of them will take watch outside the door. Just in case.

Then I climb into bed, place the down pillow over my head, and scream and scream into it, until the energetic fury finally leaves my limbs. Depleted and exhausted, I turn over.

This is a new obstacle I wasn't expecting, but I will handle it just as I have everything else.

Eryx the con artist will not be around for long.

⊱ ┄ ⊰⟩ ⊷ ◯ ⊶ ⟨⊱ ┄ ⊰

CONSCIOUSNESS CREEPS UP ON ME again and again in the night, my new troubles refusing to let me remain in blissful sleep. When Medora's knuckles rap on the locked door, I let her in.

"We need to get me dressed quickly, Medora. I have errands to run."

She selects a light yellow day dress for me with white ribbon cinching around my waist and wrists. Bows are spaced ten inches apart along the hemline. I pick opal earrings and a single white gold ring to complement the outfit. Medora pulls my black hair up into a coiffure, with strands falling down my back. One of my best features is my neck, so I often wear my hair up when I need to distract a man.

"I think I'll wear makeup today," I say, and Medora's brow shoots up in surprise. I normally don't bother with powders. I don't need them, and with them, I often cause accidents in the street. But that's exactly what I need now.

An accident to befall this impostor.

Medora lines my eyes with black, applies pink gloss to my lips, traces my brows, and deepens the blush on my cheeks.

When I'm all dolled up, I exit the room. Kyros is walking up the stairs just as I'm descending. He looks up, loses his footing, and just barely manages to catch himself on the railing. Since he's a very coordinated young man, I deem my outfit and face suitable for today's battle.

As I enter the dining room, I'm appalled by what I find. Eryx has made himself comfortable in *my* chair at the head of the table. He has two gentlemen seated on either side of him, though *gentlemen* is a rather generous term.

As I enter the room, the two extra men bolt out of their seats and make for the wall behind Eryx to stand at attention.

So they're not gentlemen at all, but servants? Most likely the "goons" Kyros had mentioned last night.

"Enough of that," Eryx says. "You haven't finished your breakfasts."

The first of the men clears his throat before saying, "You have company." This man looks a little older than Eryx and much, much rougher. Really, he's kind of terrifying with grizzled features. Ginormous arms. Trousers that barely seem to contain the thick muscles of his thighs.

The other is not nearly so enormous as the first, but Eryx still wouldn't want to challenge him to an arm wrestling match, I'd wager. While the first man has dark hair and features, the second has golden hair and bright blue eyes. He has a scar visible on one hand. His eyes widen as he properly assesses my features.

"You didn't mention she was downright gorgeous," he says, and his companion smacks his shoulder.

Both men avert their eyes, looking to the floor. They wear workman's attire. Simple cotton pants and shirts that I'm sure are much darker in color than the day they were purchased. Really, I should have assumed they were hired hands when I first entered the room. Though they haven't the manners to be well-trained household servants.

Honestly, now that they're both standing, they look more like bodyguards.

At the breakfast table?

I should have guessed the con would need more than one man to pull it off. Just how many will the constabulary have to round up and toss into prison once I expose the ruse?

"Duchess," Eryx says, realizing I'm here with them. He doesn't react at all to my appearance, which I find all the more frustrating. "Please do forgive their manners. It's been quite some time since they were in polite company. Won't you be seated?"

He motions for a servant to remove the dishes belonging to the men now stationed along the wall. A fresh bowl is laid out at Eryx's right. He rises from his chair and pulls out mine, as though intending to help me sit.

It is an odd sight, since the man isn't wearing anything close to resembling something appropriate for a duke. He's done up in all black. Pants, boots, long-sleeved shirt. No vest or jacket, and his shirtsleeves are rolled up to his elbows.

Highly scandalous.

He appears to have bathed since last night. His medium-brown hair has less volume, though it's still wild in appearance, but at least he's no longer dirt-streaked. There are hollows beneath his eyes, making him look as though he didn't sleep a wink last night.

I do a slow sweep of the room, making eye contact with each of my waitstaff, though they seem just as confused by the newcomers as I am.

This is so very, very wrong. But there's nothing to be done for it at the moment.

Right now, I have a choice to make.

I've let down my guard. Been myself around the servants. Shown too much outrage and competence in front of Eryx to pretend to be anything other than I am. So what part do I play now?

I can take the seat meant for me. Pretend to be obedient and inno-cent so Eryx will let down his guard.

Or—

I can sit at the other end of the table and show my defiance.

I refuse to pretend for a second longer in my own home.

So I ignore the duke's invitation, and I take the other end of the table, where I can sit and be Eryx's equal.

The fake duke doesn't move as he watches me. Xandria from the kitchen staff jumps forward to pull out my chair for me. When I sit and look up, my eyes lock with Eryx. He is the first to blink and retreat to his seat, and I feel a small thrill as though I've won some victory.

One of the fake duke's companion's laughs at my brazen move, and the other one smacks him again for it.

"Good morning, Duchess," Eryx says, ignoring them.

"Good morning," I say, leaving off his honorific.

"You still do not believe I am who I say I am."

"I am cautious; that is all. The late duke never spoke of you."

Eryx keeps his eyes on my face as he says, "I doubt my grandfather did much speaking if he had you around."

"He was bedbound for our entire marriage."

"Isn't that what I just said?"

"On his *sickbed*, you imbecile. I was here caring for him, more nursemaid than wife. And where were you? No doubt drinking and whoring your way about the world, if you are as you say: a Demos."

Eryx leans back in his chair, letting it rise up on the back two feet.

"What are you doing?" I ask, appalled. "I just had the wood refinished."

"Whatever I like," he returns, rough arrogance seeping through his tone.

I change tactics. "I find it reprehensible that you value the efforts of the servants so little, as they recently spent hours laboring over the restoration of this table set, but I suppose a con artist does not care one wink for the efforts of others."

The silence is earth-shattering.

Until the legs of the chair snap onto the floor once more.

That's two wins to me.

"Think what you will of me," he says. "That doesn't change who I am. It will only change my opinion of you. Odd that you're not trying to garner my good graces since your future is entirely in my hands now."

"I am a duchess, dowager or not. With that title comes respect and privilege. You cannot take those from me, nor can you throw me from this estate. Legally, there's nothing you can do to me. Whereas you, little boy, might want to be very careful, as I can make your life utterly miserable."

He puts a hand to his temple. "You mean you haven't already started? Gods, help me."

Eryx kneads the sides of his head, eyes closed in thought. When he slams them open with a small smile, I have to force myself not to recoil.

A man with an idea is a dangerous thing.

"You know what, Duchess? I think you and I had a rough start. We met under unusual circumstances, and we've done nothing but bicker since then. Perhaps we could start over?"

"To what end?" What game is he playing now?

"We clearly have need to work out this mess, and I think it might go more smoothly if we aren't at each other's throats. Here, I'll start. My name is Eryx Demos, and I am pleased to make your acquaintance. I would like to formally apologize for scaring you last night. I wanted to explore the manor before the servants had a chance to change anything, to see how it was being run in my absence. I should have spared more thought for the comforts of you and the staff."

"I was not scared," I lie.

"No? Because you often find strangers in your bed?" He thinks himself funny. His face hasn't changed, but humor lights his eyes.

"I only invite attractive strangers to my bed, so you were clearly out of place."

A snort from behind the duke, and yet another responding smack.

"Stop hitting me, Argus!"

"Keep your stupid gob shut, Dyson."

Eryx presses his lips together before turning around. I can only imagine the look he shoots at the two men. They quiet instantly and hold themselves straighter.

When Eryx turns back around to face me, he looks perfectly calm. "We seem to keep baiting each other. That's probably my fault. I've been away for so long. I don't know how to talk to members of the aristocracy anymore."

"You could stop talking altogether," I offer.

That calm facade shatters, and he shoots me a glare. "We're supposed to be playing nice, Duchess. You're making that supremely difficult."

"You're the one who barged into my home, intent on taking everything I own. How exactly do you think I should be treating you?"

"I'm trying to make the best out of a difficult situation."

"The best for you. Not me."

He grinds his teeth. "You're impossible."

I know, and it is the most delightful thing in the world. I have spent far too long playing the simpleton, keeping silent, minding myself. But *speaking*, it is the most glorious freedom. I've missed it terribly, and Eryx seems to bring out a side of me that has long since been kept dormant.

In the most mocking tone I can muster, I say, "It is a pleasure to meet you. I've never met a con artist before. For some reason, I thought you'd be a lot cleverer. No matter. My name is Chrysantha Demos. You must have thought me an easy mark, so I'm sorry you were mistaken. The dukedom is in my perfectly capable hands, and it will stay that way."

His eyes narrow. "Finish your breakfast, Duchess. We shall go pay a visit to Vander to settle our disputes. I think we both need to know exactly what is in that will."

CHAPTER

5

I order Kyros to ready one of my personal carriages. The pink one, because I know it will bother Eryx the most. He rolls his eyes upon seeing it pull up in front of the main entrance. Kyros hops off the back and holds the door open for me. I slam the door shut before Eryx can climb in after me. He's donned that ridiculous floor-length leather jacket again.

"The duke has his own carriages," I say. "And until your identity is confirmed, I'm not about to allow a potential criminal into my carriage, now, am I?" I tap twice onto the roof, and the driver sets off, leaving Eryx in the dust with a wide scowl on his features.

The kingdom of Naxos is spread out over a mountain range, with the main city sprawling across the full length of the largest peak. The duke's holdings are only one mountain over, so the drive is not longer than a few hours.

I spend the time trying to relax myself. I'm in a carriage alone, away from that horrible man. I hadn't realized how tense my muscles had become until I fall against the rose-cushioned seat. I pour myself a glass of wine from the hidden bar and finally feel my muscles unclench.

I doze against the seat, since I barely slept the night before. When the carriage comes to a stop, I make sure none of my makeup has smeared. When I deem that I look pristine, I enter Vander's building, Kyros and Doran trailing behind me.

When the secretary sees me, he bolts for Vander's main office, likely determined to beat me this time. He announces my arrival to Vander, who then sends him away to make tea.

"Mr. Vander," I say as I enter. "Have you already forgotten our last conversation?"

Vander doesn't so much as blink as he straightens the glasses on his nose. "I assure you, I have not, Your Grace. For what purpose has your presence brightened our offices?"

I'm impressed by the light tone he uses. He must loathe me dearly, yet he likes my money enough to put up with me.

"A man barged into my home, claiming to be the duke's heir. I assume you would not allow me to be blindsided by a stranger entering my home, so I'm here to get answers. I need your help getting the law involved so I can have this criminal removed by force, for I'm quite confident he will not exit voluntarily."

Vander smiles.

Smiles.

He's definitely in on it.

"Why," I bite out, "is some boy claiming to be the duke's grandson?"

"Some boy?" a voice says, and it takes me great effort not to look heavenward. Eryx enters the room. He wears no top hat, nor carries a cane, but Vander's assistant takes that dreadful leather jacket from him. Really, he looks like a highwayman with it. His companions, Argus and Dyson, try to squeeze into the room after him.

"Wait outside with the duchess's footmen," Eryx orders.

"But—" Dyson starts, yet the more brutish-looking Argus pulls him along and closes the door behind them.

"Your Grace." Vander says the honorific with an exaggerated weight. "Do take a seat, please."

The hair on the back of my neck stands on end as I realize I'm about to be tag-teamed by these two morons. I ready myself for battle.

Eryx occupies the chair next to me, and I scoot mine over a foot so my skirts don't brush his legs.

"Was that really necessary?" he asks.

"Obviously."

Our gazes swivel to Vander simultaneously.

"Ah, yes, well. This is all a bit awkward, but I'm afraid, Duchess, that the late duke updated his will."

"When?" I ask immediately.

"Before his death."

I purse my lips. "It would be truly remarkable if he'd done so after his death, now, wouldn't it?"

Vander coughs awkwardly and loudly into a handkerchief. "Forgive me, Your Grace. I wasn't thinking. The duke changed his will after your marriage."

"When?" I ask again. "Surely you have the exact date written down?"

A pause. "I'm afraid not. As long as I possess the most current will at all times, it's not necessary to note the date."

"And how are you to know if it is the most current version if you do not note the date?"

Vander says absolutely nothing in response. He's eyeing Eryx, as though he expects the scammer to help him come up with a more clever response.

"I cannot fathom how my late husband entrusted you with all of his affairs when you seem entirely unsuited to the most basic of tasks, such as writing down a simple date."

"Oh, leave the man be," Eryx says. "Mistakes happen. It means nothing."

"Nothing?" Apparently my future counts for nothing, but I will not be silenced so easily. "Where, then, did this change of the will take place? Here in the offices?"

"No, of course not," Vander answers. "The duke was bedridden."

"Then tell me, Mr. Vander. *How* exactly did this change happen, because I was at the duke's bedside for the entire two months of our marriage, and I don't recall seeing you in the manor once."

The room goes silent, and Vander's confidence evaporates. His face turns white. Eryx looks only mildly inconvenienced.

"I'm certain I sent an assistant over to handle the proceedings," Vander puts out lamely.

"Really? Which one?"

"Oh, well, I don't rightly recall—"

"You're telling me that my late husband, your *biggest* client, wanted a major change to his will and you didn't handle it yourself?"

Vander swallows.

I bite the inside of my cheek. "Do you want to know what I think?"

"Not really," Eryx says.

I ignore him. "At best, it sounds like your assistant made a mistake. That this inferior, untrained individual bungled up the last will and testament of my dear husband. And worst? I think this man"—I point to Eryx—"is no heir of the duke at all. I think the two of you are in cahoots. Tell me, Vander, did you put this plan into motion before or after my last visit? Is this payback? Or did you arrange for this when you thought I was a simpleton you could steal from?"

The solicitor reveals nothing, so I press on. "What did he promise you, Vander? Just how much of the duke's fortune has he agreed to hand over in exchange for giving him wealth and a title?"

If it were possible, even more color has fled the solicitor's face.

"That is a wildly inaccurate accusation," Eryx says.

"Prove it," I nigh spit out, "because I promise you I will not rest until the truth comes out. If I find out you've erred in the slightest, Vander, you will have hell to pay. Or you can come clean right now. Set the matter straight, and I will forgive the injury. We can go our separate ways, and the king never need be brought into this matter. Now, is there anything you'd like to say to me?"

This is a lie. I'm ruining this man whether he comes clean or not. His fate has been decided.

Vander squirms in his seat. He looks helplessly over at Eryx, who has leaned on the back two legs of his chair, as though he hasn't a care in the world.

The solicitor rolls his lips under his teeth and looks away from me, as though he might be tempted to say something he shouldn't if he doesn't physically restrain himself.

"Really, you'd rather have him as an ally than me?" I ask. "Perhaps you should ask yourself who you're more afraid of."

Eryx snorts.

"Fine," I say. "I shall hire a private investigator to look into the matter."

Eryx rolls his eyes. "There's hardly any need for that."

"I disagree."

He sighs. "Vander, show her my birth certificate. And my mother's for that matter. Give the duchess the proof she so desperately wants so we can put this matter to rest."

"Of course, Your Grace." Vander leaps up and runs toward some cabinets. He rummages through paper after paper until he finds what he's looking for.

With shaking hands, he offers me a small bundle.

"Could you try not to look guilty?" I ask the man. "That might go a long way in helping me to believe your story."

"Sorry, Your Grace."

I flip through the papers slowly, reading every single line. There's a birth certificate for an Ophira Demos, daughter of Euphrosyne Demos and Hadrian Demos, Duchess and Duke of Pholios. Two seals have been pressed into the wax at the bottom, the late duke's and the late king's. So unless these two managed to steal from the king himself, Pholios has a daughter.

The next sheet is Eryx's birth certificate.

Mother: Ophira Demos

Father:

It's blank.

I look up.

Eryx sees what I hold and says, "I'm a bastard, if you must know. No father claimed me, but I don't need one. My mother is the duke's daughter. Hadrian claimed me as his grandson in his will, his legitimate heir."

The certificate also bears the king's and duke's seals. Though, I note that while the king's seal looks old and worn, the duke's seal looks much more fresh. The wax isn't so dulled, and there isn't a speck of dust pressed into the grooves.

But that doesn't matter. I can't prove all my claims true off one small detail. I can't even follow through on my threat to take this matter to the king. My sister hates me, and the king loves my sister. They're not going to listen to a word I have to say.

I feel my heart pick up its beating. *This is all the proof Eryx needs to take everything from me.*

After a few silent beats, I say, "Two pieces of paper do not explain why Vander looks as though he's about to perish from fright or why no one seems to have heard of you before. Not to mention the fact that the duke's seal looks like it's only recently been administered. Am I to understand that the duke only recently learned of your existence and then randomly desired to turn everything over to you instead of the wife who kept vigil at his bedside? How remarkable."

When I'd questioned the staff after breakfast, none of them knew the duke had sired any children. Even more peculiar, I found that none of the staff had worked at the estate long enough to have been there when a child would have been born. Had Pholios fired them all? For what reason?

Or are all these certificates, including the presence of the king's seal, entirely fabricated?

"Fret and whine all you like, Duchess," Eryx says. "It will not make me any less real. I am here. I am staying, and now all that's left to learn is what the duke left you."

"Right!" Vander exclaims, reaching for a briefcase he'd lodged under his desk. He riffles through more papers until he comes up with what must be the will. The solicitor clears his throat.

"'To my grandson, Eryx Demos, my only living relation, I leave my lands and title, the manor and all its holdings.'"

He drones on about the tenants residing on the dukedom and the yearly incomes from the land. I perk up when he gets to the end.

"'And to my wife, I leave an allowance of fifty necos a month and any gifts she has received during our courtship and marriage.'"

I nearly choke on my next breath at the amount. *Fifty.* A baron's daughter would receive a higher allowance. Fifty necos barely covers a day's worth of shopping.

Vander sets down the paper and looks up, having finally collected his features now that he has something to do.

"May I see that?" I ask calmly, despite the storm brewing within me.

"Certainly," Vander says, "but let me warn you that any destruction of legal documents is a punishable offense."

"I'm not about to destroy anything." I take the paper, read over it myself to confirm all the man's words, then double-check the seal. It appears legitimate.

Fifty necos a month. That's what Eryx and Vander think will appease me?

"How generous the late duke was," I say, managing a careful tone.

"I rather thought so," Eryx says, obviously referring to his own acquisitions rather than mine.

"What of my investments?" I demand.

"Of course," Vander says, riffling for another paper. "Your investments in electronic advancements are raking in astronomical amounts of money. However, since these were made with money earned from the dukedom, that revenue is the sole property of the Duke of Pholios."

I think steam might be coming out my ears. Apparently, I've unwittingly made this impostor even richer.

I don a mask of indifference, hiding behind it as I have so many times before in my life. I cannot act rashly now. I need to think. I need to plan.

I spent years scheming to get my hands on this freedom and fortune. I used the law to protect myself, finding the one possible hole in the system that favors women: dowagerhood.

I hadn't anticipated someone using illegal means to take my fortune and control over the estate from me.

These men have no idea who they're dealing with.

"Now that this is all finally settled," Eryx says, "now is the perfect opportunity to discuss your future, Duchess."

"Excuse me?"

"The dukedom is mine, and I hardly want you to stick around. So let's discuss your options."

"You cannot kick me out," I snap. "The estate is my home." Regardless of whether I get to control it.

"Don't think of it as me kicking you out. Think of it as me generously setting you free."

My hands tighten into fists, burying into the material of my skirts. "Could you please speak plainly?"

"I had hoped to be more delicate, but plain might be the best way to ask this question." Eryx looks meaningfully to Vander.

"Oh, you want me to— Right." Vander coughs for the millionth time. "Your Grace, was your marriage with the duke . . . consummated?"

"I beg your pardon!" I shriek at him.

"It's not a trick question," Eryx steps in. "It's merely a way out for you. If the marriage wasn't consummated, then you can easily have an annulment. You wouldn't be beholden to the estate, nor the duke's last wishes for you."

"You honestly mean to steal the meager stipend you've left me?" I stand from the chair and round on this—this man-child!

"It is hardly meager, and it matters not to me. I'll double it, if you'd like."

My eyelids thin. "In exchange for what?"

"Whatever you say in this room will be uncontested. The duke is not around to confirm or deny your words. So, was your marriage consummated?"

He wants me to lie—or tell the truth. Whichever gets me to say what he wants to hear. That the duke and I never had intimate relations, that our marriage can be rendered void. Why does he wish for me to vacate the house so badly? It's enormous. We could both live in the place without once bumping into each other, not that I have any desire to share what is rightfully mine.

I have no intention of giving Eryx what he wants, so I lie. "The marriage *was* consummated." The words taste bitter on my tongue, but I don't falter.

Eryx sighs. "Perhaps you are daft. I'm trying to give you an out, woman. You could start over. Find a happy marriage this time around, a true one with a man you could love. Isn't that what every woman wants?"

Not me. I crave freedom. Marriage is the exact opposite of that. "I will not lie to obtain what you want. Besides, I hardly see how renouncing my claim as dowager duchess helps you or me."

"You could return to your family. Live with them. Surely you want that? You would keep all your gifts from the duke and your allowance, and as I stated previously, I'm happy to double it."

What he says might sound reasonable to anyone else. We clearly do not get along, and I gain more financially by taking Eryx's offer.

But I *won't*.

Because if I agree, I go back to my father an unwed, unsullied debutante back on the marriage market. Father can try to marry me off again. Alessandra may have changed the law where brideprices are concerned, but that doesn't mean Father can't threaten me with disinheritance if I don't wed the next man of his choosing. I'd be back to being beholden to the men around me. I won't do that again.

I worked damned hard to get myself wedded to the duke. I put up with *hell* to get my hands on that fortune, on the freedoms afforded to me as a dowager duchess. I will never give that up. And if I stay, if I remain the dowager, I'm only one person away from reclaiming all that should rightfully be mine.

Eryx needs to go, not me.

I will make sure of it.

"I'll ask one more time," Eryx says. "Think carefully about your answer. Was your marriage to the duke consummated?"

I take in his arrogant features and condescending tone. He fully expects me to play along. He thinks he's about to take this all from me, and I'll just go willingly. Because he's a man. Because he's big and intimidating and already threatened me once with a dagger and revolver.

What he doesn't realize is that since letting the real Chrysantha out, I *cannot* hide her away again. I will not play the fool again. I will not cater to the men around me again. I did my time, and now it's time for me to shine.

Whether it takes days, months, or years, I will be rid of Eryx Demos, and I will have all that is rightfully mine.

I smooth the skirts of my dress, still standing tall. "Listen carefully, little man, for I will not say this again. Hadrian Demos and I consummated our marriage on our wedding night."

Eryx's eyes narrow, while his lips turn down into a scowl. "You said he was bedridden. He barely had any strength."

"Shall I draw you a diagram of how we made it work? Is your imagination or your knowledge of intimate relations so lacking? Do you need me to explain how I climbed atop him? How I—"

Vander squeaks, and his hands cover his ears. "Your Grace, that is more than sufficient!"

Eryx's face has gone blank. I have no way of knowing if he believes me or not, but that is of no matter. As he stated before, the duke is gone. No one can refute my words. They must be taken as fact on the matter.

"In that case," Vander continues, "the duchess is to remain living at the Pholios Manor. She will take up residence in the duchess suite and resume her duties as lady of the house until such a time as His Grace marries."

I'm watching Eryx's face, so I see him grimace at the mention of his own marriage.

"Must she stay in the duchess suite?" Eryx asks. "Surely a room in the attic would be more than suitable?"

I put on a nasty smile. "If you don't like it, I suggest you marry quickly, *Your Grace*." I say the last words ironically, as though they're an insult instead of an honorific.

"I am *not* marrying," Eryx says. "And I will not have only a door separate us at night."

"Scared an accident might befall you in your sleep?" I ask innocently.

"Hardly."

But he won't say anything more.

"In that case, I'll resume residence in the master suite, and you can find a room more suitable to you in the attic," I announce.

A dimple appears between Eryx's eyes, and I realize he's furious. "Is there nothing legally I can do to be rid of her?" he asks Vander.

"I'm afraid not, Your Grace," Vander says. "Until such a time as either of you is married, things will remain as they are now."

Eryx snatches on to that bit of hope. "Her marriage?"

"Then she would, of course, move in with her new husband."

Eryx relaxes. "Then there is an end in sight."

"I am *not* marrying again."

Both men look at me critically, ignoring my declaration entirely.

"She'll marry again," Vander says.

"The proposals will come," Eryx confirms, talking with Vander as though I am no longer in the room. "Just look at her. So long as she keeps her mouth shut, someone will offer for her."

I have never in my life wanted to slap someone so badly. I have been silenced for *years*, and the mere mention of him suggesting I do so again turns my violent thoughts *murderous*.

I can't think past the strong emotion for several beats.

"You forget that I have to accept," I say between clenched teeth. As a dowager, no one can accept proposals for me. Not my father and *certainly* not the new duke.

"Someday, another man will make you an offer you can't refuse," Eryx says. Quieter, he adds, "I'll make sure of it."

Just what exactly does he intend to do? Bribe men to offer for me? I suppose he has the money to pull strings. But I'm not about to accept another man's hand, not when there's a perfectly good fortune just waiting for me to take it back up.

"Knock yourself out," I say. "In the meantime, I've a manor to run."

And a duke to get rid of.

CHAPTER 6

I alternate between self-pity and fury during the drive back home as I make my plan to reclaim what is mine. When my beautiful carriage rolls to a stop in front of the manor, little Nico comes running down the front steps. After helping me out of the carriage, Kyros swoops his son up into his arms.

"I missed you, Papa."

"I missed you, too." He pulls golden locks out of the boy's eyes and kisses his forehead.

"Papa, why does the duchess look indignant?"

Kyros turns to me, giving me a chance to answer.

"Because an impostor is trying to take my home from me."

"What does *impostor* mean?"

"Someone pretending to be someone they're not."

"Like when I pretend to be a great lion come to eat all the deer in the forest?"

"No. An impostor pretends to be another person, not a creature."

"Oh, so if I went around acting as if I were Papa?"

"Exactly."

"I should not like to be Papa," Nico says. "Papa doesn't have nearly so much time to play as me."

A second carriage pulls up behind mine, and the pretend duke jumps out without waiting for one of his men to open the door for him. He meets my gaze briefly, scowls, and then strides past us all into the manor, his henchmen in tow.

"Is that the impostor?" Nico asks.

"Yes. He pretends to be the master of this house."

"But you're the master of this house."

"Exactly, Nico."

"He looks nothing like you. He's not a very good impostor. Shall I be a lion today and gobble him up?"

I finally look away from the doorway Eryx disappeared into. "No, I think today we should gobble up sweets from the kitchen. What do you say to us seeing what Cook is up to?"

Nico squirms out of his father's arms and starts dashing toward the servants' entrance to the side of the house. "Race you!" he calls over his shoulder.

I follow after him, eager to fortify myself with sugar.

I TRY NOT TO GRIT my teeth as I watch my things moved back to the duchess suite the very next day. Thankfully, I've also refurbished this room since Pholios's death, though I did it in a light blue, thinking perhaps one day I would have a lover move in. I pictured a man lounging in dark silks ready to pleasure me whenever I want, day or night. I was preparing to ask Sandros if he'd like to move in and leave Zanita's, though after what happened to him the night Eryx Demos showed up, I doubt he'll want to come around anymore. The doctor said he'd be fine in the long run, but a nasty bruise was forming when I ordered a couple footmen to return him to Zanita's. I've given the madam a name and full description of Eryx, should she wish to press charges.

I expect to see the servants moving the fake duke's belongings into the master suite next door, but I find no one coming or going as I rearrange my things in my new room. Odd, but I have much more important things to occupy my mind.

Like how I'm to be rid of Eryx Demos.

I can think of plenty of things I'd like to do. Poison his supper. Push him out of a moving carriage. Set a couple of starving wolves loose in his rooms. Those are quick solutions, but they are not smart ones. The duke cannot perish under any strange circumstances. Everyone will look to me as the primary suspect, especially as my new reputation and character become widespread.

That means I'll have to try legal tactics first.

"Kyros," I say, finding the footman in the hallway.

"Yes, Your Grace?"

"I have something that I need done . . . quietly."

"Your business is your business, Your Grace. I don't see why the duke need hear of it."

I smile at him. "I'm in need of a private investigator. Could you go into town and find me one with a great reputation and send for them? They are to use discretion when coming to the manor."

"Of course, Your Grace."

"Thank you."

I would go and do it myself, but I have a solicitor to deal with. A promise is a promise.

Vander thought me an easy mark. He thought he could just hand over all my property to some stranger and I wouldn't put up a fuss. I've acted too well for too long.

But he wasn't the only one I had fooled. I walk into my parlor and pull out a pen and paper from the desk.

Dear Father,

Such unexpected news has reached me. Mr. Vander, the solicitor whom we share, has informed me that the late Duke of Pholios has a grandson. An Eryx Demos has taken up residence in the manor.

It's so strange, considering the duke never mentioned having so much as a child. Not to mention the newcomer looks nothing like the duke. He also has no hints of an aristocratic upbringing. One would think he was a member of the working class with the way he dresses and carries himself. He does frighten me at times.

Mr. Vander tells me the duke changed his will sometime during the two months of our marriage so that this estranged grandson inherited everything. So curious, since I never saw the solicitor or any of his employees come by the estate. You know I was by the duke's side every hour of the day, but I must have simply forgotten the meeting.

I was initially writing to tell you that I wanted to gift you a monthly sum of money, but then I remembered the new duke is in charge of the money now. I am unable to help with your earldom's finances. I shall do my utmost to remain in the new duke's good graces and be the best lady of the house I can be, as is my duty.

All my love,
Chrysantha

I give the letter to Doran with instructions for the footman to deliver it immediately and straight into my father's hands. I've no doubt that I dropped enough hints without being entirely obvious. Father lived with me for years and never once suspected I was acting the entire time.

By midday, I peek my head into the master suite, only to find that it is unchanged. No clothes in the wardrobe. No chests or trunks containing personal items. Not even a book on the nightstand.

Odd. Very odd. Did Eryx come ahead of his belongings?

When I ask for the location of the fake duke, Mrs. Lagos directs me to the study.

"His Grace said he was going to familiarize himself with the accounts," she says. "Perhaps you might offer a helping hand. He seemed a bit overwhelmed."

I laugh. "I'll do that."

"That boy is in over his head."

"He's only a few months younger than I," I say. Not to defend him but to see what Mrs. Lagos will make of that.

She harrumphs. "Women age up quicker than men. You might as well be twenty-five compared to him."

"Don't let His Grace hear you say it."

"Oh, he shan't. You, however, are always fun to gossip with, Your Grace."

"Thank you, Mrs. Lagos. I hold you in high esteem as well."

She walks on with a blush in her cheeks.

Squaring my shoulders, I make for the late duke's study, where he kept all his account books, correspondences, and everything else of import. After Pholios's death, I used the room to handle the accounting, but for anything else, I prefer to use the parlor, where more natural light enters in through the windows. Or be outdoors in the gardens. The study always felt stifling, even with the improvements I made to it. Perhaps I should have knocked out the outer wall and put in more windows?

Something to consider once Eryx is gone.

I don't knock, because whatever else, this is still my home. Not to mention that would be a sign of respect. Since I haven't an ounce of it for Eryx, I barge right on in.

He's buried in papers. They clutter the floors and desk. I believe I even see one stuck to the bottom of his unpolished boot. His hair is as unkempt as ever, and he has the top button of his shirt undone. Highly scandalous, yet again.

"I see your bodyguards are not in the room with you. Aren't you afraid someone might murder you in the study?" I don't know why it amuses me to keep bringing up his death. Perhaps because it will make me seem less suspicious. Perhaps the idea is titillating enough to carry me on another day. Or maybe I simply look for ways to belittle the man, because it is the little things in life that provide the most enjoyment.

He looks up, and I realize that he's wearing a pair of reading glasses. Something about the sight is . . . off-putting. Normally, Eryx looks like a barbarian who lives in the woods and slays panthers with his bare hands. But with the glasses? He looks studious. He looks *smart*. He somehow looks the part of a wealthy duke.

I hate them.

I hate him.

Attractive and *man standing in the way of everything I've ever wanted* should not go together.

Eryx scoffs. "They're not my bodyguards. They're my valets." His eyes drift to the right corner of his gaze as he finishes the lie.

I won't call him out. This time. "In that case, you ought to fire them."

"Why?"

"Have you seen yourself? What are they doing with your hair? And what are you wearing? You look like an orphan."

Eryx removes the glasses from his nose and plops them on the desk. "Because I don't spend exorbitant amounts of money on clothing or hair pomade or whatever else gentlemen are expected to pamper themselves with? I'm a man, not a peacock. And speaking of money—" He reaches for a stack of papers before him, so there must be some method to the mayhem around him. "Would you care to explain these?"

He brandishes them in the air like they're a weapon.

"What are they?"

"Bills. From the dressmaker, the shoemaker, the jeweler, perfumeries, cosmeticians. Then there's the carpenter, the mason, needleworkers, painters, an arboretum, and the list goes on."

I roll my eyes. "Have you missed all the signs of renovation throughout the manor? Did you think the finished rooms always looked this impeccable? Pholios didn't exactly have an eye for these things, and the manor went years without a lady to maintain it. Since I spent all my time married to the late duke at his bedside, I hardly had time to perform my duties as duchess. I've only recently managed to begin updating everything."

"And the dresses and jewelry? Am I to understand you were in need of updating as well?"

"I am a lady. We always need pampering. If you had any sense, you would visit the tailor. Speaking of which, where are your things?"

"What things?"

"Your clothes? Personal belongings? Last I checked, the master suite was still as I left it. Since you made such a fuss over my vacating it, I assumed you'd wish to move in immediately."

He puts his glasses back on and resumes reading whatever he had been. "I already did."

"In the time I walked up to the study?"

"Just before lunch. You missed the cedar chest on the opposite side of the bed."

"You—you have only a single chest?"

Eryx sighs. "Again, I'm not a peacock. A man needs naught but a single coat, five shirts, and two pairs of pants."

I bite the inside of my cheek. "I cannot tell if you are joking."

"I'm quite serious. You can wear one pair while the other is being washed."

I cannot speak for a full five seconds. "That's it! I could abide everything else, but this just *proves* my point all the more. There's no way you're a nobleman! You haven't the manners nor the style nor anything else to suggest good breeding. Where did Vander find you? A gutter somewhere?"

"Duchess, I have spent the last five years in the king's army, killing and conquering in the name of Naxos, out on the front lines. The fact that I'm still alive should tell you several things. First of which, that I'm a damned good soldier, and second, I don't give a damn what you think. Third, I'm sick of killing and quite eager to take up a quiet life at this country estate.

"Now," he continues, returning his attention to the papers before him, "what about these expenses? Men's clothing. Expensive colognes. Male jewelry. What the hell is all this? Do you parade about as a man half the time?"

He is such an idiot. I just stare at him.

He blinks once. Then a look of surprise crosses his features. "Am I to understand that you have a lover you're financing?"

"Who did you think the man in my bedroom you so rudely knocked unconscious was?"

His mouth pops open. "I thought he was a servant. When he refused to leave, I had to use force. You mean to tell me that was your—"

"It's none of your business, really."

He looks back down at the paper before him. "Why are you paying for so much? These expenses are ridiculous. Has the lord no—"

"He's no lord. He's . . . my mistress." Or was about to be. I hadn't actually gotten around to asking him.

I appear to have finally shocked Eryx into silence. Then: "You're *paying* him for—for favors?"

"For sex," I clarify, since Eryx seems rattled by the whole discussion.

"*Why?*" he asks, clearly dumbfounded. "Have you seen yourself? A woman like you doesn't need to pay for such things."

I let a smile grace my lips. "Is that your way of offering?"

His eyes dart down to my mouth at the same time he barks out a vehement "No!"

I said it to rattle him. I have more interest in being around a wild boar than I do this man. I laugh and flick a lock of hair off my shoulder. "Then I shall continue to spend my money as I see fit."

Eryx finally manages to collect himself. "Except, none of this was your money. You've been spending *my* fortune."

A feeling of dread settles low in my stomach as he prattles on.

"I'm halting all the renovations to the manor. Your role as duchess permits you to rearrange furniture, not decimate this historic home. As for all of your personal purchases, I shall take them out of your stipend, which means you shall receive your first one in approximately . . ." He pauses to do some quick math. "One year's time."

Eryx's form shifts in front of me, and it takes me far too long to realize that *I'm* the one shaking.

"You can't do that!"

"I can, and I am."

"For what reason? You have money aplenty! *I've* made you the wealthiest man in the city with my investments! You don't need to take anything from my stipend. You're just being petty."

"Is it petty to remind you where you stand? Then perhaps you shouldn't have told me I look like an orphan."

"Is your ego so sensitive? Are you so insecure that you cannot take a joke?"

"Considering both my parents no longer walk this world, perhaps you can glean why I take such high offense."

That shuts me up. For about a second. "Perhaps I'd be more inclined to feel sorry for you if you weren't stealing my money, lands, and manor." And if he weren't a man. He already has such an advantage in the world. It's hard to feel sympathy for him at all. His parents are dead? Well, at least the law forbids anyone from trading him for money. Never mind that particular law is now fixed. It wasn't at the time I suffered for it.

He says nothing as he puts his signature on some document before him. I try a new tactic. "If I have my stipend, I'm likely to spend more time out of the manor spending it."

"No, Duchess, I'm feeling petty enough to put my foot down on this issue. And I'll be monitoring all the items in the manor, should you try to pawn something off. I will come for you, not the servants, if anything goes missing, including my family's heirlooms, which I noted you've stored in the attic. You may go now."

I don't slam the door in my wake, but I do raise a certain finger to the closed door where the duke cannot see. Precisely at that moment, his supposed valets approach and see the gesture.

Argus raises a single brow, while Dyson salutes me.

"You just keep putting the prick in his place, Your Grace," Dyson says. "I haven't had this much entertainment since we visited that brothel in Pegai. When are we due for another outing, Argus?"

"Don't use such language in front of the lady, and there will be no outings. His Grace has far too much to do."

"Not even a short one? Perhaps we sneak away for an hour while Eryx is handling some boring business in town?"

"That's *Your Grace*," Argus reminds him, "and I don't think you could fill a whole hour of a woman's time if you tried."

This time Dyson is the one to give Argus a pummeling. "I'll have you know I've kept scores of women up all night with my prowess! I shan't have you disgracing my good name in front of the lady."

Dyson puts Argus in a chokehold, but the bigger man slings his elbow into Dyson's stomach. He doubles over, yet strikes out with his leg, sending Argus flat on his ass.

At the noise, Eryx throws open the door to his study to find Dyson hunched over, Argus on the floor, and me staring at the two of them in astonishment.

"Quit showing off for the duchess and get your sorry hides in this room at once."

Argus rolls onto his feet, grabs Dyson by a scrap of his shirt, and hauls him into the room. Eryx doesn't spare me a glance as he shuts the three of them within the study.

If those two men are valets, then I'm the empress of all seven kingdoms.

CHAPTER

7

can't remember the last time I was so incensed. No one has been so antagonistic toward me in my life. So few have known me well enough to truly get under my skin.

In less than twenty-four hours, this stranger has managed to take away my control over my home *and* my money.

In the morning, I don't wake to the sounds of hammering and footsteps carrying heavy items throughout the manor. I also don't wake in my beautiful master suite to the image of cherubs darting through clouds.

I'm back where I started, in the damned duchess suite. Second in power once more.

Once Medora finishes helping me dress, I walk through the manor in silence. In the entryway, the grand staircase is only half finished, the dark tiles partially replaced with white marble. The intricate metalwork beneath the banister is halfway painted with gold. The mismatched sight makes my skin itch.

In the ballroom, half the drapes have been torn down, with the other half untouched. They're a gaudy bright red that some ancestor, likely before Pholios's time, selected. Who knows what became of the gold draperies I'd purchased? The old chandelier was removed from the ceiling and is resting in the middle of the floor. Apparently the fake duke didn't even allow the workers to remove it before sending them off.

Light spots on the wall show where paintings once hung. Eryx has likely halted my shipment of new purchases to add life and color to the place. Mismatched furniture lines all the corridors. The windowsills are covered in sealant, from where a hasty patch job was done so as to not let any air into the manor, but it looks awful. Most of the windows weren't even able to be replaced yet, so they, too, are mismatched.

Outside, the hedge maze is only mostly finished. The sculpture for the water fountain will never arrive. The lawn is partially trimmed. I don't even see the gardeners out and about watering the plants, which they usually do at this time.

When I return indoors, I realize the quietness is due to more than just the missing workers. Where are all my servants? Damasus isn't walking the halls. I can't find the maids anywhere in the library or my parlor doing the dusting. It takes me ages just to locate Mrs. Lagos.

"Where is everyone?" I ask her.

I realize then that her eyes are red and glassy, but she holds herself as tall as such a short woman can.

"The duke," she says, and *duke* comes out with such vehemence that I nearly step back, "has ordered that I let go half the staff. I've just finished informing the rest of them."

I can't speak for a full five seconds. "What?"

"I had to send them away. Without places to live or their final week's wages. I begged the duke to allow me to—"

Before she even finishes, I'm stomping from the room. I tread the stairs like a rhino in a charge. Ruining my life wasn't enough? Now he goes after my staff? Big mistake. I fairly kick open the study door.

Dyson sits sideways in an armchair, balancing a knife by the tip on one of his fingers. Argus leans against one wall with his arms crossed, and Eryx—he's seated in *my* chair, looking at *my* account book.

"What have you done?" I shriek at him.

Dyson drops his knife, and Argus nearly loses his balance. Eryx's eyes narrow as he looks up.

"You've let go half the staff?" I continue. "Am I to understand that these two idiots will be preparing our meals and cleaning the manor?" I gesture to the two idiots in question. "Or are you planning on cultivating the garden and dusting the bookshelves yourself? You do look more suited to that task than lounging in that chair."

Eryx returns his attention to the desk. "I've hardly been lounging. I've had to go over all your purchases and double-check your math to ensure you haven't bungled anything up."

"Don't change the subject. We're going to hire back everyone you've let go, and you're going to personally apologize to them all for the stress you've caused by making them homeless and destitute."

Argus and Dyson go still. Each man holds his breath, as though waiting for something to happen.

"I'm not doing that," Eryx says, not looking up from the account book.

"This is a massive estate. It needs a full range of staff members to keep it running. You can't just—"

He finally looks at me, his demeanor totally unaffected. "I can and I have. That will be all, Duchess."

I stride farther into the room, walking right up to the edge of the desk. "Is this more punishment? You mean to give me more work to do with only half the staff to manage the estate? Does it make you feel like a big man to exercise such control over people's lives?"

Eryx rises from the desk, showing me that he doesn't need to do a damn thing to be a big man. I sense movement behind me. In front, I see Argus take a step forward, his eyes glued to the duke. Eryx stays his grunts with a raised hand.

What were they going to do? Physically restrain me?

"The only thing I mean to do is be rid of you. If getting rid of half the staff accomplishes that, then I'll consider it a success."

My mouth drops open. "This isn't about money at all, is it? You're not being meticulous with the accounts because you're worried a few necos have gone missing. You're looking for proof that I'm unfit to rule this estate. You mean to force me to leave at the mere thought of living in less comfort and leaving all the renovations half done. You think that will accomplish anything? Well, you're sorely mistaken. The only thing you've managed to do is to turn all your remaining staff against you and earn even more of my ire."

"Oh no," he deadpans. "Not more of your ire. Anything but that."

My vision goes red, and just like it did the day my husband died, I feel my brain detaching from the rest of my body. Of its own accord, my hand reaches for a glass paperweight on the desk and throws it at Eryx's head.

In a move too quick for my eyes to follow, Eryx catches it and sets it back down on the desk calmly.

Ooh. Anger as I've never known takes hold of me. I retrieve the paperweight once more and throw it on the floor by the window, where it shatters.

"Have fun cleaning that up yourself," I say, "since you've hardly any staff to do it for you."

"Unlike you, labor doesn't scare me."

He does not get to have the last word!

"I hope you burn in hell with all the devils for your crimes."

"Pretty sure I'm already there," he says, looking meaningfully my way.

"And you're going to stay there, because I'm not leaving!" I turn from the room and exit the door before turning back. "Obviously I meant the estate in general. I'm leaving this office because I can't stand the sight of your ugly face, you entitled ass."

I slam the door behind me, then brace one hand against it as I try to get a hold of myself.

"W-o-w," Dyson says, dragging the word out into three syllables. "I've never seen a woman so mad. You've driven a lady to swear."

"She'll need to get madder than that if we're to be rid of her," Argus says.

"Shush," Eryx says. "She's still here. I can hear her breathing on the other side of the door."

I jerk away from the room as though I'd been burned. Then I flee.

⊱⊱⊶⊙⊷⊰⊰

I THOUGHT MY SISTER was the only one who could get under my skin like that, but that was before I met Eryx Demos. Ruining other people's lives just to try to get to me? That's a new low.

Anytime I feel as though I might burst from the fury I'm desperately trying to control, I imagine myself sitting astride Eryx with a pillow covering his head. When I remove it, I see Eryx's eyes, unseeing in death. That's what I want. I want him dead, knowing it was me who killed him, just like my husband.

Yet I can't have that.

I can't have anything close to that.

But the image sustains me as I lie awake in bed that night.

When Kyros knocks on my door, eagerness replaces my murderous thoughts. Finally, something *to do* about all of this.

"Your guest has arrived, Your Grace. I've taken him through the library. No one else knows he's here."

"Well done, Kyros. You have my deepest thanks. Will you send for Medora?"

My maid helps me to re-dress enough to be suitable for company. Then I pad quietly to my favorite place on the estate.

The man I find within is young and strong. Perhaps late twenties. Deep obsidian skin tone. His head is shaved, though he keeps a short beard. He's in a fine jacket and tailored clothes, so he must do well for himself.

"Your Grace," he says, bowing at my entrance.

"Thank you for coming, Mr.—?"

"Tomaras. Ilias Tomaras. At your service. I understand you are in need of some investigatory work."

"Indeed." I explain the situation for the second time that day. This time, however, I include all my suspicions and any details that might seem pertinent, like the strange exchange with Vander.

Ilias takes careful notes on a paper pad before him, which I like. It is beyond satisfying to have a man stand still and just listen. He is on my side, unlike everyone else, and he carefully takes in every word I say.

"I can see why you have concerns. They are definitely warranted, and I am happy to look into the matter. Have you kept any correspondences of the late duke's?"

"I'm afraid not. I threw out everything of his upon his death."

"That may slow things down, but it will certainly not stop me. Is there anything else I should know?"

"The fake duke employs a couple bodyguards of some kind. One of them is a really dangerous-looking fellow. He calls them Argus and Dyson."

"Perhaps I will look into these two men in addition to the new duke. Find their connection."

"That would be wise."

Ilias nods. "I think this is all I need to get started. There's just the matter of my pay."

"Of course."

"For a job like this, I charge three hundred necos. I require half up front and half upon delivery of the requested information."

Only now do I remember that I have access to a monthly stipend that has been *cut off* until such a time as my personal purchases have been paid off. *I have no means of paying the man.*

I have grown far too accustomed to having endless funds at my disposal, clearly.

In an attempt to save face, I say, "Thank you for your time, Mr. Tomaras. I shall send my man to you with your first payment shortly. I am most eager for you to get started. With the new duke in control of the accounts, I shall have to make arrangements to acquire your pay. I will be in touch very soon."

Ilias doesn't waver at all at my proclamation. He tips his head. "Your Grace."

"I trust you can see yourself out?"

"Certainly."

Mr. Tomaras leaves, and embarrassment heats my cheeks. I had the man come all this way, only to not pay him for the job. Being a broke duchess is humiliating, and I am furious that Eryx has put me in this position.

He's not even the real duke! He has no claim to my money, but I can't even hire a man to invalidate him because I first need money. Perhaps that was all part of his plan when he cut off my stipend entirely.

I realize now that all my regular expenditures have to go.

I refuse to cry as I write a letter to Zanita, halting Sandros's visits for the foreseeable future. I feel so pitiful, a penniless duchess who now can't afford male companionship.

When I finally return to my bed, I lie completely alone. No Sandros. No release. Just pent-up energy and a name to curse into the dark hours.

Eryx Demos—if that's even his real name—needs to go.

I suppose there are only two courses of action before me. I can return some of the jewelry and other fine things I've purchased, which will be embarrassing and make me look destitute, especially with how I fawned over everything in the stores. I just know word will somehow get back to my sister, and I *cannot* have that. I can't even have Kyros pawn something for me, because everyone will assume he stole it and look for a reward from the duke for turning him over.

That means I need to find a way to get the money from Eryx.

Begging is out of the question, and it's beneath me. I could try to steal it by going through Eryx's things when no one is watching, but Eryx knows I want the money and is just waiting for me to do something that will allow him to take legal action.

So that leaves trading or blackmail.

If there's something Eryx wants, I need to learn what it is, get it, and trade it for the money I seek. Or, if he has a secret he wants kept hidden, I need to learn it and force him to pay me for my silence.

It will be tricky, because I can't use my traditional means of obtaining information. Normally, I just pretend to be vacant and aloof, and men will say all kinds of secrets in front of me. Eryx will never make that mistake with how outwardly antagonistic I've been toward him.

Which means I need to resort to spying.

Until I can pay Ilias Tomaras for the job, I'll have to play the role of investigator myself.

CHAPTER 8

force myself to wait before taking action. Eryx is clearly on high alert after my display with the paperweight. He may have no idea what I'm capable of, but that doesn't mean he won't keep a close eye on me, expecting retaliation for the stunt he pulled with the servants. Fortunately, the members of my book club remain on the estate, as well as Kyros. Most of Cook's staff are gone, and half the stable hands and groundskeepers have been forced to leave. I've done what I can to find them all positions elsewhere and offer letters of recommendation, but there's no denying their lives are forever changed because of the impostor.

Eryx Demos will get his, of that I'm certain. I just have to choose my moments carefully.

Patience and I are old friends. We sat hand in hand as we played Father like a fiddle for years and years, subtly pointing his head where we wanted it, letting him think my ideas were his. I would have been married long before nineteen if he'd been in control. He had no idea that I was reading his correspondences before he ever received or sent them. Never once suspected that letters went missing. Or that he was reading forgeries at times.

I became quite the practiced hand at imitating handwriting and opening sealed letters without leaving a trace of evidence.

I had to bide my time until I found the perfect match: an old, dying man with no heirs.

I hadn't taken into account the possibility of someone else playing my game, trying to take what was mine by the same means.

Physically, I don't think I'm in danger. If the pretend duke intended to murder me, he would have done so by now. Unless he, too, is biding his time so my death looks like an accident.

I suppose it will come down to who can play the game best.

While I wait to strike, I learn many useless things about the duke.

For instance, he made a face at dinner when the kitchen staff brought out roasted duck. He ate his meal quietly, though I noticed he didn't eat as much as he normally does. When we had strawberry short-cake for dessert, he asked Cook for a second helping.

When I stroll through the library during the day, I'll find some tomes missing and then returned later in incorrect locations. I know exactly what he's reading, and it irritates me that we have the same taste in books. Or that we both read so voraciously.

The strangest thing is when Eryx disappears from the manor for hours at a time, requesting no carriage or horse. He traipses off into the wild greenery at the edges of the estate, and I get the sense that he's not just off catching some air. No, he's up to something, but when I ask the remaining outdoor staff if they see anything, they have nothing to report. Some even offer to tail him, but they inform me that the duke just disappears without a trace.

"He's impossible to follow," a groundskeeper says. "It's like tailing a ghost."

Perhaps Eryx was telling the truth when he mentioned serving in the army. That would explain those skills.

It doesn't, however, explain what he's up to.

The man is as much of a hermit as I am. He doesn't attend social functions. He doesn't update his wardrobe.

He also doesn't spook any less easily. If he's alone in a room, and I happen to accidentally sneak up on him, he rounds on me with his revolver and knife extended.

"Honestly, you need to calm yourself!" I snap at him after the third time it happens. "One of these days you're going to shoot me!"

"If I shoot you, Duchess, it will not be an accident."

Chilling words, but I don't drop my irritation. "Put those away at once! Must you carry them through the hallways? Are we expecting an invasion any time soon?"

"Instincts acquired in the army are hard to drop."

Yet, I still don't believe him entirely. For his "valets" trail along after him most of the time, long after the duties of valet should be required for the day.

Is the duke in danger? Does he suspect someone is after him? Need I be concerned? (Not for him, of course, but for me, since we live in the same household.)

I pose these questions to Eryx once, but he merely says, "Don't be absurd," in the most condescending tone fathomable.

Karla and Tekla approach me one afternoon, dusters in hand.

"Your Grace," Karla says. "You asked us to keep you apprised of anything interesting popping up in the papers."

I had. After that day when Lady Petrakis divulged everything that my sister had been up to with her new edicts, I realized I needed a way to stay better informed. My maids/book club friends love reading the gossip columns and other things involving the nobility. I knew I could count on them to keep me apprised of anything important.

"Is it my sister?" I ask warily.

"No," Tekla says. "I'm afraid it's nothing terribly exciting. Just rather strange. A nobleman has gone missing."

"Who?"

"Lord Andris."

That is strange. Usually noblemen go missing when they accrue gambling debts or frequent unsavory parts of town. As far as I know, he's not involved in anything shady that I've overheard. In fact, the only thing I do know about the viscount is that he served in the army for a handful of years. He regularly bragged about some award he received.

Hmm, Eryx claimed to have served in the army.

Eryx, who walks around with bodyguards trailing him and weapons on hand.

"How long has he been missing?" I ask.

"Two weeks."

Which is also, coincidentally, how long Eryx has been in town . . .

The connection is too flimsy for me to really make guesses, but it is odd.

"Thank you," I say. "Do keep me posted on anything else of note that happens, especially any more disappearances."

"Of course, Your Grace," Tekla says.

"Once I have money again, I promise to tip you both."

"Oh, nonsense," Karla says. "A chat between friends doesn't warrant an exchange of money."

She's too kind, but I will be paying them for their service once I have the means to do so.

Which requires more spying.

I try to get a sense of Eryx's schedule in the following weeks, but he never sticks to one. He never goes for walks at the same time nor reads at the same time nor goes over the accounts at the same time. It's as if he's trying to make it difficult for someone like me who wishes to snoop through his things.

But my chance finally comes one day when Vander visits the estate.

He, the duke, and the two valets, Argus and Dyson, enter the study, Vander shooting me hateful looks all the while. I pretend not to notice.

"Is my presence needed?" I ask before Eryx shuts the door.

"Definitely not."

"Shall I send for tea?"

"Go away, Duchess." He slams the door, and I hear him grumble, "Damnable woman," on the other side.

I walk away purposefully, then slip off my shoes and tread back toward the door. I even try holding my breath, since Eryx somehow managed to hear it last time. To be fair, I was incensed and breathing heavily then, so perhaps I'm being overcautious.

"I'm all but ruined!" Vander shrieks. "That girl wrote to her father about us. Lord Masis has been visiting my offices constantly. He's even convinced all his associates not to use me since I now neglect to time-stamp my documents and send assistants to do jobs better carried out by myself."

"Quiet down, Vander," Eryx says. "It will be all right."

"I have no clients left. They've all run to my competitors to do their business!"

"I will take care of it," Eryx assures him.

I can't hold my breath any longer, so I tiptoe back toward where I left my shoes and slip them on as I breathe once more.

With a grin, I glide toward the master suite, prepared for some snooping.

Whether or not the servants are on my side, I decide it's best not to be seen entering the duke's rooms. I'd hate to imagine the conclusions drawn before I could refute them. The thought makes me want to gag. Instead, I enter the duchess suite before approaching the door joining our rooms together. Naturally it's locked, but I have a skeleton key that works on every door in the house. It was, after all, mine until Eryx cast his toxic shadow over the place.

The room is . . . wholly unchanged. Just as beautiful and perfect as I left it, save my bed, vanity, and other furniture, which are now in my current room instead of this one. The more masculine furniture that used to be in the duchess suite has taken its place.

And yet, the place looks lifeless, for Eryx has made no personal touches. On the one hand, I'm relieved to have the room unmolested, but on the other, it's really quite sad. Two pairs of trousers. Most gentlemen would faint at the thought.

I go to the cedar chest I missed the last time I perused the room. It bears no lock, and when I peer inside, I find a beat-up canteen, a torn red scarf, a well-worn book titled *The Adventures of Voleta Mavros*, and a handful of medals bearing Eryx's name.

Well, it appears he was at least telling the truth about being in the army. I read the inscriptions on the round brass pendants. *For Fervor. For Bravery. For Cunning.*

I know next to nothing about the army and the different honors awarded to the fighting men and women, but these would seem impressive—

If Eryx hadn't been awarded them. I wonder if they're like children's tokens given out at parties. Everyone receives one.

As I stand, I realize there were no clothes in the chest. Only personal items. I try the wardrobe, but it hasn't been filled since I last checked. The washroom is completely empty. No soaps or hairbrush or shaving cream, though Eryx is always well-shaved. Or perhaps he cannot grow hair on his chin? Oh, I shall have to prod at him about that one.

I examine the comforter on the bed. It still smells of laundry soap. Not a hint of male on it. I can only come to one conclusion.

The duke is not staying here. He made such a fuss over having the master suite, and yet, he does not sleep here. He doesn't even keep his things here, except for one chest.

Well, that poses two new questions.

Why isn't he sleeping here? And where is he sleeping instead?

Since I never see horses coming or going, I doubt he has a lover somewhere he meets up with. Besides, no one in their right mind would agree to be in close quarters with that abhorrent man.

And then a strange thought occurs to me.

Is it me?

Does he not wish to be anywhere near me? As if I were so distasteful that he cannot bear to sleep one door away from me? Surely that cannot be it.

But why else would he shy away from the most comfortable room in the house? If it's truly all the pink giving him headaches, then why not redecorate? No builders or architects have been by. It's not as though he has anything in the works.

Something is very, very strange indeed.

>-!-<>--O--<>-!-<

WHEN THE SOLICITOR LEAVES, I pounce upon Eryx.

"Did you have a nice chat?"

He rubs his thumb and forefinger against his brow. "Not exactly."

"Excellent. What did Vander want?"

"I called for him."

"Well, what did you want?"

"That is none of your concern." I'm sure his deep tone, harsh-set face, and imposing height would silence anyone else—but everything he says feels like a challenge I have to accept.

"If you're having trouble with the accounts, I can offer my services. I am, after all, older and wiser than you." Also, I need to get into that room for more information about Eryx. And if he is bungling up the accounts, I cannot let that stand! That's my money.

"I am more than capable of handling all the accounts, despite the ridiculous charges you made before my arrival."

"The only ridiculous thing *is* your arrival."

He growls. "Do you need something? Or is there a reason you're still buzzing in my ear?"

My jesting tone turns serious. "This is my home, too. I wish to be notified of any changes."

"For gods' sake, the man was here to discuss *you*, not the house or the accounts!"

"Me?"

"Yes, thanks to our soon-to-be Shadow Queen, dowries, instead of brideprices, are exchanged upon marriage agreements. I needed Vander's advice on a sum appropriate for you."

I blink several times before I can find my words. "I beg your pardon?"

Eryx looks right at me. "You are a nuisance. Everywhere I turn, there you are. At my dining table. In my library. Walking the grounds. Sitting in the gardens. You have an uncanny talent for being precisely where I wish to be."

Do I? The man must be quiet as a mouse, for I have never noticed him stumbling upon me. Only the other way around. And I don't divert my plans just because he's already occupying a room in the house.

"The rooms in the manor are quite spacious," I say. "There's plenty of room for the two of us." Not that I like sharing with him, either.

"I disagree, and I want you gone from my house."

I cross my arms over my chest. "It is a manor, not a house, and it's not *yours* but *ours*."

"Only until you are married. A matter that I intend to hurry along."

I scoff. "You cannot marry me off against my will. You don't have that authority. I am a dowager. My life is my own."

"Yes, I wasn't speaking of forcing anything. Merely providing an incentive."

"Incentive," I repeat stupidly.

"Yes, you seem quite fond of spending money. So Vander and I had a talk. Upon your engagement to the man of your choosing, I will grant you a dowry of ten thousand necos. Per the Shadow Queen's edict, this money is for your personal use, and your future husband will have no right to it. In addition, you will receive your monthly stipend as stipulated in my grandfather's will. And if you marry well, I'm sure you can negotiate an additional stipend from your new husband. You will be wed and rich. I will be alone and happy. We both win."

Ten thousand necos. I've never heard of such a large sum being exchanged in a marriage agreement. In fact, I thought the seven-thousand-necos brideprice my father received was exorbitant.

I'm stunned. I'm greedy for it. And yet—

"Why the hell do you want me gone so badly?" I say, personally affronted.

"Because you're awful," he says, as though it were obvious.

"Oh, *I'm* awful. What about you? Moody and broody. Arrogant and stupid. Poorly dressed and ill-mannered. Waving guns around and making enemies of all the staff. No one wants you here, and since there's legitimate concerns over your real identity, you'd think you'd tread a lot more lightly."

He steps forward, invading my personal space. "If you're so concerned that I'm not who I say I am, then why don't you take the matter to the constabulary? Or the king? Do something about it if you're so sure you've got everything figured out."

He's got me there. I can't go to the king, because my sister has his ear. I can't go to the constabulary, because they're not going to risk angering a man in such a position of power. They will always believe a duke over a duchess; that's why I have to hire a private investigator. But this feral man has all my money!

I have no retort, for I'm fuming over the reminder of my cutoff stipend.

"Listen," Eryx says, his voice taking on an uncharacteristically gentle tone. "I am not required to provide a dowry for you, because I'm not your father. I'm doing this as a kindness."

I snort. "After you just said I'm awful and you want me gone? You're doing this for yourself."

"Fine." His voice returns to normal. "I'm doing this for myself, but you can't deny how it helps you as well. Look at it as me taking care of both our interests."

"I have no interest in being married again."

"Don't judge marriage so quickly. You didn't exactly get the cream of the crop last time, did you? This time, you'll get to pick your partner. You can probably have whomever you want. I've seen the number of correspondences that come for you. I know you have options."

"And those options will be taken away the second I marry. I will be beholden to my husband."

"But you'll be wealthy."

"Is that what you'd choose? Bondage over freedom for the right price?"

He flicks his long hair out of his eyes. "*Bondage* is hardly the right word."

"How about prostitution, then?"

"Excuse me?"

"That's what I'd be trading. Sex for money."

"That's not—"

"Isn't it?" I ask, cutting him off. "Men need heirs to pass on their titles. That's why they take wives. Else they'd be content with mistresses forever. A wife is but an object, a vessel for his progeny."

Eryx quiets for a moment. "I hadn't thought of it that way."

I'm absolutely shocked that he took a moment to even consider my words.

But then he says, "So find a man *you* desire. Flip the tables. Fall in love. Change the game."

"Oh, just find a sexy man, is that it? What happens when he opens his mouth? Seriously, it's like you haven't met a man."

"Need I remind you that you were paying for the company of a man? If you found one tolerable man, then surely you can do so again, this time with a nobleman who doesn't need anything from you."

I clench my teeth in frustration. "I paid for the company of *several* men, and the only reason they were tolerable is because they were being paid to be so!"

Eryx closes his eyes for a solid thirty seconds, as though he wishes to pretend I'm no longer here. When he opens them again, he appears calmer. He looks over my head as he says, "You will be happy again. This time will be different. You have full control over your courtship now. You can refuse anyone."

"I thought I already did, for I'm refusing your offer. I don't need your dowry. I don't want it."

His hands clench into fists as his eyes jump to mine.

I take a step back.

Because not only does he look ready to hit something, but also his eyes have changed color. They're a bright amber instead of brown.

And they're glowing.

"Fifteen thousand," he says.

"What?"

"I'll up it to fifteen thousand necos. Your dowry."

I finally process the words, looking away from those eyes. "No!"

"Twenty. That's my final offer."

Twenty thous— That's unheard of. It's beyond exorbitant.

I'm insulted.

"Why do you hate me so much?" I demand.

"I do not hate you."

"Lies! You barge into my home. Steal my room, despite not sleeping in it. Steal my money, despite not needing it. You've fired half my friends, left the place in a complete state of disarray. Now you wish to pawn me off on someone else, just so you can have this enormous manor to yourself. Did I wrong you in some egregious manner that I'm unaware of?"

"It's not you."

"Is it because I suspect the truth? That you are not who you say you are. Is it because I can bring your dark secrets to light?"

Eryx looks away from me, his body tensing like a bowstring. I hold my breath for a few beats, waiting to see what he will do.

When he turns to face me, his eyes are back to normal.

"It is because I wish to be alone."

CHAPTER

9

There is no denying it.

Before, I could excuse it as a trick of the light. But just now? From a foot away, I watched his eyes change from dark brown, to glowing amber, to brown again.

Eryx is hiding more than just his treachery in stealing this estate from me. I can't even begin to put into words what it might be. Perhaps I should be frightened, but the mystery pulls me in like a wave being pulled by the moon. I *will* get to the bottom of this, no matter what the truth reveals.

It occurs to me that my initial assumptions were all wrong. The firing of the servants, sending away the men refurbishing the house, trying to be rid of me—it's not all solely to enrage me.

It's to get as many people away from him as possible. He was telling the truth just now when he said it wasn't me. It's him. There's something about him he doesn't want people finding out. He needs as few people on the estate as possible to keep his secret. Somehow, his "valets" are involved. They know and are helping him hide it. Of that, I'm certain.

Before I can decide what to do with this new information, a letter arrives from Father:

My dearest daughter,

Thank you for telling me about the new duke. It is highly surprising and suspicious. I've put as much pressure on Vander as I can manage, but there's nothing more I can do. I tried writing to your sister, but I suspect she is burning my letters before even reading them. No help will come from there.

I'm not sure why I bothered to tell you that. You clearly aren't worried about the new duke, but I am worried for you. We know nothing about this man, and he appears to be taking advantage of you by cutting off your access to your late husband's money.

Might I propose you look at considering marriage again? If we find you another rich husband, this time one who won't die for some time, we can better secure my our futures. I've put together a list of some suitable matches. You are a dowager now, so you'll have to take charge in this matter, but I have every confidence in your securing a new husband.

Your loving father,
Sergios Stathos, Lord Masis

I toss the letter and list of names into my hearth to be burned. I knew there was nothing my father could do to help me be rid of the duke. I only needed him to make Vander sweat, which he did, motivated by his own selfish interests, as usual.

I can't imagine what he'd do if he learned the fake duke offered me twenty thousand necos to remarry. Probably kiss the man's boot.

As usual, the only one I can depend on to get things done is myself. I have three items on my to-do list:

1. Secure money to hire a private investigator to find proof of Eryx's deceit.
2. Figure out Eryx's secret.
3. Learn where he's sleeping at night.

If I can legally prove that Eryx is in the wrong, I can be rid of him. If I learn his secret, I can blackmail him and be rid of him that way. I should cover both bases to be extra certain. And I'm convinced that item number three will inform item number two.

I walk through the manor, checking all the guest rooms for signs that a pompous, insidious man is occupying them. It takes over an hour, for the manor is enormous, but I find nothing. No rumpled sheets or clothing or anything at all to suggest they're being occupied.

A distasteful thought occurs to me, so I try asking Mrs. Lagos about it.

"Has anyone been through to clean the unoccupied servants' quarters?"

"Certainly, Your Grace. Though we may be shorthanded, we don't leave messes."

"I wasn't calling into question the skill of the staff. You're all wonderful. I merely wondered if there was a room that should have been unoccupied that wasn't?"

Mrs. Lagos cocks her head to one side. "No."

I confide in her. "The duke isn't sleeping in the master suite. I'm trying to figure out where he runs off to at night. Have the maids been ordered to clean new quarters?"

"If he's sleeping somewhere other than the master suite, the staff has not been informed of it, Your Grace." Her face pales. "Do you think there's a mess somewhere that needs cleaning? Should I ask—"

"No," I say quickly. "Do not disturb the duke on this matter. If he wanted something done, I'm sure he would have told you. I'm getting the sense that he does not want anyone in the house to know where he is nesting."

"Nesting?"

I nod. "Like an irritable badger."

Mrs. Lagos covers her mouth in an attempt to hide her giggle.

I MAY NOT HAVE learned where Eryx is sleeping at night, but there's no doubt in my mind that I'll find something useful in the study. But it's hard to tell when Eryx and his men aren't inside. I absolutely cannot be caught snooping through his things.

So I wait for the right moment.

In the meantime, I turn to the library.

I'm in my most comfortable day dress. A pink so soft it might be mistaken for white. The sleeves are three-quarters the length of my arm and loose, rather than tight about my form. Ribbons pulled into the shape of roses have been stitched at the top of the sleeves and along the skirt in a random, trailing design. I wear my hair up, my ears free of earrings today. No makeup. Just me.

I've already finished the next pick for book club and passed it along to Damasus for reading. We won't meet for another week, so I've plenty of time to select and finish a new book. As a mood reader, I generally don't plan out my reads ahead of time.

But today, I'm looking for a specific book. *The Adventures of Voleta Mavros.*

My fingers skim along the alphabetized shelves, looking for the author's surname. When I find it, I pull the book free by the spine. It's the same title I found in Eryx's cedar chest, though this copy is new, likely not opened since purchased. I can't be sure if I bought it or if it already existed in the late duke's collection. No matter.

Since Eryx is a man of few belongings, this book clearly means a lot to him.

I take it and venture outside to find a spot to read, settling for the gazebo at the center of the unfinished hedge maze. At least this structure was finished before the planting came to a halt. The workers built it first so they wouldn't have to carry construction materials through a maze before reaching their destination.

A storage bench resides underneath the white-painted trim. I select a blanket from the compartment, shake it out, and make myself comfortable. Then I begin to read.

The story starts when Voleta is six. She's a wild girl who doesn't like to do as she's told and gets into all kinds of mischief. She thinks to climb the tallest tree on her father's grand estate, only to realize she has no idea how to get down. She sneaks into the kitchens at night, knocks over a container of flour, and manages to coat herself in the white powder, leaving a trail of child-size footprints back to her room. In the summer heat, she's too impatient to put on swimming clothes before jumping into the river against her governess's caution. The heavy skirts pull her down until she is saved by the supervising adult.

There are happy instances, too. She rescues an abandoned kitten in the busy streets. Plays dress-up with her younger brother. Rides on her father's horse and pretends to take charge at the head of a cavalry. As Voleta grows older, she grows no less wild, though she does learn from her mistakes.

It's not to my usual tastes, for there's no romance nor high-stakes adventure, but it's a cute story for a child.

The fact that Eryx owns it is puzzling. Perhaps his copy has sentimental value, like the dented canteen or that scarf. The canteen, I assume, is from his time in the army. And the scarf? Perhaps a token from a lover? Then, remembering this is Eryx, I amend myself. A female relative. He said he was an orphan, so perhaps it belonged to his mother.

I finish the book in a matter of hours, and my limbs are cramped from sitting in the same position. I stretch my arms over my head before ducking out of sight beneath the railing at the edges of the gazebo.

Eryx stomps across the grounds of the estate, going for one of his "walks." Normally, Dyson and Argus will either accompany him, or they'll stay at the manor while Eryx goes off on his own. But today, a carriage rolls up to the manor, and the two henchmen climb in, Dyson enthusiastically so.

It would seem he's finally getting his free time in town.

This is my chance.

I wait until both parties are out of sight before sprinting back to the manor. I pass by only a handful of servants, who curtsy or bow, skirting the edges of the halls to allow me easier passage. When I reach the door to the study, I let myself in with my skeleton key.

I start at the desk, flipping through all the parchment scattered about there. I find the receipts to all my purchases in one pile, correspondences in another pile. Within the drawers are even more papers. Some are the beginnings of letters. Others are scraps with bits of mathematical formulas, which Eryx appears to have been using to handle the accounting. I'm pleased to find his numbers are correct when I compare them to the books.

It's tedious work, sifting through all those words, most of them meaningless. However, I do find one interesting letter from the solicitor:

Your Grace,

I have made the changes we discussed. I think you will find that everything is in order upon your arrival.

There is yet one matter that I failed to bring to your attention because I thought it trifling. Your grandfather left a widow behind, but I think you will find the dowager duchess to be most amenable upon your arrival. She is a quiet little thing and, pardon my saying so, utterly simple in the head. You won't even notice she's around, so please do not find yourself unwilling to go through with this because of her existence.

Your faithful servant,
Simonides Vander

So he made plans with Eryx *before* trying to steal money from me.

The letter doesn't contain anything I didn't already know, but hearing Vander's description of me is irritating nonetheless.

There are allusions to things that might prove to be condemning. *Unwilling to go through with this.* Or *changes we discussed.* It could refer to Vander changing the will. Their scheme could be what he fears Eryx being unwilling to go through with. But it is too vague to be evidence of anything. A chief inspector would laugh if I presented it before him. Eryx's unwillingness to go through with taking up the title could have only to do with his humble background and lack of desire to become a duke. The *changes* referenced could simply be some bit of money Eryx wanted moved around.

I open the drawers, sorting through even more letters, hoping to find something actually condemning within. It isn't until I reach the very bottom of the last drawer that I find a slip of paper crumpled into a tight ball. The parchment is plain and bears no address or signature. After smoothing it out as best I can, I read,

I hear you're calling yourself a duke now. I didn't know a gutter rat could climb so high. That's some real fancy caste system you've got over there in Naxos.

There's a glob of something brown on the parchment, as though someone spit on it. I slide my fingers away before continuing to read on.

Sounds to me like you've got access to all kinds of money now. After what you did to me, I'm owed. I hear you have yet to be formally recognized as duke before the king. Sounds like your situation is awfully precarious. It would be a real shame if certain information were brought to light before your title was made official, or after, for that matter.

I want five hundred necos by the end of the month.
I'll write the address you can drop it off at down below. Nice
doing business with you. I'll be in touch again real soon,
friend.

I read the letter twice, just to be sure I've remembered all the important bits.

At first, I have to stifle a giggle. Eryx is being blackmailed. But I sober up quickly enough, for that means someone is trying to dip their filthy fingers into *my* money.

The desire to confront Eryx and demand to know what he did is nearly overwhelming, but I stifle it. I have to be smart about this. Does this letter have anything to do with the reason Eryx sneaks off the property during random times throughout the week? Is there some scheme beyond stealing everything from me? Whatever it is, his past appears to have caught up with him.

But this paper lay buried and crumpled at the bottom of a drawer. Clearly Eryx has no intention of paying this person off, else he would take care with the listed address.

My back snaps ramrod straight as a new thought occurs to me.

This blackmailer . . .

If this note were found, if it were made known that someone was trying to take advantage of the duke—

They'd be the first suspect if anything were to happen to Eryx . . .

If it comes down to it, I could kill the fake duke and have a scape-goat.

I return the letter to where it was hidden and exit the study, locking the door behind me once more. If I could skip in my long skirts, I would.

There is an end in sight. If I have to turn to something desperate, I can get away with it. Not only that, but it sounds like whoever wrote that letter of blackmail has information that could condemn Eryx. I wonder if it has anything to do with his glowing eyes? No matter, perhaps the blackmailer will expose Eryx before I ever need lift a hand.

I'm here to take the safest route possible to getting what I want. I can play the long game and avoid committing a crime unless I have to.

Besides, that letter has given me an idea for getting the money out of Eryx to pay the private investigator's fee.

><>-O-<><

WHEN ERYX COMES OUT OF the woods late for dinner, his eyes widen in surprise to see me waiting for him at the dining room table. I never wait for him. Dinner is served at six o'clock sharp. Normally, if I can avoid seeing his face at all, I will take the opportunity.

"Duchess, what are you doing?"

"Waiting for you, of course."

He looks down at his chair, examining it from multiple angles before taking a seat. "Thought perhaps you'd put a needle on it or something."

"That's not a bad idea. I'll try to remember it for next time."

He rolls his eyes before digging into his food. "What do you want?" he asks with a full mouth.

Distasteful.

"I have a proposition for you."

His eyes narrow suspiciously. "What is it?"

"It's occurred to me that we could help each other out."

"You've considered accepting the generous dowry I've offered, then?"

I force myself not to frown at the reminder. "No. I remembered that you have yet to be formally recognized as duke before the king. Unless, of course, you've managed to walk all the way to the royal palace on one of your little hikes?"

He takes a drink of water, his eyes remaining fixed on me. I've clearly piqued his interest.

I continue. "I've said before that the king is about to become my brother-in-law. I would be willing to put in a good word for you publicly, increasing your chances of a smooth transition."

I've surprised him. I can tell by his silence.

And it *would* be surprising, if I had any intention of following through with it. No, Eryx Demos will either be in prison or dead before I have to do any such thing.

"In exchange for what?" he finally asks.

"I want my stipend reinstated immediately and doubled as you so generously offered."

Eryx puts his hands on the arms of his chair and surveys me. "Where would this public good word you'd put in for me take place?"

"My sister's wedding is fast approaching. Not only will everyone of importance be there, but the king is likely to be in a good mood. I think that will be the best time."

Eryx grins slowly. "Done. I'll have the money deposited into an account for you."

When I don't get up from the table right away, he asks, "Is there something more you wanted?"

"Let's pretend for a moment that I sing your praises before the entire nobility and you have all the documentation necessary to prove your identity."

"I *do* have all the necessary documentation."

"The point is that will all count for very little if you show up to the wedding acting like an animal."

He grunts. "Back to insults so soon?"

"If you were to sit as you usually do, tipping back in your chair, not only would you be shunned from society, I doubt you could even get an audience with the king."

"You're being melodramatic," he says as he returns his attention to his food once more.

"I'm not. Odell Vassos was shunned from events for wearing a dress that was so out of fashion, working-class girls were wearing it. I'm assuming you thought you'd get away with wearing one of your two pairs of pants to the wedding?"

He doesn't answer.

"Regardless of who you say you are, you clearly weren't raised to be a nobleman. Or if you were, you're very out of practice. We have two months left before the wedding. Let me help you to prepare for it."

Spending more time with him will be dreadful, but it's the only way I'll get to the bottom of his glowing eyes.

"In exchange for what?" he asks, his eyes narrowing.

I look down at my immaculately shaped nails. "I'm a busy woman. My time costs money. I want three hundred necos for lessons and help-ing you to update your wardrobe. On top of that, you will let me hire back the servants who have yet to find new jobs and allow me to finish the renovations to the estate. And"—I pause to take a breath—"I'm moving back to the master suite, since you're clearly not using it."

He is silent for a long, long moment.

"I will give you five hundred necos, and we will forget about the renovations and servants."

"*Three hundred.* There are only five servants who have yet to find new employment. And the estate cannot continue in this manner of disarray. What if the king and future queen should wish to come visit? Do you think seeing the place like this will earn you goodwill?"

He searches my face, as though looking for some hidden treach-ery. Unlike the first offer, this one is real. I will have to help him, but it's a sacrifice I'm willing to make. I need to get that money to pay Mr. Tomaras.

He says, "You may renovate *one* thing at a time. The workers are to be confined to the space in which they are working. I don't want a hundred extra people in the manor at all hours."

"And the servants?"

"Fine. Hire five of them back."

"Three hundred necos it is, then. I want it in my account by tomorrow, along with my first stipend. I'm also moving back into my rightful room immediately."

Eryx shakes his head as he takes yet another bite of food. "How did Vander ever mistake you for a simpleton? You're craftier than a fox."

"Perhaps Vander is the simple one."

"Perhaps so. Do you know, Duchess, I believe that's the longest we've spoken without any malcontent."

"If you continue to act like a reasonable human, I should think we could keep it up. Now, tomorrow morning, we're to go into town. You've money to transfer, and then we're going shopping. It's about time you owned your third pair of pants."

CHAPTER

10

Bright and early the next morning, I usher Eryx along to the tailor, where we look at endless swatches of fabrics.

"How about this one?" I ask, pointing to a dark pink brocade.

Eryx glares at me. "You know very well how I feel about pink."

"No, I know how you feel about dusty rose. This is magenta. Entirely different."

"Call it what you like, it's still awful. No pink."

The tailor, Mr. Asker, orders an attendant to whisk away the material. Argus and Dyson silently stand in a corner, observing.

"How about blue, then?" I ask, pointing to a vibrant swatch.

"I told you. I have no wish to look like a peacock."

Gods help me. "This is what men wear. It is the height of fashion. I cannot assist you if you remain unreasonable."

Eryx turns to the tailor. "Do you have anything darker? Or less colorful? Maybe both?"

"Certainly, Your Grace," Mr. Asker says. He snaps his fingers at his assistants. They flee to the back rooms for more fabrics.

I sit on the nearest chair while we wait, remembering the look on Mr. Asker's face when we first entered the shop. It was priceless.

The distaste for Eryx's workman's clothes and leather jacket! I had to refrain from laughing.

When Mr. Asker's men return, a series of blacks and browns and dark grays are presented. Eryx perks up.

"No," I say.

"Yes," he says. "This is much better."

"You cannot order your entire wardrobe out of three swatches of fabric. Everyone will think you're wearing the same outfit every day. This is not suitable for a duke. You need color. You need variety. This is boring. Why am I even here if you're going to disregard everything I say?"

Eryx turns to the tailor. "What's your opinion, Mr. Asker?"

"While I could make you a handful of appropriate attire from these colors," Mr. Asker says carefully, "I'm afraid the duchess is correct in stating that other courtiers will think you're wearing the same outfit repeatedly if we overdo these swatches. You will likely stand out and be the topic of gossip."

Dyson says, "As if the fancy folks won't be gossiping about his return as is."

"You need to blend in," Argus says.

Eryx groans. "I know."

"If I may, Your Graces, propose a compromise?" Mr. Asker asks.

"Please," Eryx answers.

Mr. Asker leaves to fetch more fabrics with his assistants, and I cross my legs where I sit, maintaining an upright position. I give Eryx a studious glance.

"We'll fix your posture," I tell him.

"My posture?"

"You slouch, and your face is too stern when it's at rest. No one is going to wish to approach you if you look like a grouch."

"Would the courtiers prefer I put on a fake smile?"

"I don't know. Let me see it."

His lips turn up, and it is the most disturbing thing I have ever seen. Like a grimace with lips pointing upward.

"No, that's definitely not better," I say. "Can you really manage nothing more natural?"

"This is me being natural."

"Well, it's unsuitable for company."

Eryx puts his back to me.

"Do not fret. We will work on it."

I'm simply dreading the forthcoming lessons. While they were the only thing I could think of to get the money I needed, I've no doubt Eryx means to fight me the whole way. I don't know how much of this forced proximity I can take.

At least Eryx transferred the money I requested, and I don't think anyone has noticed that Kyros has made himself scarce, visiting Mr. Tomaras with his requested sum.

Things are finally underway.

That knowledge has to be enough to get me through the rest of today.

When the tailor returns, he presents a display of fabrics on the tables before us. "These might help to expand the duke's options, Your Graces."

I'm impressed. Mr. Asker has found fabrics that combine the best of both our tastes. Deep black brocade with silver designs. Navy blue with bronze. Gray with a faint green sheen to it. Browns with purple stitching. Rich dark swatches, with mere hints of color. Tasteful, yet reserved. Endless varieties that even Eryx can't turn his nose up at.

"Yes, these will do," I say. The tailor and I both turn to Eryx.

"Very well," he says. "Just nothing in pink. I'll take—"

"All of it," I finish for him, lest he say something about requesting only two outfits. "We require full formal attire, including shirts, jackets, vests, cravats, and dress pants. He will need day clothes for less formal events, as well as evening attire for when he's entertaining."

Without waiting for any input from Eryx, I step forward to help Mr. Asker put together fabrics for different outfits. The tailor takes Eryx's measurements, and then informs us the clothing will be done in three weeks' time.

As we exit the shop, Eryx asks, "Where to next?"

"The cobbler's. You'll need shoes to go with your new attire."

"I have—"

"One pair already. Yes, I know. And you may wear that pair to your heart's content while traipsing about the property on one of your stomping rampages. But in polite society, you will wear what I deem appropriate."

Eryx's fists clench so tightly his fingers turn white. I watch his eyes closely, but I don't see a change there.

Still, Dyson takes a step forward, as though to intervene. Does he think the duke might actually strike me? I had thought that if the man were the violent sort, he would have already done me bodily harm by now.

Argus puts a hand on the other man's shoulder and pulls him back. I look between the two of them questioningly before returning my attention to the fake duke.

"We can be done with all of this now, you know," I remind him. "If you'd rather leave the estate and let me resume my role as sole owner of the dukedom, we can go our quiet, separate ways."

He forces his hands to relax. "No. To the cobbler's. We must attend the wedding. I'm hopeful you might meet someone you like. Twenty thousand necos are just waiting for you."

"Why don't you try holding your breath until I accept them?"

>─┼◆>─O─<◆┼─<

AFTER WE RETURN FROM the city, I wait eagerly in my rooms for Kyros. When he arrives, it is late in the evening, though the young man doesn't look tired at all.

"My errands went well, Your Grace," he says. "I was able to deliver the offers for immediate rehiring, and Mr. Tomaras says he will start right away and will provide an update as soon as he can."

"Perfect. I hope you know how much I appreciate your loyalty to me, Kyros."

"I am happy to serve."

Still, I tip the man, placing a coin into his hand. His fist closes, trapping my fingers against his palm. I look up from the contact, a question in my eyes.

"I'm sorry about Sandros and the others. Really. I know that your . . . visitors made you happy, but . . . I can't help but wonder if there is someone else who could make you happier? Someone who didn't need payment, for your presence is reward enough."

The words are innocent by themselves, but the heat in his eyes speaks to something else entirely.

"Just something to consider, Your Grace," he tacks on. "I shan't bring it up again. I am and always will be your friend and dutiful servant." He releases me and retreats down the hall.

I'm left standing with my hand still outstretched and my breath caught.

That was an invitation if I've ever heard one.

But from Kyros?

It's not that I've never taken notice of his attractiveness. But he is my servant and relies on me for his income, or rather, he did before Eryx showed up. I would never have thought to overstep.

But is it still overstepping when I'm not the one suggesting the arrangement?

I could be happy with Kyros, I think. Isn't friendship the perfect foundation for a romantic relationship? The fact that he's my servant is actually preferable. I will always be the one with the power, the money, the security. That actually makes Kyros a perfect candidate.

He could never really hurt me or control me, which I find extremely appealing.

I will think on it. Practice seeing Kyros in a new light.

⊱┈⊰⊱⊖⊰⊱┈⊰

IT SHOULDN'T SURPRISE ME at all that Eryx is a terrible listener, even when it comes to lessons he is paying for.

"Sit up," I instruct.

"I am sitting up."

"No, you're slouching."

"There's only one way to sit in a chair," he says.

"No, there isn't."

We sit across from each other in opposite chairs, no table or anything between us. Argus and Dyson, as usual, stand in the corner of the parlor, watching the exchange.

Good thing, too, because I might murder Eryx right here if he doesn't start to cooperate.

I stand and walk over to the man. Looming over him, I place my hands on his shoulders and force them against the back of the chair.

"Back straight. Shoulders against the chair. Legs together."

"Legs together? That can't be right."

I tap his boot with my slipper to scoot it where it's supposed to be. "No one wants to see a man with his legs spread open."

He crosses his arms. "I would argue that—"

"Uncross your arms. And for gods' sake, do not lean back in your chair."

A cheeky expression crosses his face. "You mean like this?"

He tilts the chair back on two legs.

But he should have known better with me standing right there. I place my slipper under the seat and tilt the frame back far enough for gravity to do its job.

Eryx's arms windmill, but he can't right himself in time. Both he and the chair slam to the ground.

"Oh, you're dead!" he says, scrambling to his feet, and that thing happens to his eyes again. They lighten to amber as they zero in on me.

There you are.

I run as a laugh escapes from my lips.

Not nearly fast enough.

Eryx grips me by the waist, spins me to face him, hoists me over his shoulder, and marches me across the room. I notice that Argus and Dyson have both left their positions by the wall. They're halfway to us before Eryx waves them off.

"I'm fine," he says to them.

That makes one of us.

"Put me down at once!" I insist, smacking at his back.

Eryx dumps me onto the nearest sofa, flat on my back. My hair has come free in the scuffle, and as I try to get it out of my eyes, I feel the world tip sideways.

Because he's pushed the entire sofa back on two feet before letting it fall. I roll off the backrest in a tumble before coming to a stop a few feet away.

Eryx's grin is dark as he reaches down a hand to help me up. I'm trapped between him and the floor, but that doesn't stop me. I take his arm, only to pull him to the ground beside me. I use his body to shove myself upward, but he catches my arms, and I land sprawled over the top of him.

"You fight dirty," Eryx says, capturing my flailing limbs so I can't hit him. Though I can't see his face, I feel a smile in the words. "You would have done well in the army."

"This is not gentlemanly behavior! Release me."

"You started it. I'm merely finishing it."

"You will not come out on top!"

"Won't I?"

He rolls our bodies so that I am tucked underneath his long, strong form. His messy hair spills around his face.

"I did not mean that literally. Get off me!"

"Not until you surrender."

"Never."

I try to buck him off, but it does nothing. He has me thoroughly pinned. I glare up at him, finding his eyes a glowing, wolfish amber. Interesting, since I've only noticed them surfacing before when he was angry.

He's not angry now. No, he's playful, if anything. Playful and . . . something else.

His face is very close to mine.

"If you expect these lessons to continue, you need to stop being an ass," I say, irritated that he is winning the scuffle.

But it's as if Eryx doesn't hear me. He's staring at me with the most peculiar expression upon his face. It's almost surprise? As though he just now realized who was underneath him. Who he's deliberately annoying.

He does a sweep of my face, starting with my chin and ending at my hairline. When his eyes rest on mine again, he says, "If ever you find yourself in this position again, Duchess, go for the eyes or throat."

"If you ever try something like this again—"

"I don't mean me. We are jesting with each other, aren't we? I mean, if you ever come up against someone who truly means you harm. Eyes or throat or groin. The vulnerable parts of a man."

I don't know what to say in return. Is he giving *me* a lesson now? I'm not about to thank him when he's still on top of me, despite my requests that he shove off. I wriggle underneath him, trying to free myself, but the movement seems to do something to him.

His eyes are burning, they shine so bright, and he's gone very, very still.

For one brief moment, I forget who he is and who I am. I take note of things I never have before. Like the fact that he smells like the earth after a rainstorm. The natural wave to his hair. The bob in his throat. The way his bright eyes make the rest of his features sharper. More masculine. I can see the curve of muscles in his arms as he uses them to prop himself above me.

Like a lover.

That last thought finally snaps me out of it.

"What are you doing?" I demand, silently applauding myself for keeping my voice steady.

He blinks, as though coming to, and rises. I ignore his offered hand, standing on my own and brushing out my skirts. But the energy in the room has shifted. Eryx is still staring at me as though he's just seen me for the first time, and I cannot stand it.

I leave, shutting the door to the parlor with a slam. I halt when I'm five feet away because I hear their voices.

"Do you want to talk about what just happened?" The question comes from Argus.

"Shh. She's not gone yet," Eryx barks.

I take one more step away before holding my breath.

"It was nothing," Eryx continues after a pause. "She caught me off guard, is all."

"I wasn't sure whether to step in or leave the room." This from Dyson.

Eryx scoffs. "It wasn't like that."

"If you say so."

"She's been my enemy since the beginning. I never had a chance to see her as anything else."

"And now?" Argus asks.

"She's still the enemy. I just lost myself for a moment."

"Lost yourself?"

"Surely even you can admit she's the most beautiful woman you've ever seen."

"Don't let her hear you say that," Argus says.

"I would never! Can you even imagine how unbearable she'd be then? It's awful enough now."

Dyson laughs.

"It's those eyes," Eryx continues. "They're mesmerizing."

"I imagine her eyes were not all you were admiring from your position spread-eagle atop her," Dyson says.

"Oh, piss off."

Dyson snickers.

I pad several more feet away before daring to take another breath. Yet my heart is pounding as though I'm in danger.

It wasn't Eryx. It wasn't the chase or the way he caught me and held me. It wasn't the way we were touching or even the way he looked at me at the end. As though, for just a moment, his sole objective wasn't to banish me from the estate.

No, the danger comes entirely from me.

I looked right back at him. I looked, and I saw someone I didn't want to disappear from my life. I saw someone I *wanted*, just for the smallest amount of time.

And that is terrifying.

I avoid Eryx the next day, refusing to enter the dining room for meals. I have my breakfast brought up to my room, before hiding between the stacks in the library.

Tekla and Karla are in here, too, dusters in hand, removing books and wiping the shelves clean. Karla sneezes from a bit of exposed dust, and Tekla reaches over to brush a strand of hair free from her face that came loose in the action. Both girls blush and turn away. Tekla goes to inspect a different bookcase, though I'm certain I just saw her finish cleaning it.

When Kyros starts wandering the library, looking through the shelves, I admire him from afar. Imagining him undressed and in my bed.

Yes, I can see it.

He has a child, so he obviously knows something of the bedroom. He's kind and funny, and I adore his son. Being with Kyros is effortless. Perhaps being with him romantically would be equally effortless and fill the void in my life that Sandros left.

The one my delusional self tried to fill with Eryx in a fit of dementia.

Kyros finds me before I can come to a decision. "There you are, Your Grace. The duke requests your presence in his study."

My face falls slightly.

"I could, of course, tell him I've been unable to find you anywhere?" he puts in.

That brings a smile to my lips. "Not to worry. I will heed his summons. This time. Walk with me?"

Kyros seems surprised by the request, but he follows a step behind me as I exit the library, and I slow my pace until he is level with me, purposely keeping our bodies even. The footman notices at once, and he doesn't try to stop me. He matches my gait, standing just close enough that I could brush him with my fingers if I reached out.

"How is your family?" I ask him.

"You are kind to ask, Your Grace. Mother is recovered from her fever, and my sister just accepted a marriage proposal from a merchant dealing in spices."

"I'm happy for her. When is the wedding so I might send a gift?"

"You needn't do that, Your Grace."

"And if I want to?" I challenge.

"Then, of course, I wouldn't dream of trying to stop you."

"Good. Write it down for me, so I don't forget."

"Thank you, Your Grace."

I bite my lip as we climb the stairs, wondering whether I dare say what I think should be the next step for us.

"Chrysantha," I say at last.

"Hmm?"

"My name. I wish you would use it, please. If—only if you'd like, of course. It is not an order."

Kyros halts in place, and though I want to keep moving, I stop with him, turn to face him. His eyes have widened, and he doesn't say a word for a few seconds.

"Chrysantha," he tries. "I love the sound of it."

"Thank you, Kyros."

We continue walking, but neither of us says anything more. I think enough potentially life-altering things have been spoken between us in the last couple of days.

"There's no need to announce me," I inform him before stepping past him into the study.

Argus and Dyson stand over the duke's shoulders, like henchmen ready to do their evil lord's will.

"Duchess," Eryx says, "take a seat, won't you?" He points to the soft cushions on the other side of the massive desk. I thought I'd find him buried in papers again, but his hands are clasped together in front of him, as though he'd done nothing but sit there as he waited for me. Those damnable glasses are on his face again. The ones that make him appear more attractive.

"I'll stand," I say, placing my hands on the back of a chair, should I need support. I don't know why, but I feel terribly uncomfortable, as though I need to hide myself. The chair is the only barrier I can use right now.

"Argus, Dyson, kindly leave us," Eryx says.

Argus's eyebrows lift. "You're sure?"

"Quite."

"We'll be just outside, should you need us."

Dyson offers me a wink as he strides past. I hear the door close behind the two men after they exit.

I don't like this. It feels as though they're guarding the door, should I wish to run. Why does my heart start picking up its rhythm again? This is Eryx. Man-child. Impostor duke. I am the one in control here. Who cares if he called me the most beautiful woman he's ever seen?

Eryx says nothing for the longest moment, and I cannot bear the silence.

"Well?" I ask.

"I wish to apologize for yesterday. I thought we were being playful, but I clearly crossed some line with you, and if you tell me what it was, I promise it won't happen again."

I roll my eyes. "What do you want from me now?"

"Excuse me?"

"You're trying to be polite, so what do you want?"

"Nothing. I wish only to figure out what went wrong so that our lessons might continue without any strain. You've been hiding from me today, so I assume the offense was grave."

Those intense amber eyes rise to my vision, and I try to think of an answer. Any answer that makes sense other than *I was distracted by your physique, and I'm avoiding you so it doesn't happen again.*

Finally, I manage, "Gentlemen do not touch ladies without permission." Unless, of course, they're married to them. Then they can do as they please, according to the law. I wonder if Alessandra has plans to change that one.

"It was because I touched you?" he asks.

"You took things too far. That tumble on the ground was entirely inappropriate." Actually, it *was*. It's his fault we're in this mess.

"You pulled me to the ground, you will recall."

"You lingered far too long. No matter how *mesmerizing* you find my eyes, I expect you to behave like a gentleman."

His jaw tightens. "I *am* a gentleman, despite being out of practice. I assure you I meant no harm, Duchess. What happened yesterday shan't happen again. I am deeply sorry that you were made to feel uncomfortable."

"You will forgive me if I don't take you at your word. I've never met an honest man, and I certainly don't expect a con artist to be one." Why am I arguing with him now? Just accept his apology and move on!

He sighs, yet his voice remains calm for once. "Think of me however you would like, but I assure you, I am not my grandfather. I'm aware of the kind of man he was." He pauses for a long moment before asking, "Duchess, did he hurt you? Is that why yesterday frightened you so? Did he—"

I put a stop to that immediately. "Let's get something clear, Eryx. We are not friends. We do not have discussions like this. You're trying to kick me out of my home. You're trying to take everything that should be mine. The private occurrences that went on in my marriage are none of your concern, and you don't get to ask about them."

"You say we are not friends, yet you call me by my given name," he says, his tone soft.

And I nigh explode. "I do not recognize you as the duke, so I will not address you as such or any other honorifics attached to it. I will not call you Pholios, because that is the name of the man who—" I cut off, remembering myself. "I suppose I could call you by your surname, but since it is also my surname, it feels strange. Perhaps I should dispense with any names at all and call you by that which I think only in my thoughts."

He grins, as though he finds my last statement amusing. "If you're to call me Eryx, then might I call you Chrysantha? It's only fair."

Fair? Fair! Men do *not* get to utter that word in a world that favors them in every single space of life.

"You will not call on me at all unless it is to uphold the terms of our agreement."

Eryx shuts his eyes before slowly opening them again. "Very well. Let me assure you I will not touch you again unless permission is given."

"Oh, it shan't be given."

"No? Then how are you to teach me to dance?"

My teeth hurt from how I've ground them together in the last few minutes. "Do not call on me again until it is time for tonight's lesson."

"Understood, Duchess."

CHAPTER

11

I can handle an angry, fuming man. I can handle an antagonistic and lecherous man.

But I was utterly unprepared for whatever it was that Eryx was trying to do just then. Apologize? Try to understand? Connect with me? Sympathize?

I have no interest in such things. I will not allow Eryx to humanize himself to me. I will not allow myself to become tricked by some false modesty or self-awareness that is wholly contrived. Men can put up fronts, just like I do to get what I want. I've no interest in seeing what it is Eryx wants from me this time.

Things are strained at the dinner table that evening, but I prefer it to anything else. I will not let down my guard around this man and allow him to hurt me more than he already has.

"A spoon is not meant to be slurped from, nor shoved into the mouth," I say after Eryx samples the first course.

He looks to the spoon clutched between his fingers. "Right. I think I remember this one. In the army, we often had to eat quickly. I got into the habit of shoveling food into my mouth with haste." He corrects himself with his next spoonful, raising it to his lips before tipping the contents into his mouth. After swallowing, he says, "My mother did teach me all this, but I lost a lot of good habits while fighting for my life. And there were certain things she simply could not teach me. For example, we didn't exactly have access to fancy silverware so I might discern when to use each one."

"Silverware," Dyson chimes in with a scoff, "is a luxury we gutter folk didn't have."

What is Eryx doing? Telling me about his life and his mother? He needs to *stop*. We are not to become *familiar* with each other. I'm here to do a job and that alone.

Eryx looks down into his bowl of celery soup. "This, at least, has far more flavor than that street water we were given to swallow in the army."

Argus grunts in agreement. "General Kaiser and the nobility would have their fancy five-course meals with meat and grains while we were given moldy stews."

I explain, course by course, how to properly eat food and use the correct utensil for each meal. By the end of dinner, I'm absolutely fed up with watching Eryx's mouth. He missed a spot of celery soup near the end of his chin, and I've been too proud to mention it. Occasionally I'll stare at it. It gives me a small spark of joy to realize he has no clue it's there.

It's a pity when he finally manages to clean it after he wipes his mouth for the fifth time after sampling a bite of braised pork.

"Those bites are too big," I state.

With the next, he opens his mouth less wide.

Unamused, I say, "I was, of course, referring to the size of the slice you put into your mouth and not the width of your jaw."

He grins. "I know. Sometimes it's terribly fun to prod at you. No need to be so lifeless."

"If I wished to be prodded at, I would get myself a husband."

Eryx chokes on his next bite. He hacks and coughs for a good two minutes, while Argus and Dyson fight back laughter in the corner.

"Duchess, was that a sex joke?" Eryx asks, tears streaming down his face.

"I was being less lifeless."

"You constantly surprise me."

"Maybe if you spent more time getting to know me instead of trying to get rid of me, you'd find you actually like me."

The silence has weight to it. I can feel it pressing against my skin. *Look up*, it says. *See what look he's giving you.*

No.

I meant that rhetorically. I don't *want* him to get to know me. I just detest how much he detests me!

Or at least, he did in the beginning.

Now my eyes are mesmerizing, and he's sharing stories about his childhood and his time in the army. And I notice things like his mouth and the way he smells so divine.

Damn it all.

I hadn't realized these lessons would change things. I didn't think he'd want to share stories with me or joke with me or elicit heavy silences.

He needs to stop. I need him cold and distant and detestable. Enough sharing and pretending to care. We are to remain just as unreachable to each other as we are when seated at opposite ends of this table.

As usual, I try to follow Eryx after dinner. I wait five beats after he disappears from the doors. Less time than I usually give him before following.

My slippers are silent on the carpeted floor, an added benefit I hadn't considered when selecting the depth of the plush.

Just as I leave the dining room, Eryx's figure disappears around a corner. I tiptoe to the edge of the hallway and peek around it.

He's vanished.

Thinking he must have taken the stairs more quickly than I anticipated, I hurry toward the staircase and bolt up the first flight before pausing and listening.

Nothing.

Absolutely nothing.

I suspect he knows I'm trying to learn where he's sleeping. He takes such care to ensure I can't follow him wherever it is he lays his head at night. I wander the halls aimlessly, hoping to catch a whiff of him, even though I know it's useless. He's onto me, and that is terribly upsetting.

I end up in the library, scanning the shelves, thinking to select something to take my mind off the infuriating man living in my manor.

Those amber eyes flash into my vision, and instead of heading straight for the fiction, I detour to the nonfiction. History has never interested me. Why should it? It's always about men stealing each other's kingdoms or killing each other. Men doing great deeds. Men going on adventures. I'm sick of men having the spotlight. The history of women is barely recorded, which is why I retreat to fiction, where we're finally given our due.

Though I suppose Alessandra will make a grand appearance in the history books for generations to come.

I don't know why I bother to browse through the titles on the history of Naxos or look through volumes on different kingdoms of the world. What exactly do I expect to find? Something telling me why Eryx's eyes glow amber when he's incensed? Even as something so unnatural is presented before me, my mind still tries to find a rational answer.

Perhaps there are people in other parts of the world who have amber eyes. I haven't been anywhere except Naxos. My knowledge is limited.

The hour grows late as I flip through page after page, index after index, with no results. My head slumps against my forearm as I lay down on a settee with my current selection. I feel my eyes start to drift, but I'm far too comfortable to move . . .

➣—┼◂▸•—O—•◂▸—┼◂

I KNOW I'M DREAMING because I'm standing in an impossible landscape. The floor is made up of clouds. Candles float above my head with nothing to suspend them. I hear the soothing sound of rushing water, but there's none to be found. In fact, the only object I can see is the bed. Not a bed, exactly, but a mattress laid on the floor, draped with sheets and blankets. I watch them rise and fall with the deep breathing of whoever is sleeping there.

Because it's a dream, I don't experience any fear, only curiosity. I tread over to the bed, until I can see the head resting on the pillow.

It's Eryx, and yet, not Eryx.

His messy hair is even more tangled than usual in sleep. His skin looks darker when he lies underneath a white down comforter. He appears more like a boy than a man like this, resting with impossibly long lashes against his cheek.

And then . . . there are the horns.

Two of them protrude from just above his forehead and angle toward the back of his head, reaching maybe four inches in length and coming to sharp tips. They're black at the roots, slowly turning a deep purple at the tips. They're not reminiscent of any animal I've seen before, so I haven't the faintest idea from where my mind conjured them.

Because this is my dream and I can do what I want, I approach the sleeping figure, kneel on the floor, lace my fingers through his hair, and trail them along his scalp. The motion lifts a section of hair, revealing the shape of an unusually pointed ear, before my hand snags on a tangle, and amber wolf eyes shoot open. When they catch sight of me, Eryx rolls away, nearly landing himself on the cloud floor.

Instantly the fluffy white tufts turn to darkest black, and I hear the sound of thunder, see the flash of lightning beneath my feet. The floating candles sputter in a sudden breeze that I can't feel on my skin, but I can still see Eryx perfectly.

"Have you ever even seen a hairbrush before?" I ask him, undaunted by the transformation the scenery has taken. "Truly it's astonishing how messy that mop on your head gets."

Eryx sits up, the blankets falling from his shoulders, revealing a hardened chest that is most definitely *not* boyish.

"What—what are you doing here?" he asks, looking around as though he can't believe where we are. When he opens his mouth to speak, I note his canines are longer than usual.

"Me? This is my dream. You're the interloper here. Now even sleep isn't a respite from you? You really can't leave me be, can you?"

I sit on the bed, where he has warmed the space with his own body heat, and lay myself out in the spot now unoccupied. The sheets are comfortable, though the mattress is harder than I'm used to. I close my eyes, hoping I'll fall into a deeper sleep without company or even dreams. I could really use a true break from everything.

Eryx snatches the blanket from atop me and somehow manages to wrap himself in it while lying on the other side of the bed.

"What are you doing?" he asks.

"Trying to make you disappear. Now give that back."

"This is *my* bed, and you need to leave. Get away from this place right now."

I roll my eyes and body at the same time, turning toward him and propping my head up on my hand. My dress gapes open slightly at my neckline, but I do nothing to stop it because, again, this is only a dream, so who cares?

Yet Eryx's eyes dart downward before he catches himself and brings them right back up.

I lift a single brow.

"Will you stop lying in that position?" he asks, and his eyes lower once more, as though he can't help it. Finally, he just slams them closed.

"What are you wearing?" I ask, ignoring his question. Why did he wrap the comforter so tightly about himself?

"A pair of undergarments," he says.

I feel a smile take over my lips, and I reach out for the edge of the blanket.

"Let go," he demands.

"This is my dream," I say. "Now drop it."

"No."

"What are you trying to hide from me?"

"Nothing!"

I pull as hard as I can, but not even in sleep can I will myself to be stronger than he is. Fine. I plump the pillow beneath my head before snuggling deeper into the mattress.

"You *really* shouldn't be here," he says.

"And where is here?" I ask, eyeing the storming clouds. "Is it one of the gods' heavens?"

"Certainly not."

"Right, you're here," I say. "What was I thinking? Then tell me what my brain has crafted, why don't you?"

"Your brain?"

"Yes, this is *my* dream. Do keep up, Eryx. Even my dream self can't conjure a more intelligent version of you."

His glare is more dangerous than ever, with his eyes glowing and his teeth bared, but even now I don't fear him.

My subconscious has transformed him into a monster. An incredibly attractive one, but a monster nonetheless.

"What are you hiding from me under that blanket?" I ask. "Did you grow an extra leg?"

"No."

"Are your feet webbed?"

"No."

"Do you have a tail?"

He hesitates just a heartbeat too long before saying, "No."

"You do! You have a tail. Let me see it."

"No! Chrysantha, get out of here."

"I thought we already established I couldn't because this is my dream. Now stop being a killjoy and just show me."

He picks up his pillow and throws it at my head. After a surprised jolt, I add it to the one already beneath me.

"Why are you always in a bad mood?" I ask.

He tries to run a hand through his hair, but it snags on the same tangle I found earlier. His voice deepens. "What is the matter with you? Why aren't you terrified of me? You're lying right next to me, vulnerable. Completely open. Don't you know I could rip out your throat?"

"Oh, will you? Maybe that will rouse me from this horrible dream."

"Always jokes with you."

I shrug. "I've never gotten to speak them aloud before."

"What?"

And because this is a dream, and I decide it would be interesting to see what happens next, I tell him the truth. "I've always kept it bottled up. The joking. The anger. My temperament. Myself. I had to if I wanted to find a husband."

"I don't understand."

"I learned at a very young age that men preferred women who they could control. So I pretended my whole life to be an idiot so others wouldn't be careful around me. When Father was musing about the perfect husband for me, I knew his plans and even was able to direct them. You see, I couldn't have just *any* husband. I needed a rich one who wasn't long for this world. Pholios fit the bill. I knew he would die soon, and then I could inherit everything. I just had to let my father think it was his idea. He'd been trying to pawn me off on some of his rich friends. Orrin, Lord Eliades, was one he initially tried. But Orrin was young and healthy, and I didn't want the match because I would be stuck with him for decades. But I knew about Pholios, and I just needed my father to be mindful of him.

"Do you think my father would have talked business in front of me if he'd known I was paying such close attention? Would he have left me alone in his office when he needed to run out for errands? I stole his seal and wrote letters on my father's behalf to Pholios, asking him to come up to us and make a proper introduction of himself, because he had a daughter of marrying age.

"Father didn't suspect a thing. Even when Pholios suddenly started talking to us as though he'd already had conversations with my father, he went with it. Because how could anything different have happened?

"I orchestrated everything. From our first meeting, to our courtship, to our eventual marriage. Every step I played a hand in. Father and Pholios were none the wiser.

"And then Pholios died, and I was free to be me for the first time in forever. I had months to enjoy it with the servants and my lovers." I turn to Eryx. "Then you showed up. I was brash and intelligent in front of you because I didn't know who you were, and by then, it was too late. I was stuck with you knowing who I was and unable to use my usual ways to get rid of you."

"You mean to say that you haven't found a lover who will have you without the incentive of money?"

I cannot read his tone, but I certainly don't like the pathetic light he paints me in.

"I'm not in the market for a lover. I'm only interested in having a mistress. Do pay attention, I was talking about my past. You're focusing on the wrong things."

Eryx blinks approximately five times before the words make it through his thick skull. "So you had your family convinced you were a simpleton?"

"Not my family. Everyone. The whole court. Everyone I've ever met. I've been playing this part for seven years."

"That's a long time to be someone you're not."

"It would have been worth it if you hadn't shown up. Then I would have had the rest of my life to be happy."

He rolls his eyes. "Only you would say you couldn't be happy. You live in complete luxury. You've never gone without shoes to wear or food to eat or a roof over your head. You want me to feel bad for you because you no longer can pay a man to suck your p—"

"Don't you dare finish that crude sentence! It's not about the money! What I've always wanted most was freedom, yet you try to convince me to marry again—taking away what little freedoms I have now. As it is, I'm beholden to *you* in too many ways. Just like your grandfather before you."

"You are not beholden to me in the ways you were to him."

"Oh, so I should be content to be only partial property, is that it? You don't get it. No one gets it."

So many women seem content with their lives. Being traded about for money. Forced to produce heirs. Living lives not wholly their own. They don't even see it as a burden. Some of them *like* it.

I am not content to live a life that is not wholly mine.

I would rather die.

"You are not the only one who has led a hard life," he says. "You are not the only one who has had to live to the whims of others. You are not the center of the world."

"No, but I'm the center of *my* world, which is why I have to look after myself. No one else will."

He pauses for just a moment. "Go a full day without food. Then tell me that isn't worse than being a lady."

"You think you deserve to take what's mine because you grew up destitute? I'd have rather gone without food than dealt with Pholios constantly touching me and trying to pull me into his bed. You don't understand. You will never understand. Stop trying to compare my life to yours. You are a man, and you will never know what it is to suffer as only a woman can!"

The last words are shouted, and they startle me awake.

It's the middle of the night, and I'm still in the library, the book I'd been reading weighing down my chest. It falls to the floor as I rise and retreat to my room.

CHAPTER

12

try to put the absurd dream from my mind, yet as the days continue on, I find myself staring at the fake duke, imagining him with those horns and pointed ears and canines.

"What?" Eryx asks at dinner one night, while I'm staring at his forehead.

"Nothing," I say, returning my attention to my food.

Eryx shifts in front of me, possibly sharing a look with his bodyguards.

Thankfully, he hasn't caught me staring at his ass, as I try to imagine what his tail might have looked like . . .

It isn't until I collide with someone in the hallway that I realize I might be ruminating on the dream too much. Thankfully, I catch my housekeeper before she lands on the floor.

"Mrs. Lagos, forgive me. I wasn't looking where I was going."

"It's quite all right," she says. She brushes off her skirts before straightening the shawl about her shoulders. I do a double take.

"Is that cashmere? From Michalis's?"

Her cheeks deepen in a blush.

"Mrs. Lagos, do you have a rich secret admirer you've yet to tell me about?"

"No." She won't meet my eyes.

"That simply won't do. I must know who gave it to you. I thought I was fun to gossip with?" My lips turn up into a pout.

"It's not that, Your Grace. I'm afraid I will cause you distress if I tell you who gave it to me."

"Don't be ridiculous. Anyone who would gift my friend such a thing is—" I finally put two and two together. "It was the *duke*?"

Mrs. Lagos looks down at the floor as though ashamed. "He felt bad for all the stress he's put on me. Letting so many of the staff go, managing a shorthanded estate. He only wanted to make amends."

"Surely you wouldn't fall for such bribery?"

"Of course not, Your Grace," but as she continues on, I see her patting the new shawl.

I continue toward the main doors, for I'd planned to take a walk today. Damasus enters just before I reach the exit.

"Pardon me, Your Grace," he says. His hand goes to his chest, where I notice a brooch pinned to the lapel of his jacket.

"Is that silver?" I ask him.

"No." A pause. "Forgive me, Your Grace, that was a lie. Yes, it is silver."

"The duke gave it to you?" It's more an accusation than it is a question.

He nods. Slowly.

"That's it," I mutter.

Then I go find Eryx.

It takes the better part of fifteen minutes, but I finally spot him in the library, clearly looking for his next read.

"You're giving the staff gifts?"

He spins around, his hand going for his revolver, but he thankfully does not draw it. He puts his back to me once more.

"Is that a problem?"

"It will be when they leave their employment because your gifts are worth more than their annual salaries."

"They won't leave. They all like you too much."

"Yes, and that camaraderie was earned. You're trying to bribe people into liking you."

He turns to face me and crosses his arms, leaning against the stack of books behind him. "First you're mad that I let so many of the staff go. Now that I'm showing them how much I appreciate their efforts, you're also incensed? Do you worry that I will turn them against you?"

"No."

"Then why are you upset?" His expression turns haughty. "Is it because I did not get you a gift?"

I grit my teeth. "Certainly not."

His eyes flash amber, and he turns himself back around. "Then what is wrong, Duchess?"

"You. It's always you that is wrong."

And because I will not be outdone by him, I send Kyros into town with specific instructions on what gifts I wish to purchase for every member of my staff. I don't care if it costs my entire monthly stipend. Eryx doesn't get to win.

⤞ ⟡ ⬩ ◯ ⬩ ⟡ ⤝

THAT NIGHT, WHEN I approach my rooms for the evening, I find a small box on the floor beside the door. For some reason, my heart picks up its rhythm and my skin heats.

I survey my surroundings, confirming there are no witnesses, then bend down to retrieve it. I shut myself within my room and stare at the present.

What did he get me? Earrings? A necklace?

I told him I didn't want a present from him. I was very clear on the topic.

But it wouldn't hurt to just open the box. To see what it is. Has he paid attention to my jewelry preferences? Is the gift thoughtful, or was it something random he saw in town?

The hinge swings upward at the slightest touch. After unfolding the tissue paper, I find only a short note nestled against the velvet.

So you did want a gift from me.

I hurl the box across the room.

"No," I say aloud, as though he's here to argue with. I didn't. *I don't.* I was just *looking.*

When I've composed myself, I put the note back inside and place the box exactly where I found it. As though I'd never opened it.

By morning, it's gone.

>—¡—◆›—◦—‹◆—¡—≺

"A second nobleman has gone missing," Karla tells me before the next book club meeting. "It was tricky snagging a copy of the morning's paper. Apparently there was a recall on the printing. We think it's the king's doing."

Tekla nods. "He can't have the aristocracy panicking when he wants them all fixating on his upcoming nuptials."

"Oh, it's going to be the wedding of the century," Karla says, nearly swooning at the thought.

"The missing nobleman," I prompt.

"Oh, right. This time it was Lord Kazan."

Yet another viscount who served in the army. Hmm. "If the king is forcing the papers to recall the printing, then we likely won't hear about the next disappearance."

"I suppose not," Tekla says.

"I wouldn't worry, though, Your Grace," Karla says. "It's only men who are going missing."

"I'm not worried," I assure them. I'm only concerned with what this means, and why Eryx walks about the house as though expecting an invasion. Does he suspect he's next? Or is it the blackmailer he's worried about? Could the kidnapper and blackmailer be the same person?

The only thing I know for certain is that whatever is going on, Eryx is somehow caught up in it.

>─┤◄►─○─◄►┤─◄

The time for Eryx's money drop with the blackmailer comes and goes, yet neither Eryx nor his goons leave the manor. I know because I trail the three of them like a loyal dog. Unfortunately, I'm not as careful about it as I think I am.

I round a corner and run straight into Eryx, who had clearly been waiting for me.

"What the devils are you doing, Duchess?"

I rub my nose where it pressed into Eryx's solid chest upon impact. It's not hard to don a mask of innocence. "I'm observing you, obviously."

His eyes narrow. "To what end?"

"I don't want you to make a fool of us at my sister's wedding. I need to ensure you're practicing what you've learned in our lessons."

He rolls his eyes. "You can hardly expect me to act the same in private as I would at a public event."

"What better way to practice than to make good habits at home?"

"I'm not changing every bloody thing about me just so you can feel more comfortable in public. Now. Back. The. Hell. Off."

"Swearing in front of ladies is not—"

His nostrils flare, and something about his face changes. Before I can place it, Eryx takes a step closer to me, nearly treading on my slippers, and I leap away.

"Everything all right?" Argus magically appears from behind Eryx, and he places a hand on his shoulder firmly. "Eryx?"

Eryx blinks. "Fine, I'm fine. Just . . . get her away from me."

Dyson materializes beside Argus. Both men squeeze their way into the space between the fake duke and me.

I step around them. "What's the matter with you? You didn't look right for a second."

"I'm coming down with something. You don't want to catch it, so you'd best back away. My head is pounding, and my temper is a little short."

"Your temper is always short."

"Duchess, be gone, damn you!"

He disappears before I can say anything further, and his bodyguards block my attempts to follow.

"Leave him be, Your Grace," Dyson says.

I turn my wrath on to the other man. "You do not order me about."

"Wasn't an order. Merely some advice, but I suggest you take it this once. I promise you won't like the consequences otherwise."

Consequences! Just wait until they both receive the consequences of helping Eryx with the con. I spin around and leave.

I have no immediate destination in mind, but both men walk behind me.

"I shan't follow His Grace again." Today at least. "You don't need to accompany me."

Argus expels a breath that could be a grunt or a scoff. It's hard to tell.

"Great, now I've got his bodyguards trailing me, is that it?"

I see the man's lips turn up out of the corner of my eye. "You've got it all wrong, Your Grace."

"Surely neither of you thinks me stupid enough to believe you're valets?"

"We don't think you're stupid at all," Dyson says. "In fact, you're far too smart for your own good, yet you can be completely dense at times."

"Excuse me?"

"We were in the army with Eryx. Same regiment. He saved both our lives."

Argus stops in the hallway, bends down, and begins rolling up the cuff of his pant leg. I think to stop the man from baring his leg to me, but I'm far too eager for some actual answers, so I wait until he has the garment pulled up past his knee.

"Gunshot wound to the leg. The Pegains put up a good fight before the end. They had us on the run, and with me injured, there was no way I could keep up, but that wouldn't stop a man like Eryx. He threw me over his shoulder as he ran, fought the bastards while bearing my weight. He's the reason I'm alive today."

I look Argus up and down, taking in his considerable bulking muscle. "Did you put on some muscle since the conquering of Pegai?"

The man laughs. "Eryx is stronger than he looks, and when he's determined enough, even my weight is no struggle for him."

How can that be? Argus must be twice his size, but what cause would he have to lie?

Dyson reaches for the hem of his shirt, lifting the right side up past his first few ribs, revealing a line of scar tissue.

"Got sliced up like a filleted fish. Eryx got to the bastard before he could finish me off, then proceeded to help me hobble to safety, knife still stuck in my flesh, and him wounded almost as bad as I was. Course that didn't slow him down. The man only gets more fearsome when injured."

I look between the two men. "So you're with him now because you owe him life debts?"

"Yes, but that's not a debt we could ever repay to a man like Eryx," Argus says.

"Why are you here, then, if not for his protection?" Are they merely his friends come along to profit from this scheme of his to play the false duke?

Argus and Dyson share a look, before the former carefully says, "Did it ever occur to you that we're not here for his protection, but yours, Your Grace?"

They leave me blinking stupidly in the hallway, all else completely forgotten.

I chew on Argus's words for the rest of the night, seeing Eryx in a new light.

What sort of horrors did the man witness in the war? And, remembering the blackmail, I wonder what sort of horrors Eryx must have committed. I know that soldiers can suffer trauma, that some are prone to episodes and night terrors and what have you. Perhaps Eryx is suffering in ways I haven't begun to pick up on. Maybe if I push him in just the wrong way, I could call forth a temper that's blinded by trauma. Add his strange eyes into the mix, and where does that leave him?

If it's such a problem, then is it wise that Eryx be seen in polite society *at all*? And how dare he allow himself to ever be alone with me if he might suddenly have a violent episode of some sort!

Is this the real reason why he sent away so much of the staff and then the workers? The fewer people about, the fewer people he'll violently attack?

I find this infuriating.

Not only is he taking everything from me, he's also putting me in danger with his very presence.

My ANGER AND DETERMINATION HAVE always been stronger than my fear. To prevent my snapping at or verbally assaulting the man, I stay out of Eryx's path, except when necessary. We undergo our lessons, always with Argus and Dyson present. I don't push Eryx any more than I need to, with Argus's warning still fresh in my mind. And Eryx seems, for once, not to be making a joke out of everything.

He can now sit and eat without giving me secondhand embarrassment. He manages to catch himself before swearing on a couple of occasions, though on others he seems to not even realize when foul words come out of his mouth.

We go over appropriate topics of conversation in the presence of both gentlemen and gentle ladies.

"How could you possibly know what is appropriately said when gentlemen are alone?"

"When are you going to learn that I know everything?"

When we're not in the midst of lessons, I try to do more snooping, but I'm no closer to learning where he's sleeping or why he's being blackmailed.

Thankfully, I do not dream of the man again. It's bad enough dealing with him during the daytime.

As the day of my sister's wedding grows closer and closer, I spend time arranging the perfect outfits for Eryx and me. Though his new clothing arrives, Eryx does not touch it. He's much too fond of his workman's attire and black leather jacket.

Things are progressing too slowly. I have no idea what I'll say to Kallias or Alessandra when I see them, especially concerning the fake duke. All I can do is bide my time. Keep my head down.

And then the day, or rather night, I've been waiting for arrives. Not the wedding. Something much, much better.

Ilias Tomaras returns to the manor.

Kyros escorts me to the library, and I ask him to wait outside the door should I need him. He accepts this duty without question.

Ilias Tomaras looks just as he did last time. Impeccably dressed despite the late hour. The man doesn't seem as though he's tired in the slightest.

"Mr. Tomaras, I'm so glad you've come. Thank you again for your discretion."

"Of course, Your Grace. I'm happy to have some things to report, though not as much as I would like."

"Please go on."

"I started with the mother, Ophira Demos, Pholios's daughter. She was born here at the estate and lived here until the age of eighteen."

"So he did have a child?" *Why has no one heard of her?*

"Yes, just the one, but she was disowned by her father and banished."

"Disowned? For what reason?"

"I have been quietly gleaning information from some of Pholios's old friends at the time by blending in at their clubs. No one seems to have a clear account of what exactly happened. What I do know is that Ophira had an affair with the late Shadow King."

My mind whirls. Is Eryx the late king's bastard?

I see those amber eyes behind my closed eyes. Is that what it is? But to my knowledge, the Maheras line all possess the same shadow magic. No variations. And I never saw Kallias's eyes flash amber during my stay at the palace, but then again, I never saw him angry.

Those thoughts all run through my mind in the span of a second. Right before Tomaras utters his next sentence.

"Though, it was reportedly sometime after the affair ended that she became pregnant."

Oh. "So someone else is the father?"

"Definitely. And since the late duke let an affair with the king slide, I can only assume that her new lover was not of her station. Someone her father thought was beneath her. Whoever he was, he didn't marry Ophira once she became pregnant, so we can also guess that he either couldn't afford a wife or had no interest in one. I believe the pregnancy is the reason for the ostracism."

That is . . . so terribly sad. What a horrible fate for any woman. "Where did she go?"

"This is what took the most time, but I eventually tracked her down to a remote city in Estetia, called Dimyros."

"I've never heard of it."

"Nor had I. I did some digging. It's small as cities go, and its greatest boast is its flocks of sheep."

"Sheep?"

"They raise them there; the people pride themselves on having the best fatlings of the year. Most of the world's wool products come from Dimyros, and it would seem that Ophira took a job tending flocks."

It's remarkable that she managed to get so far on her own, but I can understand Ophira's need to be away from her father. I'm glad she found an alternative for herself.

"I'm unsure whether this next bit is relevant, but there were unusual rumors circulating through Dimyros," Tomaras continues.

"I'd like to hear them."

"There were strange disappearances. Sheep, other livestock, and even some of the city folk would disappear. The bodies would be found later, sometimes nothing left of them but bones with strange, inexplicable bite marks."

I feel the hair rise on the back of my neck. "Why did this information stick out to you?"

"Because according to records, these attacks didn't happen until after Ophira arrived in the city. The timing isn't precise. They started a few years after her arrival. So I'm sure it's nothing at all. There were mutterings of Ophira being shamed and cursed by more than just her father. That misfortune followed her wherever she went."

"And do you think there's any truth to that?"

"I don't believe in devils or gods."

"What of the Shadow King?"

"I'm a man of science, facts, and reason. I've never seen the king myself, but I know that the inventions of Naxosians are remarkable. If someone wanted to appear as though they were cloaked in shadow, they could find a way, scientifically."

He wouldn't say such things if he'd seen the king in person, walking through solid walls, but now is not a time for arguments.

"What then?" I ask. "Did she give birth? Was there really a child?"

"Oh yes, Eryx is undoubtedly her son."

At that, my face falls. He really is the duke? Truly? After I felt so sure about all my suspicions. "There's no chance that the man occupying this house is an impostor?"

"There's always a chance, Your Grace, but I find it unlikely in this situation. What you've shared with me matches everything that turned up in my research. The boy grew up in Dimyros and joined the Naxosian army as soon as he was old enough to pass for fifteen, which was closer to thirteen, I believe. He wanted to provide a better life for his mother, so he left. She didn't protest, as far as I can tell. In fact, many of her neighbors suggested she wanted the boy to be a trained fighter."

"Curious."

"I thought so, too, unless she was looking for a way to perhaps impress her father and get herself and her child back in his good graces."

"That would make sense, I suppose."

Ilias nods. "Eryx apparently had a knack for killing. He rose in the ranks of the army very quickly and received all manner of awards."

Yes, those I'd seen.

"And then his mother died around eighteen months ago."

So soon? I hadn't expected that. "What was the cause?"

"Some said suicide. Others said she simply wasted away. I heard reports that she stopped eating. Stopped getting out of bed. Stopped everything. The boy had no idea until she was already gone."

"A woman doesn't just stop taking care of herself. What could have been the cause?" I ask.

"It could have been madness. Or perhaps she heard false word that her son had perished in the army. Whatever the reason, it seems as though grief took her."

It wasn't the passing of her mother, I reason. Pholios's wife died long before that. "How strange."

"Indeed, there appear to be a great many strange things where the new duke is concerned. He grew up in a town with strange disappearances, his mother dies under unusual circumstances, even his unit in the army was said to have an unheard-of knack for staying alive. Many attribute it to Eryx's prowess on the field."

For some reason, the horns and canines from my dream flash into my mind. I shake them away.

"So that's it, then?" I ask. "There's nothing more I can do? He truly owns everything and is who he says he is?" I breathe in disappointment as hope leaves me with each exhale.

Mr. Tomaras holds himself tall. "There is one more avenue of searching I'd like to exhaust before I accept the second half of my payment, Your Grace, but I would prepare yourself. The evidence is not pointing toward the answers you're looking for."

My body feels twice as heavy as those words settle in my mind. Eryx Demos really exists. He is the duke.

But *what* is he?

I finally allow the thoughts I've denied to pervade my mind. Amber eyes. Mysterious deaths. A dream that feels less and less like a dream the more I think on it. The bodyguards here to keep me safe.

Or are they here to keep me from learning the truth?

"I shall see myself out once again, Your Grace. Until next time." He bows deeply, and I precede him from the library.

Kyros escorts me back to my rooms. I'm lost in thoughts of all that was revealed to me, when he asks, "Did you learn what you were hoping to?"

"Unfortunately, it would seem that Pholios has a grandson. Eryx is who he says he is."

"What of Vander's guilty face when you met with him?"

"I don't know," I answer honestly. "Mr. Tomaras has one more avenue of searching he'd like to try, but he told me to prepare myself." I sigh. "The man's dead, yet Pholios is still hurting me from the grave."

"I'm so sorry, Chrysantha."

"He was a pig. He cast out his pregnant daughter, leaving her with nothing. He was more despicable than I imagined."

And now he's left me one more mess to clean up. Eryx and I are fighting for an estate and a title that can only belong to one of us.

I still intend to win, no matter the cost.

The law can't get rid of Eryx Demos for me?

Fine.

I'll resort to plan B.

Eryx is dangerous, and there's something unnatural about him. I may not know what it is, but there's no denying that keeping him around the estate is a bad idea.

He needs to die.

I already have a scapegoat: his mysterious blackmailer. All the aristocracy still think me an idiot. It's time to take action.

"Is there anything else I can do for you, Chrysantha?" Kyros asks as he sees me to my door.

I meet his eyes, and they are heated.

Amid everything else that's been happening, I nearly forgot about his unsaid proposition. I do miss companionship in my bed, but I know now isn't the right time. Not when I cannot get thoughts of murder from my mind.

I reach out my hand and take Kyros's gloved one. "Not tonight, but perhaps . . . later."

I let the suggestion of more linger in the air, and it is enough for now.

CHAPTER
13

I put on a pair of sturdy boots, tying the laces up my calf. I don't call for Medora to help me change my dress or put on my cloak.

I don't want anyone to have any clues as to what I'm up to today. However, only mere moments after entering the foliage of the nearby woods, I hear a shriek of "Duchess!"

Little Nico lowers himself from the nearest tree, jumping the last few feet and catching himself on his hands and knees on the mossy ground. He slaps his hands together to remove any loose dirt before throwing his arms about my skirts.

"Good day, Duchess," he says.

"Good day to you, too. What are you about this afternoon?"

"I've spotted a bird's nest up in the tree. I'm waiting for the eggs to hatch."

"Have any of them moved yet?"

"No, and the mother hasn't come back since I scared her off while discovering the nest."

I take his little hand in mine and start walking. "You'd best leave the eggs alone, else the mother might not come back. Then the babies would die."

"Oh," he says. "She would be most indignant if her babies died. I shall leave the tree alone."

"Wise decision."

"What shall we do instead?" he asks.

As we trot along the worn path, he jumps on sticks, cracking them underfoot, or picks up rocks to throw at the trunks of trees. I hadn't any experience with young boys until moving to the estate, but they are quite destructive little things.

"I'm going to pick some wildflowers," I tell him. "I'm sure you'd find it terribly boring."

"Not at all. I shall help you find the best ones!"

I don't want an audience for this part, but I doubt Nico counts. After all, he's already forgotten the bird's nest from two minutes ago.

We pick our way through the woods until we come to an open field laced with blossoms. Daisies and dandelions and morning glories and irises. Nico rushes forward and grabs handfuls of the plants, yanking some of them out by the roots in his enthusiasm. He doesn't seem to care whether the flowers look fully ripened or if anything looks like it needs more water. All flowers are created equal in the eyes of a four-year-old boy.

I show him how to make crowns out of daisies, and he spends some time perfecting his new skill before rushing toward the nearby stream to look for bugs and frogs. I keep him in my line of sight as I begin selecting my own blossoms.

Foxglove. Water hemlock. Nightshade.

They all grow naturally in the uncultivated forest surrounding the manor. I've been taught all my life to stay away from these plants, not to touch them, and certainly not to eat them. With my gloved hand, I pick a few of the belled flowers from the foxglove, berries from the nightshade, and clusters from the water hemlock.

Ensuring Nico isn't looking this way, I place my finds within a leather pouch I brought along with me. I turn my soiled gloves inside out before pocketing them. Then I search for some harmless flowers to take back with me to the estate. I call out to Nico when I'm done. He barely acknowledges me as he tries to catch water skippers hopping across the slow-moving sections of the stream. He's drenched up to his waist and couldn't be happier for it.

His childhood is so different from what mine was. So much freer, though he doesn't get to spend time with other children. There aren't any others to be found on the estate. Perhaps I should find a way to change that. We could hire on new help. Perhaps single mothers who need work? Something to look into once Eryx is gone.

I hand my bundle of flowers off to Tekla once I enter the estate, asking her to find a vase for them. That night, I steal a small teapot from the kitchen when no one is looking. Since I regularly frequent the kitchens, no one thinks my presence odd. I am fond of baking from time to time, so I regularly pop in to try out new recipes from Cook's books.

I fill the pot with water and place it atop the roaring fire in my room. I add the pouch of petals, berries, and clusters. I'm not entirely sure how much it takes to kill a man, so I figure it couldn't hurt to brew a lot of everything, letting it all soak in the boiling water, drawing out the poison from the plants into what I hope is a more concentrated form.

A mixture of the three deadliest plants found on the estate.

When I deem that my concoction has had enough time to stew, I pour it into a glass vial and stopper it with a cork. I flush the remains of the plants down the toilet, then wash and return the pot to the kitchens in the dead of night.

It seems careless to poison the duke so close to when I went picking wildflowers. No, I need to wait just a bit. Let no one be able to put this together.

I am not like Alessandra.

If I kill a man, I'm not going to be caught.

⊱ ⊰

I WAIT A FULL week before putting my plan into motion. My sister's wedding is this weekend. I'm cutting it close, but the delay was necessary. Caution is paramount when plotting murder.

When I go through the meal schedule with Cook, I arrange for an extremely spicy and potent dish on Thursday, a foreign curry heaped with herbs and vegetables. Something that will hide the foul smell and taste of my home-brewed poison.

The trickiest part, by far, will be getting the poison into Eryx's bowl when no one is looking. There are so many attendants standing near the dining table in case they are needed. The kitchen is full of staff preparing meals for all in the household.

I arrive at the dining room early and have to make a scene just to give me a moment alone with Eryx's food. I knock over a glass of wine, which trails onto one of the chairs and the waiting carpet underneath.

While everyone rushes to assist with the cleanup, I unstopper my glass bottle, pour the poison into Eryx's bowl, give it a quick stir, and return to my former position before anyone else rises off the floor. The table has to be lifted so the rug can be taken out for cleaning or replacement. The chair is ruined, the white upholstery having no chance of recovery from the bloodred stain.

It is just as everything is being set to rights that Eryx emerges with his cronies in tow.

"What is happening?"

"There was a spill, Your Grace," Xandria says.

"You are kind to cover for me, Xandria," I say, "but it was my fault. I'm afraid the chair didn't survive, and the rug isn't looking much better."

Eryx pinches the bridge of his nose. "You're going to insist on spending more money to replace them, aren't you?"

"Quit fretting like a pauper. Should you like to have a bare dining room? What will guests think when they see an odd number of chairs at the table?"

"That the duchess cannot count?"

"Precisely!"

Eryx smirks as he seats himself. He takes a whiff of the food in front of him. "Smells delicious. Do give my regards to Cook," he says to the nearest of the kitchen staff.

As I reach for my napkin, I utter the words I prepared for tonight: "You need a haircut." I glance at the medium-brown mess of tangles atop the fake duke's head with disdain. (I don't care if Tomaras says Eryx is legitimate in his claims, he will always be the fake duke to me as the title should be mine.) Talking about future events with a man I don't plan on seeing in the future only further cements my innocence.

"You need a muzzle," he replies.

I sigh with feigned impatience. "The wedding is this weekend. You must look presentable. We've come a long way with your manners, but your appearance is just as important. Please go get a haircut and *not* from Argus or Dyson. I doubt either man has ever held a pair of scissors. Go see a barber. Ask him for something gentlemanly. You cannot be seen with that mop upon your head."

Eryx gives me a look so dark I swear it leeches warmth out of the room.

"Fine," he bites out.

He sits with his eyes closed, breathing heavily, as though he needs to control his temper before he can even pick up an eating utensil. His temper seems to be getting shorter and shorter of late, though I've no idea as to what could be the cause.

I'm already a few spoonfuls into my meal, watching Eryx as I always do, in case I need to correct his manners. When he faces his food and grabs a spoon, my leg trembles from under the table. My whole body raises in temperature as he brings his first taste to his mouth.

There's a moment where I doubt. One small moment in which I think to stop him, to call out a warning that he shouldn't eat the food. A second where I can reverse what I've done and stop a man from dying.

And that moment passes right by without me saying a word. Eryx swallows his spoonful, wincing slightly. "Little stronger than I'm used to," he says, "but I'm sure I'll acquire a liking." He drinks some wine before taking another spoonful.

Another.

Another.

My leg shakes all the more fiercely. How long does it take for the poison to set in? I cling to my prepared reaction, readying for my surprise and shock.

Eryx puts a hand to his stomach, and his breathing picks up.

Finally, I think.

A jolt goes through his body, and he reaches for his wineglass again, taking a large swallow. Then he presses a hand to his mouth.

"What are you doing?" I ask him. "Use your napkin, not your hand to wipe your mouth."

"I'm not—" He convulses again, and something pours from his mouth. At first, I think he might be vomiting, if one were to vomit . . . black.

And then, I notice that whatever is coming out of his mouth isn't falling to the ground. Gravity is not claiming it as it would a liquid. Because it isn't a liquid at all.

Smoke.

No, not smoke.

Shadow.

I've been close enough to the Shadow King to recognize what that is.

Black shadows trail from Eryx's lips, floating upward, floating downward, floating outward. Eryx slaps both hands to his mouth as he sees the blackness oozing from him, but that doesn't stop it. It only flows from his nostrils instead.

What the devils did I do to him?

"Eryx?" Dyson asks.

The servants all take a step toward him.

"What is happening?" I ask, true alarm creeping into my voice.

He flees the dining room, Dyson and Argus on his heels. When I look back to the table, where the shadows had started to flow over the dishes, I see that they have vanished, as though they were never there at all.

"Did you see that?" I ask the servants.

"His Grace seemed quite unwell," Xandria responds.

"Was that smoke coming out of his mouth?" another servant asks. I don't catch which one.

"Looked like it," Xandria says. "Though I've never seen His Grace with a pipe before."

All the waitstaff look equally confused by whatever the display was. Our minds are quick to find rational reasons when the impossible is presented before us, but I know better by now.

"I'm going to check on him," I announce, shoving out of my chair. "Please clean up dinner. I doubt either of us will be returning."

I race after the three men once I'm out of the dining room, fearing that they've disappeared back to wherever Eryx is hunkering for the night. But I can hear them, specifically *him*, moving about up the stairs.

Groans guide me as I place one hand on the railing and use the other to raise my skirts as I ascend. Turns out the fake duke only made it as far as a guest room before sheltering himself within.

I place my hand on the door and push. "Eryx?" I call out. "Are you all right?"

Someone slams the opening door closed, flinging me back. I nearly lose my footing from the force of it.

"Best stay away, Your Grace," comes Argus's voice. "The duke's come down with something. You wouldn't want to catch it."

"That's utter nonsense," I say, outraged to have been kept out of a room in my own house. "You let me in this instant, Argus."

"I cannot, Duchess. For your safety, you must stay on the other side of the door."

A pained gasp comes through the crack under the door, and a small twinge of guilt courses through me. I hadn't thought his death would be painful. I just imagined him falling over dead after the first bite passed his lips.

"He sounds like he's dying," I murmur. "I'll call for a doctor at once."

"No!" comes a shout. This time from Eryx. "No doctors."

"Are you honestly too proud to accept medical assistance? You said you were sick. Let me ring for someone to help."

"Duchess, I forbid it!" he shouts before a nasty cough takes over.

"There, there," Dyson says, and I think I hear him slap the other man on the back.

"You cannot forbid me anything."

"Damnable woman!" More coughing. "I will cut off your stipend again if you ring for a doctor."

Oh, he wouldn't dare! "You don't want me to ring for a doctor? Fine, let me in."

"No," Argus calls back.

"Fine. I'm sending Kyros now."

The door flies open. Eryx barely stands, with Argus keeping him up on one side and Dyson on the other. He's got his face pointed toward the floor, and I see little spirals of shadow drifting upward, disappearing when they crest over his head.

"What are you?" I ask, even though the question should be ridiculous.

Eryx coughs, and more shadows spill from his mouth. "I'm just having a bad reaction to whatever was in that curry."

"A reaction that makes you breathe out shadows?"

"Don't be preposterous. I have a pipe in here. It's supposed to counteract the reaction."

"No, you had shadows coming out of you downstairs, too."

"Nonsense."

"Why are you lying to me? Why don't you want a doctor to come? What the hell is happening?"

He growls, but the sound turns into another cough. "This has happened before. Don't worry yourself. I'll be all right. I just need to let my body fight this off. Perhaps don't put that curry on the menu again."

"I'll ask you again, and this time, do *not* lie to me. Your eyes change colors. You have shadows spooling out of your mouth. *What* are you? The late Shadow King's bastard?"

Mr. Tomaras said that wasn't possible, but was he mistaken? There's no ignoring those shadows.

Eryx goes rigid. "I'm not— How did you— No." He grunts as another bout of pain takes him over.

He's going to continue to refuse to give me answers? Fine.

I say, "I sure hope you're not still sick by the time of the wedding. I'd hate for the Shadow King to see your abilities. He probably wouldn't accept you as the duke, then."

Eryx turns his eyes on me, and they are glowing a golden amber. He snarls at me, like an animal, and I see elongated canines.

Just like in my dream.

Argus and Dyson haul him back into the room before anything else can happen. The door slams in my face.

My heart pounds a rapid rhythm as I begin to walk away. What would Eryx have done if Argus and Dyson hadn't held him back?

The man doesn't have trauma from the war. He's not a man at all. He's something else entirely, and he's got two hired hands to help him keep from revealing it. What would he do without them? Would those horns sprout from his head? Would he rip out my throat with those canines?

And what would the Shadow King do if he found out someone with such powers existed? Would he see the man as a threat?

Most likely.

I need answers.

Despite the fear and the uncertainty, I let myself into the room next door to the one Eryx is in. I press my ear against the adjoining wall and attempt to slow my breathing, though I don't think he's likely to hear it while in his state.

"What do we do?" Dyson asks.

"Nothing," Argus says. "Just got to let the poison fight its way out of his system."

"Must have been that bastard, Sarkis."

Sarkis. That must be the name of the blackmailer.

Eryx groans again.

"This is ridiculous," Dyson says. "He's healed from bullet wounds faster than this is taking."

"He's not fighting off a concentrated attack. The poison is moving through his bloodstream."

Another five minutes passes, and then Eryx's breathing smooths. I hold my breath.

"You all right?" Dyson asks.

"I am now." Eryx's voice sounds perfectly normal.

"We'll catch Sarkis," Argus says. "That bastard will pay for what he's done."

"We have a bigger problem now. She knows."

"She doesn't *know*," Dyson argues. "She just knows something is off."

"We should kill her," Argus says, and I have to fight not to let a gasp escape me.

"No!" Dyson responds. "I like her. Besides, she's too pretty to die."

There's a pause, where they likely turn to Eryx for his command.

"Don't kill her. I'll watch her closely at the wedding. She won't say anything to anyone. Dyson is right. She doesn't even know what she knows."

"Fine," Argus says.

Though I'm straining for air, I force myself to wait.

"She thinks you're the Shadow King's bastard. Maybe you should encourage that narrative," Dyson says.

"That's barely better than the truth," Argus argues.

"It's far better than the truth," Eryx says.

Then the door to their room opens, and when I can no longer hear their footsteps, I draw in a deep breath.

I didn't kill him. He's perfectly fine.

He doesn't suspect me, but I'm not necessarily safe.

Shit.

I can't seem to catch on to a single thought. Not with Argus's suggestion still begging for attention.

He wanted to kill me!

When I make it to my bedroom, I lock the door, then stare at it.

I debate calling for Kyros. I would feel much better with another body in the room, but I know I wouldn't be inviting him into my bed for the right reasons.

Besides, two men barely restrained Eryx, and likely only because he doesn't want to hurt them. I have a feeling Kyros wouldn't stand a chance against Eryx if he really wanted in here.

He ordered his men not to kill me.

That has to be good enough for now.

While I lie in bed waiting for sleep, Eryx's sounds of pain follow me into my dreams.

CHAPTER

14

I spend the next day shut up in my rooms. Medora doesn't question it, and Eryx doesn't seek me out. Thank the gods, or devils, rather, since they're the ones more likely responsible for Eryx's appearance in my life.

He's not the Shadow King's bastard.

But what is he, then?

Is there another family line with powers? Who was Eryx's father? I wonder if that is the line of research Mr. Tomaras wanted to explore. What will he find if he discovers the truth?

For the first time since Eryx moved into the manor, I'm faced with the true reality of my situation.

I'm not safe.

Eryx is inhuman. Inhuman hearing, for how else can he hear my breathing on the other side of doors? Inhuman healing. Inhuman eyes. Inhuman canines. He has some sort of shifting powers, as far as I can tell, for the physical aspects aren't obvious all the time.

And then I think of my dream.

If that was somehow real, then there must be a mental component, too. Can he read my thoughts?

My body goes weak at the mere idea of it, but I reason against it. If that were the case, he would know it was me who poisoned him. Not that Sarkis fellow.

If I make one wrong move, Eryx could decide to be done with me. He has two physically intimidating men working for him. Men who would die for him, protect his secrets for him, *kill for him*.

I thought I knew the game we were playing, but it turns out to be far more deadly than I believed.

So what choices does that leave me?

I think through every possible option: I could abandon the estate and return to my father; marry again and move in with a new husband; or stay exactly where I am and pretend nothing is the matter with Eryx, hoping that he and his goons never think of me as too great a threat.

Those aren't really options at all. They're merely ways to stay safe. To remain subjected to the wills of men.

I would rather die first.

That means I need to keep playing the game to see where it leads.

Eryx worries I will go to the Shadow King and reveal what I think I know. He still has no idea that Kallias won't care one whit what I have to say.

Tomaras couldn't help me. The king won't help me.

Which leaves me only one option.

I need to resort to my acting skills. If I can get closer to Eryx, convince him to trust me, and learn everything that's really going on here, then one of two things will happen: I'll either find the proof I need that he's inhuman—proof that even the Shadow King can't ignore—or I'll learn his weakness and find out how to kill him.

Those are the only outcomes I can live with.

From this day forward, I need to play Eryx Demos as I would any other man. For the best way to get him to reveal his secrets is to convince him he's helplessly in love with me. I wouldn't even consider it, except I already know he finds me attractive. He's lost himself in my looks before.

But this will be tricky. I can't be too obvious or he'll see through my charade in a heartbeat. I have to maintain my air of disdain around him, while convincing him to find it charming. I must continue to act like I hate him but make him see me as the thing he desires most because he can't have me.

As my plan comes together, I go from frightened to excited.

I still have a chance to gain everything I've ever wanted.

⤜⊹⧫⊶○⊷⧫⊹⤏

I NEVER WANTED TO go to this blasted wedding. Alessandra is sure to be unbearable. My wedding was small, with only a handful of guests in attendance. It took place in this very estate, for the duke couldn't travel far. Alessandra will no doubt make comparisons about not only the venue—a palace compared to an estate—but also her young, handsome husband, compared to my shriveled, old one, as she put it.

But the consequences of not attending far outweigh those of attending at this point. I will not receive another letter from my sister telling me how grand the event was, accusing me of jealousy being the reason I didn't show up.

Besides, I've realized that putting in a good word for Eryx with the king will do two very important things for me. One, it upholds my end of the bargain with Eryx, so he'll continue to think I'm playing nice. Two, anything I tell the king is likely to be disregarded, for Alessandra will probably encourage him to do the opposite of what I want. So if I express that it's my dearest wish for Eryx to be officially recognized as the Duke of Pholios?

It will be interesting to see how this goes.

I wake early so as to have the entire morning to prepare. I haven't been seen by society at large since before my own wedding. I have to look perfect for my reentry. I've heard it's in poor taste to wear white to a wedding when one is not the bride, so naturally I commissioned an alabaster dress. It's long-sleeved, though my shoulders are bare. Pearls trail down my bodice and over my skirts in swirling lines. A V-shaped neckline shows off my delicate collarbones, stopping just short of my breasts. I clip a sheen of fabric to the back of my head, subtle enough for anyone else who looks at me to pass it over, but enough for Alessandra to fixate on its intentional semblance of a veil.

I paint my lips a deep red. I don't wear gloves, but diamonds drip from my ears and neck. Medora even threads some through my hair, which she's styled in an intricate coiffure, little curling strands trailing down my neck.

I descend the steps into an empty receiving room. It would appear that I managed to prepare myself more quickly than the fake duke.

So I wait.

And wait. And wait.

Anxiety takes root in my belly. It's bad enough that I'm nervous about seeing my sister again, especially since Sandros isn't escorting me. I have no one to show off. Then there's the fact that Argus wants me dead, Eryx is some sort of monster, and we might be late to the wedding I have zero desire to attend.

I begin to pace, while Damasus stands silently nearby. I consult the grandfather clock against the far wall.

"Damasus, could you check on what is taking so long?" I ask the butler.

"Of course, Your Grace."

He takes the stairs nimbly, and I check the clock once again.

I wish I could take my own carriage, but arriving separately runs the risk of Eryx making a fool out of the two of us. I don't trust him out of my sight for a moment at a public event. Not to mention, a private carriage ride is the perfect time to work my charms on him.

I tap my foot impatiently. Just then, Kyros walks by, holding a bouquet of flowers from the garden. He pauses when he sees me.

His gaze travels from the top of my head to the bottom of my feet. Then our eyes lock.

I wait for a flutter of butterflies to take root in my stomach at the connection, like they have countless times with Sandros.

Only, there are none.

"The wedding is today," Kyros finally says, as though remembering why I'm dressed so exquisitely.

"I thought it was your day off?" I ask.

"It is."

"Then why are you picking flowers?"

He looks embarrassed, before saying, "I was going to leave them for you to find later . . ."

"Oh."

Kyros is as handsome and kind as ever, but when I look at him, I don't feel anything at all. How can that be? I thought my mind and body needed time to adjust to the prospect of seeing him as more than a friend. But . . . I feel nothing amorous when I look at him.

I need to say something. I need to do something, yet nothing comes to mind.

"I hope you have a wonderful time, Chrysantha. May the reunion with your sister be painless, and I hope you're able to dance. Everyone needs a chance to see you in that dress."

Then he continues on through the manor. I'm too confused by my body's lack of reaction to respond.

What the devils is wrong with me?

Damasus descends the steps and takes the spot at my side. "They are coming, Your Grace. The holdup was merely an issue of learning how to tie the cravat."

It takes some effort not to frown. "The cravat?"

"Yes, it would seem neither His Grace nor his valets have ever done one before. After a brief lesson from myself—and a considerable amount of time spent untangling their previous efforts—they are now ready to go."

Leave it to Eryx not to know how to put on his own clothes. The man is hopeless.

Really, he can never expect to live this one dow—

I lose every thought in my head at the sight of the figure that appears at the top of the stairs. Strong brow, wide neck, fierce features. He descends with all the grace I've been forcing upon him during our lessons. Upright, unslouching.

He looks so very tall when at the top of the stairs, and it's incredible what an outfit that actually fits does for the man's physique. The vest and jacket spread across a broad chest. The pants stretch tight over muscle-clad thighs. The cravat puts more focus on his facial features. Those full lips and sharp cheekbones and piercing eyes. In his workman's clothing, he looks scary and intimidating. But put on clean formal attire and he looks *deadly*. Dangerous in and of himself, and then wealthy enough to thoroughly destroy anyone.

And his *hair*.

It's been cut much shorter, just barely reaching past his ears. Whatever pomade the hairdresser put in has held overnight, slicking the locks back and exposing his smooth forehead for once.

"Eryx," I blurt.

He takes a cautious step toward me, as though he's expecting me to bolt at any second. At first, I'm confused, but then I realize *he thinks I'm afraid of him*. Because I know he has powers. Because he tried to lunge for me when last I saw him.

I really ought to be afraid. I was when Argus suggested killing me. But right now, looking at him like this, I don't feel fear at all.

I feel . . . butterflies.

I raise myself as tall as I can, maintaining a look of superiority and ignoring the sensation in my stomach. "Are you quite finished making me late for the event of the century? Or does someone need to teach you how to open a door for a lady as well?"

After his initial look of shock, he steps forward to open the front door while I stare at his back. The ensemble I've chosen looks remarkable. Black pants, red vest and jacket with swirling white designs that match my dress without being obvious. The black cravat ties the whole outfit together. He turns toward me as the door opens, and I survey the front of him. It's spectacular, really. Combine the clothes with his figure and features, and he looks—

"I know," Eryx says, looking down at where I'm staring. "I've become a peacock." He pulls at the cravat as though it's preventing him from breathing.

Right. That's why I'm staring. The clothes. It has absolutely nothing to do with him. The butterflies flutter all the more fiercely.

Stop that, I order them.

"I think you look rather dashing, Your Grace," Damasus says.

"Did she pay you to say that?" he asks with narrowed eyes.

"Certainly not," I put in, finding my voice. "As if you need anyone giving you a bigger head than you already possess."

"I look ridiculous."

"You look— Well, who knew you were hiding all of that under that wild hair of yours?" I gesture to his face.

Eryx grunts. It's as though he has no idea how handsome he is.

Thank goodness.

"Shall we?" he asks before striding for the carriage.

"Wait," I say. "You must take my hand."

He turns and stares at my proffered hand as though it is a snake. "I must?"

"Yes, when escorting a lady to an event, you must take her hand."

"We're not at the event yet."

"Then consider this practice. Honestly, do you think I'm any happier about this than you are?" I'm certainly not, but I need to give him reasons to touch me.

After an exaggerated sigh, he takes my hand in his gloved one. He stares at me, as though looking for a reaction. After all, the last time he touched me he got into trouble.

And at that, that look, while touching him—

An electric heat passes through my fingertips and floods my entire body.

For gods' sake!

"Let's go," I say, tugging him along after me. I retreat into tutor mode. "You may tuck my hand into the crook of your arm or hold it upright, like so." I demonstrate. "When we reach the carriage, you're to hand me up into it. When we exit, you will do so first, before reaching to help me do the same."

He scowls as we walk. "I didn't realize ladies were in need of such help."

"We're not. Think of it as an opportunity for men to think about someone other than themselves."

One of the footmen lowers the hidden steps to the carriage, and Eryx hands me up into the seating area before following within. I note that Argus and Dyson join the coachman in the driver's seat, both dressed in the livery of footmen to blend in. Just a quick shout away.

I take one cushioned bench, Eryx the opposite, our bodies facing each other, but our faces looking pointedly away. When the carriage lurches into movement, I feel Eryx's eyes on me.

With nothing else for it, I turn.

"What?" I ask.

He looks as though he's unsure of what to say, but he settles on "I thought it was rude to wear white to a wedding?"

I smile but say nothing else. Eryx has no idea of the relationship between me and my sister. He wouldn't understand, and I have no desire to explain it.

"At least it's not pink," he mutters.

"What did the color ever do to you?"

"It's distasteful—and you can close your mouth right now. I don't wish to hear your comment about me being just as distasteful to match."

I close my mouth, almost embarrassed that he predicted my comment perfectly.

"Remind me how long of a ride it is to the palace," he says.

"A few hours."

He massages his temples. "I don't think I'll survive it."

That's rich, considering he's the one who is inhuman and can kill me with those sharpened canines. Though his teeth look perfectly normal at the moment.

His eyes snap open, and he catches me staring at his mouth.

Again.

"Something you wanted?" he asks, his voice lowering.

He keeps looking for a reaction from me. What does he think? That I'll scream? I suppose I've led him to believe that I've been hiding in my room because I fear him, rather than plotting his demise.

Perhaps I should fear him, but so far, the only thing that I've found terrifying is Argus's suggestion of killing me. Eryx's monstrous shape doesn't concern me.

And why the hell is that?

"I want answers," I say.

"Not going to happen."

"Oh, come now, Eryx. How does answering a few questions do any harm? I'll start with something simple. Does it hurt when your canines lengthen?"

He doesn't answer.

"Do you normally keep your hair long to hide your ears sharpening into points when you lose control?"

Still nothing.

"Is there fur on your tail?"

His eyes phase to amber, and he crosses his arms over his chest, as though that will keep the truth contained within him.

I reach out and poke his knee.

"Stop that," he says.

"Or what?" I poke him again.

He captures my wrist in one hand. So I use my free hand, this time jabbing him in the chest. His other hand shoots out, immobilizing my arms.

I kick him.

When he lets out a grunt, I see the flash of his elongated canines. He steps atop my feet, pushing his knees into my own so I cannot rile him any further.

Or so he thinks.

I blow a stream of air into his eyes, puffing up a strand of hair that's fallen onto his forehead.

And then out come his horns. They sprout from the top of his forehead, just like in the dream. He snarls at me.

"There you are," I say, taking in every detail I can see, as though it is wondrous. On some level, I suppose it is.

"What is the matter with you?" he asks, his voice going deadly. "Are you trying to get yourself killed?" He leans forward and pins my arms above my head on the wall of the carriage.

"You're not going to kill me."

"You overestimate my control."

He's so close, those teeth so close, and yet, I don't feel afraid. Quite the opposite. I feel . . . in control. Because I brought out exactly what I meant to. The proof of what he is. I can bring this monster out as easily as breathing.

And it is *terribly* exciting.

"You're not going to kill me," I say again, this time sharper.

"So sure of yourself?" He smiles. It is a wicked smile. A seductive smile. A *deadly* smile.

And then he strikes.

He goes right for my throat, and I brace myself as my stomach sinks. I'm certain that I've miscalculated him, and I might very well be about to die.

But pain doesn't come. There's a pressure, oh yes, but nothing more. Two points of contact, his lower canines, I realize a moment later, touch the base of my throat. The pressure isn't gentle, but neither is it bruising.

I don't have time to blink before he starts raking his teeth up the side of my throat. Something like a whimper comes out of me when he finally gets to the edge of my jaw, and that is what makes him pull back.

Glowing eyes fix on me before he finally releases me and returns to his side of the carriage.

Only then does a true sense of horror set in.

Because that sound I made, that whimper?

It wasn't one of fear. And that is more terrifying than anything else.

CHAPTER

15

Clearly I need to get myself a new lover. If my body is finding Eryx appealing, then it's definitely been too long.

But I can't very well do that while I'm trying to seduce him. He would surely know about the ruse then . . .

I don't press him for more information during the rest of the ride, and he doesn't even bother to look my way. No, he seems to be concentrating very hard on *not* looking at me, as though if he does so it will trigger something.

There's a tingling on the side of my neck for the whole journey. I cannot seem to get rid of it, as though he managed to leave something behind. But even though I touch the spot, there is nothing physical to find.

It becomes impossible to stop thinking about his teeth, his mouth. His horns and canines have long since disappeared, but I can still imagine them clearly. While he knows I'm staring, he only shuts his eyes against it.

He mutters, "Damnable woman," more than once.

And then, finally, at the end of what must be the slowest carriage ride in all of history, we arrive at the palace of Naxos.

The carriage door opens, but Eryx doesn't move.

I say, "You're to exit first. Do you remember?"

"I remember everything," he says in the most exasperating way possible. Then he descends, and his hand shoots back into the carriage for me. I reach out to take it, and the same sensation on my neck travels to my hand.

What the devils is he doing to me?

When my feet hit the ground, he tucks my hand into the crook of his arm.

The palace in Naxos is a massive gothic structure, all in black, down to the shingles. Winged gargoyles stare down at us from their perches, and some of them remind me of Eryx when he is transformed. I eye the tail of one, with its smooth length and triangle of skin on the end.

The armed guards eye us as we enter through the front gate. Their rifles are slung over one shoulder, and they're all done up in the black-and-white uniform of palace guards.

We pad along a red carpet through the massive front entrance. Hundreds of vases line the entryway, each full of a dozen black roses. The chandelier is lit with ebony candles, and someone has even melted wax onto the banister, leaving black swirling designs.

A servant leads us down a hallway, which I know will let out into the throne room. Unsurprising that they're holding the wedding in here, since it'll make Alessandra's coronation afterward that much easier.

The room has been decorated to my sister's sinisterly gothic tastes. Black and red everywhere. Midnight rose petals dot the crimson carpets. Ebony chairs with scarlet cushions for us all to sit. Flowers ring the columns, held together with some sort of wire, the blossoms making swirling designs that look eerily like shadows. I glance toward Eryx to see if he has any reaction to it.

He looks perfectly relaxed, though I can feel the tension in his body from where my hand is still tucked into his arm.

We're led to our seats, which are, unsurprisingly, at the very back of the room. My sister said in her letter that she'd save me a front-row seat, but she clearly changed her mind.

Eryx leans over to me. "Wouldn't a duke be positioned closer to the front?"

"You haven't been recognized as the duke yet, or have you forgotten?"

He doesn't need to know the real reason why we've been relegated to the back. My sister wants me here so she can gloat, but she doesn't want me to be in any place of honor.

I can't even blame her.

"But you're her sister. Wouldn't she want you close?"

I don't answer that.

We are among the last to be seated, which prevents us from interacting with the other guests, thank the gods. Besides, everyone's attention is facing forward, toward the thrones. No one has noticed our appearance—the mysterious new duke and the recently widowed duchess.

From the corner of the room, a quartet starts a romantic, slow-moving song. That must be the king's cue, for a shadowy figure appears through one of the walls near the front. He takes position up at the dais, just in front of the two enormous thrones.

Kallias Maheras is a sight to behold even without his shadows swirling about him like living flame. Black hair, bronze skin, godlike features. He is dressed in all black, from the sheath holding the sword at his side to his shining boots, to his silky cravat.

I don't watch him for long, though. I'm more interested to see Eryx's reaction to him.

He eyes the king with an unwavering focus that I have yet to see from him. His face doesn't change, but his eyes glow amber and then fade in the span of a second. He sizes up the king, as though taking in some sort of competition.

Competition for what?

And then Eryx notices me watching and looks pointedly away from the Shadow King.

I file that away to examine later.

Two men stand to the king's left: Rhouben Contos, heir of a viscount, and Petros Leva, second son of an earl. They must be close friends to the king if they're standing in such an esteemed position. Strange that I hadn't noticed the connection before. I spent quite a while at the palace trying to win over the king last year. I didn't notice him spending much time with anyone at all.

Standing opposite to the men are Rhoda Nikolaides, a dowager marchioness, and Hestia Lazos, daughter of a viscount. They have on identical red overskirts, with black pants underneath. My sister's friends. Such a small inner circle, when I compare it to my entire household staff, who have all become so dear to me.

Some sort of marriage official stands behind the king. He and the man exchange pleasantries, the official bent over with age, while the king stands tall and strong. The shadows flicker and swirl about him, as though giving away the man's excitement.

They look just like the shadows that poured from Eryx's mouth the night I poisoned him.

He's not the late Shadow King's son. That has already been confirmed twice over, but there is no denying that there is something familiar about Eryx's abilities.

"Stop that," Eryx whispers.

"I'm not doing anything."

"You're looking between me and the king."

"So what?"

"Whatever you're thinking, you're wrong."

"I'm thinking that you look even less like Kallias Maheras than you do your supposed grandfather. You have none of the same features."

Eryx purses his lips together in a way that suggests he's entirely fed up with me.

The room goes quiet when the king's shadows suddenly vanish. Kallias turns to survey the door at the end of the hall and freezes in place as though some otherworldly power has hold of him.

Everyone adjusts in their seats to see what has caught his attention.

And then we stand.

For my sister has made her appearance.

And she's not wearing white.

No, Alessandra's dress is blacker than a sky without stars. Her skirt is full, her sleeves long and tight, and she's got so much chiffon layered about her that the material shifts when she moves.

Like shadows.

She wears her hair down, trailing behind her. A ruby necklace adorns her throat while matching earrings dangle almost to her shoulders. Her lips are painted just as red as mine.

Alessandra strides forward alone. I see that Father was not invited to give her away, nor does he appear to be seated anywhere in front of us. But she looks better that way. Walking as though she needs nothing and no one. She belongs to no one. She is choosing a life with the king. She doesn't take note of me when she walks past. No, she sees nothing but the man at the end of the aisle waiting for her.

And I realize for the first time that she is in love with him.

My sister is not an actress. Not a talented one anyway. Not like me. That devotion in her eyes, that single-minded purpose with which she strides toward the king cannot be mistaken.

I feel sorry for her.

By loving the king, she is giving up her power. If he knows how much she cares, he will use it to try to control her.

She should have been more careful.

⪼—┤⟡⟶○⟵⟡├—⪻

THE CEREMONY IS DULL, and the coronation is even duller. I watch stone-faced as a crown is placed on my sister's head. People cheer, as though they're genuinely happy to have a queen, and not like they're just putting on a show for the king.

At least . . . the women do. Many of the men do not seem pleased. How dreadful that my sister is making laws that prevent them from exploiting women in so many ways.

Alessandra looks radiant as she stands and appraises her people. She looks genuinely happy, as though she has everything she's ever wanted.

And then, through the clamor of clapping hands, whistles, and shouts, her eyes land on me.

I know what the Chrysantha of the past would do. She'd turn up her nose and look away. By seeming superior, I've ensured that Alessandra never pays too close of attention to me. She was the one I most worried about learning my true nature. A part of me still wants to treat her that way. The petty side of me that still cannot fathom how she managed to snag a king while I labored night and day to secure a match with a slimy, handsy duke.

But as I truly look at her for the first time in years, I realize I don't have to be that girl anymore. Playing the simpleton doesn't gain me anything anymore. As a dowager, I am in control of my life for the first time, and I'm just one person away from having everything I've ever wanted. Now I'm about to potentially use my sister and her husband to get it.

So I incline my head toward Alessandra. A sign of respect, and even a congratulatory nod.

Her eyes widen for a single beat. Then she composes herself and looks to her husband. The two of them lead the way out of the throne room and into the ballroom, where we're all to enjoy refreshments and dancing.

Row by row we're asked to join the queen and king for the celebratory ball. I watch as dukes, marquises, earls, viscounts, and their guests all stroll by in a self-righteous procession. No one bothers to glance toward the barons and other lesser nobility in the back as they precede us from the room.

When it's finally our turn, Eryx takes my arm once more. I can hear a full orchestra playing from the open doors to the ballroom. A herald announces the guests one by one before they're allowed entrance. Eryx and I wait our turn.

"Lovely ceremony," he says.

I make a sound that doesn't really pass for agreement or disagreement.

"You didn't think so?" he asks.

"It was fine."

"If it wasn't the ceremony, then what was it? Do you not like the choice your sister's made? Do you think she should have held out for someone better than the *king*?"

"I don't really care what choices she makes." I did once. Her choice drove me to murder. But being here and seeing her again are giving me some clarity. I thought we were competitors, that by playing the same game only one of us could win.

But perhaps the truth is more complicated than that. We always wanted different things. It doesn't have to be her or me. While it hurts to see her in such a position of power and respect while I'm still working so damn hard for my happy ending, it doesn't mean that I should blame her. No, the blame rests solely upon the shoulders of the men who drove us to make the choices we did.

When we finally reach the front of the line, we give our names to the herald.

"Their Graces, Eryx Demos, the Duke of Pholios, and Chrysantha Demos, the dowager duchess."

Heads turn, even those belonging to couples already dancing. I give a cursory glance over the crowd as we enter the room. Many faces stand out, those of my would-be admirers who sent me letters, and I glance right over the tops of them before we can make eye contact. I don't have any desire to inadvertently encourage them. The men of the nobility have enough audacity as it is.

When I finally manage to block out all the men ogling me, I realize something that I hadn't taken into consideration before.

Eryx is young, rich, and unwed. That alone would cause a stir at any public event. Add to it all the fact that he's dangerously attractive, and it's a nightmare.

Now that Kallias Maheras is wed, Eryx Demos is the most eligible bachelor in the world.

Ladies and their mothers are practically frothing at the mouth at the sight of Eryx. And when they finally compose themselves enough to shut their gaping jaws, they jostle one another to be the first to approach.

"Your Grace, won't you please introduce us to the duke?"

"Of course, Lady Petrakis," I say. "This is the Duke of Pholios. Your Grace, this is Marchioness Petrakis and her daughters, Lady Violetta and Lady Evadne."

The two young women curtsy opulently, then look up at the duke through their lashes in the most obviously flirtatious way. Eryx bows grandly in return. I'm almost proud of the gesture, for it is one I made him practice at least a hundred times.

"Lovely to meet you. I'm terribly sorry, but you must excuse us. The king and queen are expecting us."

No, they're not, but I don't ruin his lie. I find a bad taste in the back of my throat at the way ladies are stepping over one another's skirts to get closer to Eryx. I've no desire to stick around.

"Of course," the marchioness says, "but I hope you will come seek us out again before the night is through."

Eryx looks like he wants to grit his teeth, but he keeps his smile in place. "We shall do our best, but I'm afraid we've already made many promises tonight. As a gentleman, I wouldn't dream of making another one unless I was absolutely certain I could keep it."

One of the daughters sighs at his response. I close my eyes to hide their rolling.

Eryx tugs me after him deeper into the room before another word can be said on the matter.

"That was awfully diplomatic of you," I say. "I've never seen you that patient with someone in all the months I've known you."

"You've only witnessed me interacting with you," he points out.

"So you can spare patience for strangers but not the woman you share a living space with?"

"Precisely."

A man elegantly maneuvers through the swishing skirts to be the next to approach us. I'm not sure how he manages it without knocking someone over.

I whisper to Eryx, "Watch and learn," before the man intercepts us.

"Your Grace," the Duke of Simos says, staring me down. "I feared the worst, since I never heard a response to my letters."

I stare at the new man's cravat. "Forgive me, Your Grace. I meant to reply, but I simply became so overcome any time I would imagine your impressive figure while trying to compose a response."

Eryx barely manages to conceal a snort. I only catch it because I was waiting for his reaction to the words.

Simos doesn't know what to say at first. Finally, he mutters, "Thank you for the compliment, Your Grace. Might I have the pleasure of a dance?"

"Oh," I say, taking a slight step backward. "If I can't manage a letter, I surely won't be able to handle a dance without swooning. As a gentleman, I know you wouldn't have me embarrass myself in front of so many people, now, would you?"

Simos's voice drops in tone. If I were watching his face, I'm sure I would find it crestfallen. "Of course not, Your Grace. I hope you will recover your nerves. Please do write me, if—if you can manage."

The man walks away with less confidence than when he approached.

When I turn back to Eryx, the man looks dumbfounded.

"What just happened?" he asks.

"It's called acting."

"*How* did that work?"

"It's a simple and highly effective play I've perfected over the years. You deliver information that will be disappointing to hear but appeal to their vanity while you do it. They can't very well argue with me or beg further without refuting the compliment I'm paying them. Most men are far too vain to argue on their looks."

"How can they possibly take you at your word? You, swooning? Over that soft-handed man."

"I hadn't realized you'd found an opportunity to hold his hand."

Eryx grumbles, "I don't need to touch him to know he hasn't done a day of hard labor in his life."

"And that's a bad thing?"

"I said it was nothing to swoon over."

"And who should I be swooning over? You?"

He stumbles over his next words. As though he's unsure whether he should encourage the notion or vehemently protest it.

Before he splutters out a response, more courtiers approach us, asking for an introduction to the new duke. I listen as Eryx carefully refuses the not-so-subtle hints of salivating mothers that he should dance with their daughters. As soon as one party leaves, another takes its place. Men approach, begging me for dances, and I let them down with gentle words that appeal to their egos.

After several women leave our sides, dejected, some of the men in the room start approaching Eryx, thinking perhaps the reason he's not dancing is that his preferences lean in another direction.

"Would you care to dance?" Petros Leva, friend of the king's, asks Eryx without any preamble. He doesn't bother to introduce himself, despite the fact Eryx has no idea who he is. Petros eyes the fake duke up and down before meeting his eyes.

Eryx seems to lose his voice at the request.

Petros turns to me. "Is he all right?"

"He might be swooning."

"Wouldn't be the first time this has happened to me. Really, no one is prepared for me before they see me."

"It's those delightful freckles on your cheeks." I smile. "Why didn't you ask me to dance?" Petros is known for liking both men and women. I hadn't ever thought I'd be competing with Eryx over something like this, but now that I was the second choice, I can't help but feel put out.

"You're prettier than he is, but I am loyal to your sister."

The response is the last thing I expected to hear. He must be close to Alessandra if he knows the nature of our relationship.

"Thank you for the invitation," Eryx says before I can change the subject, "but my interests lie elsewhere."

"Pity," Petros says. "But I daresay you are giving everyone else in the room hope by refusing to dance with the women."

"I'm afraid I don't have any interest in dancing at all. We're on our way to speak with the king and queen."

"Is that so?" Petros does a sweep of the room.

Kallias and Alessandra are seated at chairs against the far wall. At this rate, it'll take us another half hour to reach them.

"Well, this I have to see. Follow me."

Petros starts walking toward our monarchs, and Eryx and I hurry to follow. When anyone tries to approach, Petros shoos them away.

"Their presence has been requested by the king and queen. You can harass them later! Don't you give me that look, Leta Trakas. You've accosted the young men in the room long enough. Go dance with your husband!"

Before I've mentally prepared myself, I'm staring down my sister. She's eyeing her husband as though she's conflicted about whether to stay for the party she's planned or move things to a private location. No one can fault her for that.

"Alessandra."

My sister's eyes land on me. In a haughty voice, she says, "That's *Your Majesty*, Chrysantha."

"Your Grace."

"What?"

"If you're going to insist I call you by your title, then you must use mine. I am a duchess, after all."

"Devils, there's two of you," Eryx mutters under his breath, too quiet for anyone other than me to catch.

Alessandra says nothing, clearly caught off guard by my snarky response. To dispel the tension, I say, "Thank you for the invitation. It is good to see you happy. You look radiant. You made that dress yourself, didn't you? You've always had such a talent for sewing."

She cocks her head to the side, as though she can't quite tell what to make of me. Am I in earnest? Or is there some hidden barb in my words? Or am I buttering her up because I mean to ask something of her?

When still she says nothing, I press on, "And it is good to see you again as well, my king. You couldn't have found a better match than my sister."

"I know that," he says, and when he looks at Alessandra and sees her conflicted face, he leans forward, whispering words too quiet for me to hear. I wonder if Eryx can decipher them.

Alessandra shakes her head, answering no to whatever the king asked. "Who is your guest?" she asks me. "I heard you had taken up with a man. From Zanita's?"

Her tone makes it clear that she thinks me a hypocrite, and I suppose I was, chastising her for sleeping around when I went and did the very same thing. The difference is that the chastising was an act.

"No," I say, "sadly I had to let Sandros go. This is Eryx Demos, my late husband's grandson and the man who would take up the title of Duke of Pholios. I wanted to make an introduction."

Alessandra gives Eryx a careful perusal. The king says nothing, letting his wife take the lead on this matter.

"Was your lover more or less handsome than this man?" the queen asks.

Startled by the question, I look to Eryx, who seems equally perplexed. I don't know what game she's playing, but I'm doing everything I can to keep calm and get through this encounter.

So I give her question the consideration it deserves. I imagine Sandros standing next to Eryx. He would be a bit shorter and leaner, but his face was the stuff of poetry.

I say, "The same."

"Hmm."

Alessandra reaches over to take her husband's hand in hers. She plays with his fingers as she continues to survey me.

Finally, she asks, "What do you want?"

For Eryx to disappear from my life. I say, "At first, I wanted to ask that you deny the man the dukedom so it would remain in my care."

Eryx's breath hitches, but I press on.

"However, after spending some time getting to know him, I have to admit that he makes a fine duke. It is my wish that he be recognized formally by Your Majesties as the new Duke of Pholios."

That perplexed look has yet to leave my sister's face. She still doesn't know what to make of me. Alessandra turns to Eryx. "Leave us."

I wonder if he'll dare to disobey, when I know leaving me alone with the king and queen is the literal last thing he wants to do.

He says to me, "I won't be far."

It's a threat more than a promise.

"You too," Alessandra says to Petros, who has remained within hearing distance all this time.

"Spoilsport," he says to her good-humoredly, but he obeys as well.

And then I'm alone with my sister and her husband.

CHAPTER 16

nce Eryx is gone, Alessandra leans forward in her chair.
"What game are you playing?" she asks me.
"Game?"

"Yes, you aren't behaving like your usual self."

"For the first time in my life, I'm allowed to be my real self."

"And what does that mean? A man finally tempted you into bed and now you're climbing down from your high horse?"

I can't help but smile. This is the first real conversation we've had in years. "No, I'm no longer dependent on Father or anyone else for my survival, so I don't have to be the woman men want me to be."

Alessandra narrows her eyes. "And what woman is that?"

"The airheaded beauty who wants nothing more than to please her father because she's too stupid to want anything for herself."

Alessandra sits up straighter in her chair. She eyes me from head to toe as though meeting me for the first time. I suppose in a way, she is.

"I had Father wrapped around my finger for years, and you were none the wiser to my antics. I had the whole world fooled, and now I have everything I've ever wanted." Almost. "So there's no point in keeping up the ruse. Not with you, at least."

I keep my eyes locked on hers. There is no looking away or backing down. This is me.

Kallias turns toward his wife as though waiting for her to do something. She finally schools her features and asks, "And what is it that you've wanted?"

"Freedom. As a dowager duchess, no man can tell me what to do. My life is my own." The only thing I need now are the unlimited funds to go along with it.

"You mean to say you wanted to marry Pholios?"

"Who do you think planted the idea into Father's head?"

Another pause. "Let me make sure I've got this right. You pretended to be an idiot for . . . *seven years* so you could control your own life, and it *worked*?" The last word comes out at a higher pitch than the rest.

"Yes." I press on. "And I owe you an apology. Probably about a hundred, actually. You see, I knew that if anyone was to pick up on my ruse, it would be you. I kept you at a distance to protect myself. I was self-righteous because I knew it would infuriate you and make you want to stay away from me. I was rude and condescending and judgmental all to play this game. You didn't deserve any of it. I chose my own survival over you. I didn't think I had any other choice. I regret how I hurt you over the years."

Alessandra stands. "Kallias."

"Yes, dearest?"

"I would like to dance."

"Then let's dance." He holds his hand out to her and leads her toward the center of the ballroom. She doesn't say another word to me, but she stares at me until another dancing couple blocks her vision.

Alessandra isn't one to keep her thoughts to herself. I must have truly startled her for her to be speechless. Or perhaps she just needs time to process it all.

At least she hasn't thrown me in prison or something else drastic, I suppose. I hadn't expected our conversation to go that way at all, but once we were talking, I couldn't stop myself from coming clean. I have no idea why.

Because if I can find an ally in Alessandra, she can help me to be rid of Eryx? Perhaps.

But never mind that. I need to find Eryx. I sure hope he hasn't found a way to embarrass me in the short time we've been apart. I turn in place, looking for his pomaded head. He's walking across the room, not far from the dais.

Was he eavesdropping?

But of course. How else could he be sure that I didn't spill his secrets? I hope it's the first step in getting him to trust me. But all hell could have broken loose if the king and queen had caught him.

He doesn't look my way as he approaches a small group of men. Is that because he actually wants to talk to them or because he doesn't want to face me after catching him spying? I observe him for a moment. He pats one of the men on the shoulder, and they shake hands before widening the circle to admit him. Either he's making friends astonishingly fast or he knows these men.

I'm surprised that I do not recognize most of them. I thought I knew all the courtiers.

To gently insert myself into the conversation, I approach slowly and take Eryx's arm once I'm certain he's seen me. While it would be difficult to fit his pistol and serrated knife in the tight outfit he's wearing, I wouldn't put it past him. Spooking him in this crowd would be a nightmare.

Eryx places a hand atop mine and pulls me forward, effortlessly including me in whatever conversation is happening.

"Gentlemen, allow me to introduce Her Grace, Lady Chrysantha Demos, dowager Duchess of Pholios."

Each of the four men surrounding him bows.

"You must be the most fortunate man in all of Naxos," the first one says. He's older than the rest of the group, with graying temples and wrinkles about his mouth. "You inherited a dukedom that just so happened to come with such a lovely lady of the house."

I think he meant it as a compliment, but I don't delight in being relegated to "lady of the house." I am its rightful owner and master.

"Your Grace," Eryx says to me, "let me introduce you to General Kaiser and two of his underlings, Captain Rodis and Captain Zogafros. And this is—"

"Lord Barlas," I finish for him. Yet another man who sent me letters right after the death of my husband. He already has a mistress, one whom he's kept for years. Either he means to replace her with me, or he intends to have a short tryst. Either way, I'm not interested. He's not a bad-looking man, but I've never cared for his character. I curtsy to the group.

"I'm afraid you caught us in the middle of a rather boring conversation," one of the captains says. I already forgot his name.

"Yes," the other agrees. "We were talking about the war efforts in Estetia, which must be dreadfully boring to someone like you, Your Grace."

I'm torn between correcting the man or stating that the only thing I find boring about the topic is the company.

But Lord Barlas speaks up. "Why don't you join me for a dance, Your Grace, and we can leave our fighting men to their chitchat?"

I open my mouth, prepared to deliver some sly rejection, when Eryx grips my hand more tightly. "Lord Barlas, what a kind offer. The duchess would be delighted." He passes me off to the other man like money exchanging hands.

I'm so startled by the move that I can't form a word of protest. Up until now, Eryx and I had made a game of rejecting our admirers. Now he's hand-delivering me to one?

How dare he?

I'll kill him. This time for real.

The last thing I see is Eryx disappearing behind a group of people, still engrossed in conversation with the men from the army.

And then I've nowhere to look but at the earl before me.

"Your Grace, I have to tell you how divine you look tonight. You put all the other women in the room to shame."

"You hardly need to pay me a compliment by insulting the other women in the room," I state.

He laughs as though I've said something funny.

"Where is your mistress tonight?" I ask, trying to keep my tone pleasant.

"At my home, waiting for me. Parties overwhelm her. She doesn't like to go out."

Doesn't like to? Or he doesn't let her?

"Tell me, Your Grace, did you receive my letters?" he asks.

"I didn't. They must have gotten lost in transit."

"Pity. I'll have to write you new ones."

"Perhaps you should spend time focusing on the woman you're already keeping."

"There's no need to be jealous. You have my full attention right now. Enjoy it while it lasts."

Just who does he think he is? One of the gods' gifts to this world? Hardly.

I swear it's the longest dance I've ever been subjected to, and it doesn't help when I catch sight of my sister and the king dancing.

They're almost indecently close to one another, with his hand low on her back. They're staring into each other's eyes like they can't get enough.

I feel that familiar rage try to overcome me again. There my sister is with a man who loves her. Who's treating her well. How does Alessandra keep doing that? What secret has she learned that I haven't? Why does she get what she wants when here I am, yet again, subjected to someone who thinks more of his polished boots than he does of me?

It takes a moment, but I direct the rage where it belongs, staring daggers at the man holding me.

When the five-minute-long dance ends, the earl tightens his grip on me. "Let's do another."

"My lord, as the sister to the queen, I have many duties to perform tonight. You must excuse me to see if she needs anything."

"The queen is preparing for another dance with the king."

"I'm feeling fatigued. I'd like a drink."

"After the dance."

He sweeps me along into the next song. No matter how I try to pull away, his grip tightens, and his left hand strays far too low.

On the next step, I tread on his foot. Hard.

He grunts, and though he must be surprised, he doesn't let up.

So I do it again.

"Your Grace, surely you know the correct steps to the dance," he says.

"Surely you know when a lady is trying to tell you no."

He ignores me, and my gaze tinges with red as I plan how I will exact vengeance on this man who dares to touch me unwanted.

This dance is longer than the first one, and I feel a bruise forming from where he's adjusted his grip from my hand to my arm to get a better hold on me.

When a third song starts, I debate kicking him in the crotch, everything else be damned, when a shadow looms over us.

I look up, startled to find Eryx with his eyes a shimmering amber.

"May I cut in," he says. The words are no less than a demand.

When the earl tries to splutter out some reason why Eryx cannot in fact cut in, Eryx reaches out, grips the earl's wrist, and squeezes.

I hear a *snap*.

Lord Barlas shrieks as he doubles over, clutching his injured arm, and finally releases me. Thankfully, the sound is lost in the music that has picked up its tempo. However, Eryx doesn't appear to be done with him. He places a hand on the man's shoulder, and I have every intention of watching what he will do next to the earl, but I remember that we are in a public place and shouldn't cause a scene.

I throw myself between the two men, bumping against Eryx's extended arm. He turns that murderous gaze on me.

"Dance with me," I say.

He doesn't seem to hear me, but I dare to grab his arm and place it at my waist. Then I take the other in my grip. On the next beat, I spin him away from the injured man, whom no one else appears to have noticed.

When Eryx's eyes land on me, they don't dim. His body is rigid, though it manages to move as I direct it. He clearly doesn't know the steps to this song. And why would he? It's not as though I've taught it.

I lean forward. "Your eyes, Eryx. Get yourself under control."

He shuts his eyes immediately. "I wasn't done with him."

"You are in a public place."

"I don't care. He was *hurting* you."

"I will handle him later."

"And how do you plan to do that?"

"I'll think of something. Perhaps pay off his mistress to leave him."

Eryx's eyes open; they're a little less amber and a little more brown. "That's not punishment enough."

"It's the only kind of punishment I can manage."

"That's why I intend to handle him. Men like that don't deserve to live."

I falter a step. "Are you saying that you would kill that man for me?"

His eyes widen, as though he's just realizing the truth of what he's said.

And meant.

Those butterflies start up in my belly again.

I look away from his face, at our joined hands. His white undershirt pokes out from his jacket. The sleeve is tinged red.

"Is that blood on your wrist?"

He looks down to where my gaze is. "No."

"Then what is it?"

He cannot come up with a single lie, and it's foolish to even try. What could possibly be mistaken for blood?

"Are you hurt?" I ask.

"No, it's not mine."

I don't know if that's better or worse.

"Where have you been?"

"The men's room."

"At least that's a better lie."

His whole body tenses.

"Stop that," I say. "Focus on getting yourself under control. Then we can leave."

"I can't," he says through his teeth. "I still want to kill him."

"Don't think about him. Think about me. Focus on the dance."

A few couples finally notice Barlas and help him off the dance floor. If anyone suspects what really happened to him, they don't approach us. At least the earl has the good sense not to accuse a duke.

"This"—Eryx pauses—"actually isn't horrible."

"And why would dancing be horrible?"

"Most people don't usually enjoy things they're not good at."

"I think you and I can both agree that you are certainly not anywhere close to *most people*."

Eryx takes a deep breath through his nose. "You're very good at distracting me."

"Better than Argus and Dyson?"

"Much."

"What do they usually do when you shift?"

He starts to say something, then catches himself, as though remembering he's talking to me.

"Eryx, your eyes are still blazing. We need to get you calm."

"How the hell am I supposed to be calm when I handed you off to a man who—"

"Because you know I will make you suffer for it. When we get home, I'm going to make you wish you'd never met me."

He smiles. "I don't doubt it." Then his face falls. "You must know I had no idea. I didn't think anything bad could happen in such a public place."

"That's because you don't know all the tricks men pull in public places and get away with. How would you? They don't try that kind of stuff on those who have the strength to fight them off."

Eryx's eyes blaze brighter, and I look around to see if anyone has noticed. We're safe for now, but he really needs to stop.

"No one," he says, "*no one* is going to touch you like that again. I will make sure of it."

I want to scoff, but I don't. I realize that he's not saying it out of any sense of ownership. No, Eryx has tried very hard to get rid of me from day one. He means it because he has a sense of justice. He would step in for any woman he saw being treated that way.

So I don't correct him or tell him to stop saying silly things like that.

Instead, I tease him. "And how will you make sure of that? Are you going to follow me everywhere I go? Are you going to kill every man who touches me in some untoward way? Would you like a list of the men who have done so in the past? There won't be many courtiers left in Naxos then."

He pulls me closer. "*Who?*"

"Gods, I was joking. Relax."

"Who?" he demands again. "Are they in this room?"

"Please, you must calm down if we're to get you out of here unseen. I was trying to lighten your mood with a joke, not stoke your temper."

"Suddenly you care about my well-being?"

"After you just made a show of looking after mine, yes."

That finally has his muscles unwinding. The music picks up, and Eryx has to concentrate very hard to follow my lead. His fingers splay against my back, and I wonder if he even realizes he's done it. As though he's trying to grip more of me.

So as not to step on my foot, of course.

"Look at me," I say. "Don't watch your feet."

"If I don't watch my feet, then I will injure you."

I grin. "You won't. You'll get a better sense of my movements by watching me. Trust me."

He looks up, and a tight, squirming feeling spreads through my chest.

I ignore it, instead enjoying the crinkle on Eryx's forehead from his concentrating so hard. His eyes dip down to my mouth.

"Are you laughing at me?" he asks.

"No, I just think you're adorable when you're concentrating."

"Adorable?" The word sounds ridiculous when it comes out in his deep voice.

"Yes."

"Now I know you're making fun of me."

I roll my eyes. "Relax. It's almost over."

And for a moment, he does. His body loosens, and his limbs fluidly follow me. The amber glow leaves his eyes.

"Good."

And then the music slows again, and he's still looking at me. Because I've told him to.

Eryx pulls me closer, without even thinking about it. His thumb draws a soothing circle against my back as his gaze intensifies. A sheen of amber reenters his irises.

I squeeze the hand in mine, as though trying to snap him out of it, but Eryx squeezes back, mistaking the gesture.

"Your eyes," I whisper.

He blinks, as though coming to, and they fade back to their usual brown. I do yet another carefree glance about us, just to make sure no one saw.

My eyes land on my sister and the king, who are dancing just two couples down from us. Kallias is staring at Eryx, and my sister is staring at me.

My stomach drops, but I offer Alessandra an encouraging smile. Why was she watching me? Why is the king staring at Eryx? Did he see? And if he did see, why isn't he doing anything?

When the song ends, I usher Eryx from the room before anything else can happen.

CHAPTER

17

n the carriage, I realize something is missing for the first time.

"Where are Argus and Dyson?"

They escorted us to the wedding. They waited with the staff during the ceremonies, and I remember them tailing us inside the ballroom. Where did they go after that?

"They wanted to stay in town overnight to enjoy the city."

"Hmm. That's the best one."

"What?"

"The best of the lies you've told this evening. That one was almost believable."

Eryx massages his temples as the carriage takes off. "And why are you so sure it's a lie?"

"I'm to believe they left you alone during the middle of a public event where you could have exposed yourself, which I might add, you nearly *did*, to enjoy the city? After they've been trailing you around your own home, protesting the few times you've requested to be alone with me? No, you've all been up to something tonight. Something illegal, I might guess, considering the fact that you disappeared from the ballroom for over ten minutes and returned with blood on your sleeve—and Argus and Dyson didn't return at all." My voice takes on a teasing lilt. "Are they disposing of a body for you?"

Eryx's whole body freezes in place, and my eyes widen at his reaction.

"I was joking!"

But it's too late. He's given away the truth, and he knows it.

He turns murderous eyes on me. "You. Need. To. Go."

"As in out of this carriage?"

"As in out of my life. You're going to ruin everything."

I lose it. For a while, all my schemes fly from my mind, and I am helpless to do anything but give that accusation the response it deserves.

"Oh, *I'm going to ruin everything*? Did you forget the part where you strolled into my life, stole my home, my money, and my peace of mind? I tutored you for months on etiquette! Helped you find decent clothing! I just put in a good word with the king on your behalf! What more do you want from me? You don't have to trust me, but what else do I have to do for you to finally respect me?"

He doesn't soften the slightest at the rebuff.

He turns his head to look out the window, signaling he's done with the conversation.

It's only as the carriage pulls back into the manor that I realize I didn't bring up the fact that he's a monster, and I've kept that secret, too.

Curious that it didn't even cross my mind at all.

I HADN'T ANTICIPATED THE consequences of attending my sister's wedding. Apparently, people had avoided calling on me directly because they thought I might still be grieving my husband. But showing up to a social function and dancing with two different young men proved to be all the invitation my would-be suitors needed.

Everyone in the blasted country seems to think that the mysterious Duke and Dowager Duchess of Pholios are taking callers.

The day after the wedding, Damasus finds me reading in the garden. "Your Grace, there is a Lord Varela here to see you."

He hands over the earl's card, and I don't even glance at it. I refuse to entertain gentleman callers. Best to stop these habits right from the get-go. This is my home, and I will not have it soiled by the presence of overeager dandies.

"I'm out of the house today, Damasus."

"You certainly are. I shall inform him at once that you are not at home."

"Thank you."

My butler leaves with a bow.

Twenty minutes later, Damasus returns.

"Now there is a Lord Regas at the door."

"I'm still out of the house."

"Of course, Your Grace."

In another hour, Damasus is back again.

"You're kidding," I say.

"I know very well you have no wish to see any callers today, or ever, really, but I'm afraid the duke admitted Lord Moros into the manor before I could inform him you were not at home. The duke is requesting your presence in the parlor."

Of course he did. After last night's conversation, I'm sure the fake duke intends to invite all manner of gentlemen to come see me, hoping to entice me with marriage once again.

The damnable nitwit.

I mark my place in the lovely romance novel about two gentlemen who must bridge the gap between their social classes to be together, and march into the parlor.

Eryx is laughing at something the baron has just said, and it is a rare and highly unusual sight. It draws me up short, makes me angry, even. How dare he get some joy out of my misery? But we have company, so I paste on a wan smile.

Moros notices me before Eryx does, and rises as I enter the room. Eryx is a full second behind him as he remembers his etiquette lessons.

"There she is," Eryx says. "I knew the duchess would be eager to chat with you today. Chrysantha, Moros has the most delightful stories to tell about fishing mishaps."

"I'm certain the duchess has no desire to discuss fishing mishaps, but I'm sure we'll find some common ground," the handsome man responds. He must be in his late thirties, but he's aged quite well. A bold mustache sits beneath his nose, and he has a full head of hair, straight teeth, and bedroom eyes.

"Perhaps I should leave you two to it, then," Eryx says, walking around the tea table centered in front of the sofa the two men had been sitting at.

"You will do no such thing," I state.

"Duchess," Eryx says, embarrassed as he tries to block me from sight of the baron. As though my whole self must be offensive, rather than just my words and tone. "He really seems quite lovely. Just give him a chance," he whispers in a lower tone.

"That is the Baron of Moros," I state in the same tone.

"Yes, I'm aware."

"Eryx, he's *married*."

That has Eryx spinning to look at the man. "No," he whispers to himself. "Moros, are you already wed?"

"Ten years and counting," the man answers. "It's been so lonely. I am in the market for a new mistress. I thought the duchess and I might come to an arrangement."

Eryx swirls back around to me, eyes wide.

"Unless you intend to start whoring me out," I say to him, "I'm going back to my garden. Next time, perhaps talk to me before you go on inviting gentlemen into the manor on my behalf."

I stride out of the room, book still under my arm.

I try to get back into my novel, I really do, but I'm so terribly furious. I had been interrupted during the first kissing scene of all places, and now I can't properly enjoy it while I'm distracted by thoughts of clawing Eryx's eyes from his skull.

I'm unsure how long I sit there feeling sorry for myself when I'm interrupted yet again. I swear if Damasus has news of another caller—

"I'm sorry, Chrysantha." Of course it's Eryx.

"You ruined my reading time."

"I had no idea the man was already married. I wasn't trying to sell you or anything, I swear. I'm not that kind of man."

I laugh at him, because he can't hear how ridiculous his words are. "Eryx, that's exactly what you're trying to do. You offered me twenty thousand necos to get married. You don't care who you have to pay to be rid of me. You're just upset you were mistaken and didn't find someone who could take me for life."

I rise, suddenly needing movement, and head for the trail that goes across the grounds and into the neighboring woods.

He follows.

"It's not like that, and you know it," he argues. "I'm not like your father. I'm not selling you to the highest bidder. I'm trying to give you a comfortable life with someone you love and enough money to give yourself all the things you could want. After everything you've learned about me . . . I thought you'd be more eager to get off this estate. I'm only thinking of you. Why can't you see that?"

"You're not taking into consideration what I want. That's all that matters, and that's why you're exactly like my father."

"What do you want, then?" he snaps, and nearby birds flutter away from the overhead branches.

"I want my manor back. I want my land back. I want my money back. I want to find out who and what you really are. I want to be safe and comfortable. I want you gone!"

But he can't give me any of those things. Why should he even want to? He doesn't care. And he somehow has every right to them.

"You're not even trying!" he yells back. "You could have all of those things. Just not here on this estate. You could find love and happiness with a young man who will respect and cherish you."

"I don't want love and happiness! I want freedom. I want to be left alone. I don't want *to try*. I've been trying my whole life to be someone else to give my father what he wanted. To get what I wanted. I'm done. I endured Pholios for *two months*, until death finally claimed him. I'm supposed to be my own woman now, yet I'm somehow beholden to *you*. You *summoned* me today. I listened only to protect Damasus from your wrath. You have too much power over the people I care about!"

The surrounding woods go completely quiet after my outburst.

"What . . . what did you endure?" he asks softly.

"You don't want to hear about it."

"Yet I'm asking. I want to understand."

"Why? What will understanding do? Will you suddenly leave me alone when you hear about how Pholios criticized and yelled at me every day? Will you up my allowance if I tell you how he pawed at me every chance he got? Will you give me back the dukedom if I tell you about the bruises he left? If I make myself pitiable to you, will you suddenly behave like a decent person?"

The longer I talk, the more the shift happens. First, his eyes. Then his ears. Finally, his horns and canines sprout at the word *pawed*.

I have the distinct urge to step backward, to give room to the massive form before me, but I hold my ground, determined to cling to my righteous fury.

His voice is deeper than before as he says, "If he weren't already dead, I'd kill him myself."

"You can't just say things like that!"

"Why not."

"Because they make you sound like you care when you clearly don't!"

He growls at me, the sound somewhere between human and animal, as though contradicting me with the noise alone.

I reach out, grab one horn, and pull his face down to my eye level. "I do not care what you look like, Eryx Demos. You will not win arguments by shifting in front of me."

His eyes are trained on my mouth, which is right where I need them, but my traitorous body reacts to that gaze. My breath catches, and my heartbeat gallops as though trying to escape my chest. I feel myself start to move closer, as though he has his own force of gravity and is pulling me in.

I remember all too well how those elongated canines felt against my neck. Now I'm imagining them pulling on my lips.

Reason is a faraway thing, but it seems to push through my traitorous thoughts to reach the forefront of my mind.

It's too soon to give him what he wants. He needs to be begging for it. Only then will you learn his secrets.

At the last second, I shove his face away from mine.

"Pull yourself together before one of the groundskeepers sees you."

Eryx blinks, then slams his eyes closed, concentrating. The horns shrink until they disappear beneath his skin, like swords sheathing. His ears turn from pointed to round. His canines retract. When he opens his eyes, they're still amber, though no longer glowing.

"So that's it, then?" I ask, continuing the conversation. "No progress today? We're exactly as we were twenty minutes ago?"

Eryx says in a gentle voice, "I'm so sorry for how you were treated by my grandfather. It wasn't right. It was an abuse of power, and I hope he burns in one of the devils' hells for it. But just because one man behaved that way, it doesn't mean that all men—"

"Do. Not. Finish. That. Sentence."

His eyes narrow at my tone.

A mirthless laugh escapes me. "You want me to put my trust in another man? Just hope that the next one won't abuse his power? *I* want to be the one with the power: the power to remove myself from those who treat me poorly, the power to protect myself, the power to always make my own decisions about my body and my life. Neither you nor anyone else can put a price on that freedom. So you and your twenty thousand necos can leave me the hell alone."

There is a prominent silence in the wake of my words.

Eryx, for once, seems to be rendered speechless. We stare at each other, my breaths coming out quickly from the force with which I delivered that little speech.

When Eryx drops his gaze, he says, "You deserve that power. Of course you do. I'm sorry that I cannot give up mine for your sake. I need it right now."

"I hate you," I whisper.

He hears it, but I don't wait for his response. I leave, and this time, he does not follow.

>⊷⊷○⊷⊷<

I TAKE THE REST OF the day to cool down. Something happens to me when I'm near him. I lose all reason and turn into a chaotic mess of rage.

I messed up. I'm supposed to be slowly charming him, yet I exploded on him. I told him I hated him, which is true, but not conducive to seducing him.

There has to be a way to get him to trust me. At the very least I need to catch him off guard. Eryx doesn't get to have the upper hand again. I'm sick of him parading into my personal space whenever he wishes. I need to go to the one place where we'll be on even footing.

Or, better yet, where I might just have the high ground.

Testing a theory, I take a blanket with me to the library that night. The last time I dozed in this room, I dreamed of Eryx. More than that, he *visited* my dream somehow. Or I was in his. Either way, it seemed to bother him. Must be terrible to have someone else insert themselves into your safe space.

I curl up on the settee and will myself to sleep.

Of course, it takes hours, because even my own body is conspiring against me.

But when I'm finally in blissful darkness, it happens. My eyes open to a room outlined by fluffy white clouds. I bend down to scoop at them, but nothing comes off the floor into my palm. Shrugging, I make my way over to the bed.

I debate the best way to do this part. I'm sorely tempted to rip the sheets from him so I can finally catch a glimpse of that tail, but it feels like a line that should not be crossed. Sighing, I settle for kicking at the mattress.

Eryx jolts awake, as fully transformed as the last time we met like this.

"Not again," he groans.

"Afraid so," I say, crossing my arms over my chest. "We need to have a chat."

"We just had one a few hours ago."

"Well, I want another one."

Eryx looks over the side of the bed, as though hoping his clothing will materialize. No such luck. It must be out of the dream's range.

What a pity that fully muscled chest will have to stay on display.

"You could tuck the blankets under your chin to preserve your modesty," I offer.

He glares at me. "Talk. Then be on your way."

"First, I want to apologize," I say, trying not to choke on the falsehood. "I was short with you earlier. I said some things I didn't mean."

"The part about hating me?"

"Let's not dwell on details. I think we both say things we don't mean when we're enraged. The point is that I think you and I can come to a unique understanding now that we have a better idea of where the other stands."

"Meaning?"

I twirl a lock of my hair between two fingers. "You know that I'm not leaving this estate. You know that what I want most is control over my own life. To escape the restrictions men have always placed upon me. I know your secret."

He flinches, but I press on. "Bits of it, anyway. This presents us with an opportunity."

"It's too late in the evening for discussions like this. Will you just spit it out?"

That draws me up short. "You often have dark circles under your eyes. Is it because you're not really sleeping when this happens? Does this happen often?"

"Focus, Chrysantha. You have a proposition for me."

"Right. If you leave me alone to live my life as I see fit—control of the servants, the manor, my own money—I will help you. But no more talk of marrying me off or anything like that."

He rubs at his forehead. "What do you think I need help with *now*?"

"Keeping your secret. This isn't a threat. This is me offering to help you control yourself. There have been multiple times now where I've helped you rein in your glowing eyes. I seem to tame the beast somewhat, and I think I could help you make real progress in not slipping up in the future. If you keep at this much longer, the staff are bound to notice something is up."

"You *bring out* the beast. Now you insist you know how to *tame him*?"

"I do that on purpose. Getting a rise out of you entertains me. I think with some real practice, you could get this all under control."

"You don't even know what you're dealing with! How can you want to put yourself in danger like that?"

I lie. Again. "You protected me from Lord Barlas. You've never hurt me before, and I don't see why you would start. And . . . well, you could tell me what I'm dealing with. Help me help you."

"So you can have more ammunition to use against me?"

"Whatever do you mean?"

"If you knew everything, you would truly have the upper hand on me. I feel like we're barely on even fighting ground as it is."

"How can that possibly be true? Why do you think I pose such a threat to you? No one will believe me if I tell them what I've seen."

"Because you have a connection to the Shadow King, and while no one else will believe you, he might. And he might see me as a threat to his kingdom. You saw the way he stared at me at the wedding."

Ha, as if I could ever get an audience with him. Perhaps everyone's ignorance of my relationship with my sister is the only thing sparing my life right now. "Why should the Shadow King see you as a threat?" I have my own theories, but I want to hear his.

Eryx looks down at his blanket. "The Maheras line claims that their shadows are a divine right to rule, even though the truth is that the shadows were a curse from a devil. Devils love to make mischief in the lives of humans, though few are strong enough to manifest on this plane physically. Even then, they're only able to do so after centuries of building their strength. The Maheras line was cursed by the most powerful of them all, and they don't want any threats to their crown. If anyone with abilities makes them public, they are immediately executed in private. How can the shadows be a sign of a divine right to rule if other people have powers?"

"That's it, then?" I whisper. "You were cursed by a devil?"

"No, Chrysantha. I'm something much, much worse."

Goose bumps rise on my flesh. "Why are you telling me this?"

"To help you see what you're dealing with! You don't want to be on this estate with me. You don't want to help me. You should be looking after yourself."

At least it takes little effort to summon my defiance. "And what if I told you that's the opposite of what I want? I do want to be on this estate. I am looking after myself. I do want to help you, and I'm not scared of you or whatever devilish abilities you possess."

Eryx grips both of the horns on his head in frustration. "You're not listening to me. I don't know how else to say this. My hold on the monster is tenuous at best. I may not be able to hold him back from you."

I stare at his forehead. "Are you saying there's two of you in that head of yours?"

"No. It's just me, but it's how I differentiate between being in control and out of control. When I lose myself, the shift happens. I'm not in my right mind."

"What about now?"

"I'm sleeping. I always shift when I sleep, because I'm not conscious to hold my human form."

I smile.

"What?" he asks, defensive.

"It's nice to understand. To have some answers."

He shuts his eyes tight. "I'm asleep. I'm not as careful with my words as I should be. That's why you shouldn't be here."

"Does that mean if I prod you enough, I'll get the whole truth?"

"No. I'm not *that* tired."

"Fine, but can we come to an arrangement?"

He looks astonished. "How do you still want to push this? What do I need to say to make you run?"

I cross my arms. "What do I need to say to make you realize that I'm not afraid? You need to trust that I mean what I say."

He looks up. "It's a terrible idea. Your worst yet."

"Let's just give it a try. What's the worst that could happen?"

"I could kill you!"

"You've had plenty of opportunities to do that. Obviously neither you nor the monster wants that."

He grumbles something that sounds a lot like "You'd be terrified if you knew what the monster did want." Eryx shudders.

"And what does the monster want?" I ask brazenly.

Eryx swallows, but his face turns determined. "Nothing that I can't control."

For some reason, the memory of his teeth against my neck surfaces.

Now I'm the one shuddering. "Then it's settled," I say. "We'll start tomorrow. That means I should let you get your beauty sleep."

"I haven't agreed to anything!"

"No, but you didn't refuse, so I'll take what I can get. I'll see you tomorrow. No valets. Hopefully they'll still be in town disposing of that body."

Eryx bares his teeth in a growl right before I shut my eyes tightly, willing myself to wake.

CHAPTER 18

'm far too excited to sleep, even after I return to my rooms. I'm certain it's just the prospect of Eryx finally letting me in. It doesn't have anything to do with seeing more of his monster form. Or being in close proximity to that rumpled hair, arrogant features, or chiseled body.

I'm much too practical for that.

Still in my nightgown, I traverse to the parlor, unable to stay turning in bed any longer. I seat myself at my desk, reach for the lamp, and procure a fresh page of parchment.

I'm not quite sure where the letter will go, all I know is that I have this desire to write to my sister. Probably because I need to soften her up for once I finally have the information I need to expose Eryx.

Dear Alessandra (or must I address you as
  Your Majesty in private, too?),
Only as I write this do I realize that we've spent so
much of our lives conversing through letters. We've
always written to each other on birthdays and special
occasions. Or when we had something to gloat about.
  I would like to change that.

I'm not writing to you today to gloat or send along fake well-wishes. I'm not entirely sure why I'm writing at all. But I enjoyed seeing you at your wedding. Though the words we exchanged were brief, they felt real, and I would like for there to be more of that between us.

So here is my attempt to share more real words.

- *I love reading. It's my favorite activity. I prefer romance and action in my stories, everything that my life is not, I suppose.*
- *I adore living out in the country. My garden is one of my favorite places. I like to smell the flowers and watch the butterflies.*
- *One of my servants has a little boy of four years, and he's such a delight. I'm teaching him to play the piano. He likes to help me pick wildflowers or joins me on walks through the property.*
- *Feeling safe and in control are two things I've come to cherish.*

This all probably sounds very simple to you. You're ruling a country, and I admire that you have the stomach for that. I've always wanted a life that is free from scrutiny. I am content to finally have it.

If you have the time, I would love to hear from you.

Sincerely,
Chrysantha

I read through the letter several times, trying to decide if I should actually send it. Will she laugh in my face? Will she even read it? I suppose I won't know unless I try.

When Doran wakes, I'll send him off with it.

I spend the rest of the wee hours of the morning reading. I'm not entirely sure what our first monster training lesson should be like. It'll obviously be much different from any other lesson we've had before. How am I to get Eryx to open up to me while thinking I'm helping him?

I expect something will come to me when it's time.

Yet, as I take the stairs down for breakfast, I glance out the large windows leading to the east side of the manor, only to see Eryx striding toward the woods.

I groan and roll my eyes. It'll surely be ages before he returns. He's likely off to see what's become of Argus and Dyson. They have yet to return, and it's possible something went wrong.

My staff doesn't seem to take note of the way I barrel through my breakfast. I rise from my chair as I'm placing the last bite into my mouth. Time is of the essence. I gather my skirts in one hand as I bolt for the library. Once I reach the doors, I spin about, eyeing the hallway right and left.

The two times I dreamed of Eryx, I was in the library. I'm almost certain that this has to do with the proximity to where Eryx is sleeping. For why else would he not take the master bedroom? He feared appearing in my dreams every night and not getting any sleep. Which means he must be near enough to this spot without being too near the servants.

The kitchens are to the right, far down the hallway. The servants' quarters are beyond that. So he can't be staying anywhere in that direction. To the left is my parlor, the entryway, the dining room, the receiving room, and ballroom.

He can't be sleeping in any of those. I or the staff would surely have noticed.

If I travel up a floor, I'm met with the guest rooms, which I've already searched.

So what else does that leave?

Deciding I need to think outside the box, I head outdoors and look at the library windows. As I scan the estate from the outside, I wait for a burst of inspiration.

Nothing is forthcoming.

Has the man built himself a burrow in the woods? Surely that would put him too far from the library, not to mention the house in general.

I start to walk, taking in the beautiful flowers and well-maintained trees. Since hiring back one of the groundskeepers, the exterior of the estate is looking much better.

I halt in my tracks as I spot the wooden doors almost at ground level.

The cellar.

Surely not.

I approach the lock fastened across the doors with growing trepidation. He couldn't possibly. It's unhygienic and likely full of spiders and *why is he making me go into the cellar?*

My skeleton key fits into the lock without so much as a whine as I turn it. Darkness lurks far below, where the sun doesn't reach. It's the one part of the manor that wasn't updated with electricity. There was little reason for it.

But I spot a lantern hanging on a hook just inside. The interior is full of oil while the exterior hasn't a speck of dust anywhere to be seen.

Someone is certainly using the room.

I light it, then begin my careful trek down into the cold area. Rows and rows of shelves house wines and food storage. Most of it is coated in dust, though a path has been worn along the ground. Evidence of foot traffic.

The room keeps going and going. I've never had cause to come through here before, and I really hope this is my last visit as I spot a fifth cobweb.

I try to orient myself as I imagine what the floor above me looks like. The servants' quarters would be back that way. Then here are the kitchens. Yes, I can hear a slight commotion above me as the staff work to clean breakfast and prepare lunch.

That means the library would be about . . .

I round a corner and come to a standstill.

Someone has laid out floorboards on the ground to cover the dirt. A plain mattress with a white comforter rests right on the ground. And as I step into the space, I catch a smell.

That of the earth after a storm.

He's been living here, between two shelves of canned fruits. I am horror-struck. I wouldn't dream of letting one of my servants sleep in such a place, yet he has been hiding down here in an attempt to keep me from learning his secret. Were his accommodations in Dimyros better or worse than this? Why do I care?

A broom lies off to the side, to keep the floorboards clean. A small chest nearby reveals another pair of pants and a handful of shirts. Next to a bucket of water, I find a handheld mirror, a razor, and soap.

Good gods.

And then, as I survey the far side of the room, I find a single piece of parchment, staked to the wall with a dagger similar to the one Eryx keeps sheathed on his person.

When I approach, I'm able to read the scribblings.

~~BEMUS ANDRIS~~

~~TARASIOS KAZAN~~

~~URIAN STRATOS~~

~~TYPHUS VALIS~~

~~CALLISTUS LIAKOS~~

~~KYMUS PANOS~~

The first two names are the lords who have gone missing, the ones mentioned in the paper, as reported by Karla and Tekla. Has the king managed to cover up the rest? I try to recall if I saw any of these men at the ball. I don't think I did, but it's hard to be sure. I continue to read.

ORESTES SARKIS
~~GENERAL KAISER~~

The next two names stand out in stark relief. I know them. Sarkis is who Eryx assumed poisoned him. It's the man who has been blackmailing him. And I just met the general last night at the ball.

His name has been crossed out, the line of ink darker than those before it.

Because it was struck out last night.

This is a hit list.

Also in dark ink is a new name that's been added, written sideways along the margins because there's no more room.

ZOSIMO BARLAS

My body goes hot all over.

Eryx added this name last night. After the earl mistreated me. Even though Eryx broke the man's wrist. He said it wasn't enough.

Clearly, he meant it.

And I feel light, as though I could float. I feel my heart surge as though it is growing. Those butterflies flutter in my chest as I think of the man who wants to protect me, even though he's so desperate to be rid of me.

And then my eyes finally reach the very bottom of the list to take in the last name.

KALLIAS MAHERAS

I start laughing uncontrollably.

So much is finally coming together. The reason why Eryx was so opposed to me being in the house with him. The reason why he wasn't sleeping in the duke's chambers. The way he so readily agreed to attend the wedding with me.

He needed the title of duke to get close enough to these men. So he could end them. He ran off at the wedding so he could dispatch the general. Argus and Dyson are burying his body somewhere, hoping it won't be found.

And Eryx has only two names to go if I exclude Barlas. Sarkis, who, for some reason, has evaded Eryx all this time despite his abilities, and *the king*.

Just how does he expect to get away with the last one? And who's going to rule the country after that?

Well, Alessandra would, but she and the king have no heirs. There wouldn't be anyone to pass the kingdom on to. Not to mention the huge target on Alessandra's back without Kallias around to protect her.

I'm not really concerned for my sister. She can clearly handle herself. I'm not even too upset at the thought of the king dying.

It's Eryx's arrogance. What the hell does he think he's doing? He can't get away with this. This is stupid and ridiculous. And why? What have all these men possibly done to him? He's only been in town for a few months!

It must have something to do with Eryx's time in the army. What other connection could the general have possibly had to Eryx? And Kallias controls the army, so that must be the connection between all the men.

Still, I memorize the name Orestes Sarkis. I will have Kyros run the name by Mr. Tomaras for further investigation. Maybe he can find the exact connection to Eryx.

Then I pick up my skirts and head back out the way I came. I've no desire to be caught, and I have much to think about.

>-!-+>-O-<+-!-<

I MAKE MYSELF COMFORTABLE in the flower garden, where I have a clear view of the woods, and wait. For once, they don't disappoint me.

Approximately three hours later, the world's dumbest trio emerges.

They're streaked with dirt and blood and devils know what else. Eryx single-handedly drags a large buck behind him, its eyes closed in death.

"We're having venison for supper!" Eryx calls out as they approach, then veers for the kitchens.

"It's a good cover story," I praise. "You're finally getting good at the whole 'deception' thing. When you're finished cleaning the general's blood off you, don't forget we have our first monster training session."

Argus mutters a very naughty word, and Dyson exclaims, "How! How does she know that?"

Eryx smacks Dyson's chest, warning him to be quiet.

"When are you idiots going to realize that I'm an asset to you? You'd be smart to keep me close, rather than try to shut me out of your schemes. And before you suggest killing me again, Argus, I've informed my sister that if anything happens to me, you're the first person she should question."

It's a bald-faced lie, but it shuts the man up.

"What do you want now, Chrysantha?" Eryx asks, his face calm.

"I'm not threatening you. Believe it or not, everything I do is not a ploy. I merely wanted to offer a suggestion."

"And what's that?"

"Plant evidence of the general's murder on Lord Barlas. He was seen talking to the general at the ball, and the man has it coming."

With that, I walk inside the manor, leaving the three of them to clean up.

><+>+O+<+><

WHEN ERYX FINALLY COMES TO find me, he's wearing one of his new pairs of pants. It's a simple black pair but sewn in a fashionable style. He wears a white long-sleeved shirt, rolled up to his elbows.

"Hmm. Yet another reason why one should own more than two pairs of pants," I say.

"To replace pairs that get ruined after murder?"

"Precisely." I grin.

Eryx is astonished. "How can you joke about this? You clearly know I just killed someone. That doesn't have you fazed even slightly?"

"I'm sure you had your reasons."

"I think perhaps you should see a doctor."

I arch one brow.

"Something is wrong with you. You don't react in fear when you know a literal monster is standing across from you. You don't blink at the thought of murder. I'm starting to think *you're* not human."

I scoff as I look around my parlor, then reach for my teacup. "Maybe you've just never trusted anyone with your secret. Of all the people who have figured it out on their own, how many rejected you?"

"Including you? Two."

Sarkis must be the other one.

"That's my point, though," I say. "I don't reject you because of what you are. I hate your role in my life. That's entirely different. Besides, we're here to change that. You need to learn to trust me."

"If you were to break that trust, you could ruin everything."

"Your petty revenge schemes rank low on my list of priorities."

"Is that what you think I'm doing? Killing men who hurt my feelings?"

"Is it not?"

Eryx grits his teeth. "General Kaiser was a selfish prick who treated his men worse than dogs. Good men died who didn't need to because he was given far too much power with little supervision."

Power that Kallias Maheras gave him.

"And now you've set that to rights."

He nods proudly.

"Did you mean to kill him? Or did you let the monster out?" I ask, even though I already know it was premeditated. I'm covering my tracks, lest he suspect I found where he's sleeping.

"It was intentional."

"Has it ever . . . not been intentional?"

His silence is answer enough.

"This is why you need me. I can help you."

I expect him to argue or flee from the room without another word. Instead, he surprises me. He sits opposite me, on the second sofa across the tea table.

He's finally admitting he needs help. Or he's trusting me. Either way, I need to encourage this.

"Can you help me to understand? What happens when you lose control?" I hope it's a safe question. I need to ease him into this.

Eryx bites the inside of his cheek, then glances at the ground. "The monster is all my baser instincts. He is the worst thoughts I've ever had. He wants to take. Take anything he fancies, take any life that inconveniences him or threatens what's his."

"I think I can follow that."

"The problem is when the monster and I want the same thing. In the case of the general, we both wanted him dead. Keeping the monster at bay is nearly impossible then."

"But you were talking to him. Your eyes weren't glowing then."

"The monster isn't completely stupid. He can bide his time as long as he knows he'll get what he wants. It's when I get enraged or—" He cuts himself off. "When I get enraged, I shift."

"I've seen you shift when you're not angry."

"This is embarrassing, and I don't want to talk about it. Can we just focus on the—"

"You also shift when you are impassioned. Just say it. There's nothing embarrassing about that."

"Impassioned. Such a delicate way of putting it."

I narrow my eyes. "You're the one embarrassed, not me. I thought only to protect your delicate sensibilities."

"Very funny."

"I'm not trying to be. Men are the most sensitive individuals I have ever met, yet they claim it is women who are always close to hysterics. I can confidently say the reverse is true. Now, let me see if I understand this correctly. If you experience really strong emotions or have an intent that's aligned with your baser instincts, you have a hard time not shifting."

"Yes."

I think for a moment. "Which is your true form?"

"They both are. I was born looking human. The shifting came as I got older."

"And it's a result of . . . ?"

"Nice try. We're not there yet."

I smile. *Yet.* That's a good sign.

"All right," I say. "What have you tried doing to rein yourself in in the past?"

"Everything."

"Such as?"

"Pain. Inebriation. Distractions. Things like that."

"What kind of distractions?"

"Argus or Dyson will try to take my mind off what is setting me off."

"And does that work?"

"Not really."

I cross my arms. "*You* need to be what calms the monster. Not them.

You will only gain control over him when he sees you as the one in charge."

"Now you're the monster expert?"

"No, but I know about impulses. I've spent years mastering my own. Do you think I enjoyed playing a simpleton? Do you think I didn't want to verbally assault men when they would belittle me? I had to be in charge. I had to keep my end goal in mind. Surely this is no different."

He purses his lips. "If it were that simple, I would have figured it out before."

"What brings you peace?"

"What?"

"Peace. The opposite of war? Is there a place or thing or person that makes you feel whole? Calm?"

"A person? Definitely not. I've never been in a place that was peaceful. My whole life there's been danger."

"What about a future goal? Something you're trying to attain?"

He thinks a moment. "I suppose I am trying to achieve peace in my own life."

"By killing?"

"Among other things."

"And what's the end goal? When will you be done and your life perfect?"

"When my enemies are dealt with, then I can finally rest."

I examine the dark circles under his eyes. "Then think of that. Imagine you're finally at rest because the work is done. And that can be achieved only if you stay in your human form."

"This is ridiculous."

"You being unable to control your emotions is ridiculous. You're like a child, throwing tantrums."

"I am nothing like—"

"Killing people who upset you because you know no other way to deal with your problems."

"They deserved—"

"No one can even blame you with the upbringing you had. First your grandfather abandoned your mother, then your mother abandoned you. You will continue the cycle. It's all you know."

His eyes glow amber. "I know what you're trying to do, and it won't—"

"Why didn't you kill your grandfather? He was all that stood between you and wealth. Why let nature take its course? You knew the kind of man he was, yet you let him continue on. Let him continue on with me—"

His black-purple horns sprout from his head. I might feel guilty for pushing Eryx in this way, but I'll do him no favors by coddling him.

"You have no honor. No sense of justice unless it directly benefits you. Firing people from the estate to protect your secrets. Stealing this dukedom away from me because you think you're more deserving. You probably wouldn't have even stepped in to save me from Lord Barlas if it hadn't been your fault in the first pl—"

He growls and launches forward, leaping clean over the tea table without hitting a single cup. He lands before me and covers my mouth with the palm of his hand.

"For once will you shut up?"

I slap him away. "Not until you shift back. Find your peace. Think about the goal."

He slams his eyes closed, and I keep talking. "Your father didn't care about you or your mother. You're probably what scared him away."

His eyes crinkle from the attempts to block me out.

"Argus and Dyson only stick around because they owe you. They don't actually care about you. They told me they hate that they're bound to you."

He cracks open one eye. "That's ridiculous."

Fine, he wants me to play dirtier. I can do that. "I don't actually care about helping you. I only don't want you to embarrass me because our names are tied together. If you go down, then I do, too."

His eyes fly open. A hand reaches behind him to adjust the back of his pants, which tells me his tail has sprouted and he needs more room.

"Focus!" I shout at him. "How hard is it to do one simple thing, Eryx? Just don't be a monster. Be what you need to be to find your peace."

His mouth snaps at me, stopping just shy of my neck. An audible *click* sounds from where he stopped himself at the last second.

"I told you this would be dangerous," he says on a growl.

"And I told you I'm not scared of you. Control yourself. How do you expect to run a dukedom when you can't even keep your eyes brown? Will you kill all our tenants when you inevitably reveal yourself to them?" I hurl the accusations at him, unsure if they're meant to convince him or me of his faults. "The first woman who pushes you too far, begging for a dance at the next party—will she meet your wrath? How many innocent lives will you take so that you can keep your secret?"

"Apparently, all of them except yours."

In the seconds it takes me to parse that out, Eryx finally catches himself. He shifts back to a perfectly normal, albeit far too handsome for his own good, man. We should feel accomplished. He did it. Yet I feel as miserable as he looks.

"We're not doing this again," he says.

I stare at his back as he leaves.

CHAPTER 19

Well, it could have gone worse, I suppose.

Eryx could have killed me. He could have not sat down with me to begin with. I could have never found his list of names.

But we're finally getting somewhere. And I know something of his plans. I just need more proof.

And I need to convince the fake duke to have another go-around. He needs to open up more. To feel safe. To let me in the way he has both Argus and Dyson. Never mind that making him miserable made me feel miserable. This is what's best for me.

But now he's not talking to me.

"Eryx," I call out as he's leaving the study the next day.

"No," he says before disappearing down the hallway.

Argus steps in front of me when I try to follow.

At dinner, he has his "valets" sit beside him, not bothering with pretenses any longer. The three of them chat like the best friends they are while they pointedly ignore me.

Dyson shares some story about when his childhood friend growing up broke his nose. "He only found out the next day it had been all a misunderstanding. I didn't actually kiss Calandra Karahalios."

Argus and Eryx burst into laughter, the first man slapping the table. I narrow my eyes at the gesture, but not one of the three men pays me a lick of attention.

There's an enormous surge in my bank account, despite everything. Eryx regularly deposits large sums. I don't know if he thinks he's buying my silence or paying me to stay away from him. Regardless, we've come to no formal agreement, so I've no intention of doing either.

About a week later, a letter arrives to distract my efforts. My sister actually sent me a response. I hold it between my fingers for several minutes before finally opening it.

> Dear Chrysantha (no honorifics are necessary in our letters),
> I hate reading. I can't think of anything more dull, but I'm glad you have something to do in the countryside. I suppose it's unsurprising that life at court holds no more excitement for you. You were able to spend all the days of your youth attending parties and balls and other functions, while I was forced to stay at home and hear about them after the fact.
> I was sick of being ignored by everyone simply because I was the second daughter. There are some real words for you. I don't think our childhoods could have been any other way when society was made for you while hindering me.

There's a little scratch on the parchment, as though she wasn't quite sure what to say next, before adding,

> I've spent so long resenting you. A lot of things were out of your control, but some were within your control. You could be so cruel with your words. The only way to protect myself was to cease caring about you at all.

I've taken some time to consider it, and I've decided to stop resenting you. I am glad my life turned out the way it did. I became who I am because of you. You, Father, Hektor—you all played a part in shaping me. I turned into not only an excellent queen but also a woman who goes after what she wants by any means necessary.

You and I, we did what we could to survive. I've found my happiness and peace. It seems that you are close to finding yours as well.

So I will play nice, for now. If I catch any whiff of deceit from you, then I'm done—for good this time.

Love has made all the difference. Having Kallias changed everything, and I can only hope that you find that for yourself, too.

I'm sorry about your lover. I've heard rumors that the new duke is the reason for his disappearance from your life. I don't know if he fears having a worldly woman living under his roof or what the issue may be, but I will not allow that to continue. I changed the laws for a reason, and if he isn't respecting that, then you tell him he will have me to deal with.

How is Zanita's, by the way? I've heard it's a marvelous place. If I weren't happily married, I'd investigate it myself.

All my best,
Alessandra

I retrieve a blank parchment and immediately scribble a reply.

Alessandra,

I wish we could have swapped our roles. I would have loved to stay at home and receive no attention. I thought the only way to survive was to stomach it and find an ideal situation for myself. I am sorry I did not give more consideration to you. Thank you for sharing that pain with me so I can better understand.

Here is another truth. I was so jealous of you. The way you were so free and ignored, left to your own devices. You had real relationships, and I was left thinking I would be soiled goods if I didn't do exactly as Father wanted. I wish I could have been like you. With your edicts, you really are changing women's lives for the better. You saw the good you could do with your power, and I am proud of you for it.

Zanita's is marvelous. I highly recommend it. Thank you for the threat I can use on the duke should he become too bothersome. And remember, if ever the king does anything to upset you, you can threaten him with visiting Zanita's.

I hope she takes that as the joke it's meant to be.

It's okay. Reading isn't for everyone. What do you do for fun aside from sewing? I hope you are able to take some time for yourself, despite how busy you must be.

Sincerely,

Chrysantha

I send it off with Doran that day.

"THIS ONE WAS MY FAVORITE YET," Karla says at the next book club gathering.

"Agreed," Tekla responds, and the two sigh contentedly.

I will admit, this one was perhaps the most romantic tome we've read for book club, and that's really saying something, considering that's basically all we read. Even Damasus chooses books with romance in them, even if the main plot is a high-stakes adventure.

"I don't think I really understood the romance in this one," I say. Though the steamy scenes were excellent, they didn't feel earned with the buildup to them.

"What's not to understand?" Damasus asks. "The two men were smitten with each other from the start."

I raise a brow. "They *hated* each other at the start."

"Exactly," Karla and Tekla say in unison. They turn to each other and laugh at the coincidental timing.

"Hate is not love."

"Of course not," Tekla says, "but it's remarkable how often the two coincide."

I'm brought up short. Did we all read the same book? Surely we cannot be talking about the same thing.

"They're both such strong emotions," Karla says.

"That doesn't make them the same emotion. They're on opposite ends of the spectrum!" My voice comes out louder than I intend. So I tack on a "Pardon my outburst."

"I don't mean that they blur because they're so strong," Karla says.

"Then what do you mean?" I ask.

"When you hate someone so fiercely, they have to be worthy of that hatred. You wouldn't ardently hate someone who was beneath your notice or someone who didn't compare to you in wits or charisma. You have to be on equal grounds to hate someone so much. And that level of hate inherently comes with a level of respect. You're recognizing that they're an actual threat. That they compare to you."

Tekla nods vehemently. "And when that level of hatred comes with that level of respect, it's all too easy for that passion to turn from one form to another."

The hair at the back of my neck stands on end, and goose bumps erupt on my arms. I do a quick look around the library. If I didn't know any better, I'd say someone was watching us.

"I had never thought of it that way," Damasus says. "I rather like that description."

"That's why love stories about enemies turned to lovers are so popular," Tekla says. "It's the level of feeling. That intensity. It's so dynamic."

"Of course," Karla says, "not all heated relationships need to start off that way." She looks sheepishly at Tekla. "Friendship is just as good and powerful of a start for a courtship."

"Definitely," Tekla says. The girls' eyes meet, and Damasus and I hurry to look elsewhere.

My eyes land on two amber orbs floating above the dark crevice of a row of books, but I blink and they're gone.

I keep my voice from quivering as I say, "I thought the two men in the story were awful to each other. The words exchanged, the closed fists that were thrown—how can you really come back from something like that?"

"Do not siblings treat each other abominably when they truly love each other deep down? Can't two lovers do the same?" Karla asks.

"No," I assert. "No, love should be soft and caring. It should be given without insults and antagonism."

"What world are you living in?" Damasus asks with humor.

Karla laughs. "One where the duchess pays men for favors. For her, love is only present when she's the one in control."

Tekla pinches her arm.

"What?" Karla asks.

And then she sees my face.

"I'm sorry, Your Grace. That was a joke. I didn't mean—"

"What do you know about love?" I snap. "You two have been making eyes at each other, but you're both too afraid to actually start something. At least I go after what I want!"

The girls' cheeks heat, and Damasus rounds on me. "Your Grace, I don't think that was appro—"

"And you! You've been single as long as I can recall, Damasus, so what do you know?"

The butler's eyes darken. "I do not experience attraction the way others do, but that does not mean that I don't like reading these books and discussing them. When did this meeting turn so sour?"

I glance around the room, looking for those eyes, wondering if I'm seeing them because they're really there or because getting rid of Eryx has become an obsession. The duke can't really be listening in, can he?

When I don't see them anywhere, I relax. No, of course he's not anywhere. He has much better things to do than listen in on a silly discussion of a romance novel. I'm simply overtaxed by everything that's happened in the last month.

And my friends are not the ones I'm angry with. I'm frustrated with myself for expending too many of my thoughts on a fake duke.

"I apologize for my harsh words," I say, first looking each of the girls in the eye, and then the butler. "I'm not myself today, but that's no excuse. You are my friends, and you deserve better treatment. It shan't happen again."

"I didn't mean for what I said to come out the way it did," Karla says, her eyes not once daring to look at Tekla. "You were so mistreated by the late duke. No one thinks poorly of you for your choices. We all do what we must to survive. To find happiness. I think that looks different for everyone."

Though her hand trembles, Tekla reaches out until her fingers grasp Karla's. The second girl doesn't pull away.

"Damasus, I have something I'd like to discuss with you out in the hallway," I say abruptly.

"Of course, Your Grace."

We both leave the library, and Damasus doesn't bother asking if I truly need something when we close the doors behind us. He departs one way, and I flee in the other direction.

I feel wretched for my behavior. My hatred of Eryx is no excuse to take out my irritation on my staff. I need to be better. I'll give the girls the rest of the day off so they can spend some time alone together, figuring out what they want from each other. And Damasus could use another raise.

Then I remember I have to speak with Eryx before I can make changes like that, unless I want to pull the money from my personal stipend.

My temper flares again, and I shut myself in my room so no one need witness it.

⋗⋯⋄⋯◯⋯⋄⋯⋖

I DON'T LET ERYX STEW FOR longer than a few more days before I visit him in the one place where he cannot escape me.

"Bloody hell!" he shouts after I kick his mattress. He groans when he sees I've entered his dream yet again.

"How do you keep finding your way here? No, *why* do you keep finding your way here?"

"You're avoiding me."

"I do that when I don't want to see you."

I stare at my fingernails. "I appreciate the deposits to my account, but I cannot do my part of the bargain if you won't let me help you practice some more."

"You and your bargains. I don't want them anymore. Just take my money and do what you want with it. I don't care. Just leave me alone."

"Why? I thought we made real progress when we practiced together. I brought out the monster, and you reined him back in."

Eryx flexes his fists. "I wanted to rip your throat out for the things you said."

"So that's the real reason you won't try again? I hurt your feelings? You know I didn't mean any of it. I was only trying to rile you."

"I know that."

"Then what's the problem?"

"There isn't one."

"Great, then I shall see you first thing after breakfast for our next lesson."

"Chrysantha!"

"What?"

He stands, tucking the comforter in at his waist. It doesn't go willingly. Finally, he just holds the whole thing at his side as he crosses the cloud-covered floor to reach me.

"I can't do them anymore," he says.

"Why?"

"Because . . . you—"

"Yes?"

"You remind me of my mother."

The words nearly wake me from my own dream. "I *what*?"

I can't remind him of his mother. He's supposed to want me. He can't want me if I remind him of his mother. Mothers aren't sexy.

"You don't resemble her physically, obviously. But she would try to give me lessons about my form, convincing me to shift, and I don't like it."

"She tried to help you control the monster as well?" Is that why she died? Did he snap and kill her finally?

"That's not what I said."

"If she wasn't teaching you control, then why would she . . . ? She wanted you to *bring out* the monster?"

"Yes, she would try all manner of ways to get me to shift. Just like you did. I don't want to deal with it again."

"Why?"

I worry that he won't answer or that my question was too vague.

Eventually, he looks up.

"My mother raised me for a single purpose. She *conceived* me for a single purpose, and everything in my life was predetermined by her until we were separated while I served in the army. Even my enlisting was due to her insistence."

"What did she want from you?"

After a pause, he says, "Vengeance. I was to be her means of exacting vengeance."

He turns around, heading back for his bed, having said his piece.

My eyes travel to his ass.

Or just above it, rather, where a little triangle of black-violet peaks above the comforter.

The tip of his tail.

My mouth falls open. "Why is it purple?"

Eryx freezes and looks over his shoulder. As soon as his eyes land on it, it winks out of sight. He ignores me as he crawls back into bed.

"No more verbal assaults to get you to shift," I say. "I can work with that."

"How do you plan to work with that?"

"You've said it before. Angering you isn't the only way to get you to shift."

Those amber eyes look at me in surprise as I force myself to wake up.

Let him stew on that thought. Let him toss and turn on his mattress as he thinks on how I intend to make him impassioned and force him to shift.

A large smile stretches across my lips as I return to my room. Next time, I'm not going to seek him out. Oh, no. Eryx is coming to me. I've just ensured it.

Feeling proud of myself, I drift off to sleep in my own bed this time.

I'm unsure how long I'm out before a thundering crack echoes in my dreams, but when I shred my eyes open, another loud crash sounds, followed by my door swinging off its hinges and smacking into the ground. At first, I assume it's Eryx. Who else would have the strength to do such a thing? And he's so fresh in my mind after yet another visit.

But it is not Eryx filling the hole where my door once stood.

CHAPTER 20

Dozens of men slosh into the room, like an unsteady tide. I hear one of them hiccup, and another laughs and smacks him on the arm.

"Don't see no monster in here," one of them says.

Another turns on his heel to properly inspect the whole of the room. When his face catches the moonlight, I recoil.

He's harsher-looking than Argus. Apelike arms, full scraggly beard, stern face.

"Sarkis, does this look like the master suite to you?"

This is the man who has been blackmailing Eryx?

"Aye," says Sarkis. "Yet there's no master in here." He burps loudly and strides toward my bed.

I leap off the other side, my stomach sinking as my heart tries to pound its way out of my chest. Why are these men here?

For the first time, I wish that Eryx didn't sleep so far away from me. These men are here for him. Not me.

"Why are you in the duke's bed?" Sarkis demands of me. "He been tupping you?"

"You do not get to barge into my room and ask lewd questions."

The man takes another step forward. "I'll ask anything I like of you."

"Yeah," another says, "cooperate or we'll do you in like we did that butler fellow."

Damasus. "Have you hurt my staff?"

I come around the bed, thinking to pass them all and check on Damasus and the rest of the household, but an arm snakes around my waist.

"Where do you think you're going?" one of the men asks.

Another says, "You're already dressed for bed. Best you climb back into it, and I'll follow."

I try to twist out of the arms that hold me, but they're tight like a vise. A flare of panic rushes through me. I claw at the face of the man holding me.

"Ah," he shrieks, finally letting go and raising a careful hand to his marred flesh. I back up to the far wall, putting as much distance as possible between them and me.

"Damasus!" I call out. "Damasus, can you hear me? Are you all right?"

"She scratched me!" the man I struck says, turning a bleeding face to Sarkis.

"You shouldn't have touched the lady," their leader returns. "That's not why we're here. We need to find the monster and deal with it."

"Maybe this will help." Another nameless man steps forward out of the crowd. I press myself against the wall of my room until my back hurts, but I can't stop him from getting within reaching distance.

He slaps me across the face.

I gasp as I flinch away from the blow, my hand hovering over the stinging skin.

"You need to scream for us, lady," he says.

"What?"

"I said scream." He grabs my hair, pulls me up by my roots, and I whimper and gasp at the pain, trying to kick outward, but the angle is wrong, and I can't make contact.

"Don't think she cares for your methods," another brute says. "Let's try mine."

I scream before the knife makes contact with my skin, but once it does, my voice turns more shrill. He starts at my wrist, raking the steel upward slowly and deliberately while the other man holds me in place.

I fight back with all I have, twisting and thrashing. When that doesn't work, I try to go limp, but they're too strong. My pained exclamations are the only constant as that knife makes a path upward, my voice increasing as he presses the metal ever deeper.

And then a shadow moves in front of me. The man with the knife goes flying against my wardrobe, wood cracking before he hits the floor. The man holding me is startled and turns, finally releasing my arms.

I'm too scared to look at the damage. The pain seems to come from everywhere on my forearm, and I feel the blood oozing downward, dripping from my fingers. My screaming has turned to sobbing, and I can barely see through my tears as another one of the brutes goes flying up into the ceiling, smashing through the hanging chandelier before denting the plaster. Another man breaks his fall when he comes careening back to the floor, and glass rains down atop them both.

The shadow continues to move impossibly fast. It flies toward the man who'd been holding me in a hard-to-follow streak. The next thing I know, he's airborne and shattering the glass of my window before disappearing outside.

Now I'm not the only one in the room screaming.

Shots go off, and I drop to the floor, slipping in the puddle of my own blood. I want to cover my head with my hands, to turn my face into the plush rug, but I can't seem to look away from the shadow and what it might do next.

Rationally, I know it's Eryx disposing of the men one by one, but when I see men unload their revolvers into him without slowing him down, it's easy to imagine him as something else entirely. The bullets ping to the ground uselessly once his healing abilities force them free from his flesh. I don't hear the sound, but I see them rolling about the floor, dented on one side from the impact. I know because one stops just shy of the rug I lie atop. I pick it up and squeeze it within my grasp, giving myself something tangible to feel as I behold all the savagery around me.

Eryx picks up a man and snaps him in half over his knee. He pulls another's arms out of their sockets. He sends a punch into another man's knee, and I hear the patella shattering before the man goes limp on the ground. Eryx crushes his skull underfoot, and the intruder doesn't move again.

One by one they fall to him, and I lie there with my head turned to the side, watching it all as if I were still dreaming, only this is surely a nightmare.

Eryx cracks the neck of the last standing man, and everything goes impossibly still.

The lights turn on, though they're dimmer than before with the chandelier partially ruined above us. Still, the true horror of the situation dawns on me as I see everything in excruciating detail.

The broken furniture, broken bones, broken glass. The oozing blood, oozing brain matter, oozing spittle. At least one man pissed himself before he died, or after perhaps, and another's face is frozen in a scream in death.

And yet, amid all that carnage, there is beauty, too.

Because I can see *him*.

Amber eyes, pointed ears, sharp canines, horns protruding from his skull. He looks so big from where I lie on the floor. He managed only a pair of pants and boots before trudging up all of those stairs. How did he even know I was in danger? He's so far away, clear down in the cellar . . .

Bullet holes spatter down his front, but instead of blood dripping—

It's shadow. Black shadows seep from his wounds, pooling at the floor before he tramples them underfoot. Because, yes, he's moving.

Moving toward me.

He falls to his knees, hands shaking as he looks down at me with amber eyes. I think I might still be whimpering with pain.

Softly, he says, "Can you stand?"

I shake my head vehemently.

"That's all right. You stay right there, then." His hand reaches for my injured arm. His horns and fangs retreat as he shifts back to human.

I flinch before he even comes close to making contact.

"Easy," he says. "I'm not going to hurt you, Chrysantha. You don't need to be afraid of me."

And, despite everything, I let out a snort. "Me? Afraid of you? Please."

His puzzled expression looks absolutely comical with his wolf eyes on display. "Then, why—"

"My arm hurts, dammit. I don't want you touching it!"

He sways backward as though in astonishment at my answer. As he shakes his head at me, as though he can't believe what he's seeing, I catch sight of something behind him.

It's Sarkis. He must have hidden behind the door before Eryx appeared in the room, waiting for his chance. Now he approaches Eryx while his back is turned, the man carrying the thickest sword I've ever seen.

More than that, Sarkis looks different than he did before. Are those pointed ears peeking out from his hair? And the barest hint of horns. Not like Eryx's. No, they're half the size and an eerie yellow.

I don't think before the words are out. "Behind you!"

Eryx spins around, his hand seizing Sarkis by the throat.

That sword moves, slashing across Eryx's chest. More shadows pour from him. Eryx throws Sarkis away from him, and the second man somehow manages to land on his feet, though he loses his sword.

"This ends here," Eryx shouts as he throws himself onto the other man. Sarkis should be dead. How can he handle all of Eryx's unnatural strength? But the man blocks his blows and returns some that have Eryx reeling.

At the first injury that should draw blood from Sarkis, shadows flow from him instead.

"You did this to me," Sarkis yells as he wipes at the wispy blackness.

"I saved your life!"

"No, you made me into a monster."

"No, I accidentally gave you my abilities. You became a monster all on your own."

Sarkis lunges, throwing Eryx onto his back. He lands not far from the sword, but he can't quite reach it.

Forgetting my own pain, I rush over and kick the sword the rest of the way. When his fingers curl around the hilt, Eryx brings it up and swipes it across the other man's throat, severing head from shoulders.

No shadows seep from the wound.

There is nothing but dead flesh atop of Eryx. Because that's a wound even the shadows cannot heal.

Decapitation is the only way to kill him.

I can't do that.

Not that you want to, a smaller voice intones. *You just actively helped him escape death.*

Yes, because an unknown monster was in my room and might have killed me next.

Eryx shoves the dead weight off himself before standing.

"Thank you," he says before scrutinizing my arm.

I dare to look. The knife made it halfway up my forearm; my skin is split wide, blood still seeps from the cut. Something white peeks at me from around some of the red muscle—

I nearly faint when I realize it's my own bone.

I bite the inside of my cheek to stay awake, not daring to move my arm. "Damasus," I mutter. "They said they hurt him. You need to—"

"Take care of you," he says. "I'll be back with supplies."

"No, please. Check on him. On the rest of the staff. No, wait, I'll do it." I sway forward before I can even take a step. Eryx catches me by the shoulders, and I'm so close to him that the shadows pouring from his wounds brush against me.

They're neither cool nor hot to the touch. Merely wisps of movement, as though the slightest breeze were brushing my skin before continuing to the floor.

"Easy," he says. When he looks at my arm, his fangs drop down from his teeth again, making him look feral. "They cut you."

"I'm aware of that."

"In my own damn house."

"Not a house. Not yours." The words come out weak.

His eyes flutter closed, his jaw tensing, but for once, I don't think it's because of something I said. "This is my fault," he whispers.

"Fine, then. Stand there in self-pity. I have my staff to look out for."

"I'll do it if you promise to sit still until I can call a doctor."

"You can't do it."

"Why not?"

I gesture to the pools of shadow at his feet.

"That'll stop in a moment."

I stare at the spectacle, at the impossibility of what I'm seeing. The shadows look so much like the Shadow King's, and yet they clearly work differently.

I've still got the bullet grasped tightly in my fist.

Running footsteps come from down the hall. I throw myself in front of Eryx, as though I can shield him from the staff seeing his abilities, but it is only Argus and Dyson.

"What do you need?" Argus asks.

"Send for a doctor. Chrysantha is hurt badly."

Argus looks like that's the last thing he wants to do, but Dyson says, "I'm on it."

When I look back to Eryx, his wounds close up, and the shadows dissipate. His eyes fade to a deep brown.

"Damasus," I prompt as my vision starts to fade in and out.

"Right," Eryx says, "Argus, go find all the staff. Assess who needs the most help. Then go—"

I don't catch the rest.

⤛━◈━◦━○━◦━◈━⤜

WHEN I OPEN MY EYES, it's to the feeling of a sharp pinch in my already-throbbing arm.

The wound hurts worse than when it was first administered. It smells of alcohol, and as I turn, I find a needle in my flesh, the start of a single stitch. I'm no longer in my bedroom but back in the duchess suite yet again, presumably because there are fewer dead men in here.

When I look up, I find some kindly old doctor observing me. "Good, you're awake," he says, pulling the needle the rest of the way through my skin. "I'm sorry for the pain, Your Grace, but I couldn't have you drink this until you were conscious." He holds out a glass for me.

"What is it?" I ask.

"Laudanum. For the pain."

"I can't have it. I have a terrible reaction to it." I have since I was a child.

"Then I'm afraid this is going to hurt quite a lot. At least you were out of it for the cleaning portion of my administrations."

The longer I'm awake, the more my memories surface. "Damasus," I blurt. "Have you seen my butler?"

"Not yet, Your Grace. The duke was very clear that you were the priority."

I snatch my arm away and then grimace at the bout of pain that brings on. "Go to him," I demand.

"Your Grace, you have an open wound."

"Which you just said you've already cleaned. I can wait. You will see to all of my staff first."

"But the duke—"

"Will be upset by the delay. Now move. I assure you I will not allow you to work on me until my staff have all been seen to."

His faces bunches up tight, but he finally says, "Yes, Your Grace, but I'll have to inform the duke you are refusing care."

"You do that. Just go."

I try not to look at my arm as I gently settle it on the bed beside me. It throbs sharply with every beat of my heart. I let out a soft groan, but I stand by my decision. Damasus can't die. No one is allowed to die. They can't—

The door slams open, and I startle, then gasp in more air at the pain.

"You're refusing treatment?" Eryx barks.

"I told you I wanted Damasus to see the doctor first. You didn't listen."

"Damasus's injuries are not as serious as yours!"

"I don't care."

Though I can't move much, I turn my head away from him, ending the conversation.

"Fine," he says, and I expect him to leave the room. Instead, I hear the splashing of water. What is he doing now? I turn to find him in the washroom, soaping his hands thoroughly.

"What do you think you are doing?"

"I may not be a doctor, but I had to do this dozens of times in the army. If you won't let the professional see to you, then you get me."

He dries off his hands before seating next to me. He reaches for the discarded medical thread and needle.

When I meet his eyes, they flash amber, daring me to argue.

It's not as though I could run. And I have a feeling Eryx will just knock me out if I don't cooperate this time.

"Fine." I turn back away, leaving my arm exposed.

When I feel the chair beside me move again, I brace myself for pain. But the suspense is too much, so I turn back toward the spiteful man.

"What happened back there?" I ask. "You fought those men off, and then we were talking. Argus and Dyson showed up. I don't remember anything after that."

The needle hovers over my skin, and a guilty look crosses Eryx's features. "You swooned," he says.

"Swooned?"

"Yes, got too close to me, I expect."

At the furrowing of my brow, the needle goes in. I wince, jerking at the contact, preventing me from reacting to his ridiculous statement.

"That hurts!"

"I know, but you have at least ten more stitches to go."

I feel a tremble start to work its way out, so I try to keep myself talking. "How wounded is Damasus?"

"They roughed him up pretty good. He has countless bruises, but nothing was broken except his nose, which the doctor will need to right. The butler was in good spirits when I saw him, and I'm sure he's handling his administrations much better than you are."

He pulls the medical thread through my skin and pulls it tight. I bite down, just barely missing my tongue.

"You bled much more than I originally realized," Eryx says conversationally. "It's remarkable you were alert for as long as you were.

Finally got your arm elevated, and that helped to slow things down considerably. All the staff wanted to be in here by your side, especially that footman Kyros. But I ordered them all away." He dips the needle in again, and I just barely manage not to cry out.

I glare at him. He's donned a fresh shirt since the attack, and there's not a scratch on him.

And the levity with which he speaks, I don't know why, but I feel as though I cannot trust it.

"How did you know I was in trouble?" I ask.

"I heard you scream."

"All the way from the cellar?"

Now it's Eryx's turn to wince. "Yes, from the cellar. How long have you known?"

"Not long. I finally figured it out with the proximity to the library."

"Too smart for your own good, as usual."

"I had to snoop. You're a mystery, and I don't like mysteries. I like knowing everything."

"I can see why I'm so frustrating to you, then."

"You can't begin to glean the list of your frustrating qualities, Eryx. Shall I state them for you? I— Ack!"

He ties off another stitch and closes his eyes against my shriek of pain. His face bunches tightly, as though he were trying to fight off a bout of something. Anger? Fury?

At me?

"Tell me why," I say, needing another distraction.

"Why?"

"Yes, *why* did you come?"

He doesn't say anything, so I continue. "They would have killed me. Then you would have been rid of me finally. No more prodding you to tell me your secrets. No more worrying if I'll reveal what I know. You would have been free of me, had the dukedom all to yourself. I thought perhaps you brought those men here to do the job for you."

He raises those eyes to mine, stilling the needle before the next stitch. "I am the reason they came, but it was no invitation to do you harm."

"Then it should have been a fortunate turn of events for you. So I'll ask again, why stop them? Why expose your abilities to me yet again? You would have had everything you wanted."

I watch as his eyes turn amber once more. "Not everything."

I don't say a word as he does the next stitch, hoping he'll continue. He says nothing until another whimper of pain escapes me despite my best efforts to hold it in.

"If you don't know, then you're not as clever as you think you are," he says finally.

Is there something he needs from me? Something he can have only so long as the dowager duchess is alive? What am I missing here?

Eryx leans over my arm and blows a long, cool breath over my stinging, raw flesh. "Tell me why you called out a warning, Chrysantha."

"Excuse me?"

"You told me about the man who'd snuck up behind me. I was already wounded, bleeding shadows everywhere. Did you think to stop me from more pain? Or did you think he might have been able to kill me and want to spare me? He could have, you know. I'm not entirely invulnerable. He could have killed me, and you would have had everything. The manor, the estate, the servants, the money." A pause. "Your lover returned. It all would have been yours again. The thought had to have crossed your mind, so why call out a warning?"

"You'd just saved me," I say. "I owed you one."

"So now we're even? Next time I'm in danger, you'll let me die?"

"Yes."

He smiles, showing off those sharpened canines, and my heart skips a beat at the sight of them. But then he's back to seriousness and focusing on my stitches once more.

"I'm so sorry that you are hurt, Chrysantha." His voice cracks, surprising us both. "It shouldn't have come to this. I never thought Sarkis capable. If I had thought for a second that you were in danger, I promise I would have done something more. I never meant to let my past harm you."

"Who were those men? Why did they want you dead?"

"Sarkis was in my regiment in the army. There was an incident with the enemy. We were both injured. I threw him over my back and carried him to safety, but he had prolonged exposure to my shadows while my own wounds healed. They flowed into his open injuries."

My mouth rounds into an O.

"He inherited some of my abilities. The supernatural strength and healing. At first, he was glad of it. He liked how unstoppable we were in the army, but he wasn't as cautious about being seen. The king had a warrant out for his arrest. I was worried that Sarkis would reveal me, too. I tried to put him down and failed. Naturally he turned against me after that. He's been messing with me ever since."

I grit my teeth through the next stitch. "And you didn't think I should know about him?"

"I told you. I didn't think he was a danger to you."

"You need to start trusting me with things like this. We could have had hired hands on the property. We could have prevented this."

"I'm . . . not used to putting my trust in others."

I look pointedly at my arm. "When the consequences affect more than just yourself, you might want to consider it."

He winces. "Noted."

Eryx returns his attention to my arm, pulling a little too tightly on the next stitch.

"At the risk of seeming pathetic, this *really* hurts. Could you try to be gentle? Not all of us have supernatural healing."

"You're not pathetic. This is a very deep cut. You're going to have an impressive scar."

A scar? "I've never had a scar before."

"Stop frowning. Scars are good. They mean you survived."

"I only survived because of you." I was helpless. Entirely outnumbered with nothing but my nightclothes on for protection. I cannot remember a time when I'd felt such terror.

"No human person could have taken on so many barehanded."

"Then today, I am grateful you are not entirely human."

I bite back a sob at yet another stab of the needle, and Eryx hardens his jaw. "Last one." He ties off the stitch, spreads some sort of soothing ointment over the line of sewed flesh, and begins wrapping the wound.

Eryx returns to the washroom to clean himself up again. On his way to the bedroom door, he says, "Rest up, Duchess. Your body needs to heal."

I'm already throwing the covers off me. "I will do no such thing. I need to check on Damasus. My room has been destroyed. It'll need to be cleaned. Someone will need to speak with the constabulary when they arrive. I'll need to order new furniture."

"It's always the bloody furniture with you."

"If every little thing about me irritates you, you can always leave."

"Every little thing about you does not irritate me."

"All evidence to the contrary." I try to step around him, but he steps with me, continuing to block my path.

"Do you respect me?" he asks suddenly.

"What?"

"Do you hate me so much because you recognize on some level that we're equals?"

My stomach falls at the words. He *was* at book club listening in!

"We could never be equals. Not when you hold all the power," I say.

"And if I didn't?"

"Then I'd hardly have cause to hate you, now, would I?"

His eyes flash amber, and I try to parse what I've said to upset him. I can't think of anything, so I fire back, "Do you see me as an equal?"

"I respect you."

"But you don't see me as an equal?"

"I see you as . . ." He trails off, but his eyes never leave mine.

"Something to hurt? To kill? So what? You said you could control the beast."

"I can control the beast."

"Then why are you glowing your eyes at me? You're being strange. I—"

Eryx steps soundlessly toward me, and I back up as far as I can go when I see his canines descend. When I strike the wall, I hold my injured arm away from it so as not to hurt it further. Eryx runs a finger down my neck in the same path where the beast once ran his teeth.

"You've never been afraid of what I am. I like that. The beast thrills at that. I see you as something more than an equal, Chrysantha. You're so much better than me."

"I already knew that."

And as though the sarcastic comment is more than he can bear, his eyes lower to my mouth before his lips are upon mine.

CHAPTER
21

The sudden pressure startles me, yet at the same time, I had to know this is where things would lead. For this is always where they lead. It's what men want from me. I'm a rare beauty. Something men want to claim and make theirs. They always want to take, take, take.

After the initial meeting of our closed lips, he pulls back ever so slightly, so a hair's breadth rests between us. He drags in a deep lungful of air, breathing me in. Or steadying himself. He holds so still for a solid second, I think he might be wrestling with himself.

Our foreheads touch. He playfully nudges my nose with his. Then his lips descend. Just not to my mouth.

He brushes his lips along my jawline. I hardly know why I'm allowing this. Perhaps a morbid curiosity?

When he stops at my ear, he whispers in a deep growl, "Tell me where you like to be kissed."

Those words—they do something to me. Something inside me stirs. Something that has been dormant too long. A restless energy crackles beneath my skin, and I throw all sense out the window.

I pull up the long sleeve of my nightdress, exposing the wrist of my uninjured arm, and draw a slow circle on the veins just below my hand. "Here."

With amber eyes on mine, he grabs my arm and brings the limb toward his mouth, watching me as he kisses the skin there. Liking what he finds, he slides my sleeve up and up, exposing the inside of my elbow. His teeth and lips travel upward until he can kiss the pulse point there. His tongue darts out to kiss my flesh, burning me with the quick stroke.

I force my breathing to remain calm, but I'm far too excited now. "Here," I say, touching with two fingers the base of my neck.

He steps forward, takes my hand from the spot, laces our fingers together, and pins our locked hands to the wall above my head as he leans in. I feel his hot breath first, tickling my sensitive skin. His lips are endlessly patient as they work at my neck. Endlessly obedient when I call out "harder" and "lower."

He works his way down, down, past my neckline, at my command. Giving, giving, giving.

Aside from where his hand grips mine, where his lips brush me, we are not touching. He doesn't grab at me, doesn't paw at me, just gives me exactly what I ask for.

And for once in my life, I cannot stand it.

I pull my hand free from his, and he straightens, thinking perhaps I mean to stop him. Stop this. Instead, I grab his face and bring it to mine so I can be kissed properly. Except, he stands perfectly still under my ministrations. Doesn't engage. Doesn't return my kisses.

I hold him at arm's length so I can look at him. His eyes are so liquid, his fangs peak out from under his lips, and he stares at me with something that can only be described as wonder.

"What's wrong?" I ask.

"Nothing, I—I've just never done this before, and I don't want to hurt you or for the beast to get out or—"

"Never done what before?"

He looks sheepishly down at my lips.

Kissing. He's never done kissing before. How is that possible? Those lips of his are perfect for kissing.

"You won't hurt me," I say, nearly mad with the wanting of a proper kissing. I don't just want to be kissed. I want to be devoured. To be made senseless. "Do you feel out of control?"

"Not right now."

That takes me aback. "Then what?"

He reaches out and grabs a strand of my midnight hair. He starts twirling it around one of his fingers. "You've been hurt by all the men in your life. I don't want to be another one. I need you to tell me what's okay. I don't know where to touch you or where to kiss you. I don't know what's too hard or too soft, with my extra strength. I don't want to hurt you," he repeats.

I have no response. None. I'm so baffled and touched. This has never happened before. No one has ever said anything of the sort to me before.

Even Sandros, who gave me pleasure, never once asked what I wanted. He gave and he took, and I went along with just about every-thing because I wanted to try everything. But this? Having a real choice—is it true? Or just something he thinks I want to hear?

"You've truly never done this before?" I ask, because I'm not sure what else to say.

"No woman has ever known my secret. I couldn't risk being this close to anyone before. I can't keep it concealed when I'm . . . impas-sioned."

"Is that what you feel for me? Passion?"

"You. You make me forget all my rules and reasons for everything. You make me want to believe it's possible not to be alone forever. You make me want to claim the whole world and gift it to you on a silver platter. You are unlike anyone I've ever known. And gods, but I love your mouth. The way it smiles. The words that come out of it. How it feels against mine. Just looking at your lips makes my mouth water."

I bite my lower lip, trying to think of anything to say in response. Anything at all. But as if he can help it no longer, he kisses me again. His movements are clumsy at first, as he tries to figure out how our lips work together. But that lasts only a matter of seconds before I'm drowning in his kisses. And damn him, but it feels so good to be kissed again. When his movements slow, I think he's going to stop. But I realize he's only giving me control again, allowing me to set the pace.

Gods, this is incredible. In control yet out of control. Feeling as though I could do anything. When I go to wrap my arms around his neck, I hiss and pull away, my hurt arm throbbing.

"You're injured," Eryx says aloud, as though reminding himself. "Shit, what am I doing? I'm so sorry. We should get you into bed."

I arch a single brow his way.

"I meant alone. You need to rest and heal. I will take care of everything else."

He doesn't leave immediately, instead staring after me as though waiting for something.

"What?" I ask.

"Do you find that agreeable?"

Agreeable? Is he serious? "You get one taste of me and suddenly you're going to act as though you care what I think? Why bother and just go back to bossing me around as you always do?"

He scoffs and, upon finding me in earnest, says, "Is that what you want? For things to remain as they were before?"

"Don't you? Surely you've had a slip in judgment?"

"I've had a slip in judgment?" he questions.

"Well, I certainly can't be held responsible for my actions. I'm on laudanum." The lie is too easy to find. Too easy to use to protect myself.

Eryx's expression turns to one of horror. He looks around the room, and then his eyes land on the cup the doctor left for me. The one I didn't drink, but Eryx likely comes to the conclusion that it was for me to have more of if I felt I needed it.

He rakes his hands in his hair, even pulls out a few strands. "I'm so sorry. I didn't know. I never would have—"

He cuts himself off and strides out of the duchess suite without a backward glance, but the door doesn't slam in his wake.

I'm beyond exhausted, arm throbbing, but even after I climb into bed, my mind won't let me find oblivion. It fixates on that horrible man, on his kisses and gentle words. On the way I hurt him by allowing him to think he took advantage of me. The guilt is consuming, but I can't let it win.

Eryx . . . said the right words, did the right things, but I cannot trust any of it. Men will say and do whatever they can to get what they want. He's had a taste of me. He will either lose his obsession or want more. Either way, I can work with that.

>─┼─◆>─○─<◆─┼─<

During the next fortnight, I observe constables coming and going. Men from the morgue arrive to collect the bodies. A special cleaning staff admits themselves into the manor to do a thorough cleansing of the master suite. I don't know if I can stay in there again after this instance. Too many awful things have happened in that room now. Perhaps I should wall it off and let it crumble over time.

I have no clue what Eryx tells the constabulary, but I'm sure he gets Dyson and Argus involved, so it's more believable that three men took out over a dozen intruders.

I visit Damasus, who's finally recovered enough for visitors.

"I didn't open the door for them," he says during one of his first lucid moments when they lessen the pain medication he's on. "Never would have let anyone into the house so late in the evening. They busted the door in, asked me where the master slept, but I didn't tell them anything."

No, that had been poor Tekla, who told them exactly where the master suite was so they'd release Karla. They threatened all kinds of harm on the girls before locking them into a cupboard on the first floor.

"I didn't think I'd done any harm," Tekla said when she saw me and my injuries. "I knew the master wasn't sleeping there. I thought they'd find only an empty room. I didn't think for a moment I was putting you in danger, Your Grace. I'm so terribly sorry." I throw my arms around her as she cries, reassuring her that I was perfectly fine and all was well now.

I can't help but be bitter toward the pain Eryx put my staff through. Damasus's broken nose, Tekla's and Karla's terror, Mrs. Lagos's white face when she saw the destruction done to the house, Kyros's alarm when he couldn't find Nico right away during the intruders' attack.

Eryx needs to stop thinking he can handle everything alone.

Medora changes my bandages for me each day. The front door to the manor is replaced. The master suite smells of cleaning chemicals. My skin is healing.

We can patch up plaster. Replace broken wood, pound out the dents to the brass. But wounds to the soul cannot be fixed so readily.

I haven't seen Eryx once since the attack. I don't even know if he's still at the estate.

We keep doing this to each other: offending the other and then avoiding. It has to stop. We should just be speaking to one another. Or yelling it out. I need to stop letting him get to me.

The doctor returns to the manor to check up on everyone. He removes my stitches before seeing to Damasus. I observe the exchange, wanting to ensure everyone is in peak condition. When the doctor is finished, he heads to the study, likely to collect his pay from Eryx.

They chat for some time before the man leaves, and I stare at the closed door.

It's time to engage Eryx again. I cannot let this continue. I must be so close to the truth. If I can get the rest of it, we can be done with this whole charade. His secret consumes me. I feel as if I could just get my hands on the full truth, then my next move will become clear. Everything will make sense then.

When I let myself inside, Eryx is seated at the grand desk with his head in his hands while Dyson sits sprawled over the arms of a large chair in the corner and Argus stands with his arms crossed over his chest.

Three sets of eyes look up.

"May I have a moment alone with you?" I ask, staring down the pretend duke.

He looks . . . disappointed somehow, but he says, "Yes, of course."

I walk to the center of the room, then glance back and forth between the other two occupants.

Argus rolls his eyes before plucking Dyson out of the chair and marching him out of the room.

"Don't do anything I wouldn't do," Dyson says before the door shuts.

I turn to Eryx. "You told them?"

He rubs a hand along his brow. "Dyson is as tactful as ever."

"Bragging about your conquest?" I ask, my voice bitter.

He swallows. "Hardly. I needed advice. I . . ."

"You what?"

His eyes narrow. "I don't know anything where you are concerned."

Oh, but he wants to. I can see it. I just need to get him to open up.

I go right for the jugular. Looking pointedly at my exposed, healing arm, I say, "You have brought fear and pain to this household, and it's time you stopped."

He swallows. "How do you propose I do that?"

"You can start by telling me everything. No more secrets. No more lies. No more surprises. Just let me help you."

"I don't know how," he says. "I've carried on this way for so long."

"Well, enough is enough. You take some time to think of everything you need to share with me and how you'll share it. In the meantime, I'm going to make arrangements for your next lesson."

"I told you, I don't want you throwing more insults my way. I can't—"

"I won't. We're taking a new approach. You have"—I look at the clock on the wall—"four hours to compile all that you wish to. Then we're going out together."

"Out?"

"Yes, to a brothel."

CHAPTER

22

"This is a terrible idea," Eryx says as the four of us stand outside the entrance to Zanita's.

"Yeah, he's going to kill someone," Argus says unhelpfully.

"He's not going to kill anyone," I say. "That's why you two are here. To make sure that doesn't happen. If you can't do that, then I see no reason for you to be here."

A look of panic crosses Dyson's face. "We can do that. We are the best at that! We absolutely need to be here."

"Then let's not delay any longer."

"Wait," Eryx says, staying me with an outstretched hand. "How is this going to work? What exactly do you intend to do?"

"Just relax and follow my lead. I have already devised the perfect cover story."

"Yeah," Dyson says. "Chrysantha has thought this all through. You should really be more trusting."

"And you should stop thinking with your prick," Eryx fires back.

"If Chrysantha can help you get this under control, you can start thinking with yours!"

"Dyson!" Argus bellows before Eryx has the chance.

"What? It's not like he wouldn't be more fun to be around once he can finally get some of that pent-up energy out of his system."

Eryx looks ready to swing his fist, so I step forward and take his arm.

"If anything starts to go poorly, we'll leave immediately," I offer.

"What if I'm exposed?"

"That's the point!" Dyson shouts.

"Not that kind of exposure."

"There isn't a soul in here who we can't buy off," I offer. "And most will explain away anything unusual in terms they can understand. The servants at the manor have already done so on your behalf. Now come along, Your Grace. We have an heir to make."

"Wh-what!" he stammers as I open the front door and step through.

It is just as I remember, from the sensual candlelight to the sweet fragrance of roses. Many of my past lovers sit back on cushioned seats or take strolls about the room. It would seem Zanita has even acquired some new workers.

"Welcome," Zanita says. "I'm Zanita. What can we do for you?"

I appreciate that she pretends she doesn't know who I am, though it's hardly necessary in this case.

"Hello, Zanita. It's been a while. I've gotten myself married since the last time I saw you."

"Is this the lucky man?" she asks, turning toward Eryx. She doesn't bat an eyelash at my announcement.

"He is, and I'm afraid we need some help."

"Of course. Are you looking for a third? It is one of the few exceptions we make to servicing male clients."

Pushing aside my pride, I pull forth the lie. "Actually, the problem is my husband doesn't find me attractive enough to perform. We need to produce an heir. I'm hoping you have a woman who can help him get in the right mindset so I can then take over."

The madam eyes my face and figure before turning to the duke. "You like fair-haired women, then?"

Eryx is speechless, likely still reeling from my explanation.

"Precisely," I say for him.

"I think I have just the girl for you. I will explain the situation to her and send her up. Here." The madam hands us a key from her ring. "You will take room thirty-seven. Your men will need to wait outside the room." She eyes the "valets" warily. "I have my own staff on standby should anything go poorly."

"That won't be necessary," I assure her. "The men will wait outside."

"What?" Dyson says, looking up from a woman he'd been eyeing.

I take the key. "Let's go."

I lift my skirts as I take the stairs, three men trailing behind me.

"Of all the— This is such a stupid plan," Eryx says. "We're paying a woman to—"

"Get you impassioned. Then we can practice. It's such a clever ruse I've thought up, isn't it? She can come in and out of the room as many times as necessary. And we can return as long as we need to. It can take a while to produce an heir, you know."

"I don't want to become impassioned."

"Do you want to get a grip on the monster? Do you want to continue your life this way?"

We reach door thirty-seven. "Don't let him stray," I say to Argus, obviously referring to Dyson. "You two have a job to do."

"Understood."

Unlocking the door, I step foot inside, and Eryx reluctantly follows. I try not to laugh at the pink wallpaper, crisp white blankets and pillows, or sweet-smelling fragrance. Eryx must loathe it, but he doesn't say a word. I don't think he's really even seeing our surroundings.

"You could try looking less unapproachable. You'll scare the woman away before we can get started."

"Maybe I don't want to be approached."

"This is the only way. You said you didn't want me bringing out the monster with words, so now we're stuck with option B. Once you get this under control, you can go to a brothel for real. Besides, it's been far too long for me. I intend to make use of this place after we're done here for the night."

"What?" he asks, his whole body tightening.

"You will recall that I had to stop visiting because you cut off my stipend. Now that it's returned, I don't intend to spend tonight alone when we're already here."

"No." The word is low, fierce, and demanding.

I spin toward him. "Hmm?"

"You're not staying the night here. I'm not doing this. We're not doing this. This is outrageous."

"Eryx, what do you—"

He stomps to the door, opens it a crack. "Change of plans. Send the girl away when she gets here. We'll be using the room, though. No questions. You two spend the evening however you think is best."

"Don't have to tell me twice," Dyson says at the same time Argus manages, "But—"

Eryx slams the door and locks it before turning back to me. When he does so, his eyes have shifted to amber. "Why do we need another woman in the room when you and I can manage just fine on our own?"

My heart speeds up at the words, and I have to swallow before speaking. "Because you couldn't pay me enough money to do that job." The words come easily, but the force behind them is somewhat lacking.

"Really," Eryx says. He prowls toward me like a panther.

I back away slowly, but there's not far for me to go. "Yes, I detest you. I'm only doing this for selfish reasons. There's no reason for me to give any more than I already have. You've taken enough from me as it is."

My back hits a wall and Eryx's arms come down on either side of me. He leans forward just as his horns sprout from his head. His lips trail across my neck before coming up to my ear. My hands instinctively curl around his arms, I thought for the purpose of pushing him away, but they simply hold on.

"I don't need another woman in this room to consummate our marriage. I don't want anyone else in this room with us." He hovers over my lips but doesn't touch me again.

"That was just a story."

"A pitiful one at that. The madam almost didn't believe it. As if anyone would need help with such a thing when it comes to you. Have you seen yourself?" His lips skim the top of my head. "Silky raven hair." They reach my forehead. "Golden skin." He kisses a closed eyelid. "Brown eyes that sparkle when you've something mischievous to say." He hovers above my mouth again. "Ruby lips."

Still he doesn't kiss me.

I open my eyes, thinking perhaps he's moved, but his face is still right there.

"I know my secret is safe with you, so let me assure you that your secret is safe with me," he whispers.

"What secret is that?"

He licks his lips. "That you like me."

"I do not."

"The doctor and I had an interesting chat before he left today. You told me a wicked lie."

"I—"

He kisses me then, and I don't even try to push him away. Because he knows. He knows, and that means I can't pretend anymore. Not with him, and not even with myself.

I can't deny it: I want him.

Just right now. Just for tonight. Let me have him before I get rid of him once and for all.

And once the decision is made, I let go.

Forget about the money or the manor or anything else. In this room, there is just this man and me. This man who is also a monster. My fingers slide through his hair, bumping up against the root of a horn, and for some reason that only makes this more exciting. Because I am taming this beast. This beast wants me.

And *gods*—I want him.

I kiss him with everything I have, but it doesn't seem to be enough. His kisses don't soothe. They set me aflame. I might combust right here if he doesn't do something.

But he doesn't attempt to remove my clothes. He barely touches me with his hands, as though he's too scared to break me. How hard is he fighting to keep the monster in check? And what might happen if he finally let go?

The thought is thrilling, and I step away, prepared to tell him to throw caution to the wind.

But seeing him, I realize that there is still something I need from him. The final piece of the puzzle to getting rid of him, and my body is the only incentive I have at this point for obtaining it. Once he has me, he won't give up anything more.

"You're holding back," I say.

He blinks through a sensual haze, likely reining in his instincts. "So are you. I have a monster to keep in check. What's your excuse?"

I pull out my acting skills, let them wash over me. "I'm sorry about the laudanum lie."

"You weren't ready for me to know you actually wanted me."

"I wasn't."

"And now?"

"I want you."

His eyelids flutter at the admission, as though he wants to close his eyes and savor the words. "But?" he asks.

Nothing, I wish to say. My body yearns to make him mine.

I ignore what it wants. "But there are still too many secrets between us. I will not have you when I don't fully know you. I want all of you. Not only the parts you think I can handle." The words come to me so effortlessly, as though I'm not even consciously thinking them up.

"Then let's fix that," he suggests.

"What do you mean?"

"We lay it all out there in the open. All our secrets."

"What, now?" I ask.

"No." He chuckles. "I can't think straight right now. I need to cool off first. But soon."

"Tomorrow?" I ask, putting a tone of hopefulness into my voice.

"All right. Tomorrow. We'll go somewhere. Just you and me."

Victory surges throughout my limbs. "I'd like that."

"Me too."

I clasp my hands in front of me, not sure what to do with them now. Within me, hunger and triumph still fight to come out on top.

"Take the carriage back to the manor," Eryx offers. "I need a moment to myself."

"How will you get home?"

"I'll manage."

"All right."

I turn around, but before I reach the door, there's pressure at my wrist. Eryx spins me around and captures my lips in another kiss.

"I'm looking forward to tomorrow," he says.

"Me too."

It's not even a lie.

>—+—+>—O—<+—+—<

THE DUKE IS NOT AT BREAKFAST, but that's not unusual for him. He promised we'd speak today, and there are many hours in a day. It doesn't need to happen first thing. So I eat what I can manage through my nerves and excitement.

I sit in the parlor afterward, thinking perhaps Eryx will materialize. He doesn't.

After fidgeting in an armchair for fifteen minutes, I start walking. I think to perhaps go outside, but that will leave me alone with my thoughts. I think it would be far better to have a distraction.

So I go to the library, where I stumble upon Kyros and Nico.

Kyros sits on one of the lounge chairs, with little Nico in his lap, a book held open between the two of them. At the sight of me, Kyros stands and places Nico on the floor.

"No need for that," I say. "So sorry to interrupt."

"Duchess, I found a new frog in the creek today. Papa was helping me to iden-i-fy it."

"Iden-*ti*-fy," Kyros corrects.

"Identify," Nico repeats. "That means figure out what it's called."

"And did you figure it out?" I ask.

"Yes!" Nico grabs the book from where Kyros set it on a side table and rushes over to me.

I bend at the knees to be on his level.

"Look, Duchess. It had stripes on its head just like this picture. It's a tree frog. Did you know some frogs like to play in trees as well as lakes?"

"I didn't know that."

"They're the tiniest frogs found in our area. The biggest only reach a couple of inches. They can be different colors, but the one I saw was green! Duchess, might I keep this book? I want to identify more frogs."

"I don't think that's a great idea," Kyros says. "You're not exactly gentle on books yet, and you might drop it in the creek."

"I would never drop it! Then how would I identify frogs?"

"He's welcome to keep it," I say. "I prefer fiction, so someone ought to find some use out of that one." Besides, it was part of Pholios's collection, and I'm happy to give away that old toad's things.

"Thank you, Duchess!" Nico grips me in a hug and runs off with the book before his father can say anything else about it.

"I hope that was all right?" I ask.

"You spoil him," Kyros says, but by the way he says it, I know he means it playfully.

"How can you not? He's the most adorable boy in the world."

"And he knows it, too."

I laugh.

"How can I be of service, Chrysantha?" Kyros asks.

"I just came to the library in search of a distraction." I meant the words harmlessly enough, but Kyros gleans another meaning from them entirely.

"I would happily be a distraction for you."

I shut my eyes, hoping to feel something, anything at all. Some heat. Butterflies. A tingle.

But this man, kind and sincere as he is, does nothing for me.

It is a wicked man I want.

"I appreciate the offer, both this one and others you've made. But I think . . ." Oh, why is this so hard? "I think I would like things to remain as they are between us. You are a dear friend, Kyros. My closest, perhaps, but I don't think there is more here for us."

Even once Eryx is out of the way, it's not going to change my lack of feelings. Maybe . . . given enough time, but it's cruel to keep Kyros waiting.

Kyros smiles sadly. "I understand. I did mean what I said before. I am and always will be your friend. Nothing could change that."

"You're too good for me," I say, and I really, really mean it.

A COUPLE OF HOURS LATER, Doran finds me in the library. I lower the new romance I'd started, about a king and queen whose marriage was arranged, yet they begin to fall for each other.

"Your Grace, the duke has asked that you please join him outside. I believe he has a lakeside outing planned. Possibly a boat ride."

"All right. Will you please grab my shawl?"

"Of course."

Once outside, I find Eryx right near the front drive. What's more, he's not wearing one of his old outfits. He has on a black coat over a blue vest. Tailored black pants and boots polished to a shine. His hair is slicked back, keeping out of his brown eyes. He doesn't wear gloves or a cravat, but everything else looks incredible on him. Most adorable of all, he fidgets in place, as though nervous.

"You—you dressed up," I say.

He startles at the sound of my voice, but at least he doesn't draw his gun. "You seemed to like it the last time."

"I did. I do. You look very nice."

"You look beautiful." His cheeks heat, and so do mine, and why is everything so strange?

"Shall we?" he asks, extending his arm. I take it with my uninjured one.

We start for the property's natural lake in silence. It isn't awkward, exactly, but neither is it relaxed.

We pass by Nico hanging upside down in a tree by his knees. He waves at me with one hand, while the other tries to hold up his shirt from the effect gravity is having on it.

I smile and wave back.

"He's a handsome child," Eryx comments. "Curious at times, though. I distinctly heard him mutter the word *impostor* last time I walked by."

I turn my snicker into a cough. "He's learning new words rapidly. He likes to test them out whenever he can. Nico also has an endless curiosity about the world and how things work or what things are called. He likes words and answers to tough questions."

"You care for him?"

"Of course. How can you not?"

"Perhaps we ought to hire a tutor for him, then. Help him on his way to a brighter future."

I stop in my tracks, and Eryx is forced to follow suit. "Do you mean that?"

"Of course."

Two words and I feel tingly all over, like he's woven some sort of spell on me. How does he keep endearing himself to me? I don't like it.

The lake comes into view, vast with trees lining the edges. I believe the late duke had fish brought in for sporting some years ago, but no one has used the place in quite some time. It's beautifully overgrown with cattails and various reeds and tall grasses. Ripples form on the surface, little fishes coming up for bugs.

When we reach the dock, I ask, "Are you isolating me in a boat so I cannot run?"

"You might want to after you hear everything I have to say, but no. I just thought it might be a nice location for an outing. You seem to be outdoors quite a lot, and I have not had a chance to enjoy the lake yet."

What a . . . thoughtful observation. Curse him.

A single rowboat is tied off at the end of the dock. A few leaves and twigs have fallen into the base, and Eryx releases me to reach down and scoop them out.

"After you," he says when done.

He helps me into the boat, which sways a little as I take my seat at the back, facing forward. Eryx takes the other bench, where the oars rest.

"Oh, um, should I call for a footman to take us out?" I ask. "I didn't even think about—"

"I can row, Chrysantha. I'm not scared off by such labor."

"I'm not scared of labor."

"Ah, so you've done some, then? Please, do tell." He uses one oar to turn the boat, until his back is to the lake; then he takes us out.

I rack my brain for one single instance of labor I've performed, yet nothing comes to my mind. I pout. "I said I wasn't scared of it, not that I had done any before."

He smiles, watching me as he rows.

My eyes flit to his arms, so tight in his jacket sleeves. The way his abdomen bends with each stroke through the water. No one would ever guess he was younger than I. I only remember when I need something to tease him with.

"Wait, I've baked in the kitchens with Cook," I say triumphantly as I remember that working at dough certainly must count. My arms are usually sore the next day.

"I didn't know you cooked."

"I bake. I . . . like sweets."

"Anyone who says they don't is a liar."

"Quite so."

After only a couple of minutes of rowing, we've reached the center. Eryx pulls up the oars and leans back on his hands in the boat as we drift.

"Well, you've got me here," I say. "Alone. Without easy escape. Now what?"

"I suppose we talk."

"The boat would make it difficult to do anything more."

He smiles at the joke. It's rewarding to see his lips turn up. So rare for him. "Then I suppose it's a good thing I chose it. We're not going to get distracted."

"As if I'm helpless to your charms."

He raises a single brow, as though to question that statement. "Sure you're not, Miss Laudanum."

"You're not going to let that one go, are you?"

"It hurt me, Chrysantha. It's hard to let it go."

"I wasn't ready to admit I liked you."

"And now?"

"I still admit nothing."

His smile grows. "It's going to be awfully hard for us to make sure we're on the same page if you don't share anything."

"Fine." What's the point in being all awkward when I'm lying through my teeth to get what I want? "I liked it. There, I said it."

"Liked what?"

"When you first kissed me. It was a surprise, of course. I thought you hated me. Even more surprising was that I liked it, as I thought I hated you even more."

"I never hated you. Well, maybe a little. Mostly I hated how easily you got under my skin. How much harder I had to work to keep the monster at bay when you were around."

"Because I wouldn't let you get away with your villainy."

"It's more than that."

"What do you mean?"

"Everything about you unleashes him. From your biting words to your hateful looks. The first time I saw you, I barely kept him in check. Not only were you stunning, you held a knife to me."

"It was a toothbrush. *You* held a knife to *me*!"

"Semantics."

"Hardly."

"I think we are a good match."

"If you think fire and oil are a good match."

"Exactly. Together, we could burn the world down if we wanted to."

I let my fingers drift below the surface of the water. Eryx is staring at me too intently. I need something else to do.

"What if I don't want to burn down the world? What if all I want is my quiet country life?"

"Then I'll burn anyone who tries to take it away from you."

I arch a brow. "And would you be content with a quiet country life?"

"These last few months are the happiest I have ever been."

"Because you've been murdering noblemen and generals?"

"Does that bother you? The fact that I've murdered?"

"No."

"Why not?"

"I'm hardly a saint. More than that, though, the first time I met you, I saw something I recognized. I understand a willingness to do whatever it takes to get what you need to survive. There's something about you that draws me in. I don't care what you've done."

CHAPTER
23

I *don't care what you've done.*

I watch as Eryx processes those words. They settle about him, like a coat that fits just right.

"Are you ready to hear the whole of it, then?"

"I've been ready since I first realized you weren't quite human."

I rest my hands in my lap and wait. Yet Eryx hesitates.

"If I were to report you to anyone, I would have done it by now."

"It's not that. I think you might see me differently after this."

"That's not possible. Trust me." The words taste like poison as they drip from my lips.

He stares at me until his eyes turn amber. Then says, "I do."

Damn, but guilt is a pesky companion for me today. I wish it were something I could swat away, like an errant bug. But I have to settle for mentally tamping it down.

Eryx takes a deep breath. "My mother was in love with the late Shadow King."

I allow an expression of surprise to cross my face, even though I know this already from what the investigator has shared with me. "She thought she would be the one to encourage him to give up his shadows.

You see, the king's power is reliant on the lack of touch. So long as he does not allow himself to touch another person, he is immortal and invulnerable, but the moment he allows himself skin-to-skin contact with an individual, his shadows will no longer keep him incorporeal around that person. He is mortal around those he touches. He will start to age as we do. It is only for the greatest, most ardent of loves that the Shadow Kings of the past have given up their powers."

My skin starts to heat. Is that what my sister has with the current Shadow King? A love that transcends power? I don't think such a thing can exist.

"But he didn't choose her," Eryx continues. "No, he chose the late queen, and my mother didn't take it well. No, that's not right. She was *destroyed* by the rejection. She loved him so much, and when he sent her away, that love turned into an even more powerful hatred. She wanted revenge for her broken heart. And that's how she had me."

I know there's more to it than that, so I wait, patiently, my heart pounding to finally be receiving some real answers.

"Her hatred grew to such depths that she attracted the attention of a demon, a different one than that which granted powers to the Maheras line."

My eyes widen at the reveal. "One appeared to her?" I clarify.

"He did more than that. He promised her revenge if she lay with him. Thus I was conceived."

It takes some effort not to allow my mouth to drop open. "Your father was a literal demon?"

"Yes. I was to be her means of finally taking revenge on the late Shadow King, and for the longest time, I believed that was all I was good for. Those early years were . . . terrible."

"Tell me," I encourage.

"I could not control the shift. I was always hungry. I preyed on the local livestock in Dimyros—a small city in Estetia—and when the farmers or other townsfolk saw me in my true form, I had to dispatch them."

He pauses here, as though waiting for another reaction. Obviously, one doesn't come.

I ask, "Why did you end up joining the army?"

"It was my mother's idea. She thought it would hone my killing skills, and I wanted so desperately to please her. When I was fully grown, I was to battle through dozens of soldiers, swarm the palace at Naxos, and kill the Shadow King."

"But the king died," I say.

Rebels were led into the palace by the late king's own son Xanthos Maheras, after the king beat the boy nearly to death for not having the power of the shadows.

"I know," Eryx says. "When my mother heard the news of the king's death, she stopped everything. Stopped eating or bathing or caring about anything. She lost her entire purpose for existing. Her entire purpose for me. She let herself die once there was nothing more for her to do in this life.

"I wonder sometimes if that devil knew what would happen. If he knew that the king would die before my mother got the chance to unleash me on him. If he fed off first her need for vengeance, and then her suffering once the king died by other means."

"Has he ever appeared to you?" I ask. "The devil who sired you?"

"No. He probably has to wait another thousand years before he can build up the strength to appear in our world again. I don't think or care about him, except that he cost me my mother. He stoked the flames of her anger, led her to the death she fell into."

A breeze blows across the lake, and a strand of Eryx's hair falls free from the gel. He reaches up to stroke it back into place.

"I'm so sorry," I say softly.

"My mother made her choices."

"That doesn't mean they didn't hurt you. Whether your mother was kind or not, that doesn't mean you didn't love her." I reach out and grip his hand in one of mine. He squeezes back.

"I wonder if I would have let her have her way. Would I have done her bidding and killed the late Shadow King for her? I would have been caught or killed, whether in the attempt or after. Her plans were not subtle. She knew that. She didn't care. I wasn't a son. I was a gift from a demon for her to control. I've come to terms with that.

"I made friends in the army. I had a life outside of what she wanted for me. I was relieved when she passed. I found my own purpose."

"And what was that?"

He hesitates before answering, "My own vengeance."

"Against the general?" I ask.

"And others. Men who've wronged me."

"I saw your list. There's still one name on it, assuming you handled Barlas."

"I handled Barlas. Argus left an anonymous tip with the constabulary. They'll find the general's half-buried body on his property, as well as the murder weapon in Barlas's study."

"Good," I manage. He deserves to spend the rest of his life in prison, if the king doesn't kill him. "And the last name?"

Eryx looks down at the water. "The Shadow King is the reason good men died. He persists in his search for power, risking lives other than his own. I lost more friends than I saved."

I think carefully before answering. "It was a job, Eryx. They were paid for their services."

"You're defending him? Why? Because he's family to you now?"

"Maybe it's because I don't want to see you killed or behind bars, unlike your mother."

"I'm not rash like my mother. I wouldn't storm the gates the way she wanted. I don't need to be seen. I could do it without ever being caught."

"Perhaps, but perhaps not. You would risk my happiness by trying."

Our eyes lock, and it takes him a moment to glean my meaning.

"After everything, you wouldn't do that to me, would you, Eryx?"

"You want me to give up years of hate for you?"

"I do."

He looks out at the still water. Were we not trapped on a boat, I think he would pace. His fingers pull at his hair, and it is a full minute before he returns his gaze to mine.

He swallows. "Then consider it done."

I am shocked by the quick relenting. I thought for sure he would say that he couldn't. That he wouldn't. It would make what comes next so much easier.

But he agreed.

And a thought hits me. One I've never had before.

What if I didn't get rid of Eryx Demos?

He does stand between me and everything I've ever wanted, but that was before I got to know him. To rely on having him around with his ridiculous hair and pompous attitude and antagonistic nature.

For the first time, I try to imagine what life will be like once he's actually gone. Just me and the servants and the manor. It's enough. It's always been enough.

No more teasing conversations.

No more monster for me to engage with.

No more hearing his laugh.

Gods, and his kisses. No more of that sensual curiosity or amber gaze.

No more of the way he's looking at me right now.

What if I could be happy with him here?

What if Eryx didn't put restrictions on me and I was an accomplice to all his schemes? What if we were a team? What if he really did treat me as an equal? What then?

The thought is almost as terrifying as it is exhilarating.

Besides, the rational voice in me thinks, I could always change my mind if he abuses me in any way. I now have the ammunition to go to the king if things change.

"Row us to shore," I say, my voice low.

Eryx's eyes don't leave mine as he obeys.

There is just something intoxicating about a man who knows the true me and wants me anyway. I never talked about anything that mattered with my lovers. Not like I do with Eryx.

He can't seem to row fast enough, and the suspense makes my muscles coil tighter, just waiting for the moment they can spring free.

Eryx tucks the oars into the boat before managing to exit without the boat rocking even the slightest. He holds a hand down to me, and I take it, letting him help me onto solid ground once more.

I take his face in my hands and pull it down to my level. His lips are still as stone as I press a kiss to them. I keep my hands cupping his cheeks as I wait for him to open his eyes and look at me.

"I do not care one whit that you're half demon. You could have told me that you *were* a demon now living on this plane, and I wouldn't care. That monstrous form is just a part of who you are, and I like it, too. I like all of it. Eryx Demos, liar, murderer, thief, demon. I don't care.

"This," I say, and I reach out to touch the skin of his wrist with my fingers. Electric heat flows through me at the contact, just as I knew it would. "This is what I care about. This connection. This understanding. You were made for me."

Eryx sweeps me off my feet and carries me about twenty feet away from the dock, where the grass has grown thick and green. He lowers himself to the ground, crossing his legs beneath him, and holds me gently in his lap. He adjusts my hurt arm, ensuring it is not in danger of being crushed between us.

Only then does he capture my lips with his own.

The kiss isn't soft or hesitant. No, Eryx knows what he's doing now. He plays with my lips, tugging and nipping at them. When I feel a sharp canine brush the tip of my lip, I let out a gasp. Eryx tries to pull away, but I move my hands to the back of his head, pulling him closer instead.

A low hum rumbles up from deep in his chest, something not quite human, and I love the sound of it. I reach out with my tongue, trace his upper lip. When his mouth opens in surprise, I explore the inside of his mouth, too.

Then I'm not in his lap anymore. No, I'm lying on the grass with his body spread over the top of me. With his hands supporting his weight, he leans down to taste me. My fingers are in his hair, and when I feel the smooth hardness of one of his horns, I grip it in a fist. My free hand goes to the other one.

And I roll us.

Straddling him now, I can feel his excitement. Looking down at his face, I can see so clearly his amber eyes, his elongated canines, the deep violet horns.

I bring out the demon in him.

Oh, and he undoubtedly brings out the demon in me.

I do a sweep of the area, ensuring no one is around to see his shift. When my eyes return to Eryx, he swallows.

"You've no sense, woman. Are you sure I'm what you want? You still ought to be afraid of me."

"All this time, I've been trying to tell you. It's you who should be afraid of me."

My hands go to his vest, making quick work of the buttons, and he freezes beneath me. My eyes meet his, and he doesn't utter a word of protest, so I continue, moving on to the shirt beneath. It's come untucked from his pants, and I splay it wide, so my greedy eyes can take in the expanse of his muscled chest. For once I get to see it not in a dream but in the real world.

When I reach down to touch him, his eyes flutter closed. But then his forehead crinkles in concentration, and every muscle in his body goes taut.

"What is it?"

"The beast. I'm trying to keep him contained."

Those words send a smile to my lips. I bend down to his ear. "Why? Let him out. He doesn't scare me."

A choking sound comes from Eryx. "You don't know what you're saying. Just pause for a moment while I calm him down."

Instead, I bend over his body and bite his neck.

His eyes shoot open, glowing brighter than I've ever seen before.

"Chrysantha," he snarls, and before I know it, I'm flipped onto my back once more. Eryx doesn't hold his weight off me like last time, and I love every inch of him pressed against me.

"Yes?" I ask innocently, but he doesn't respond.

No, his hands go to the front of my dress, ready to rip it right down the middle.

A breath of air releases from somewhere behind Eryx, and he turns, horns and eyes and teeth still on display.

Kyros stares in horror at the duke, and I can do no more than stare between the two men, waiting to see what will happen.

Eryx stands in one motion, then proceeds to stalk toward Kyros. Because the beast does not retreat, I run after him and throw myself in front of Eryx.

"Get a hold of yourself," I say.

Those eyes snap down to me, and I do not mistake the look that had been directed at the footman. A need to protect me. To claim me. To remove every other man from his path.

Eryx's nostril's flare as he tries to look over my head. I grab him by the horn and pull him back down to my eye level. "Snap out of it," I demand.

Finally, he closes his eyes, the horns and teeth receding. When I'm certain he's thinking clearly, I turn, brushing my hands down my skirts, as if I can somehow erase what Kyros just saw. As if the white material weren't covered in grass stains from our activities.

"Kyros," I say, and the man meets my gaze before focusing on the duke again.

Eryx reaches down to take my hand in his, clearly still feeling territorial.

"Let her go," the footman says, finally finding his voice.

"No," the duke says, the word more beast than human.

"Chrysantha, come here," Kyros says. "We'll get you away from him."

"No," I say, echoing Eryx's statement.

"He's a *monster*," Kyros says.

"He is no such thing."

"I'll send for the constabulary."

"Kyros, *no*."

"You'll be dead before you leave the premises," Eryx says.

"*No*." I round on Eryx. "You will not hurt him!"

"He saw me."

"And he is a member of your staff, paid to keep quiet."

Eryx shuts his eyes and breathes deeply through his nose, calming himself, searching for reason. "I don't think that's necessary," he finally says. "It's his word against a duchess's." Eryx looks over my head. "You can run for help, but you'll only end up in a place for lunatics and leave Nico without a father."

"Are you threatening my son?" Kyros asks, stepping forward.

"No," Eryx says. "I'm only showing you the realities of what will happen if you start spreading lies about me. Chrysantha likes the child far too much for me to even dream of hurting him."

"And what about her?" Kyros asks, gesturing to me with a tilt of his head.

"I would *never* hurt her," Eryx says.

"It's a bit late for that. You've taken everything from her, or have you forgotten?" The last part of the sentence he directs at me. He shakes his head, as though he can't stand the sight of me. "The queen sent another letter for you. I thought you would want it right away. Had I known you were indisposed, I never would have come looking for you."

Kyros tosses the envelope on the ground before stomping back toward the estate.

I bend down to retrieve the letter and pocket it.

My heart pounds so loudly in my ears, I cannot hear the words Eryx is trying to say to me.

Eryx spins me around. "Are you all right?"

"Me? You're the one who was just discovered!"

"Kyros can do nothing to hurt me."

"Well, he can to me. He's my friend. I don't want him to quit and take Nico with him!"

"What do you want me to do? Bribe him to stay? To forget what he saw?"

"Oh, *now* you're open to handing out bribes?"

"Chrysantha, I'll fix this."

"No, I will. Do nothing until I talk to him."

Then I march toward the manor, following after the footman.

CHAPTER

24

"Kyros!" I shout. "Kyros, wait!"

He's got a good fifty yards on me, and I hike up my skirts to follow after him at a run. I don't catch up until we reach the manor. Then I grip his arm and haul him up the stairs. His face is set in a stern line, but he follows after me. Clear up until we get to the duchess suite. I shut and lock the door, then pull him far from it so we cannot be overheard.

"Just give me a moment," I say, panting, trying to get my breathing under control. I'd been breathing quickly *before* I chased after the footman.

Then Kyros begins talking. "You knew. All this time you knew he was a monster. Was the investigator all a ruse? You already have all the information you need to get rid of the pretend duke!"

I swallow before managing to get out, "I didn't know all this time. I only just found out!"

"Yet you were kissing him! And getting ready to do far more by the looks of things." He looks down at my grass-stained dress.

"Jealousy is unbecoming on you, Kyros," I say, hurt by his words and wanting to inflict pain of my own.

"This goes far beyond jealousy, Chrysantha. He. Is. A. Monster. What the hell was that out there?"

"That was me getting him to reveal all his secrets." Never mind that I already knew his secrets before kissing him.

"Really? That was the only way you could think of to get that information out of him?"

I hold myself up tall. "Don't you dare talk down to me like that. I'm not the one who had a child out of wedlock."

Kyros bites his lip from saying something he cannot take back.

"Just so we're clear," I say, "I was *not* about to do something more than kissing with him. I was pushing him. Seeing what would bring the beast out. How else am I supposed to prove to the Shadow King that he is the monster I claim he is?"

The taut lines on Kyros's face calm. "Oh."

The problem is I'm lying through my teeth. I'm not even so sure that I want to go to the king. I'm teetering on an edge, waiting to see which way I'll fall.

I have no explanation for why I kissed him other than that I wanted to. I like kissing Eryx Demos. I've done it three times now, and I've not even begun where he's concerned.

"What's the plan?" Kyros asks. "And how can I help?"

"Is that your version of an apology?"

His eyes drift close. "Forgive me, Your Grace. I should never have spoken to you like that or questioned you or—"

"You might be employed by me, Kyros, but you know you are my friend most importantly. You always have leave to speak to me as a friend without repercussions."

"I still overstepped. I should not have shouted at you or doubted you. A friend wouldn't do that."

I have to hide my wince. Yes, he should have doubted me. I still doubt myself. I have no idea what the hell I'm doing. I just want things to make sense again.

But the only thing I seem to know for certain or want above all else is Eryx Demos.

"I need to think," I finally say. "Please don't go anywhere or say anything," I beg. "I promise that despite what you saw, he's not dangerous. He would never hurt you or Nico. Don't do anything rash. Just let me make a plan. Please."

Kyros reaches out a hand, as though he means to touch me, then lets it drop to his side. "You have my support. I will be here."

Then he lets himself out of the room.

When knocking comes later that day, I ignore it. Even when Eryx's voice asks to be let inside.

"Please, Chrysantha, we didn't actually finish speaking. I didn't get a chance to tell you what I wanted. My plan for our future."

"It has to wait. I need to think."

What *he* wants. *Our* future.

I want to hear those words, but I have to find a way to keep my friend and keep him quiet. There is very little he wouldn't do to protect me.

When Eryx's footsteps finally leave, I climb into bed. I don't let Medora in for the night. I don't care about getting undressed or anything else. I feel numb. I feel torn two different ways. I am unable to see a path forward.

Remembering Alessandra's note, I pull it from my skirts and read,

You, jealous of me? Now that is something I never suspected. Perhaps we always want what we don't have, as the saying goes.

What do I do for fun aside from sewing? I enjoy spending time with my friends. We go for picnics on the palace grounds. Kallias

and I take Demodocus, his dog, out for walks or to play fetch. As strange as it sounds, I actually enjoy problem-solving. When something happens to upset peace in Naxos or one of the conquered kingdoms, I love to find ways to fix it. Having Kallias listen to and trust me is heady. Calling him my husband is even headier.

You should come to the palace sometime. I think it could be fun to chat again face-to-face. Perhaps you might swing by for tea next week? Only if you want to. I'm sure you don't care to leave your country estate more often than you have to, so I understand if you can't manage.

~Alessandra

The last words are so hesitant that they warm my heart. Maybe there is hope for us. Maybe I can rekindle this relationship. Maybe I can do away with this inherent sense of competition I seem to have where she's concerned.

Another knock sounds at my door, though the sun has long since set. "Go away, Eryx," I call out. "I'm still thinking."

"It is Kyros, Chrysantha. You have a guest in the library."

I sit up straight.

The investigator.

He's returned to collect the rest of his payment, surely. But will he have more news for me? Does it matter anymore? I'm convinced that if I can just find a way to keep Kyros quiet, then maybe I can also keep Eryx.

Uncaring that I'm still in my grass-stained dress, I leave my rooms and accompany Kyros to the library. My friend doesn't say a word the whole way, but I offer him a smile before I enter the library, to show him that things are good between us. Hesitantly, he returns it.

"Wait here, please," I say.

"Of course."

I straighten my shoulders and hold myself with all the grace expected of a duchess as I enter the library. If Mr. Tomaras is surprised or put off by my clothing, he says nothing of it. In fact, he keeps his eyes on my face as I approach. I gesture to the armchairs before the hearth, inviting him to sit, and take the other one.

"I'll get right to the point, Your Grace," the investigator says. "You're about to be in control of the dukedom once more. I finally found what I was looking for."

My heart skips a beat. "And that was?"

"A money trail. I've gone through Mr. Vander's correspondences. In a letter to the duke, he mentioned a fondness for a particular painting. I took the liberty of searching your attic."

"Why should that have led you to my attic?"

"You stripped the house of its old decoration, and you tasked your housekeeper with selling it. She informed me that what was left is being held up in the attic. It seems your late husband was fond of a specific painter. Mrs. Lagos handed me an itemized list of all the pieces cataloged in the attic, along with what had already been bought or sold.

"I paid a visit to Mr. Vander's home and found one of the unsold paintings hanging in his private study. Its worth is estimated to be fifty thousand necos."

I clench my jaw tightly, a feeling of dread causing goose bumps to prickle on my skin. "Could you put it plainly for me, Mr. Tomaras?"

The man crosses his ankles before him. "Eryx Demos is indeed the grandson of the late duke, but his mother—and Eryx by default—was ostracized. She was cut off from his will and money. Eryx paid off Vander with this painting in exchange for writing him *back into the will* and taking everything else from you. He *was* the heir, but everything rightfully belongs to you."

My vision goes hazy, and I see red. Eryx did this. Eryx, who said he wanted no more secrets between us, was actually keeping the most chilling secret of all.

I barely manage to find my voice as I ask, "You have proof of this?"

"Of course, Your Grace." He stands and reaches for a briefcase I hadn't noticed earlier. He hands it over to me. "It's all there. The itemized list of your husband's belongings, the position of the missing painting in the house. The letters between Vander and Eryx that now read with their incrimination once you have the right context by which to observe them. In there is everything you need to bury Eryx Demos, the pretend duke."

I clutch the briefcase to my chest.

"Thank you, Mr. Tomaras. I shall fetch the rest of your payment. You've done excellent work."

"Thank you, Your Grace." He bows.

I leave the library, and though I'm weighed down by the evidence of Eryx's treachery in my hands, I feel lighter than when I entered, for the path ahead is made blatantly clear.

I actually considered giving up everything that I fought so hard for to be with him! I considered not killing him. Of sharing all of this between the two of us. If he was willing to let me have all the things I wanted, then what harm would it do?

But all this damned time he's been playing me. He was going to let me continue to think he was the rightful duke and what? Let me stay on at his side as his mistress? Is that what he would have proposed by the lake if we hadn't gotten distracted by kissing?

No more uncertainty. Eryx needs to go, and I now have everything I need to bury him.

>—+—<>—O—<>—+—<

THE FOLLOWING MORNING, I find Eryx in the study. He holds an envelope in his hands, twirling a corner on the pad of one of his fingers.

Keeping my face calm, I say, "I spoke to Kyros. He has no interest in divulging your secret and being thought of as a madman, but he has informed me that he can no longer work under this roof. Since he is my friend, I'm going into town today to help him find a new position. I figure it is the least we can do."

His eyes widen. "He's truly going to leave you? I thought the two of you were closer than that."

"So did I," I say, letting a tremble enter my voice. "I will miss him and the boy."

Eryx clenches his teeth together. "I'm sorry for the pain I've caused you. I never meant for you to choose between your friendship with Kyros or our—what we have."

I nod and step around the large desk to the chair where *I* should be seated. Leaning a hip against the edge of the desk, I take Eryx's hand.

Why is this so easy? Should it be this easy? And why does my chest feel like it's full of bricks?

"It is what it is. It cannot be helped now, but I owe him this much. To see him situated in a new place. Him and the child. Writing a letter of reference doesn't seem good enough. I'm to attend interviews with him in the city."

"You put that together rather quickly," he says.

"When you're a duchess and the sister of the queen, people are more than eager to please."

Eryx nods.

"I should return late tonight. Don't wait up." I lean down and press my lips to his in a quick kiss before heading toward the exit.

"Wait," Eryx calls.

My body tenses as I turn, but I keep my expression normal.

Eryx rises and hands me the envelope he'd been holding. He won't look at me as he laughs awkwardly. "I don't know how to do this." He swallows audibly, as though nervous.

Even now my heart swells to look at his unruly hair and beautiful lips. I have to steel myself. *Remember what he did to you.* This is all a joke to him. I know too much, and anything he says or does is just to manipulate me. Eryx never cared for me. He thinks me beautiful, of course. But he doesn't want me any differently than any other man who has. Anything contained in this letter will only prove that. Any declarations of love or poetry will be pointless.

"I understand why we couldn't speak yesterday, and I don't fault you for it. You have much on your mind, and you're losing someone you care so much for. Of course Kyros needs your time right now. I didn't sleep last night, so I wrote down all my thoughts, everything that's in my heart. Maybe during your journey you could read it. Take some time to think about it. And then I will abide by anything you decide."

I take the letter and tuck it into the pocket of my dress.

"I would rather talk," he continues, "but I realize that the turn of events doesn't make that possible right now. And . . . I need to give you space. To think about what you really want. I just ask that you let us speak again before you decide anything."

"Of course," I say, truly perplexed by the exchange.

"Then you'd best be off. Do pass along my regards to Kyros, if you think it would be appropriate."

I nod.

Eryx raises a hand and runs two fingers through one of my loose curls. "Safe travels."

And then he releases me.

KYROS WAITS FOR ME by my carriage. He hands me into the interior, before trying to climb the seat to join the driver. "No. Please join me inside, Kyros."

He meets my eyes and nods.

Then we're off.

"Did he buy it?" Kyros asks when we make it down the drive. I spot the briefcase where he's stashed it in the corner of the carriage.

"Yes."

"Then why do you look . . . sad?"

"I'm not sad. I'm furious. He claims to have feelings for me. When he did *this* to me." I gesture to the estate disappearing behind us. But perhaps, secretly, I am a little sad. For what could have been. Eryx Demos saw me in ways no one else did. Together, we could have been—

It doesn't matter. He lied. He took advantage in a way no man has ever been able to. Because he saw the real me. The whole of me.

And he thought to make me small by taking everything I earned for myself.

"I am sorry," Kyros says, and he does sound as though he means it.

I hold myself higher. "Why are you sorry?"

Kyros thinks about his next words carefully. "Because you clearly care for him."

"I do not," I say through clenched teeth.

"Perhaps not now that his treachery and monstrous form have been revealed, but before you knew . . . it's okay if you did start to care."

"That's not why I invited you to sit back here with me."

"Then why am I here, Your Grace?"

"Don't call me that anymore. Please."

He sighs. "What is it, Chrysantha?"

"Because you're my friend, and I want you here." And if I change my mind, I need a voice of reason to help me stay the course.

"Then I'll be here," he says simply.

Yet I can't escape the feeling that he's not who I want with me right now.

CHAPTER

25

The palace seems to look drearier than usual. The black stones look gray, and the gargoyles seem slumped. Even the guards appear bored.

Some messenger greets us at the front doors, asking our business.

I say, "I am Chrysantha Stathos Demos, Dowager Duchess of Pholios, and sister to the queen. Please tell her and the Shadow King that I have arrived and wish to speak at their earliest convenience."

The page's eyes widen, but he asks me to wait in an adjoining receiving room while he goes to relay the message. Kyros stands behind me as I seat myself on a plush sofa. We are there no longer than ten minutes before the page returns, which is a relief.

"The queen bids me to take you to her private receiving room. She will meet you there as soon as she can. This way, please."

I know Alessandra left an open invitation in her last letter, but that doesn't mean she couldn't change her mind. Or be in a bad mood today. Or any number of other reasons.

I'm nervous and jittery. I'm about to turn over the man I'd come to l—

The man I'd grown fond of. The one I was prepared to give up what I wanted most for. And it hurts, even if this is the right choice.

We're led through the palace corridors, past beautiful wooden furniture with roses and thorns etched into the sides. Midnight-black carpets line the floors and the upholstery is mostly done in crimson.

This is my sister's home. Once, I envied her. I envied all of this. But now it's obvious that I never would have been happy in this dark castle. I much prefer the pinks and golds of my estate. A home in the country, away from prying eyes.

Any remaining anger I might have felt toward my sister evaporates at the realization. I was jealous because she snagged herself a king while I only managed a duke. But she has duties and responsibilities heaped upon her every day. How could I have let myself think that I ever wanted that?

Because I didn't know any better. I had no chance to really figure out what I wanted for myself. I was too focused on securing my own freedom. And once I had it, I knew what I wanted. To never have to put on an act again. To not have people expecting things from me. To just be me.

I will have that again.

So long as Alessandra is willing to listen to me.

We're finally led into a massive receiving room. It's lovely. A vase of fresh flowers rests atop a grand piano. One wall is covered in stained glass depicting a forest teeming with life. The whole scene glows faintly, as though lit candles from behind were brightening the glass. I seat myself upon one of the sofas, and the page nods respectfully before shutting us within the room.

Kyros and I wait in silence for all of five minutes before I rise to explore the room more thoroughly, tracing my fingers over the beautiful stained glass. When I grow bored, I dare to open the adjoining rooms. I wonder if Alessandra suspected I would do just this. If she wanted me to see all her fine possessions. I don't care, I'm going to look anyway.

Kyros draws in a breath when I let myself into my sister's bedroom, but what I find is surprising. "The king and queen share a bedroom!" I call back to Kyros.

"Chrysantha, I don't think you should—"

"He really loves her. Look at all these outrageously expensive perfumes. Kyros, come smell this one."

"No, thank you," he says, and I think I can hear his eyes rolling.

Her wardrobe is more full than even mine. She's been sewing, for none of these designs can be found at the modiste's. The vanity is covered in face paints and lip stains. I read the labels of several, noting scents and colors I like. When that ceases to entertain me, I return to the receiving room, much to Kyros's relief, and fidget some more on one of the beautiful sofas.

"It's been half an hour," Kyros says after a moment.

"We did spring this on her. She's a queen. Probably very busy."

My legs bounce. My fingers tap on the upholstery, and I cannot believe I'm here. What if Eryx is onto me? What if he had Argus and Dyson follow me? Every minute that goes by is a chance of me being found out.

"He doesn't know," Kyros whispers, as though reading my thoughts. "It'll be okay."

"He could notice at any moment that his correspondences are missing. I still have no idea how Mr. Tomaras managed to snag them."

"It's his job to be good at that sort of thing. It will be all right, Chrysantha. Just breathe."

"I'm breathing!"

The door opens.

And my sister, Queen Alessandra Stathos Maheras, steps into the room.

She wears black pants under an open skirt in deep red, as though she thought to match her very surroundings. Some sort of corset-looking top attaches to the open skirt, black with red ribbons. Her hair is the same shade as mine in deepest ebony, though mine has a natural curl to it while hers is more wavy. She wears hers down, while mine is up.

"Chrysantha," my sister says in greeting.

"Alessandra."

A servant comes in behind her, setting tea onto the table as my sister takes a seat across from me.

"I was surprised to hear you were at the palace so soon after I sent my letter, but I'm glad. It's been . . . nice to understand each other better."

"Yes, it has. What have you been up to since the wedding?"

"A honeymoon along the coast. Then back to work at the castle."

"Was it nice? The coast."

Her smile is contagious. "The water was warm, the company was perfect, and the food was delicious. What of you? Have you read anything new that you've enjoyed?"

I tell her all about my latest romance novel, my book club, and my purchases to the library. We get so caught up in conversation that a good fifteen minutes must pass by. Alessandra has already filled our teacups twice.

When Kyros coughs twice from behind me, I realize that I've totally lost track of why I'm here. I hadn't realized that Alessandra of all people could do that to me.

"This is fun," I say.

"It is," she agrees.

"I would like to schedule something like this again, but I'm afraid I'm actually here today because I need your help."

She straightens in her seat, as though she needs to be wary. Of me. As though I'm using her. Oh, I probably went about this all wrong. But I didn't know how else to do this.

"Go ahead," she says, deadpan. "Ask."

"Last time I saw you, I told you the story of who I've been these last seven years and why. I got what I wanted. Freedom. The right to control my own life as a dowager. You've made it even better, you know. With your new edicts. I didn't have to stay in a period of mourning for a man I didn't care for in the least bit."

She shrugs. "What is the point of power if I do not use it to make things right in the world? We still have such a long way to go, but I intend to do what I can."

"And the king is so supportive?"

She smiles. "He is."

"I'm glad." And I mean it, though I am a little envious. I started to think that I could have something like that, too.

"I've come to tell you a second story. About what happened once a man claiming to be the new Duke of Pholios entered the picture. Would it be all right if the king joined us for this part? He will want to know it, I'm sure."

Alessandra taps her fingers on her thigh while she scrutinizes me. "All right. I will get him. Wait here."

She leaves.

Only ten minutes pass before she returns with none other than Kallias Maheras, the Shadow King, on her arm. Bounding in behind the king is an enormous dog with sleek brown hair. Someone must spend hours brushing him every day, for the sheer bulk of hair on him. He sniffs at my feet, before the king says, "Demodocus, come." The hound leaves me and sits at the king's side.

"Will you wait outside, Kyros?" I ask.

"Of course."

He leaves us, and my sister and the king sit. I'm not sure what Alessandra told him, but he holds out a gloved hand. I take it, and he bows over it. "Good to see you again, sister."

I'm surprised by the words, but it must be that Alessandra is starting to hold me in some regard if he's said them.

"Alessandra says you've paid her a surprise visit and that you need help."

I pick up the briefcase from where it rests beside me and set it on the table next to the tea set.

Then I tell them both about Eryx Demos. Who he is, the fact that he was ostracized. I don't mention his powers, not yet. Just the fact that he's taken what's not his, and that I bear the proof of that.

Kallias looks at the briefcase before glancing back to me. "Why not take this matter to the constabulary? If you've truly all the proof you need, then why come to me?"

I take a deep breath. This is it. There is no turning back from this point. If I reveal the secret Eryx trusted me to keep, his life is forfeit.

But that anger and betrayal is too strong for me to stop now. So I push ahead.

"Because the constabulary cannot remove him by force from the estate. You see, he is the spawn of a devil." And the rest finally comes out. Eryx's powers and true heritage. His strength. His bodyguards. The weaknesses I know of. The more I talk, the more Kallias's face grows troubled.

"You are earnest?" he asks, looking between me and his equally surprised wife.

"I swear I do not lie. My manservant out in the hallway can confirm it. He's seen the beast, too."

After a moment's pause, Kallias asks, "Has he hurt you?"

My neck flares with sensation at the memory of his teeth, but I answer truthfully, "Physically, no."

"Is he violent toward anyone else?"

I think about disclosing the fact that Eryx was the one who murdered the general and several others, but for some reason, I decide to keep that to myself.

"He's dangerous, to be sure. He has limited control over himself at times, but I have yet to see him lose control and attack anyone." The time he saved me doesn't count. "I . . . just thought you would want to know. You claim the shadows are a divine right to rule, do you not? If others have powers, doesn't that hurt your rule?"

Kallias cocks his head to one side. "So you came because you are worried his existence makes my kingship vulnerable? Has he threatened me?"

I think about the list of names in the cellar.

But Eryx said he wasn't going to pursue the last name. The king. If he was telling the truth. It's not like he hasn't lied to me hundreds of times before.

"I am doing this because he's taken what's mine. If dispatching him benefits you, too, then I am happy for it."

Kallias looks to my sister, and I cannot read the silent conversation they have.

"Then I will take care of him," Kallias says simply as he rises from his seat.

Alessandra reaches out with a death grip on his hand. He looks down at her.

"I will be all right. So long as you stay here, he cannot hurt me. Do you not wish for me to protect your sister?"

The question is terrifying, because I realize that if she told him not to protect me, he would listen. Her wants are far more important to him than my life. That is abundantly clear by the way he is looking at her.

She only pauses for the briefest moment, looking between me and her husband, before nodding. "We will be here."

Just like that, Kallias leaves us, though Demodocus remains at my sister's side. She reaches down to scratch him behind the ears.

I'm left with guilt flooding my body. I want to fix things with my sister, but now I've thrown her husband into danger's way.

"I'm so sorry," I say.

"Don't be. He means it. As long as I stay here, he is invulnerable to death."

But Eryx isn't. No, I just signed his death warrant.

My legs begin to bounce again, and I fiddle with my skirts. Alessandra hesitates only a moment before rising from her sofa and joining me on mine. She doesn't touch me, but her presence is a comfort I didn't know I needed.

"Tell me about him. This Eryx," she says. "Has he treated you poorly?"

"We argue. A lot. He can be spiteful. He took away my stipend just because I called him an orphan. Oh you should have seen the state the dukedom was in before I had leave to pretty it up."

It relaxes me to talk, to tell her about all the changes I made. I even feel better talking about Eryx. Reminding myself of the awful things he's done and why it's okay to be rid of him.

He professed to like me, to talk of a future together—when he deceived me like no other has.

I bunch my fingers in my skirts, only to feel a rustle of paper. I reach into my pockets before remembering the note that Eryx had slipped me. I turn to Alessandra.

"It's from him. He gave it to me before I left."

"Did you read it?"

"There wasn't time."

"Go ahead, then. Especially if you think it might calm your nerves."

I debate whether to read it, but in the end, I decide it will only add fuel to my hatred and make me feel better about my decision to send the Shadow King after Eryx.

My fiery Chrysantha,

I have a confession to make. Two, in fact. The first is that I lied about changing the will. The truth is, you should have inherited everything. The estate you love and have made so beautiful, the servants you've hired and built relationships with, the money that will secure your future forever. I truly am the grandson of Hadrian Demos, but my mother and I were disinherited because of my siring.

Vander failed to mention until after events were set into motion that the duke left behind a wife. In the beginning, I didn't care whether or not you existed. You were a titled and pampered lady and would continue to be so even if I was made duke. I've never had a real home, full of safety and peace. And when I arrived at the estate, I fell in love with its beauty—beauty I learned later was a result of your handiwork, though I would never have dreamed of admitting that in the beginning.

But then I learned more about you. You told me of your family and your horrible marriage to my grandfather. You told me about how trapped and helpless you feel in a world run by men. You told me how you managed to find some control over yourself by becoming the dowager duchess.

And that leads me to my second confession. One I should have been brave enough to tell you in person the moment we were in that boat on the lake. I love you, Chrysantha Stathos Demos. I love your fiery temperament and your wicked mouth. I love your intelligent mind and your love of books. I love that crass sense of humor and your passionate friendship. There is not one part of you that I don't love, so how can I possibly stand in the way of what you want? What you need and deserve?

I'm leaving the dukedom to you. I've already written to Vander to have him make everything legal. You will be the proper Duchess of Pholios, and no one will have the power to take that away from you. Though perhaps you might ask your brother-in-law to change the name? I know what Pholios has come to mean to you.

It is my dearest wish that you will allow me to stay at the estate, in whatever capacity you choose. I wish not to be parted from you, but more important, I wish you to be happy, so I will abide by whatever your wishes are. Whether they be to have this monster far, far from you or as close to you as possible to protect you and love you for the rest of my life.

I'm so sorry for Kyros. I'm sorry I had to put this in a letter because I ruined your friendship with him. Be well and safe as you journey. I am forever yours and eagerly await your return.

With love,
Eryx

I drop the letter to the floor, my eyes unable to see anything through my tears by the end. A burst of something spreads through me, replacing my horror and guilt.

Love, it must be.

I wrap my arms around myself, try to get a hold of the tears. It isn't until I take a deep breath that I realize Alessandra has picked up the discarded letter.

She scans it quickly before her eyes find mine.

"I don't understand; why would he— Oh. Do you love him?" she asks.

The tears return, but I manage a nod.

"Then what are you still doing here? Go to him before my husband kills him. I will travel with you as far as I can, but I will not put Kallias in danger by rendering his abilities useless."

I fairly leap from the settee and launch myself through the door. Kyros, still manning the hallway, falls into step with me. I'm beyond words, so Alessandra tells him, "Bring the duchess's carriage around. Quickly now!"

With his longer gait, Kyros overtakes us, disappearing out of sight.

Meanwhile, a horrible cry rings over and over again in my mind.

What have I done? What have I done? What have I done?

Why didn't I just read the damn letter on the way here? I was so clouded by my anger. So overcome with my need to be free.

But Eryx offers me what I want. Freedom and himself.

And how I want it. More than I've wanted anything else in my entire life. If Kallias kills him—

I cannot bear the thought.

The castle seems five times its actual size as Alessandra and I race through its halls and chambers. My lungs and legs ache after a short while, but I push on anyway. The only comfort I have right now is that my sister is at my side.

Who would have thought that so much could change in a day?

Servants try to stop the queen, asking what is the matter and if they can be of service. Alessandra ignores them all. She does not falter even once, though I hear her breathing just as rapidly as I am.

When we burst through the castle doors, Kyros is already there with the carriage, holding open the doors. My sister and I throw ourselves inside. Before Kyros closes the doors, I say, "Make all haste for the dukedom, Kyros. Lives are at stake."

He relays the message to the driver as he seats himself next to the man. And we're off.

I cannot think clearly. I can barely breathe for how tense I am.

"He only has a fifteen-minute head start on us," Alessandra says.

"That's all he could need to kill him."

She doesn't argue.

"Why are you helping me?" I ask.

"I would say it is because you are my sister, but I don't think that has mattered to either of us for most of our lives."

A silence falls at her words, for I cannot refute them.

"I was once in your position," she says quietly. "There was a time when I left the palace, only to realize Kallias was in danger. I feared I would be too late."

"How did you save him?"

"By killing the man who threatened him. He thought me too weak to murder. He didn't know that I would commit any manner of evils to save the man I love." Her eyes move to me. "Does that make you think differently of me? When you learned I killed my first lover, did you think differently of me?"

I get the distinct sense that she is perfectly proud of who she is, but she is unsure where my thoughts lie.

I look her in the eye as I admit, "I killed the late duke."

Her eyes widen.

"He touched me. Hurt me. I snapped. I smothered him with his own pillow. I also tried to kill Eryx by poisoning his food. He has no idea. I wonder what he'll think of that when I tell him—*if* I get to tell him."

She smiles. "I thought to poison Kallias once. I didn't go through with it, though. How fortunate that both our men survived us."

And though there is still danger to dispel, I find myself smiling in return. "We Stathos sisters are a force to be reckoned with."

"That we are. We are as arrogant as the gods, deciding who gets to live or die."

"If the gods didn't want us killing men, then they shouldn't have allowed them to hurt us so much."

"Indeed," she agrees. "We only have the one life. We have to fight to make it the best it can be. And when others abuse the powers granted them, then what choice do we have except to fight back?"

Her words ring so true they pulse within me in time to my rapid heartbeat. "I wish I had turned to you when Mother died. I should have chosen you instead of Father. Together, we would have been unstoppable."

"We have each other now. I think the past played out the way it needed to, but did you have to call me a trollop so many times?"

I manage to laugh through the tears starting to fall down my cheeks. "I did it because I envied you. Because I wanted to experience love and passion, but I thought the only way to make the match I needed was to keep myself pure. I let the laws of men dictate me. I thought it was the only way I could win. But choosing myself has been more freeing than anything else."

Alessandra crosses her legs in the roomy carriage. "And now you're choosing Eryx. A devil-born bastard who lied to you."

"Yes, I am," I say with conviction.

Yes, I am.

➤─┤◀➤─○─◀➤┤─◄

WHEN THE DUKEDOM FINALLY appears far in the distance, Alessandra knocks on the roof of the carriage. The driver halts the horses, and she steps out. "I will be here. Come find me when it's done. I will be ready. To celebrate or to comfort you. Whichever you end up needing."

"Thank you," I say. "Kyros, remain with the queen."

The man's feet have barely hit the ground before I shout, "Drive!"

A whip cracks, and the carriage takes off again. When we clear the beautiful trees and the glorious Pholios Estate appears ahead, I see the masses. My servants all surround the front doors, palace guards keeping them in check. Another set of guards comes forward, ordering the carriage to halt.

"Let us pass," I snap at the man daring to stop us.

"The king has ordered the estate evacuated. No one is allowed to enter."

"That is my home. You will let us pass at once."

"I'm afraid not, Your Grace. We have our orders."

"Drive around," I order the driver. We'll take the back entrance if necessary.

"This is as far as this coach goes," the guard barks. More men surround the horses.

I fling open the opposite side door and make a run for it. A group of guards chases after me, but I bolt for the hedge maze. At first, I worry they will overtake me, but after I make the first turn, they start to fall behind, lost within the greenery, unable to deduce what turns I make until I'm too far ahead. One guard tries to throw himself over the top of the hedges, but he only falls hard to the ground on the other side. His progress is too slow.

When I reach the unfinished center, I make for the exit on the other side. I know this path like the back of my hand. When I'm through, I don't glance over my shoulder. Instead, I bolt for the back of the house, finding the servants' entrance.

It's quiet as the grave within, since all the servants were forced outdoors. I had feared I would enter the home to the sound of shattering glass and smashing furniture.

But there is nothing.

And devils, but the estate is enormous. Where could they be? It's midday. Perhaps Eryx would have been in the study?

I try there first, but the door is locked, and I don't hear voices within. My skeleton key is in my rooms, but I don't take the time to grab it. I doubt they're behind the locked door. Perhaps Eryx had been napping when the king found him? Dare I check the cellar?

No, I've been training him on etiquette and the proper way things are done. I know exactly where the two men are.

My parlor. It's the king. Eryx would have welcomed him in the best room in the estate. The one I fashioned just for callers. He probably didn't even suspect the reason the king showed up was because I ratted him out.

I hear the voices long before I reach my destination.

"Stay back. Both of you." This from Eryx. "This is between me and the king."

Kallias says, "This doesn't have to get physical, but if it does, you will lose. I cannot be killed."

"I'm pretty difficult to kill, myself."

"Difficult and impossible are two different things."

"I said *stay back*, Argus. Leave us."

"Please, sire." I pick out Dyson's voice. "The duke is harmless. I don't know what imaginings the duchess might have shared with you—"

"Dyson, shut up for once in your devils-damned life!" Eryx barks.

There is the briefest of pauses as I finally reach the doors.

"Show me your real face," Kallias says. "Show me who you really are. I felt it, you know, something different about you at the ball. I never could have guessed it was this."

I burst into the parlor, and all four men snap their necks to me. Before I can even get out a word, the unthinkable happens, quick as the blink of an eye.

One moment, Eryx is normal with his messy brown hair and brown eyes. And in the next, he changes.

Horns sprout from his head, his canines lengthen, his eyes glow a bright amber. A tail snakes out from a hole in his trousers, thin and long save the triangle of skin at the end.

"Eryx, no!" I shout, just as he launches himself at the Shadow King. Who cannot be killed. And it doesn't escape me that he didn't change until I was in the room. When he thought *I* was threatened. Stupid, foolish boy.

Kallias is dripping with shadows. They run over his skin and float above him, undulating to their own rhythm.

Eryx's first punch goes right through Kallias, as though the king literally were made of shadow. He connects with nothing, and nearly collapses from the lack of resistance.

Then Kallias strikes. He slams a fist into Eryx's exposed lower back, and Eryx roars as he finds his footing again.

Dyson and Argus run for me. "You need to leave," the latter says.

"No, you two need to leave."

Dyson and Argus each grab one of my arms, hoisting me clear into the air.

"Put me down immediately!" I scream at the two of them.

At the sound of my voice, Eryx turns, putting those wolflike eyes on his friends. He advances a step to them, to *hurt* them, but Kallias lands another blow, this time sweeping Eryx's legs out from under him.

Argus and Dyson drop me at once, as we all realize that messing with me is the surest way to get Eryx killed.

As Eryx stands quicker than my eyes can follow, I say, "Stop. Kallias, I made a mistake. Please stop. I've changed my mind. I need you to call this whole thing off."

"It's a bit late for that," the king answers as Eryx tries to slam into his gut. His fingers cleave through the middle of the king, rippling shadows, but nothing else. Again. When Kallias goes for yet another punch, Eryx catches his closed fist.

Catches it.

Because it's not incorporeal. No, Kallias has to make parts of himself physical in order to strike Eryx, and Eryx is so much faster.

Bones crunch beneath Eryx's hands as he tightens his hold on Kallias. The king winces, then turns his hand to shadow once more. It doesn't take much time for the bones to reset themselves in the correct order. His shadows heal him just as quickly as Eryx's do him.

Kallias smiles. "This is the most fair fight I've ever been in."

But Eryx is beyond words. As he looks at Kallias, staring at those shadows he cannot make contact with, I watch in horror as Eryx reaches for that serrated dagger he keeps on himself at all times and rakes it over his own left palm, sending shadows spilling forth from the wound. With the palm extended, he reaches out.

And *touches* the king.

Shadow to shadow. It doesn't matter that Kallias should be incorporeal. Eryx's shadows are the exact same as the king's. And he shoves Kallias onto the ground. Then he grips his throat.

Shit, shit, shit.

Kallias draws his rapier and rakes it against Eryx's arm, sending more shadows flying. Eryx flinches backward from the pain of it, but keeps the dagger in hand.

"Eryx, stop!" I cry out. "Please, you need to listen to me. I'm fine. See. Come here. Come to me. I'm fine!"

But he doesn't even turn his head in my direction. His entire being is focused on the king. On my sister's husband, who unwittingly put himself in danger. If Eryx found a way to touch him when he's incorporeal, then he very much *can* die, even with Alessandra almost a mile away from the manor.

Sparks fly as rapier and dagger meet and dance. Eryx is faster, but he's limited to where he can strike Kallias with his own shadows. His own wounds. Gods, it must be painful.

Dyson and Argus stand helplessly beside me. Honestly, whatever did they possibly think they could do when Eryx was like this? He can't be stopped. No mortal man is a match for him. How could they have deluded themselves into thinking they could stop the beast from getting what he wants?

Eryx takes a slice to his side, and shadows ripple from the wound. He then uses that same side to barrel into Kallias, sending him to the ground once more. Eryx injures his own palm again so he can make contact with the king.

Kallias rolls over, despite having the breath knocked from him.

"Call him off, Chrysantha," the king says when he can draw breath into his lungs once more. "I will stop if he does."

"I tried!" I shriek back. "He's past reason now!"

Kallias has to block a series of slashes from that nasty dagger. But Eryx is too fast, and the third lands on the king's wrist, where his hand is corporeal to hold the blade.

More shadows spill into the mix.

Someone is going to die. Of that, I'm certain. And if it's my sister's husband, then any hope of rekindling a relationship with her will be ruined forever.

If it's Eryx, I will not be able to live through the guilt.

But me? This is all my fault, and my sacrifice is the only one I will tolerate in this moment.

In perhaps the most foolish mistake of my life, I advance. And the next time the two men are thrown apart, I insert myself between them.

Eryx is poised for the next strike. That dagger comes within a hair's breadth of me, but I don't close my eyes. I keep mine directly focused on his.

He halts; he doesn't land another blow.

Instead, he growls at me.

And I growl right back.

He tries to look over my shoulder, to get to Kallias, so I make another reckless move. I step closer, press my body against his, and I wrap my arms around his neck.

I kiss him.

The beast goes utterly still, and I can almost hear his brain working. Thoughts of killing to protect me fly out the window as a new desire overcomes Eryx.

He drops the dagger as he scoops me into his arms. The monster is fully out, and he doesn't recede. Not as he carries me from the room.

I don't care one bit.

"Alessandra is on the edge of the estate with my footman," I call over his shoulder. "I'll come find you both later."

Argus and Dyson try to step in front of Eryx, and he bares those canines at them both.

"Don't," I say. "I choose this. You would all do well to stay far, far away."

For I feel just as bestial as Eryx in this moment.

He tries to carry me to the cellar, but I stop him with a yank on one of his horns.

"No," I say, and I direct him to the duchess suite instead. As he ascends the stairs, he breathes deeply, taking in the scent of me. My arms rove over his chest and face, touching where I can. The bedroom cannot come soon enough.

Eryx slams the door to the duchess suite closed with one foot. He lowers me onto the bed before taking my mouth in a heated kiss. His teeth graze my lips, but they don't break the skin, and the contact is exhilarating. His clothing is in tatters from where the king slashed at it, so it hardly takes much effort on my part to remove it. Eryx does as he meant to the first time by the lake, shredding my dress under his brute strength.

He stares down at me, taking in the length of my naked body underneath his. He shudders at the sight of it.

And then he claims me.

But more important, I claim him.

⤜┄◈┄◯┄◈┄⤛

WE'RE BOTH PANTING ON THE bed by the time we're done.

Only then do the changes fade.

The horns and tail disappear. His canines return to normal. Only his amber eyes are left when he props himself up on one elbow and looks at me.

"Did I hurt you?"

I grin in response. "Did I hurt *you*?"

His responding smile is delicious, but then, as though looking at me is too painful, he sits up. Eryx runs his fingers through that messy hair, and I watch the way the muscles in his arms flex with the movement.

"You went to the king," he says softly. "You lied to me."

"You didn't seem to care about that thirty minutes ago."

His shoulders slump in shame, as though he's guilty for ravishing me. I nearly laugh at the thought, but this is a serious conversation.

"I lied to you about many things," I admit. "I killed your grandfather."

His head snaps in my direction.

"I'd had enough of his pawing and belittling. I smothered him with a pillow after he bruised me."

Eryx says nothing, so I continue. "I also tried to kill you. The poison in your curry? That was me. Not Sarkis."

Now his eyes are so wide they nearly pop from his skull.

"I thought I was in danger from you. I was convinced you were a fake, no matter what other sources said. You had stolen everything from me." I bend over the bed to my ruined dress and come back up holding his letter. "Turns out I was right on all accounts."

His eyes darken back to their usual brown, but his face is a mask.

"If it's any consolation," I say. "I didn't read it until after I told the king about you. That's when I realized my mistake." I look down to the rumpled bedsheets. "I found out about you and Vander before reading this letter. I hired a private investigator. It's the reason I agreed to put in a good word with the king for you and give you etiquette lessons—so I'd have the means of paying the man. I thought you lied about your feelings for me to manipulate me. To try to convince me to stop my investigation and let you stay. Always the superior to me. Instead, you gave everything up for me.

"And I . . ." A tear slides down my cheek. "I gave you up. I ratted you out to the king. I killed your grandfather. I tried to kill you. Gods, I can never fix this, can I?"

He wipes at the tear with a thumb. "I've killed innocents. I've killed not-so-innocents. I came here under false pretenses. I was fully ready to take everything from you."

"But you didn't, in the end."

"You didn't leave the king to kill me. You came back."

"Of course I came back, you stupid boy. I love you."

"Always with the age difference." He rolls himself on top of me as his eyes turn amber again. "We'll see how much it matters to you once I'm inside you again."

A delicious tremor runs through my whole body at the promise. "The words you said to me in that letter. I want to hear them aloud."

"Which ones?" he asks as he leans down to kiss my neck, but he knows very well which ones I mean.

"The only ones that matter," I answer.

He raises his head to look me in the eye once more. "I love you. I fought loving you, but it was as inevitable as the sun rising every day. For you are my equal in nearly every way and my superior in all the rest."

I make a humming noise. "You say such pretty words."

"No more talking," he demands. Then he claims my mouth.

>-!-+>-·-O-·-<+-!-<

I PROBABLY SHOULDN'T HAVE left the king and queen of Naxos to wait while I consummated my relationship with Eryx.

Three times.

There's just something about knowing that my sister is waiting in the woods while I'm being pleasured by this enthusiastic man that makes it all the more exciting.

I truly am a terrible person, and I smile at the thought of it.

But as I realize that Eryx is still potentially in danger from the king, I hurry to dress. Eryx goes into the adjoining room to find his newly made attire.

By the time we walk into the parlor together, it would seem that my sister and the king have already made themselves comfortable. Kyros stands behind them at the sofa. Argus and Dyson have their arms crossed as they lean against the wall. A number of the king's guards stand vigilant around the room, and I suspect they are there at my sister's request.

There is a sharp awkwardness in the air, as Eryx and I take a seat on the sofa opposite the king and queen.

"The estate is quite lovely," Alessandra says. "I thoroughly enjoyed my walk over here."

"Thank you," I say.

More silence.

The king leans forward, making eye contact with me. "Explain," he says.

I look to my sister. "Did she not tell—"

"She told me. I want to hear it from you."

I sit up taller, and Eryx's hand snakes into mine, offering strength.

"I love this man. I have for a while. I was just too blind to see it. Please don't kill him. He has no political aspirations. No wish to be anyone of importance. He's already given up the ruling of the dukedom to me. Eryx only wants a quiet life in the country, as do I."

Eryx's hand tightens in mine. "I will accept whatever punishment you deem necessary, my king. But please allow the duchess to resume control of—"

Kallias puts up a hand to halt Eryx. His face gives away nothing.

Alessandra leans over and whispers something into his ear that I don't catch. Eryx must hear it, for he relaxes ever so slightly.

Kallias looks at her with heat in his eyes, but he turns his attention to us once more. "You forged a will. You have brought undue stress upon the duchess. And you attacked your king."

Dread crawls down my spine. "Please, Kallias. He was only trying to protect me. I—I can keep him under control."

The king turns his gaze to me. "Don't even get me started on your crimes."

I swallow.

Alessandra's grin grows, and I cannot tell whose side she's on. Until she says, "I pardon them."

Kallias fights a smile as he turns to his wife. "You pardon the man who tried to kill your husband?"

"He didn't succeed. No one in the estate saw anything. No one knows anything except those present in the room. Besides, I think I like my sister and want to spend more time with her. You wouldn't have me do that from a prison cell, would you?"

Kallias rubs a hand over his chin, and I realize that the two of them are toying with us, just as they're toying with each other.

"I suppose your sister would hardly wish to see you if we killed her lover, and I can't have my queen stepping foot in a prison."

What is happening?

Alessandra rises before looking between me and Eryx. "You have one week. Then I expect you both to come visit us at the castle."

I blink. One week . . . to spend time with my new lover before she expects us to be in polite company. Gods, did they hear us earlier?

"By then, I expect Eryx to have a tighter leash on his protective instincts," she continues.

I nod, because what else can I possibly do or say?

Kallias holds out a gloved hand to Eryx, and he takes it. "Don't mistake this for tolerance. If you cross any lines or get out of control, I will hold her responsible." He points to me. "Since she claims to be able to control your actions."

A low growl comes out of Eryx, and I smack him.

"Of course, Your Majesty," I say for him.

Kallias looks around the room. "It's a lovely parlor, Chrysantha. Have a good day."

The guards follow them from the room, and Eryx and I stare at each other.

"I don't know which of the gods is looking over you two," Dyson says, "but by all accounts you should both be dead."

"I'm still of half a mind to put an end to the lady," Argus says with venom in his voice.

"Argus," Eryx says, a warning.

"She turned you in! She brought the king on us. We should leave—"

I stand, releasing my hand from Eryx's, and walk right up to the man. "Eryx and I have made peace with our pasts. Can you? I'm willing to forgive your part in all of this, so can you find it within yourself to forgive me, too? For I would have you all stay, but you're both fired as valets. Perhaps we could find more appropriate positions for you."

Argus and I stare each other down, but the man eventually relaxes.

"I won't be no footman. You cannot dress me up in that." He looks over at Kyros.

"What are your skills?"

"Killing."

"We'll . . . figure something out."

I turn my attention to Dyson, but he already has a grin on his face, so I know there's no problem there.

That leaves Kyros.

"I'm sorry," I say as I reach him.

"You made no promises to me," he answers.

"I know, but I had wanted to try. I started to, but something kept getting in the way." I dart a glance to Eryx, who looks between me and Kyros with new understanding. "I had meant to go through with all of it. Until I read a note Eryx wrote me. He's signing over the whole dukedom to me. Making it legal. I no longer wished to have the king hurt him."

"He's still dangerous," Kyros whispers.

"He is." And so am I, but I can't very well say that. "But not to me. Not to those who we care about. Eryx has already brought up the subject of hiring a tutor for Nico. I think the idea is grand, and I would love to help him have a bright future."

I can see the indecision in Kyros's eyes. While he clearly loves the idea of a better life for his son, he's still torn about Nico living under the same roof as Eryx.

"Just think on it," I say. "If you decide you wish to leave, I will of course help you to find a new position."

Kyros nods.

And that leaves Eryx.

"So what is my new role to be, Duchess? Are you hiring on anyone new?"

I lean forward to whisper lowly in his ear, "I'm in need of a new mistress."

I hear the faint sound of the door closing, before I realize the other three men have left the room. Perhaps I wasn't whispering as quietly as I thought.

"I'll not accept payment for that. You have my services for free."

"Are you sure? I'd give you a very generous stipend of fifty necos a month."

Eryx winces. "In my defense, I thought the sum was generous at the time. I had no idea how much money the wealthy were accustomed to having at their fingertips until I pretended to be a duke."

"I still have much to teach you," I say as my voice takes on a sultry tone.

"I ought to be paying you for lessons."

"You need an income for that, darling."

"I'm sure you'll find some use for me."

"What skills do you have?"

"I can manage the accounts and deal with that horrible solicitor for you."

"We're firing him first thing."

"That's probably wise. Not a very honest man, that one."

I reach out a hand to trace his lower lip, and his eyes turn amber. I'm going to have so much fun learning exactly what brings that out.

"Just be mine," I say. "That's all I need from you."

He wraps a finger around one of my curls. "I'm already yours."

"I'm going to teach you how to spend money," I say, already imagining all the fun things I can dress him up in.

"Gods help me."

Acknowledgments

I CAN'T BELIEVE I'M finally writing the acknowledgments page for this book. There was a time when I thought the edits on this manuscript would be the death of me. I was grieving. I was overwhelmed by everything I had to do for grad school, for work, for my personal life. Everything came crashing down at once, but I had so much love and support.

Thank you to Holly and Rachel, who recognized what I needed and offered everything they could to help me get through a dark time. You really are my dream team, and I'm so lucky to have had you by my side for EIGHT books now.

Thank you to the team at Macmillan, who works so hard to make these books possible. Thank you especially to Jean, Gaby, Leigh Ann, Morgan, Sam, Starr, Kristin, Jordan, Meg, the audio team, the copy-editing team, and everyone else who had a hand in this novel.

I'm beyond blessed to have so many foreign publishers who help my books reach new markets. Thank you to my Pushkin team, especially Rima, Sarah, and everyone else who works tirelessly in the UK.

I also have to give a special shout-out to my French team. Dorothy and Miriam, you are my favorite people in all of France. I adore you both. Thank you for making things so special for me when I come visit.

Special shout-out to Caitlyn McFarland who read drafts of this book and helped me plot out scenes. Thank you for being there when I needed you. Thank you to Mikki Helmer for coming over whenever I needed a write night to meet deadlines.

Thank you to my family for your support. Before I ever made any money from my writing, you were there cheering me on. I'm lucky to have you.

Finally, thank you to my fans. You make my job special and precious. I love visiting with you all online or at events. Thank you for providing a safe place for me to share my words.

A SCENE FROM THE CUTTING ROOM FLOOR

In the first draft of this book, Chrysantha decided not to attend her sister's wedding. Instead, Chrysantha agreed to accompany Eryx to social events in exchange for the money necessary to hire the private investigator. In the following scene, Chrysantha and Eryx are at a luncheon at an earl's estate, and Eryx has just issued an open invitation for a duke interested in Chrysantha to stop by the estate.

When lunch is finally, finally over, courtiers break away from the table in small groups while the servants set up all the equipment for the main event. An assortment of guns, ammunition, and some sort of slingshot-like contraption are brought outdoors, away from the tents, where plenty of seating can be found.

I pull Eryx out of hearing range of everyone else. "What do you think you're doing?"

"I told you why we are here: to find you a husband. Now, the duke is clearly interested, and you'd be rising in station, so—"

"Don't invite people to my home!"

"I think you mean *our* home."

"Never mind that. I thought you detested people. What are you doing inviting them to swing by whenever they wish?"

"They're swinging by to see you, not me."

"Eryx, *no*. I agreed to come to these events with you. I did not say I would entertain random callers at any hour of the day."

"What am I supposed to do about it now? Rescind the invitation?"

"Yes! Tell them you're an overeager boy and got ahead of yourself."

"This consistent calling out of my age is getting rather annoying. My birthday is coming up. What will you do when we are the same age?"

"Oh, there are plenty of things about you for me to complain about."

We glare at each other, but when I realize that others might be watching, I smooth out the frown lines on my face. Eryx does likewise.

"Just remember," I say pleasantly. "You started this."

"Started what?"

But we are joined by other nobles, so I am unable to answer. For lunch is over and due to our late arrival, only now are guests permitted to mingle with us.

Apparently, I should have been admiring their restraint.

For suddenly, they're battering upon us like a storm.

"Duchess, you look exquisite today."

"Your Grace, please allow me to introduce myself, I am—"

"Would you like to take a turn about the gardens, Duchess Pholios?"

"Pholios, have you considered coming round the club?"

On and on the voices merge, until I cannot tell which *Your Grace* is being addressed. Ladies and quite a few lords try to fight for Eryx's attention, while I'm accosted by men, since my preferences in romantic partners were made known during my first outing into society.

Thankfully, Lady Glaros comes to save us. The countess ushers me to a chair beneath one of the gazebos, and she hands Eryx off to her husband so he can participate in today's event.

But even in my chair, I'm accosted in new ways.

Ladies flock to me with questions about Eryx. What does he like to do? What are his talents? Where did he come from? What is he looking for in a wife? Does he have his eye set on anyone? Could I please secure an introduction? On and on and on.

And instead of telling them what I really think of Eryx, I talk him up, just as he did me.

"Oh, Eryx is a fine young man. He loves going for long walks and reading. He's very easy to please and endlessly patient. I'm unsure where he was living before taking up residence in the dukedom. I believe he's looking for a love match, someone who can woo him romantically. He has eyes set on no one and welcomes new potentials. I'm happy to secure an introduction with anyone who would like one."

I feel positively evil for the lies that spew from my mouth, but I couldn't be happier about any of them. Eryx wants to throw me to wolves? Fine, I'll send sheep flocking to him. If my days are to be interrupted by interested callers, then so will his.

"Is his grace any good with a gun?" young Lady Kormos, the daughter of a viscount, wants to know.

Since the only times I've seen him handle one are when he's drawn that revolver on me, I can't rightly say. But I answer, "He served in the army on the front lines, so I suspect so."

"A war hero," Lady Kormos says with a dreamy lilt to her voice. "Oh, do you suppose he has any scars? I do love a man with a handsome scar."

"If he does," Evadne says, "then they must be in places we can't see."

"Oh, maybe if the sport grows to be too much, he'll take off his jacket?"

I try not to gag. These women are swooning at the thought of Eryx wearing less clothing? I suppose it's my fault that I've made him out to be some honorable war hero. Little do they know he has fewer fine qualities than an irritable grizzly bear.

The Earl of Glaros takes a central position on the back lawn, raising his voice to be heard above the chittering ladies and muttering men. "Esteemed guests, I'm so very excited for the main event of this afternoon. Since it would be tedious and difficult for us all to go traipsing about the woods, hoping for prey, I've commissioned a way for us to gain our sport and allow the ladies to enjoy the view safely."

He pulls a brown disc from a pile beside him. "Behold the clay pigeon and the thrower." Glaros gestures to the mechanism before him. He places the disc into the arm of the machine, pulls a lever to pull the elastic taut, and steps on a pedal just above the ground. The disc goes flying high into the air.

In a motion too quick for my eyes to follow, the earl draws his weapon from where it's slung over his shoulder, aims the rifle, and fires. The clay pigeon shatters into a hundred pieces that rain to the ground.

A few of the lords and ladies jump at the sudden noise of the gunshot and following explosion. Most try to cover up their embarrassment. But I'm surprised to find a small number of men who didn't react at all. Those who must be quite used to the sound.

Polite applause comes from gloved ladies' hands, but the men enthusiastically clap their appreciation. Lady Glaros whistles at her husband's true aim. I find the display rather impressive and invigorating, though I hadn't expected the gunshot to be quite so loud. Father wasn't ever one for such sport.

"Who's next?" Glaros asks, and one by one the men line up for their turns.

It's quickly apparent that most men do not have the same eye for a moving target that Glaros does. Most shots go wide, and the clay pigeons only smash to pieces upon impact with the ground. Simos manages to hit his target, however, and the ladies about me clap more enthusiastically than before.

"With the king wedded, Simos is the most eligible bachelor in all of Naxos," the countess says, leaning conspiratorially toward me. "Though I suspect Pholios will give him a run for his money now. You could do worse." She leans her head in Simos's direction.

"I have no interest in marrying again."

"Even if it were a handsome man who knew his way around the bedroom?"

I'm almost too stunned to answer. No one, besides the late Pholios, ever talked to me in such a way. But I find I rather like it when it's a woman conspiring with me. "How would you know?"

"Simos has had a couple public affairs, but nothing serious. His lovers seem saddened by the parting."

Another gunshot goes off, and I have to repeat the first part of my next sentence. "I have no wish for a husband, but I wouldn't mind another lover."

The statement comes out louder than I intend, with the sudden silence after the gunshot, and many nearby coiffured heads turn in my direction.

Innocent Lady Kormos's eyes go wide. "You mean those rumors were true? You had a—a *kept* man?"

"Sandros," I say wistfully. "But that's all done now that Eryx has entered the equation. I haven't the funds I once had."

"Don't look so scandalized," Countess Glaros says to the younger girl. "Women have needs just as much as men do."

"I had no idea the duke's presence had altered your life so," Evadne says. "Oh, we must find you a new lover, then."

"Yes," the countess says enthusiastically. "Oh, I'm sure there would be countless men who would have you without the incentive of money. You are a rare beauty."

I try not to grimace at her last statement. That is what my father used to say. It was my only worthwhile feature to him. The one thing he could bargain for all the money he needed.

"We shall have to compile a list for you," the countess continues. "What are your requirements?"

Before I can answer, Evadne says, "Of course he has to be tall and handsome and good with his hands. Good teeth," she adds. "Yes, good teeth are a must."

With a smile, the countess says, "I thought I'd asked the duchess the question, but it seems you've already given this quite a bit of thought, Lady Petrakis."

The girl's cheeks go red.

"No, she's right," I say, thinking to spare her. "He must have good teeth, and I do like a tall man." For some strange reason, my eyes land on Eryx just then, remembering how he towers above me.

"It should be a love affair, should it not?" Lady Kormos asks. "Don't you want a man who wants nothing from you? You should be the prize to him. Not the things you can give him. Forget this Sandros. He clearly wasn't worthy of you."

Many heads nod in agreement, and I feel my heart warming to these ladies around me.

The conversation halts when someone says, "Hush, it's Pholios's turn!"

A couple dozen heads turn toward the duke as he approaches the pigeon thrower with a rifle held loosely in his hand. He eyes the bullets within the gun before closing the compartment and cocking back the hammer.

I watch his chest expand within his tight clothing as he takes in a deep breath. As he exhales, he steps on the pedal, releasing the clay pigeon. Before the disc even reaches its apex, Eryx pulls the trigger. The shot finds its mark, clay scraps raining toward the ground. His applause is louder than any other's so far, including Simos's.

"You ought to be an assassin with that kind of quick aim, Pholios," Glaros says to him before clapping him on the back of the shoulder.

Eryx hides a pained smile behind a forced, more natural-looking one. "Perhaps I was. You've found me out. My secret identity was not meant to be disclosed to the public."

Men and ladies laugh at the joke, but I narrow my gaze at him. As though there is something more to the words, if I can just determine them. Everything about Eryx is a mystery, and I have such a hard time deciding how much of him needs to stay that way.

"Why don't we make things a little more interesting, gentlemen?" the earl says. "How about a friendly competition between friends? Single elimination? Shoot until you're out. Winner takes all."

Some men, knowing their strengths, politely decline, but a good amount make wagers and enter in the earl's competition.

"Well, we shan't let the men have all the fun," the countess says. "I place ten necos on my husband." The women begin their own predictions. Several place money on Simos and Eryx. Some on other gentlemen, feeling the need to support their brothers or admirers.

"Well, Your Grace? Anything to bet?" the countess asks of me.

I really have no desire to risk losing any of my small stipend, but since Eryx has paid me a generous sum for his lessons, maybe it would be all right to indulge?

"I'll place ten on Pholios."

"Great," the countess says, marking the amount, and I stare out at the man in confusion. I'd meant to say the earl. I had every intention of putting on a show of good faith toward our hosts. But out came Eryx's name. As if I'd meant to say it all along. I would call back my words, if I didn't risk embarrassment over correcting myself now.

So be it.

The men take turns firing, and each time a man misses his mark, he politely cedes the game to the rest. After two rounds, Lord Livas loses. At the third round, Lord Soter barely clips his clay pigeon to make it to the next level. But after four rounds, half the men are eliminated. At five, only six remain. On and on it goes, and the countess becomes more and more engrossed in the sport as her husband rises in the ranks.

It's adorable to watch.

At the tenth round, only three men remain: Pholios, the earl, and Simos, who wasn't in the war, but has always had a hobby of shooting, nothing so garish as living creatures (Lady Castellanos informs us).

I wouldn't have thought holding a gun would be that taxing, but the earl has sweat beading on his brow, and Simos pulls off his cravat. But, in true uncivilized fashion, Eryx removes his cravat and jacket *and* rolls up his shirtsleeves. The ladies with fans beside me flutter them more energetically. And I'm at least grateful that no one seems overly scandalized by the gesture.

Simos is up first. He wipes his forehead before stepping on the pedal and releasing the pigeon. He finally misses.

"Well done, Your Grace," the earl says, clapping the man on the back. "You had a very good run."

"Thank you, I shall have to practice harder for the rematch."

"That's the spirit."

The earl goes next, getting off a perfect shot.

Eryx does the same.

They trade off, each man getting more and more tired, more determined to come out on top. The competition doesn't turn unfriendly, but it's clear both men are tired and ready to be done with the whole thing. I wonder if one will throw the match, but either they're both too proud to do so, or their formal army training will have none of it.

The ground is littered with shards of clay, and I feel a twinge of sympathy for the servant who has to pick them up, but that is nothing compared to my desire for Eryx to win. There's quite a lot of money between all the women. I should like to add it to my modest income. Even if it does mean having to listen to Eryx gloat later.

But as time continues on, I begin to notice a slight change in Eryx.

I don't think it's physical at first. Merely something I sense. A strange stillness about Eryx in between rounds. His almost too fast movements.

And then when I notice his eyes turning to liquid amber, even from this distance, I realize something very bad is about to happen.

After his last perfect shot, Eryx turns unblinking, wolflike eyes on the earl. His muscles coil, as though readying to pounce. Argus and Dyson have noticed the change, but they're both too far away to help, and I can't imagine how they intend to do so without causing a scene.

I'm not sure what compels me to do so, but I leap from my position and throw myself between the earl and Eryx.

"I think we should call it a draw," I exclaim, never taking my eyes off the threat. Eryx turns his gaze to me, and I know I'm not imagining his eyes now. There's no possible way to mistake this in the outdoors under full sunlight. There's no trick of the light or hiding beneath shadows. His pupils are dilated, and his nostrils flare ever so slightly.

"Besides, I think the ladies have had enough watching," I continue. "It's our turn, I think."

I reach for the rifle Eryx is holding, though I'm not entirely certain it's the most dangerous weapon at his disposal. He seems surprised when I wrench it from his fingers, but he doesn't immediately react.

"Now, who's going to teach me how to shoot?" I ask.

Many hopefuls raise their hands, but I all but throw myself into Eryx's arms, my lips going to his ear. "Whatever is going on with you, you need to pull yourself together!" And then, I don't know why I do it, but I blow a puff of air into his ear, as though to cool him off.

He blinks slowly, but I'm relieved to see his eyes return to normal when he looks down at my face.

"Of course, Duchess. It would by my pleasure." He stands behind me, wraps his arms around either of my hands to show me where to position them.

"Thank you," he whispers back to me, and I let my chin dip into the slightest of nods.

Eryx's muscles are strained and his breathing is labored, but he holds himself straight as he corrects my form, every line of his body taut against mine in a way that's wholly inappropriate for company. But this is a shooting lesson, so surely everyone will overlook it.

"Be ready for the recoil," he says, loud enough for everyone else to hear.

"Recoil?" I ask.

I feel his smile at the back of my head. He steps on the pedal, the clay pigeon goes flying, and when I feel the slightest pressure from Eryx, I squeeze the trigger.

The clay pigeon shatters, but I'm too distracted by the sudden pain in my shoulder to be happy about it.

Recoil, indeed.

Several ladies stand, each one eager to get their own shooting lesson, though I suspect it has less to do with the act of shooting than it does with the idea of Eryx or Simos standing behind them to correct their form.

I return to my chair at the sidelines, watching the spectacle and mulling over something that is becoming more and more clear to me.

There is something not quite right about Eryx Demos.

Something, perhaps, not quite human.